PRAISE FOR JULIA LONDON

Nice Work, Nora November

"London's latest triumph is a book that asks a lot emotionally of the reader, but it gives back so much more in return."
—*Booklist*, STARRED REVIEW

"A delightful novel about fate, second chances, and how our worst moments are only the gateways to the best moments to come. When you're finished, you'll be writing your own reverse bucket list to check off."
—JODI PICOULT, #1 *New York Times* BESTSELLING AUTHOR

"Nora's remarkable transformation is a testament to the power of second chances. Her quest to conquer her past and fulfill her reverse bucket list is bright with warm humor and poignant moments that will make you laugh, cry, and cheer for her all at once. With richly developed characters and a plot that keeps the pages turning, this novel is a captivating exploration of what it means to truly live. *Nice Work, Nora November* is a delightful reminder that no matter how bleak the past, the future is filled with endless possibilities. A must-read for anyone seeking inspiration and the joy of second chances."
—SUSAN WIGGS, #1 *New York Times* BESTSELLING AUTHOR

"Wonderful! Nora's amazing journey is fresh and heartwarming. This book is a keeper for sure!"
—SUSAN MALLERY, #1 *New York Times* BESTSELLING AUTHOR

"A touching, heartfelt story you won't want to miss! London will have you making your own reverse bucket list."
—LAURA GRIFFIN, *New York Times* BESTSELLING AUTHOR

"I love a gal with a list, and Nora November makes hers in reverse! With equal measure of heft and humor, this clever novel is brimming with inspiration, tenderness, hope, and heart. If you're looking for a feel-good story that will bring cheers and groans, laughter and tears, look no further than *Nice Work, Nora November*. It is a triumph to the dreamer, to the nonconformist, to the one who dares to take control and change her life."
—LORI NELSON SPIELMAN, *New York Times* BESTSELLING AUTHOR OF *The Life List*

"What if you had a near-death experience and decided to create a 'reverse' bucket list of the simple things we sometimes take for granted? In Julia London's new book, she makes readers understand the fragility of life, the power of self-discovery, and how important it is to take control of your own life. A thought-provoking, delightful read."
—REA FREY, #1 BESTSELLING AUTHOR OF *Don't Forget Me* AND *The Other Year*

"A poignant, beautiful, and surprising novel. Julia London's writing is heartwarming and true."
—LIA LOUIS, INTERNATIONAL BESTSELLING AUTHOR

"A book that tackles serious issues, complicated families, a heroine who fails again and again . . . and somehow remains utterly charming throughout. The perfect blend of women's fiction and romantic comedy."
—KRISTAN HIGGINS, *New York Times* BESTSELLING AUTHOR

"*Nice Work, Nora November* is a sparkling, spirited, emotionally engaging story of self-discovery and reinvention. I loved it."
—JAYNE ANN KRENTZ, *New York Times* BESTSELLING AUTHOR

"A story brimming with hope, humor, and heart. I rooted for Nora November from the very first page, and so will you."
—TERI WILSON, *USA TODAY* BESTSELLING AUTHOR

"Nora is a character you are immediately rooting for—her story is funny, moving, and carries an important message about being true to yourself and finding your own happiness. Witty, warm, and wise—a wonderful read."
—DEBBIE JOHNSON, AWARD-WINNING AUTHOR OF *Jenny James Is Not a Disaster*

"Quirky, lovable Nora grabbed me from the beginning, and I couldn't let go—or stop rooting for her—until the very last page. Julia takes you on a heartwarming story of finding yourself, starting over, and forgiveness. I love all the heart Nora has and her perseverance to keep going and hoping even when everything falls apart. She's a modern-day, genuine heroine, and I adore her! Worth every second of reading!"
—JENNIFER MOORMAN, BESTSELLING AUTHOR OF *The Magic All Around*

EVERYTHING IS PROBABLY FINE

Also by Julia London

Nice Work, Nora November

EVERYTHING IS PROBABLY FINE

A NOVEL

Julia London

Everything Is Probably Fine

Copyright © 2025 by Dinah Dinwiddie

All rights reserved. No portion of this book may be reproduced, stored in a retrieval system, or transmitted in any form or by any means—electronic, mechanical, photocopy, recording, scanning, or other—except for brief quotations in critical reviews or articles, without the prior written permission of the publisher.

Published by Harper Muse, an imprint of HarperCollins Focus LLC.

This book is a work of fiction. The characters, incidents, and dialogue are drawn from the author's imagination and are not to be construed as real. Any resemblance to actual events or persons, living or dead, is entirely coincidental.

Any internet addresses (websites, blogs, etc.) in this book are offered as a resource. They are not intended in any way to be or imply an endorsement by HarperCollins Focus LLC, nor does HarperCollins Focus LLC vouch for the content of these sites for the life of this book.

Library of Congress Cataloging-in-Publication Data

Names: London, Julia, author.
Title: Everything is probably fine: a novel / Julia London.
Description: Nashville: Harper Muse, 2025. | Summary: "New York Times bestselling author Julia London returns with a story about forgiveness and second chances perfect for fans of The Wedding People and The Husbands. After forty-two years, Lorna Lott is ready to learn where she's going with her life—even if it means revisiting all the places she wishes she hadn't been. It'll be fine. Probably. Maybe"—Provided by publisher.
Identifiers: LCCN 2025003590 (print) | LCCN 2025003591 (ebook) | ISBN 9781400245765 (trade paperback) | ISBN 9781400245789 | ISBN 9781400245772 (epub)
Subjects: LCGFT: Novels.
Classification: LCC PS3562.O48745 E94 2025 (print) | LCC PS3562.O48745 (ebook) | DDC 813/.54—dc23/eng/20250228
LC record available at https://lccn.loc.gov/2025003590
LC ebook record available at https://lccn.loc.gov/2025003591

Printed in the United States of America

25 26 27 28 29 LBC 5 4 3 2 1

If we are facing in the right direction, all we have to do is keep walking.
—ZEN PROVERB

This book is for everyone who has lived with addiction, either in themself or a loved one. Keep walking.

Chapter 1

Lorna Now

THEY CALLED HER KING KONG.

Not to her face, of course. In polite company, they said Lorna Lott was a hard nut to crack. One tough cookie. All business, no play.

Behind her back, they said something else. Lorna knew this because she had a habit of striding into conversations around the proverbial watercooler. It didn't take a genius to know that when the conversation came to a dead halt just as you entered, you were the subject. But since she had a bit of genius in her, Lorna knew to slow her steps before entering the break room to catch the whispers and comments.

As best she could tell, the King Kong moniker had popped up after the unfortunate incident during the quarterly sales conference. She'd broken the heel of her shoe by getting it stuck in a grate on the way to work—a classic romantic comedy maneuver without the requisite hunk to save her. No one in the office had or would admit to having a shoe that fit her size 10 dogs. So Lorna hobbled through several presentations, and apparently her hobble gave off a gorilla vibe. Well, she couldn't help her feet. They matched her five-foot-nine body. Her late uncle Chet used to say she was built like a farmer. "Some of my favorite people are farmers," he'd add cheerfully.

She also tended to scowl, which probably didn't help. "I'm not telling you to smile," her boss whispered at the same sales conference, "but could you look less . . . mean?" Lorna tried. She really did try.

Anyway, they called her King Kong in the break room, and she tried to laugh it off and tell herself that it didn't matter what they called her as long as they met their sales quotas. But she wasn't unaffected by the name. She was not an automaton; she had feelings and very much wanted to be liked, even in her role as a sales team leader. She just didn't know how to get people to like her. She'd been leaning into the awkward side of things most of her life, and now that she was in her forties, it was clear she didn't know how to be un-awkward.

And there was the whole low-key rage thing. The vague feeling that she needed to clock someone for no good reason. She didn't like that feeling, and she'd been working on developing a different mindset. She was a frequent visitor to the library, checking out self-help books. Edward, her favorite librarian, had nodded along sympathetically as she explained she needed to learn how to be more likable, and he'd directed her to guides that advised her to smile more, ask questions, and soften her approach with humor. Then when she told Edward she needed to learn how to harness a killer instinct to make more sales, he showed her all the books designed to help her reach a million dollars in sales or climb the corporate ladder. Those advice books tended to be a little more aggressive in their approach—work hard, know your product, don't give up, *persist, persist, slay.*

She was very good at persisting, anyway. She was a goal setter. When she had the idea to learn how to row after watching one summer Olympics, she did it, right here in Austin on Lady Bird

Lake. Create needle art? The angel on her cubicle wall was her own creation. Sing? She'd absolutely nailed it as an alto in the community choir until Jed Faris took over and turned it into a show choir singing pop tunes. Lorna did not believe that choirs were meant to sing pop tunes.

The point being, Lorna looked tough, acted tough, and knew how to achieve goals. Sure, she could be a little hard on her sales team when they lagged behind the quotas she set, but it was her job as team leader to light a fire under their butts. That she seemed "mad" or "pissed" was just their way of deflecting.

Once, a therapist had suggested she work on being more in the moment and aware of how snappish she could be. *Snappish?* That hardly seemed fair. Wasn't everyone snappish at times? Wasn't everyone subconsciously mad about something? Sure they were—politics, gas prices, extreme temperatures, tornadoes, wildfires, ice storms, barking dogs. Social media, long queues, not enough cashiers. Zoom calls, traffic, poverty, high heels, skinny jeans. More ice than soda, more bun than burger, more noodles than shrimp. There were any number of things on any given day to set off even the saintliest person. Such was the nature of modern times.

But she was working on it. And in the meantime, she was trying very hard to be likable.

So when no one even made eye contact when she came back from lunch, Lorna thought through what might have upset them. It probably had something to do with the sales team meeting she'd convened yesterday. Their cubicles were built around a "discussion pit" made of couches that were too low to the ground and sprinkled with colorful pillows that smelled like mildew. In the center was a scarred table for drinks and pastries. The pit sort of looked like a giant flower. Lorna had gathered everyone together to discuss quotas because, as she liked to say, quotas were set to be achieved, not waved at as they flew by. She'd indicated she didn't think they were working smart (she'd read that in a self-help book: *Work smart!*).

What else had she said? It wasn't *that* bad, was it? She was pretty sure she'd said worse in the past and they'd all survived. Why this should put their panties in a twist, she couldn't say. Except . . . except maybe she'd been a smidge harsh. Lorna was hard on herself, and sometimes she found it difficult to discern where her internal self-flagellation ended and her inappropriate comments during pep talks began. They tended to be the same in theme and tone.

Okay, she'd bring donuts tomorrow. People would forgive a multitude of sins if there were donuts, and even more if strawberry sprinkles were involved. She'd just pulled out her cell to check which delivery service would bring donuts when her office phone buzzed. "Lorna Lott speaking."

"Good morning, Lorna."

It was Deb, Lorna's boss. Unlike some of her colleagues who found their bosses to be insufferable, Lorna really liked Deb. She looked up to her, admired how she'd risen to the top of management with hard work and dedication. That was what got you places—whining did not get you anywhere.

"Could you please step into my office?" Deb asked.

"I'd be delighted." That wasn't a lie. Lorna popped up and briskly traveled the ten feet to Deb's office.

Deb was standing behind her desk. She was sixtyish, short and round, with a bowl-shaped head of curly gray hair. She always wore a pair of glasses on her crown and preferred a standard daily uniform, a move that was either genius or insane—Lorna could never decide. Black pants and a black cardigan or blazer. The only thing that varied day to day was the color of her blouse. Today,

Deb's silk blouse was peach colored, with tiny swans dotting the fabric. Personally, Lorna favored tailored suits. Her self-help books had taught her that suits give an air of authority. Particularly dark colors. *King Kong*.

"How was your evening?" she asked Deb. They weren't friends, exactly, because Deb's large family and many children kept her from socializing outside of work. But they were friendly. They sat together at company meetings and often had lunch together in Deb's office to talk about work.

"Good, thank you. Shut the door, please."

Lorna hesitated. Deb never asked her to shut the door, and her trouble meter began to tick. "This must be about that raise," Lorna said, and chuckled at her joke in a feeble attempt to gauge the seriousness of this door-shutting business.

Deb did not smile. "Have a seat, Lorna." She gestured to the small, round conference table where they often had lunch.

This was not good. Lorna's scalp tingled with dread. "We don't need to sit, do we? I know you're very busy—"

"Sit," Deb said more firmly.

Lorna sat.

Deb took a long, deliberate drink of water, then came around from behind her desk and sat next to Lorna. She sighed. She glanced toward the window, which overlooked several massive transmission towers, and sighed again. "Lorna, Lorna, Lorna," she said sadly.

Oh no. Lorna's belly began to somersault. She hadn't been fired from a job since she was a teen. Quite the contrary—she had worked her way up through employee of the month awards to sales achievement awards. Yet she had an uneasy feeling that something bad was about to happen. Her immediate thought was to head off whatever it was, to correct whatever mistake she'd made before Deb could act. "Is this about the new sales quotas?" she blurted. "I know they're high, but you don't win the blue ribbon for going easy."

"No," Deb said. "But the quotas are insanely high. We've discussed that."

They had, but Lorna knew what her team was capable of. She drew a shallow breath. "Did . . . did something happen at the sales team meeting yesterday?" she asked. "I mean, I know what happened, I was there, but was someone . . . offended?" *Again?* she whispered in her head.

Deb didn't say anything but emitted another weary sigh.

There was a fine line between assertive and mean, and Lorna had missed the line a couple of times. "I admit, I was a little annoyed that they hadn't met this month's threshold." And she did say something that she knew was bad, but in her defense, she had not directed it at any one person. It had been more of a collective slander. "For what it's worth, I didn't call any one individual a moron," Lorna said quickly. "I said it was like working with a bunch of morons. I didn't mean to insult them, Deb. I was just trying to be funny and make a point."

Deb looked dubious.

"Millennials, man, am I right?"

"You're a millennial, Lorna."

Right. She kept forgetting that.

"I didn't call you in here to talk about the sales team meeting, although this admission doesn't help your case."

Her *case?* Well, that tipped her right into a small eddy of anger. Her *case* should be ironclad. She was the top salesperson at this firm. She pushed them, but it wasn't like there was no reward for that push. The more sales, the more money they all made. She frowned, trying to think of what she had done wrong so she could fix it. That's what she did—she fixed things, set everything to rights. Then she went home to her small apartment and ate frozen dinners and talked to her dog and fumed like any working woman in this country would do. *Think.* "The AutoZone account," she said, sitting up. That had to be it. "I had the team stay late last week to get the specs out quicker."

"On the promise of pizza. Which you didn't order until eight o'clock. People have lives outside of work, you know."

Unfortunately, she didn't really know. "I'm so sorry. I was attempting positive motivation." She'd read all about it in her book about hitting a million in sales.

"It's not positive when they don't actually get the pizza until well into the night."

"I'll make amends to the team."

"I hope you do. But that's not—"

"Please don't say it's Franklin Industries," Lorna blurted. She had everything riding on that account. Her promotion. Her bonus. Her raise. Her house.

Deb cocked her head to the side. "Are you okay?" She leaned closer to place her hand on top of Lorna's, which, Lorna suddenly realized, was curled into a tight fist.

"What? I'm fine."

"But it looks like you're crying." Deb gestured to Lorna's face.

Damn it. She really needed to see a doctor because her eyes had recently started leaking all the time. "No, no." Lorna grabbed a tissue from a box on the table. "Everything is fine." *Probably.* "It's allergies."

"Are you sure?"

"Positive." She dabbed at her face.

"Okay," Deb said, sounding uncertain. "I was trying to say that the problem we are having is you."

More leaks. Lorna dabbed harder at her face. "Me? That's crazy. I'm fine."

"What about the email attachment?"

Lorna paused while her brain sorted through a dozen email attachments she'd sent recently. She found nothing offensive. "Pardon?"

"The email attachment in which you . . . expressed some thoughts."

She'd expressed some thoughts? What was wrong with that? Her thoughts were pretty basic and mostly about work. Or instructing others to work. Or what was for dinner, or when she could walk her dog, or what the guy who lived above her was doing at 10:00 p.m. on a Tuesday that sounded like a flash mob rehearsal. But she hadn't put any of that in an email.

"Oh dear," Deb said. "You don't know."

"I don't know anything," Lorna admitted.

Deb sighed heavily again. She reached for a plain blue folder on the table and drew it toward her. She opened it, flipped through a couple of pages, found what she was looking for, and slid the paper across to Lorna.

Lorna was reluctant to take it but forced herself to look down and read. She didn't get very far because words started to swim. *King Doofus. Most Likely to Get Punched.* These words, *her* words, did not belong in this office. She'd written them in a letter she was composing to her sister. Her sister was her sounding board. Or she would be if Lorna ever sent the letters she typed, printed out, and stuffed into envelopes. But that was neither here nor there, because somehow, Deb had *this* letter. "I don't understand," she said slowly. She looked up from all the terrible words. "This is a letter to my sister. No one else was supposed to see it."

"Well, you made it un-private when you sent it to your entire team early this morning as an attachment to the Franklin Industries specs email."

Lorna's heart nose-dived to her toes. She felt suddenly sick—she'd been up at five working from home this morning, and both the specs document and the letter had been recently opened on her computer. When she responded to an email from the team about the Franklin project, she must have attached the wrong file. "Oh no." Her voice was shaking slightly. Her eyes burned and her chest heaved with an emotion that was so hot and toxic she almost couldn't breathe. "No, Deb, you don't understand—these were jokes."

"Your jokes are not funny."

Well, no kidding, looking at this list now. No matter how hard she tried, she could not be funny. "It's . . . it's something we used to do as kids. You know, make up superlatives for people." Even she knew that explanation wasn't very helpful. Lorna winced and looked at the page again. How could she have been so careless? She felt the blood draining from her face. And the faint but steady drum of anger that this had happened in the first place. "This is so bad," she admitted. "I would never intentionally hurt them. Never, Deb. I didn't mean . . . Listen, I will figure out how to make it up to them. I'll—"

"Lorna." Deb handed her another tissue, because apparently her eyes were really leaking. "I think you know you have a problem that needs to be addressed."

That felt . . . alarming. Did she know that? Maybe a little part of her? "Look, I was careless, and I feel horrible, and I've been working a lot lately, you know that, because I really want the promotion to senior vice president for all the reasons we've discussed, and I let—"

Deb surged forward, placing her hand on Lorna's again. "As your boss, I'm telling you that you have a problem. Now, I like you, Lorna. But this isn't the first time we've had an issue with something you've said or done. It is clear to me that you have a lot on your mind and you need better coping strategies."

Lorna was shaking her head. Maybe she was shaking her whole body. She felt like she was standing outside of herself, not really absorbing this properly. Not really understanding. She kept a tight control of everything in her life and could not allow it to get out of control. Out of control was when bad things happened. "Are you firing me?" she asked, her voice scarcely above a whisper.

"No," Deb said softly. "And I don't want to. You're really good at what you do and you could go far. But I want you to get help."

"Okay," Lorna said. "I will get help. But really, I probably only need some sleep." Even as the words left her mouth, Lorna knew that wasn't what she needed. Who typed letters to her sister going through the roster of her team? Who spent her birthday picnicking at Zilker Park with just her dog? Who couldn't get invited to an after-work happy hour to save her life? And Deb, whose opinion she trusted, looked very skeptical. Lorna scooched forward. "I can see how things might look a little . . . disconcerting. I don't mean to be this way, I swear it, Deb. I *want* to be their friend. I'm having a bit of difficulty figuring out how."

Deb nodded. "It's good that you recognize you can be a little . . . much."

"Cringe, even," Lorna added helpfully.

"I know you're a good person, Lorna. But Dirk is not happy. He's questioning my judgment about you."

Dirk Kendall was the CEO of Driskill Workflow Solutions. He would have the final say about her appointment to senior vice president and the raise that would accompany it. Not to mention the signing bonus. All the things Lorna needed and had worked so hard to achieve.

"I convinced him to let me help. But, Lorna, you need to get your act together. Fortunately, at Driskill, we take mental health very seriously."

That was debatable, but Lorna was not in a position to point that out.

"I'm putting you on leave—"

Lorna gasped as if Deb had just sentenced her to death.

"—and sending you to our new wellness program. You'll be entering the day program at Bodhi Tao Bliss Retreat and Spa on the shores of Lake Austin." She smiled as if Lorna had won a grand prize. As if she should be happy about this turn of events.

Lorna knew that place—she'd sold them their workflow software and then laughed bitterly at the thought of all those spa-goers walking around in plush bathrobes. That some people didn't have to work and could lounge around all day made her a skosh furious.

"Their day program is called Leaves of Change, and it's thirty days."

Lorna's mouth fell open. "Are you crazy?"

"I most certainly am not," Deb said curtly.

"I mean . . . this isn't like you, Deb. I can't take that kind of time off. We're about to finish Franklin Industries, and you know how important that is to me." That was the sale that would put her over the top. The project that would get her the promotion and the raise and the bonus. The bonus that would enable her to put a down payment on her grandmother's house.

"Franklin Industries will not be finished in the next month. We are just now developing the proposal."

But she needed to be here to develop the proposal. This was a disaster. *That stupid letter.* Lorna straightened, making her spine stiff. That was something else she'd learned in her books—

posture mattered. "I understand. But the thing is, I am very good at my job, and the team can't really function without a leader. Also, I want to go on record and say that I don't think any of this is necessary. I promise I will make amends. And I will work very hard not to be snappish."

Deb did not look pleased. "The problem is that I don't believe you can make proper amends to your team until you address whatever is the cause of your . . . unhappiness."

Lorna opened her mouth to argue, but Deb held up a hand. "It's not up for debate. Human resources has already prepared the paperwork. All I need from you is the name of someone on your team who can head things up while you're out."

A seismic urge to beg or, conversely, to toss a chair through the window was building in her chest, pushing all the air from her lungs. It was impossible to explain to Deb how important her plans were. She had no other way to achieve her goal of buying her grandmother's house. Well, except maybe adhering to the terms of the trust her mother had left for her, and that *certainly* wasn't happening. Talk about a rage-inducing thought.

Panic like she hadn't felt in years seized her. She always had a plan. She was always working toward something. That was all she did! She *worked*. And she tried not to say rude things or get angry with people who let her down, and okay, she needed improvement. But she did *not* need a wellness program.

"So . . . you need to gather your things and sign some papers and speak to your team to get the ball rolling. Okay?" Deb leaned forward in her seat like she was about to stand.

Lorna could hardly think to speak. "I don't know if I would choose the word *okay*."

"Listen." Deb put her hand on Lorna's again, which was now balled into a fist so tight she was surely cutting off circulation. "It's going to be all right. You'll be back before you know it. Take a few breaths and work through things. I know the last few years have been very difficult for you." She stood and straightened her blouse with the tiny swans, signaling that the meeting was over.

No, Deb, this will not be all right. It will not be even remotely all right. She could feel the cracks spreading across her bubble already.

"Okay," she forced herself to say, and then made herself stand up too. "Okay."

It was not okay.

Chapter 2

Lorna Now

LORNA'S ENTIRE TEAM SEEMED ALMOST GIDDY WHEN SHE announced she'd be taking some time off.

"Thirty days?" Kendra, the newest hire, asked with more enthusiasm than she had ever shown for work. It was practically a squeal.

Lorna affirmed it was thirty days, although she was already plotting how to shorten that time. She reluctantly named Lance (Most Likely to Microwave Fish) as the team leader. He wasn't the best salesperson, but he was the most organized of the bunch. Suzanne was determined not to let Lorna leave until she explained herself.

"I just don't understand why I was given Most Punchable Face."

"It was a joke, Suzanne. A bad one," Lorna said. "I'm sorry."

"Yeah, but why did you say it about me?" She looked around pointedly at her colleagues. "Does *everyone* think my face is punchable?"

"I'm sorry to you all," Lorna said before anyone could answer. "I was just trying to be funny in a letter to my sister."

"What is funny about me looking like a serial killer?" Sheldon asked curtly. "What does that even mean? Is it my hair? It's my hair, isn't it?" he said, running a hand over his old-style flattop.

None of the other team members made eye contact with him. They were saved from having to respond when human resources showed up. Beverly Rich, who was assigned to Lorna's team and who had "sat in" on more than one meeting, was grinning like this was a birthday party and she was about to blow out the candles. "Time to go, Lorna," she said cheerfully, and gestured to the exit.

"Right." Lorna picked up her things. "So listen, guys," she said as Beverly put her hand firmly on Lorna's elbow and began to steer her toward the exit. "I'm really sorry. I know this is sudden, but I will be back, and we will make our goals, and we will get our bonuses. Don't worry!"

No one said a word until the exit door closed behind her. Then Lorna heard several people start talking at once.

Was she really that bad?

She walked out into a blistering, bright day, her box in her arms. What, exactly, was she going to do now? She spotted Raymond, the guy who panhandled at the intersection in front of their building every morning, and walked over to him. She handed him her Driskill coffee thermos and the snack bag she kept in her bottom desk drawer for late nights. She was tired of Fritos anyway. "Looks like I'm going on a little vacay," she said.

"For real?" Raymond asked, taking the proffered items. "Never knew you to go on vacation."

"I know," she said morosely. "I don't know who will bring you donuts on Fridays."

"Hmm," he said, looking thoughtful. "I'll figure out something. Enjoy yourself. You deserve a break."

He had no idea. "Take care, Raymond. Mean streets of Austin and all that."

"Aw, they're not so bad," he said as he ripped open a bag of Fritos.

She walked on, her box a bit lighter without that Driskill

thermos that leaked half the time. Why give out thermoses that were going to leak, anyway? How did that say *staff appreciation*? It said careless, thoughtless, and cheap to Lorna.

On the drive home, her anxiety turned to nausea. This was a huge miscarriage of justice, and therefore, according to her self-help books, an "opportunity." *Stand up for yourself!* She should have fought back. She should have admitted she knew she wasn't funny, that she'd made a terrible mistake, and yes, she was easily annoyed, but that didn't mean she ought to be put on leave for a month or that she had a problem. Had anyone taken the time to consider what they stood to lose in sales without her there? Of course they hadn't, because that would have been her job. She knew, without a doubt, that she could peddle workflow software better than anyone.

She was not the problem.

She turned onto her street in Central Austin, where the old live oaks with their long and twisty limbs created a canopy. Halfway down the block, she pulled onto a gravel patch for parking carved out of what once had been a grand lawn. The patch held exactly four cars. Or, rather, three cars and one giant truck that forced them all to park so close they had to squeeze their bodies out of their doors.

That gravel patch was something else to be angry about. It was an eyesore before the beautiful, pink-brick Georgian home. This grand house had once belonged to her grandparents. When she was a child, her family spent weeks during the summer and holidays here. In her preteens, they'd moved in and lived here until her mother sold it. Then it had been chopped up into four separate apartments. That was before the paint on the wooden window frames had peeled and the trumpet vine had grown wild up one corner of the house. Before the bricks in another corner had begun to crumble and one of the chimneys needed to be patched. Before that strange, musty smell permeated the central hall.

And yet, despite its run-down appearance, the house was still impressive.

She slumped down petulantly in the driver's seat of her car. Her breath had grown short, a sure sign she was getting rage-y. Her entire plan to buy back the house was in jeopardy now. She'd been saving for so long, since the moment she saw the For Rent sign on one of her weekly drive-bys a couple of years ago. She'd stalked this house like it was a cheating husband until she was finally able to snag one of the apartments.

Her great-grandfather, a honcho at the University of Texas in his day, had bought it when houses in this neighborhood were being built to accommodate the university elite. Both floors boasted a wide center hallway, constructed to encourage airflow in the days before air-conditioning. The rooms were spacious, the ceilings high and ornate. The floors solid oak. The backyard was deep and ran to a small creek tributary where Lorna and her sister, Kristen, used to catch frogs and minnows and an occasional garden snake.

When she and Kristen were girls, Nana would wake them up for pancakes and French toast, served with happy faces made using fruit and whipped cream. On spring afternoons, Nana would lay a quilt in the backyard, then serve them an English tea with finger sandwiches. The tea was iced, but Lorna still felt like a princess. In the winter, when it rained, Nana and Papa would create a scavenger hunt for the two of them, leading them to all the nooks and crannies in the house where they'd find little objects, like an empty Zippo lighter, a thimble, a deck of playing cards. When all the items were found, they were awarded with candy and permission to watch their favorite TV show—*Full House*.

Later, after her parents divorced, Lorna, Kristen, and their mother moved in with Nana, who was a widow then. Papa had died from a lung ailment as best Lorna could recall now. Lorna and Kristen had the two rooms on the top floor at the back of the house. Kristen learned how to climb out those windows and down a tree within a few weeks. Lorna had been too clumsy and too fearful of falling to try.

There was an old tomcat that came by every day and slipped into a hole in the skirting around the house and lived beneath them. Nana was allergic to cats, so they'd never had pets, but Lorna pretended that tomcat was hers. She walked every day to a small neighborhood school while Kristen was bused to a bigger middle school.

Every Halloween, they had the spookiest house, all of them eager to decorate with ghosts and witches. On the porch, they kept cauldrons of punch and candy. In the summer, their yard was the prettiest and most inviting—green grass, flowers in the window boxes, a tire swing beneath one massive oak. But the yard began to fade when Nana couldn't tend it anymore. Barn swallows built their nest in the swing.

Lorna had believed they would live happily forever in that big rambling house. But then Kristen ran away, and Nana accidentally drank herself to death, and Mom sold the house and moved them into a garage apartment, and this house was chopped into four apartments with cheap, tacky baths and kitchens added in.

Lorna now lived where the dining room and kitchen used to be. The space had been unforgivably mutilated, a bath installed in what had once been the large walk-in pantry. She intended to restore the house to its former glory when she owned it.

And she *would* own it.

Last year, her landlord, Mr. Contreras, he of the bushy crop of white hair and bushier mustache, mentioned he was looking to sell in the next couple of years, as the old house needed lots of expensive repairs. Lorna had told him then and there that she would buy it from him.

He'd looked down at her like a grand priest from on high. "Now why would a woman like you want to own a pile of bricks like this?"

She didn't know what a "woman like you" was supposed to mean. "It could be restored."

"Not without cash, baby. A *lot* of cash. The foundation alone would set you back twenty-five grand, and that's using one of my contractors. Not to mention the property taxes are skyrocketing in this neighborhood. Nah, you don't want this. No one will be able to afford a property like this except a developer. You a developer?"

"No. I sell workflow software."

Mr. Contreras chuckled as if she'd meant that as a joke. But she hadn't, because she was Not Funny. "Find yourself a good man and move to the suburbs like everyone else, sweetheart."

Well, that was easier said than done, and that was assuming she even wanted the life Mr. Contreras had prescribed. But she couldn't care less whether he underestimated her—she'd been saving like mad, pushing her team to the brink of revolt just so she could hit the highest sales mark. Thanks to her drive, everyone had made more money, and she was a shoo-in for senior vice president and its signing bonus and better salary, which, added to her savings, would be enough for a down payment on the house. It was a win-win-win-win-win.

Or it had been, until the egregious events of today.

She felt sick again. In a dull grip of panic. And furious, like she could pick up her car and hurl it down the street.

They couldn't just get rid of her, could they? For the mistake of attaching a private letter to a work email? That *attachment* was for Kristen! Which was doubly frustrating because Kristen would never read the letter. Mostly because Lorna would never send it to her sister in Florida, because she and Kristen were on a break just now.

Anyway, if that was how they were going to treat her, their *top salesperson*, then she should just find another job. That would show them. *Way to chase off your best talent, Driskill Workflow Solutions.*

Or . . . *Or.* She could at least consider meeting the conditions of the trust. But only as a last resort.

Her head was beginning to pound with the tension invading every inch of her body. She got out of her car and walked stiffly to the door. As she neared the entry, she could hear the thud of something hitting the house over and over.

Where once there had been a double door with twin sidelights, there was now a single door with reinforced glass and a keypad entry. She punched in the code and entered the building as another thud rattled the old house.

A stack of mail had been strewn across the console just inside the entry. Removal of the original door with its mail slot had necessitated the erection of a mailbox on the side of the house with four separate compartments. But, in the inimitable reasoning of the US Postal Service, they'd all been keyed the same. It had become the habit of the residents to empty all four boxes and dump the mail on the table for everyone to sort through. Lorna considered this a security breach of the highest order, but as Martin from upstairs had once pointed out, if someone broke in and stole all the offers for free window replacement estimates, no one would be harmed.

She found only two items of mail for her—both junk—and moved on to her apartment door at the base of the stairs: 1A, as it should be. She stuck her key in the lock just as Martin came bounding down the stairs with a backpack slung over his shoulder, his over-the-ear headphones on his head. The red earpads made him look like he was wearing apples. "Hey, Lorna," he said as he sailed past her.

"Martin," she said crisply. She had not yet registered her complaint about his marching band rehearsals or whatever was going on upstairs at night, but she liked to give advance notice of her displeasure. Not that Martin noticed—he was out the door before she could ask him if he wanted to know what was bothering her.

There was that thudding again.

She opened the door to her apartment and stepped inside, placing her bag on the chair at her small writing desk. "Agnes?" Usually her dog was waiting for her at the door, dancing around on her short little corgi legs. But the apartment was still.

She walked through her apartment looking for her dog. There weren't many places to look: Her space had been partitioned into a living and small kitchen area, a bedroom, and the intolerable bathroom. As she was on the ground floor, she also had an exit to the backyard with a dog door. Mr. Contreras had tried to charge her extra for that access, but Lorna had countered that the fact her bathroom was a closet ought to bring the price down. In the end, he did not raise her rent, and Agnes was free to come and go as she pleased while Lorna was at work.

The large backyard was available to all the residents, but until a couple of months ago, Lorna and Agnes were the only ones who ever used it. It was overgrown in some places, bare in others. The flower beds grew nothing but weeds now.

But then a kid had moved in across the hall from her. On the day he and his dad moved in, the kid had spotted her—or rather, Agnes—when they'd come back from a walk. "I like your dog!" he shouted at her from across the lawn.

Of course he liked her dog—*everyone* liked her dog. With a curt nod of acknowledgment, Lorna had kept walking.

"Can I pet it?" he shouted.

Lorna stopped walking. She did not want to stand in the sun and humor the kid, but she also didn't want to seem like a witch. "It's not an it; it's a her."

The boy took that as a yes and came charging toward them. His dad, laden with two boxes, was apparently perfectly fine with his son petting a stranger's dog. He'd barely even registered them before disappearing inside.

The kid had round cheeks, blue eyes, and reddish-brown hair that was in desperate need of a comb. Sweat poured off him—not that he seemed to notice. She thought he was seven or eight, overweight in a way that made her ache for him because she knew from personal experience how cruel kids could be.

As he squatted down next to Agnes, his face split with a broad smile. "I love dogs. They are my favorite animal. But also sloths are my favorite because they're really cool."

"Sloths?" Lorna had recoiled slightly. "Sloths are no comparison to dogs, sir."

"What's your dog's name?"

"Agnes."

"Hi, Agnes. *Hiii*," he said, scratching her behind the ears.

Agnes lapped up the attention like warm milk, her bobbed tail wagging hard. The kid laughed at her eagerness. Then the man came out and yelled and the kid got up. "Bye!" He ran off.

Since that day, the kid was always in the yard, and if he was in the back, Agnes was with him. Agnes adored him.

Lorna suspected Little Mr. Sunshine was responsible for the thudding and went to the back door. She turned the lock and then stepped out onto her small landing. Just as she did, a large object whizzed past her head, slammed into the side of the house, and bounced up and off again. She'd almost been decapitated by a soccer ball.

"Sorry!" the kid called out as he and Agnes chased after the ball.

"You should look where you're kicking," Lorna said irritably, but the kid was too far away to hear. "Agnes, come!"

Agnes ignored her. The kid kicked the ball again, this time sending it to the back of the lawn.

"Fine." Lorna walked down the few rickety steps onto the lawn, then followed the path that led to the creek. There used to be pavers here, but they were long gone. She could feel the heels of her sensible pumps sinking into the loamy dirt and wished she'd thought to take them off. The kid was squatting in the grass, looking down at something. And Agnes was beside him, digging furiously, kicking up dirt that landed on Lorna's pant legs until she thought to move. That's when she noticed a very big hole in a bald patch of the grass. "What's this?" she demanded, gesturing wildly to the hole.

The kid pulled the soccer ball out of it and looked up at her, blinking in the sun. "It's a hole."

"I see that it is obviously a hole, but what is it doing here? Agnes, stop that," she commanded.

Agnes stopped for a moment, turned her dirt-covered snout to look at Lorna, then gleefully resumed.

"Aggie and I dug it today."

"Why?"

He examined the hole as if searching for the answer there. Honestly! Like this house wasn't falling around them as it was. The lawn was so unkempt that a boy could see it and believe it the best place for a hole.

"Do you have a shovel?" Lorna asked, making a mental note of the complaint she'd submit to Mr. Contreras. *Children should not have shovels to dig holes for no apparent reason.*

"The shovel is over there," the kid said, pointing to a small equipment shed that was leaning slightly to the left. And there was the shovel, propped up against the wall. So typical of the yard crew—they left out equipment that the tenants' rent paid for to be stolen or taken up by young boys with bad ideas.

"But I found this really cool metal thingy." The kid dropped the ball and looked around the grass, then triumphantly produced a green metal stake, the sort that plastic fencing was tied to.

Lorna stared at it. Then she stared at his red, sweaty face. "You found this and thought, *I'll just dig a massive hole*?"

"It's *really* deep," he said proudly.

"So deep someone could fall into it and break a leg." Not to mention it was just another thing she would have to repair when she got the house back.

"Aggie fell in, and she didn't break any of her legs."

"Is that right?" Lorna asked, her hands going to her hips. "Well, first of all, her name is Agnes. Second, her legs are so short they are nearly impossible to break." She marched over to the shed and grabbed the shovel before Boy Genius got any more ideas.

"I forgot her name. Sorry, Aggie," the boy said to the dog, and leaned down to pet her head. Agnes wiggled closer to him. Traitor.

"Where is your father?" Lorna demanded as she came back with the shovel.

"He's at his job. Sometimes his job lets him come get me at school. But most of the time I ride the bus. I get off at the corner and I walk home and wait for my dad. Kenzie wanted me to come home with her one time, but Dad said I have to have permission."

"Okay, well, that's a lot of information I won't necessarily retain," Lorna said. "Second, you shouldn't be digging deep holes for people to fall into and break their ankles."

"Okay," he said.

He was terribly agreeable, this sweaty, chubby kid. She studied him a moment. In her considered opinion, he was too young to be left alone. She felt something against her pant leg and glanced down. Agnes had at last acknowledged her, the one who bought squeaky dog toys and kibble that cost as much as caviar, and was licking the dirt she'd kicked onto her clothes.

The skin on Lorna's neck began to tingle like it did when she felt she might scream. She was still holding the shovel, but instead of using it to fill the hole, she shoved the blade into the edge, filled the scoop, and hurled the dirt away. She did it again. And again.

She kicked off her shoes, hard, and they sailed across the yard. She could feel her hair fall out of the containment pins. She kept digging, fast and furious, tossing mounds of dirt, forgetting the kid, forgetting Agnes, forgetting everything but the rage that wanted to explode out of her head.

"Hey!"

She didn't hear him at first, she was so intent on the hole.

"*Hey!*" the kid shouted again.

Lorna realized in a moment of horror how she must appear to the boy. He was probably frightened out of his wits. She paused, her mind racing around all the things she could say to ease any distress she'd caused. That was probably impossible—her chest was heaving as she tried to catch her breath. Her back and chest had sweated through her clothes. Her pant leg was sticking to her skin.

"Do you think there's treasure buried here?" he asked excitedly. "Because the Indians used to live here. They might have buried something!"

Lorna paused to consider it. She doubted there was treasure of any sort, but she and Kristen had buried a box of coins back here once. "Maybe. We won't know if we don't dig." She started digging again.

So did the kid, with his metal thingy. He didn't last long. Neither did Agnes. And when Lorna finally gave up, her rage spent (for the moment—rage had a way of creeping back in when she least expected it), she dropped the shovel and fell onto her butt beside the kid. Her clothes were ruined. She was covered in sweat and dirt. And she wasn't entirely sure what had just happened.

"Are you okay?" the kid asked.

"Why does everyone keep asking me that? I'm *fine*."

"Because you're crying," he said. "Wait!" He hopped up and ran to the back door that led from the main hall. He was back a moment later with a bottle of water and a metal box. He handed her the water bottle, then put down the box. She glanced at it—it was a first aid kit.

"What are you doing?"

"You're crying," he said again. He produced a small bottle of aspirin. He opened the lid and shook two into his grimy palm. He held them out to her. "I cry sometimes too, and my dad gives me these. He cries *a lot*."

Weird. "I don't need this, but okay," she said, and took the two aspirin, washing them down with a grimace.

"Your hair is really big," he said.

"I'm aware."

"It's like a superpower. Like Samson."

Lorna snorted and took another swig of his water before wiping off the mouth of the bottle with the tiny bit of sleeve that had escaped sweat or dirt. "Not exactly," she said.

"You have to believe," the kid said. "That's what my dad says."

His dad sounded like a dolt. Believing didn't give you a superpower. "What's your superpower?" she asked as she looked around for her shoes.

"I'm still deciding," he said, and began to draw something in the dirt with his metal thingy. "My dad says you have to try different things to find out what you like. Hey, want to see my box of badges?"

She had no idea what a box of badges was but shook her head. "Maybe some other time. I need to clean up." She rolled onto her knees and came to her feet, holding on to the shovel for support.

"Can Aggie and I still play?" the kid asked.

"I don't know. Can you do it without being loud? Because you were being loud when I came out here."

He looked surprised by this news. "*Super* loud?"

"Super-duper loud," she said, although she wouldn't swear to it in a court of law. "Can I trust you to stop kicking the ball against the house?" She bent down to pick up her shoes.

"I'll be quiet. When we have quiet time at school, my teacher said I'm the quietest."

Doubtful. "Congratulations. Just keep it down. I had a terrible day. And don't fall in the hole—I don't need a lawsuit."

"Okay. Come on, Aggie!"

"*Agnes*," Lorna said again, but the two were already off like a shot across the yard.

She returned to her apartment, pausing at the threshold to kick clumps of earth off her shoes. No sooner had she closed the door behind her than the kid kicked the ball against the house again.

She stood very still in the kitchen, her eyes closed, her fists clenched at her sides. Then she stepped back to the kitchen door and watched the boy and Agnes. She'd been so happy playing in this backyard as a kid. Before everything went to hell. Nostalgia, warm and thick like honey, moved through her, filling her up. It was the good kind of nostalgia. Sometimes it made her feel sick, because not all nostalgia was good. But this was not that.

She watched the kid and Agnes long enough that if anyone saw, they might think she was being creepy. When the two went racing around the side of the house to the front yard, she finally turned away.

She heard a car door slam, then voices. Moments later, there was a knock at her door.

Lorna straightened her suit jacket, then remembered she was covered in dirt and sweat. She frantically tried to smooth her hair away from her face but felt it pop right back around, probably going off in a million frizzy curled directions. No time to fix it now. She went to the door and opened it a sliver. The man who lived across the hall with the kid was standing there, his arm around his son. She'd only seen him across the lawn, but up close, she realized he was bigger than he appeared at a distance. A little taller than her and broad-shouldered. He looked to be roughly her age, maybe a bit older, forty-five-ish, give or take. His hair was shaggy and long, almost reaching the shoulders of his plaid shirt. His eyes were nearly navy blue, and he was sporting an afternoon beard. He was good-looking. Much better looking than the men in her office. Good-looking enough that she didn't want to look away. She could see instantly what the kid would look like when he was grown: barrel-chested and strong.

He cocked his head to one side to see her better in the crack of the door. "Hi there," he said, and smiled. A very lovely smile. "I believe we have your dog."

As if on cue, Agnes trotted forward. Lorna opened the door a little wider so she could trot in, but immediately returned to peering through just a crack. "No problem."

He was still smiling, and she couldn't work out why. Was he just . . . friendly? "Everything okay?" he asked.

"All good here," she said quickly.

He nodded, then put his hand on the kid's shoulder. "Can you say thank you for allowing you to play with her dog?"

"Thank you for allowing me to play with your dog," the kid said. "Bye, Aggie!"

Lorna wanted to correct him again but held her tongue. She wasn't a complete curmudgeon.

"I'm sorry," the man said. "I got caught up at work. I hope my son didn't bother you."

"No. He's just . . . young."

"That he is. Anyway, thanks again. Have a good afternoon."

Lorna gave him a curt nod to indicate that as much as she would like to have a good afternoon, that ship had already sailed. She watched them disappear into the apartment across the hall, the man's arm around his son, the son chattering about (and she might have misheard this) missile launches.

She closed the door and turned around. Agnes had already melted onto the floor in a sploot. Her nubbin of a tail began to wag when Lorna glared down at her. "Thanks a lot."

Agnes kept wagging her cropped tail and added a happy pant to it.

Lorna's wave of nostalgia and any residual rage had already emptied out of her, leaving her numb. She glanced at the neat stack of letters on the console table next to her chair. They were all pink. All from her stepmother. All unopened.

Next to the pink envelopes was a stack of white legal-sized envelopes, all securely sealed and with premade address labels affixed. Those were the letters she wrote twice a week, without fail, to Kristen, but could not find the courage or forgiveness to send. Just looking at them made her eyes well with tears, which infuriated her. What did she have to cry about?

Unfortunately, of late, Lorna had noticed that she often felt like crying and couldn't say why. It was weird and stupid, and she operated under the assumption that if she ignored it, it would go away like that mysterious bump on her neck did.

But it was also weird and stupid to write letters to her sister she never sent. She avoided her father's calls as best she could, and when she couldn't, she kept them unpardonably short. Her attempts at humor made her sound like a psychopath sometimes, and the worst part of all was that she didn't know why she did any of it.

She didn't know why she was so closed off to the world. But she'd built and fortified a super-max bomb shelter in her that even she couldn't penetrate. The only thing she knew for sure was that living in a bomb shelter could get pretty lonely. Sometimes she really wanted to force open the door and have a look at whatever it was she was hiding from. Or missing. But mostly, she felt too scared to face it.

She looked down at her dog. "Come on, Agnes," she said, and started for the kitchen. She got some kibble for Agnes and a snack pack of Nutter Butter cookies for herself. As she stood there munching the cookies over the sink, she looked again at the stack of letters.

She turned away from them. A bone-deep weariness settled over her.

Maybe she would do this wellness thing. She didn't put much stock in things like that, but then again, she'd never actually tried it. She did not like to do things that made her uncomfortable. But wasn't she always telling her team to open their minds to the many possible roads to sales? Maybe she needed to open her mind to the many possible roads to wellness.

It wasn't as if she really had a choice at this point. She needed her job if she was going to buy this house. Sure, she could find another job, but she'd put so much time and effort into Driskill. She deserved the promotion. And she didn't want to start over.

She polished off the last Nutter Butter and fetched her phone. She retrieved the papers Beverly had so gleefully shoved in her hand as she walked out the door this afternoon and called the number to schedule her first appointment.

Hello, Kristen—

> Today I almost got myself fired because of a letter I wrote to you. Figures. Apparently, I push the team too hard to make our goals. Well, guess what? I have to push if I am ever going to buy back Nana's house, which we lost because of you. Happy now? And don't hand me Mom's old argument that it wasn't your fault but the fault of society and a lack of affordable health care. We all know it was you. You promised. You promised and promised and promised and you never did live up to your promises and now I have to go to a wellness thing. Thanks a lot.

> PS: Saw there is a hurricane headed your way. I hope you have those hurricane windows everyone talks about.

Chapter 3

Lorna Now

THE BODHI TAO BLISS RETREAT AND SPA WAS ONE OF THOSE swank West Austin places, set on lush acreage on the banks of Lake Austin. In other words, it was for rich people. There were cabins for long-term residents of the program (Lorna wondered how long anyone would want to be part of the program. One month? Three months? A year?), all on the water, all with little patios, the length of a fishing line from the shore. There were activities like paddleboarding, yoga, and nature walks. Gentle music drifted through the trees from the same apparatus that provided the soft lighting, following people wherever they went. And a scent that Lorna found cloying—incense—smothered any other natural smells.

People wandered around in slide-on sandals and those plush white bathrobes that had made her angry when they bid the job. Servers milled about with trays of orange juice and green cleanses. The whole thing was so Austin that Lorna couldn't help but grit her teeth.

She'd worn trousers and a smart jacket to her first appointment because she was a professional. And a wee bit insecure. She certainly wasn't the type to show up at the grocery store or pharmacy in denim shorts, and she wasn't the type to wear leggings to a place like this. But she was the only one dressed in this manner—everyone else was wearing loungewear. Everyone was way too casual these days.

The young woman behind the counter was all smiles and soft white linen. She had inky-black hair that hung down her back in a silky tail. Her skin, Lorna couldn't help noticing, was flawless. "Good morning," she said brightly. "You're Lorna Lott?"

Obviously. She had just given the woman her driver's license and paperwork. "Yes."

"Purrrfect," the girl said. Her name tag said Xandra, which Lorna guessed she'd spent her entire life spelling for baristas, who still got it wrong. She might have attempted a joke about the woman's name but, given her recent history, thought it better to remain silent.

"If you will come this way," Xandra said, and began to walk down a hall. "Did you bring a change of clothes?"

"What?" The first signs of panic erupted on Lorna's scalp in the form of aggressive tingling. "Was I supposed to?"

"Not necessarily. Some people like to change into something comfy."

Comfy? No one said prepare to be comfy! she silently screamed.

Xandra opened the door to a stark white room. White beanbags were scattered about the floor, and a few white chairs were arranged around small white writing desks. The room smelled of incense, and classical guitar music was playing faintly in the background, the sound competing with the trickle of a small water feature running in the corner. Lorna stepped into the room as a dark slash across this otherwise snowy landscape. *King Kong strikes again.*

She turned back to Xandra. "I think there must be some mistake. I am here for the wellness program."

"Yes, we have you down for that. This is where we start the

program. There are a few intake questions we need you to answer." She handed Lorna an iPad. It was white.

Lorna handed it back. "I already did that over the phone."

Xandra handed the iPad back to her again. "That was the initial intake. This is the more in-depth one."

Lorna slowly, reluctantly held on to the iPad. She'd thought the initial interview was invasive enough, asking her height and weight and if she was on any medications. Why did anyone need to know that?

"Have a seat wherever you feel most comfortable and fill it out. Your concierge will be in to fetch you for the morning meditation in about thirty minutes."

"I haven't signed up for any classes yet," Lorna said. "What do you mean, concierge?"

"Morning meditation is not a class. We start each day by centering ourselves. Everyone on campus is expected to participate. Your concierge will explain all." She pressed her palms together at her chest and bowed.

"Great, thanks," Lorna muttered, but Xandra had already exited stage left.

With a sigh of annoyance, Lorna looked around the room. The beanbags were interesting, but there was no way she was going to humiliate herself by trying to get up and down from one of those. She picked a desk and chair in the corner of the room, as far from the door as she could be, and swiped the iPad to get started.

The first thing the form required was a name, which annoyed Lorna, since they already had it. Same for her address. She wondered if Driskill's workflow design was responsible for this crappy interface. She would love to give that smug engineer Gordon her feedback.

She answered more routine questions, dashing off her yes-no

replies with little thought, until she got to a group of questions that gave her pause. *Are you sexually active? What is your gender preference? Do you identify as LGBTQ+?*

Wow. Nosy much? She couldn't imagine what that information had to do with why she was here. Not that she completely understood why she was here, but unless they were worried about a venereal disease, she didn't think it was germane. They had some nerve to ask.

From there, the questions became increasingly intrusive. *Do you abuse substances? If yes, what substance and how often per week? Have you had any thoughts about harming or killing yourself in the last ninety days? Do you ever have any thoughts about harming or killing someone else? Do you ever hear voices? Do you sleep through the night?*

She had the urge to harm some*thing* else right this minute.

She continued down the list, dashing off *no no no*. Frankly, she wasn't sure what embarrassed her more—that she was not currently sexually active or that she wasn't cool enough to smoke pot. Why couldn't they ask something that would give them real information about her, like did she have a dog? Everyone knew that dog lovers were generally better people than those who didn't love dogs. Why didn't they ask if she took care of her mother when she was dying with cancer? Didn't that count for something?

By the time she finished, sharp pangs of regret for agreeing to this were shooting through her bowels.

A brisk knock on the door was followed by the entrance of a young man dressed in all white, his skin as dark as her suit. "Hello, Lorna," he said.

"Hello . . . you."

"My apologies, I should have said. I am Montreal."

Lorna blinked. "Not Toronto?"

Montreal smiled. "Montreal. My sister is Toronto."

"Seriously?"

"No." He chuckled. "I'm an only child. Have you completed the intake?"

She handed him the white iPad.

"Wonderful. It's time for the morning meditation. If you will follow me."

With a grunt, Lorna got up. "For the record, I don't actually do meditation."

Montreal merely smiled.

She followed him down another white hall and into a gymnasium. At least here, there were people dressed in something other than all white. But there were a lot of those fluffy white bathrobes wandering about too. And she was the only person wearing a suit. *Great, another fashion disaster. Just buy a few potato sacks and call it.*

There were people handing out braided mats. Montreal handed one to Lorna and invited her to sit where she felt comfortable. "I'll fetch you after our morning practice." He smoothly disappeared into the crowd.

Lorna felt conspicuous. Like it was obvious to the dozens of people in here that she did not belong. She would have felt more comfortable in an office. But she found a space and put her mat down, then somehow maneuvered herself onto it, even crisscrossing her legs while praying her tight pants didn't split.

There was a platform stage at one end of the gym, a lone ottoman the only thing on it. A man with a high bun of hair appeared through a side door, walked up onto the stage, then arranged himself in a seated position on the ottoman, his legs crossed, feet on his knees. He was not wearing white, but purple and green robes. A long gold chain with some sort of emblem

Lorna couldn't make out hung from his neck. She sincerely hoped she hadn't gotten mixed up with a cult.

"Good morning," he said. He spoke softly through a mic pinned to his lapel, his pitch a little higher than she might have expected from looking at him. "Welcome, everyone, and a particular welcome to our newcomers. Could we have a show of hands?"

Lorna didn't raise her hand. She didn't want any attention. She mentally tried to squeeze herself into a smaller frame.

The man with the bun looked at the few hands that had gone up, clasped his hands in a prayer pose, and bowed his head to them. "Our morning meditation is designed to help alleviate stress and center one's thoughts for the day's work ahead. Please close your eyes and empty your mind. Let your breath be your guide."

Lorna closed her eyes. Emptying her mind was impossible. All sorts of thoughts were pinging through just now. *Will they let me leave here or is this a "Hotel California" situation? How long do we have to keep our eyes closed? Is anyone looking at me? What's the deal with his sorcerer robes?*

"Please begin by counting your breaths." He made a very loud inhaling noise that lasted forever, then slowly released it.

Lorna took a deep breath too. *I hate this. Why empty your mind when there is so much to think about? I don't have time to be here. Deb didn't have to make me do this. Man, my pants are tight. My leg is falling asleep. Did I give Agnes her biscuit this morning?*

"Breathe in, breathe out slowly," the man said.

Lorna followed instructions to let the breath reach her toes. Amazingly, she felt herself begin to relax. *This is how they get you. They relax you to the point you don't know what you're signing up for and then—whammo—you're literally drinking the Kool-Aid. How am I going to fill that damn hole in the backyard? That kid will probably hurt himself if I don't. Why do I feel so angry? I'm literally just sitting here.*

It felt like the stillness went on forever. Lorna never did empty her mind of all the thoughts. A gong sounded, and it was over. As people picked up their mats, Montreal came to find her.

"Micah is ready for your assessment now."

He led her down a marble-tiled hall, the sounds of more classical guitar and the sweet scent of incense trailing after them, to a room that was, surprisingly, painted blue. Inside was a glass-top desk and two white beanbags. Another water feature was running in the corner. The windows were big and the leaves of a tree outside scraped against the glass in a sort of soothing rhythm. On the walls were paintings of elephants and symbols Lorna assumed were mystic in some way.

"Have a seat," Montreal said, gesturing toward the beanbags. "Micah will join you shortly." He smiled and backed out of the room.

Lorna glared at the beanbag he'd pointed to. This assessment business seemed designed to intentionally make her feel out of place. First the meditation, and now she was in a room meant for either a princess or a hippie. It was clearly not meant for King Kong. But King Kong lowered herself in her tight pants onto a beanbag anyway.

The door suddenly swung open and a man with a long tail of salt-and-pepper hair down his back swept in. He was wearing silk joggers, a short kimono jacket over a Grateful Dead shirt, and thick, black-rimmed glasses. He looked like he'd just come from a tai chi class.

A pink manila folder was tucked under his left arm.

"Welcome, Lorna," he said, as if they'd met dozens of times before. He walked straight to a hot plate and the teapot there. "I like to have a little herbal tea during these sessions. May I offer you some?"

Lorna eyed him suspiciously. "What sort of herbs?"

"I've got them all. What's your pleasure?"

There was no pleasure in this, but she did like a cup of lavender tea. "Lavender?"

"An excellent choice." He turned a dial to heat the hot plate. "Allow me to introduce myself. I am Micah Turnbull, a licensed clinical social worker and an avid coach of life."

Lorna was momentarily confused by his wording. "A life coach?"

"Personally, I think that phrasing is limiting, but yes, I am. Now it's your turn. Tell me about yourself."

She hated this. He could probably look at her and know everything he needed to know. Classic spinster story, thank you. "I don't know what to say. I'm not really an avid anything."

"Fortunately, that is not required. Just tell me a little something so I can get to know you."

"Umm . . ." There was a weird rumbling deep inside her. She was pretty good at not letting anyone see her. Especially herself. "Not much to say, really. I just work a lot and that's about it. I like dogs."

He poured water into two mugs. "What kinds of dogs?"

"All dogs. But I have a corgi."

"Great breed. What about a partner? Do you have one of those?"

She shook her head. Her stomach was beginning a slow churn. It always made her feel strangely guilty that she was in her forties and did not have a partner. She'd had them. Two, to be exact. And a smattering of dates in between. But neither significant other had lasted long, and the more time went on, the more isolated she'd allowed herself to be.

"Friends?"

She thought of Agnes and Deb. While she considered them friends, she imagined Micah might not. "Not really."

"Family?"

Okay, this was getting awfully personal, and she could feel her anger meter kicking into gear. She didn't like to talk about her family. "I don't see what that has to do with . . . this."

Micah poured the tea, handed her a mug, and, holding the other one, sank effortlessly onto the beanbag facing hers. He wrapped long, tapered fingers around his mug. "So, if I've heard you correctly, you're single, you don't have many friends, maybe fewer family, and you work a lot."

When he said it that way, she sounded pathetic. "That about sums it up."

He smiled and sipped his tea. "That's a bare list, though I think there is more to you than that."

"Nope." She sounded curt, and she didn't mean to be rude. But she didn't care to look more closely at what there was to her. She was perfectly satisfied with what she'd presented and had come to terms with this version of herself. It didn't do any good to go looking around for other things to add. That could only make the picture worse.

"For example, you're a good salesperson," he said.

"Oh." She hadn't thought of that. "Yes, I am. The best at Driskill. And that's not bragging—I'm just really good."

"I have no doubt. You manage a top-notch sales team too. The best in the company is what I read."

Well. She didn't know if she'd go so far as top-notch. Notch, maybe.

"But maybe not always as effectively as you would like?"

Okay, here we go. "Gross understatement, my man," she said, trying to sound chill. Sometimes at work, when he wasn't eating fish and was being chill, she'd hear Lance say "my man" to his friends on a call.

"And you may have some unresolved personal issues getting in the way of effective management and interpersonal relationships?"

That was a strange thing to surmise and entirely wrong, and did he want her to be just annoyed, or was he going for furiously annoyed? "No. Everything is fine. Why, what did Deb tell you?"

"Deb?" He put aside his tea, opened the folder, and pulled out a piece of paper to examine. "Beverly Rich compiled the referral. Do you know who she is?"

"Unfortunately," Lorna muttered.

"It doesn't matter who referred you. It's clear to me that people who work with you care about you."

Wrong. No one at Driskill, save maybe Deb, cared about her. They were probably having a pizza party right now to celebrate her absence.

"I urge you to open yourself up to our process. The goal is to remove any internal blocks you may have to working effectively with a team. Or anyone, for that matter. And those who are able to remove internal blocks are generally much more forgiving of themselves."

That was the goal? Dumb goal. "I don't have blocks. I work effectively with a team. I told you, everything is fine. This is just supposed to be a break."

He winced sympathetically. "But *do* you work effectively with other people? Because you said just a moment ago that you don't."

"*You* said I didn't always manage effectively."

He said nothing.

"I work effectively with them. I assign work and all the other things managers do."

Still nothing.

She did not understand what she was supposed to say. "Okay, I get it. I know they don't like me, but we sell a lot of software." There. She'd admit what she knew was true.

He nodded. "Wouldn't it be great if you could sell a lot of software and also have a good rapport with the team?"

Would it? She honestly didn't know anymore.

"I'm thinking a great place to start is with some exercises where you can learn how to connect with your innermost self. I like to use consistent meditation for that."

This guy was insane. She was already composing the email in her head. *Deb, thanks for trying, but the Bodhi Weirdo Place is not going to work for my particular issues.*

"The idea is to gain mental clarity so we can really tackle issues that you identify. As you go along in the program, we'll progress to some more out-of-the-box ideas to connect you with your inner peace and effect change."

Whoa. She did not like the sound of that. "Okay, hold up," she said, lifting her hand. "I've been to therapy before, and this doesn't sound like anything I've ever had to do. This sounds made up."

"Nope. Our approach has been studied and proven effective for people just like you. What we do here is one, acknowledge the need for change, two, contemplate why that change is necessary, then three, prepare to make positive changes before actually making them. In other words, we work on giving you the tools to identify necessary changes and then make them in a way that lasts. And then, of course, we'll work on tools to maintain those changes after the program." He suddenly leaned forward, his gaze piercing hers. "Lorna . . . do you think you need to change?"

Mumbo jumbo. She could feel her body coiling up. Did her company actually spend money on this nonsense? Was there any choice but to be here? "Maybe a tiny bit," she said, holding up thumb and forefinger to show how tiny the bit was. "How far out of the box are we talking?"

Micah smiled again, which, she was realizing, was his way of deflecting. "That's up to you. But I think you'll like the direction we're going. It's all designed to help you help yourself."

"Oh, for heaven's sake," she muttered.

"For today, let's get some background. We were talking about family—"

"No, you were mentioning it. We weren't talking about it." As long as they were pursuing clarity of thought, she was happy to clarify that she was *not* talking about her family.

"You're correct. Let's do that now."

Oh boy, he was not taking the hint. Lorna put aside her untouched mug of tea. "Look, Micah, I appreciate that you're doing your job . . . although I really don't get your job, and that's on me. But I don't like the idea of getting too personal."

"Are we getting personal?"

"You want to talk about my family."

He shrugged lightly and took a sip of his tea. "We don't have to talk about it. Perhaps you could just give me a general outline. Your mother is . . . ?"

She forced herself to swallow. "Dead. Cancer."

"Oh." He put down his teacup and leaned forward. "I am very sorry for your loss. That must have been incredibly hard."

It wasn't just hard. It was torture, misery, anguish . . . all the things. The burn of tears immediately sprang to the back of her eyes. It had been several years now, but Lorna could hardly think of that time without feeling miserable. "Yes," she said. "I was her caretaker, and in the end . . ." She'd said things to her mother that would haunt her forever. "It was awful. I don't want to talk about it."

He reached for a box of tissues and handed them to her. "Then we won't talk about it. Your father?" he asked, pivoting.

Her father? Another bad topic. "Umm . . . remarried. A long time ago. He lives in Florida." Dear old Dad, who had come crawling back when it was too late.

"Any siblings?"

An image of Kristen popped into her mind's eye. But it wasn't the same Kristen Lorna had seen last. It was the Kristen of her youth. Her big sister Kristen, the lithe, tanned, blond, pretty Kristen she'd so admired. Lorna remembered always laughing then, with Kristen, at Kristen, around Kristen. Those were happy times. Her skin began to feel clammy. She couldn't remember the last time she'd been sick, but she was feeling weirdly queasy. Like she was at the top of a roller-coaster ride and waiting for the drop. "A sister," she managed.

"And where is she?"

"Also in Florida. With my dad."

"What's her name?"

She swallowed down a swell of nausea. "Kristen."

"Younger? Older?"

"Does it really matter?" she blurted. She was doing her best not to lose her cool, but this line of questioning was so . . . intrusive. She curled her hand into a ball and shoved it under a bent leg, trying to keep a grip. Micah simply looked at her, waiting for an answer. "She's older."

"And you and Kristen are close?"

Her throat was constricting, making it difficult to breathe. "No. Not now. We used to be. Look, I really don't want to—"

"When—"

"We're on a break!" she snapped. Was she perspiring? She felt so hot suddenly. She imagined dark stains spreading under her arms. She wanted to rip off her jacket.

He pushed the box of tissues closer to her. "Are you doing okay, Lorna?"

She grabbed a tissue. "I'm fine. There is something wrong with my tear ducts. Look, Micah, my sister and I are on a break because she's an addict, and her addiction has ruined my life. Is that what you want to know?" She paused to dab at her eyes. *What in the world?* Was she going to keep shouting private things at him? This was precisely why she didn't want to talk about it.

"*Ah*," Micah said, like he'd just caught on to the theory of relativity.

Like what she'd said meant anything to him. He didn't have a clue, because unless you had lived with an addict, you could not imagine how addiction could throw an entire family into a tailspin and how sometimes you really wanted to step out of the room. Or out of a life. Or out of your own body. "I really don't want to talk about it."

"Okay." He tapped on his knee a moment. "I can imagine it must be very painful."

"Enraging is more like it."

"It looks like we have a lot of ground to cover before we design a program for you."

"Nope. Think we covered it," Lorna said firmly, trying to regain her internal composure. "They are in Florida, I'm in Austin. It's all good."

"Okay," he said, and smiled again. But this time, his smile seemed piteous, and she had to get out of there before she did something terrible like smash her fist through one of his elephant paintings.

She rolled onto her knees from the beanbag to get up, wondering how she was going to get to her feet without humiliating herself. But she had no time for grace and poise. "I'm sorry, I have a prior engagement. I should get going."

"Sure, Lorna," Micah said. "We'll pick back up tomorrow. I've got a pamphlet I'd like you to read on the power of meditation as a gateway to healing." He leaped up like a cat and walked to his desk, sparing her the humiliation of sticking her ass in his face while she gained her feet.

He picked up a brochure and handed it to her. "I look forward to working with you," he said. "And if I may, I think you have nothing to lose and everything to gain from this experience."

"Uh-huh." This room—and her jacket, and her life—was unbearably tight and hot. She had to get outside and breathe. "See you," she said, and walked out of his office before a torrent of sweat broke from her forehead.

Chapter 4

Lorna Now

SHE HAD STOPPED HYPERVENTILATING BY THE TIME SHE pulled into the gravel square before her house, but feared she might have another go when she noticed that a cornice from the corner of the house had fallen and broken into pieces on the patchy lawn. She pulled out her phone and made a note to call Mr. Contreras. Normally she would call right away, but she was still feeling nauseated and perturbed that Micah Feelgood, or whatever his last name was, thought he could just start asking personal questions. She would like to know what Kristen had to do with software sales.

She banged in through the front door and immediately stripped off her jacket, still hot, still perspiring. She picked up her mail—two window replacement flyers and an official-looking State Farm envelope. She was not insured by State Farm. She shoved them in her bag and turned to stride for her door. Her mind was a million miles away, which was why she almost tripped over a long plastic piece of something on the floor.

She realized it was a toy racetrack that went down the stairs, looped three times, and then ended right here in front of the door, so that any unsuspecting person entering the building could be nailed in the shin by a small metal object.

The boy was sitting with his back to his apartment door, a book on his lap and a crumpled sheet of paper on top of the open page. His T-shirt had ridden up a little over his belly. He was beating a chewed-up pencil on the floor like a drumstick.

Across the hall, she could hear Agnes whimpering on the other side of her door.

Lorna stared at the kid. He said, "I have cookies. Do you want one? Miss Liz made them."

"Who?"

"Miss Liz. She lives upstairs. She has a cat, and his name is Garfield, and he's *super* fat."

Miss Liz? Elizabeth Foster? The tenant in 2B? "What are you doing here?" Lorna asked.

"My homework."

"I mean, what are you doing here on the floor? And what is all this?"

The kid looked confused by her questions. "There's not a chair."

Lorna sighed.

"That's my racetrack. But my car went into that hole," he said, pointing out a heretofore unseen hole in the baseboard. "You should have seen it fly!"

Agnes barked behind the door.

"Of course it did," Lorna said impatiently. "Your loops are too big. It's physics. Have you started physics yet?"

"What?"

She groaned. "Where is your dad?"

"He's at work."

What did this guy do that kept him always at work, leaving his son unattended? "Don't you know that you can't sit in the hall like this? It's getting dark outside, and anyone could come along and snatch you."

The kid looked even more confused. "But they'd have to know the code."

"The code?"

"If someone was going to snatch me, they'd have to know the code to the door."

"A minor detail," she said with a sniff. "The point is, if they got the code, they could come in and snatch you while you eat cookies and pretend to do homework. Tell your dad that."

She didn't know if he heard her, because just then Martin came in, wearing his over-the-ear sound system. He saw the kid and slid the giant cups off his ears. "Bruh," he said. "What up?" He held out his fist.

The kid bumped Martin's fist with his. "Hi! Wanna play *Minecraft*?"

"Can't right now, buddy," Martin said. "Maybe later this week." He glanced at Lorna standing there and shifted his gaze to the kid. "You okay?"

"Excuse me?" Lorna protested. "What do you think I'm going to do, steal his cookies?"

Martin shrugged. "They look pretty good." He started up the stairs, then paused. "Hey, is this a Hot Wheels track? I haven't seen one in ages!"

"Yeah," the kid said, smiling proudly. "I lost my car. But when my dad comes home I can get some more and you can try it."

"That would be fire," Martin said. "But I've gotta bounce." He jogged up the stairs to his apartment.

The kid picked up his cookies. "I like his locs. They're cool."

Lorna looked at him, confused.

The kid gestured to his own fine brown hair. "I'm going to have locs when I grow up."

Lorna guessed he would not have them, given the texture of

his hair, but she let him have that fantasy. "Okay, well . . . be careful out here. And you'd better pick up that track. It's not allowed, you know."

"It's not?"

It wouldn't be once she owned the place. "Nope." She turned and went to her apartment. Agnes tried to get past her when she opened the door, but Lorna pushed her back and shut it behind them. She was going to melt with anxiety, right here. The authorities would find a giant puddle of sweat where she'd once stood.

A loud knock made her jump a foot in the air. Agnes started pawing the door.

Lorna looked around her apartment in a panic. No one ever came in here. She didn't like anyone in here but her and Agnes.

She opened the door a crack, peering out with one eye while trying to contain Agnes. She expected to see one of her neighbors, but no one was eye level. She lowered her gaze.

"Hi," the kid said.

"Hi." She moved her leg so Agnes couldn't get out.

"Can I use your bathroom?"

A bead of sweat dripped down her back. "Umm . . ."

"I really need to go," the kid said, and began to dance around. Agnes barked again.

She did not want the kid in her apartment for a lot of reasons. But she wasn't heartless. "Okay, but hurry. You're about to give Agnes a heart attack." She pulled open the door, and the kid came through, scurrying past the dog in the direction Lorna pointed.

When he emerged moments later, he was wiping his hands on his shorts.

"Hold on, kid," Lorna said sternly. "Did you wash your hands?"

"I forgot." He sprinted back and took longer to return this

time. Finally, he came out, Agnes trotting alongside him, looking up at him with devotion.

The kid glanced around the central room. "Is this where you live?"

Before she could answer that this was of course where she lived—he'd just come in to use her bathroom, what did he think she was doing granting him access if she didn't live here—the kid began to slowly turn a circle. "*Whoa*," he said.

Lorna sighed. Her secret was out. She tried to imagine seeing her apartment through his eyes, the hundreds of figurines, the pink and white envelopes stacked on top of her desk.

"Look at all *these*." The kid's voice was full of awe. He began walking around her room, checking out her extensive collection of Precious Moments figurines. "How many do you have?" he asked, his hazel eyes wide with amazement. "Are there, like, a *thousand*?"

Her face began to heat. "No, of course not." Quite honestly, she didn't know. But there were a lot. A *lot*.

"There's, like, hundreds!" he said, excited.

"There are not hundreds," she protested. "Maybe two hundred. Or three. But not, like, *hundreds*." She was being defensive with a child, but she hadn't wanted him to see them to begin with. That's what cracked doors meant—no entry. Not that it was his fault, but still. And not that he'd taken the slightest notice of her mood—he was marveling at the figurines that covered every shelf, every windowsill, every unused surface. Sometimes she rearranged them, grouping them by animal versus person, by adult versus child. But mostly she just looked at them. Mostly she pretended these were her memories.

Mostly she was just nuts, wasn't she? Nothing said raving mad like seeing yourself through a child's eyes.

"Why do you have so many?"

"Because I like them."

He blinked, clearly unable to understand why anyone would like Precious Moments figurines this much. It was a legitimate question.

She felt the need to make him understand. "They're happy moments. Get it? Look, here's one of two kids walking two puppies. Happy, right?"

The kid looked where she indicated.

"And here's one of a little boy like you reading a book in the grass."

"What's he reading?"

"I don't know. It's too small to tell. What about this one?" Lorna tried again, noting the hint of desperation in her voice. "This is two grandparents sitting outside their little camper with their cat. That's kind of fun."

"Yeah," the kid said, nodding slowly. Lorna looked helplessly around her living area. The collection stank of hopelessness. She'd always been attracted to the figurines depicting moments of family happiness. Her grandmother had had a few, and she and Kristen used to play with them.

But . . . but she'd never experienced that kind of happiness herself. Not really. Except for a few years of her childhood that she'd spent here, in this house.

She felt something quake in her, sending an uncomfortable spasm up her spine. Every one of these porcelain scenes represented a life she wished she'd had. Couples and children and lovers and mothers and angels to watch over them all. Moments she believed she'd deserved. And over the years, the urge to buy more of the moments she'd wished for had been too strong to resist.

Was she a bored spendthrift? Or someone who struggled with mental health? She could go either way.

"I don't even have this many Pokémon cards." The kid sounded excited. "Can I touch them?" he asked, already reaching.

"Just be careful," Lorna said. "And listen, if you're going to hang out here, you need to let your dad know where you are. He probably has strict rules about you just walking into strangers' apartments."

"You're not a stranger. You're a neighbor."

"Stranger," she insisted. She picked up the State Farm envelope and a pen and turned it over on her writing desk. "Write a note to your dad and tell him you are with Miss Lott in apartment 1A."

The kid asked no questions. He bent over the envelope and began the laborious process of jotting down a note. He bore down on the pencil like he thought he had to carve his missive into the paper. His block letters got bigger and bigger as he neared the edge of the envelope.

When he was done, he handed it to Lorna. She reviewed it.

Deer Dad miss lop said I could come to her house.

"Lott," she corrected him. She wiggled her fingers at him. "Pencil, please." He handed it over immediately. She wrote in the small space he'd left in the corner of the envelope:

Sir, I have asked your son to join me in apartment 1A for his safety. Miss Lott.

"Now let's go put this on your door." She opened her door, and she, the boy, and Agnes marched across the hall (well, Agnes trotted). Lorna shoved the envelope in the space where the door met the jamb, collected the boy's things from the floor, and marched back.

This time, the kid dumped his backpack and drawings in the

middle of the floor and didn't hesitate to examine her figurines more closely. He gasped loudly. "Whales!" he cried with delight.

"Dolphins," Lorna corrected, and picked up the bag of cookies Mrs. Foster had given him. "Come into the kitchen, please."

He followed her and laughed when he entered the kitchen. "There's more!" he said, pointing at the army of figurines lined up on the windowsill and open shelves.

"All right, already, so I have a few figurines." She tried to turn him away from them, but that was impossible, as they were everywhere. Her neck felt prickly hot. Was it shame? She was hell-bent on changing the subject. "What's your name, anyway?" she asked as she helped him up onto a stool at the bar.

"Benjamin. That was my grandfather's name. Not my dad's dad, because his name is Joe. But my mom's dad. My mom called me Benny. But my dad calls me Bean. Everyone calls me Bean. You can call me Bean too."

"Okay, Bean." She'd never seen anyone with him but his dad. "Where's your mom?" she asked as she opened the fridge. Nothing was in there but a few containers of yogurt and some sparkling water.

"She's dead," the kid said matter-of-factly.

Lorna stopped what she was doing and turned to look at him. She half expected him to be joking. But Bean calmly returned her gaze. "Oh," she said. "I . . . I didn't know. I'm sorry."

He shrugged. "Do you have any juice?"

"I have milk. You want milk?"

"Yes!"

Was he ever not enthusiastic? She poured milk into a glass and set it before him. He drank thirstily.

"By the way," she said as he pulled a Precious Moments figurine of a Christmas angel to him for inspection, "my mom is dead too."

Bean paused to look at her.

Lorna nodded. She didn't know why she needed to share that with him, but it felt important. "She had cancer. Was your mom sick?"

"Nope. A bus crashed into her."

"Oh no," Lorna said quickly, wincing in sympathy. "A car wreck, huh? Was anyone else hurt?"

"Not a car," Bean said. He pushed the figurine away, then slugged enough milk to leave a mustache behind. "She was riding her bike. She liked to ride it a lot. My dad says she was a health butt." He giggled.

"I think you mean a health nut." Lorna opened the bag of cookies and handed one to him. "When did that happen?"

"I don't know," he said. "But I was six. I'm eight now." He paused for a moment and looked off toward her living room. "I was six."

She'd been much older when she lost her mother, but sometimes it still shocked her that she was without a mom.

Bean suddenly focused on her. "What's your name?"

"Lorna."

"Hi, Lorna!"

"Hi."

He dunked part of the cookie into the glass of milk. "Guess what? I'm a Ranger Explorer. Did you know that?"

"I just learned your name, Bean, and therefore could not possibly know you are a Ranger Explorer. Moreover, I don't even know what that is." She settled onto a stool beside him.

"It's for kids who want to be rangers and explorers."

"Is that what you want to be? I can see how that sort of work would be rewarding, but I'd guess it's a tough life. A lot of sleeping on the ground. And I bet it doesn't pay as well as you think."

He pressed his lips together in a perplexed frown. "But I'm going to discover the Arctic Circle," he said with all seriousness.

"Too late. It's already been discovered." She helped herself to one of the broken cookies.

"But if I want to get all the badges, I have to discover something. Right now I'm working on my science badge."

"Let me guess, you're going to blow something up."

Bean wrinkled his nose. "I can't do that! Dad and I are going to build a catapult with a rocket. You can set it on fire, you know."

"The catapult?"

"The rocket."

That sounded like a major hazard to her. She imagined him attempting this flaming rocket catapult in the backyard and setting the whole house on fire. How closely did his dad watch this kid?

Bean dipped another cookie into the milk. "I like your dog."

"Unnecessary to mention. It's been well established."

"Did you know Aggie can roll over?" he asked, sitting up taller.

"Her name is Agnes," Lorna said.

"Watch." He hopped off his stool and got down on his knees next to Agnes. "Roll over, Aggie! Roll over!"

Agnes looked at Bean adoringly, then rolled over. And rolled over again, presenting her undercarriage. Bean petted it with both hands. Then he put his face on her belly and rubbed it around. "Good girl!" he praised her. He climbed back onto his stool to polish off the rest of the cookie pieces. Lorna couldn't help but reach across and brush an upsetting bit of dog hair from his cheek.

"My homeroom teacher is really pretty," he said. "Her name is Mrs. Kimble. You know what I like to watch on TV with my dad? *Gunsmoke*. Dad says it's a really old show, but I like it because they shoot each other a lot. Dad's usually on his phone, though. Sometimes he's asleep."

She would be, too, faced with an endless round of *Gunsmoke*.

The kid nattered on, throwing out random Bean facts. He had big toes. Diego was his best friend, and he had chickens. His dad didn't like bicycles anymore. He'd thought about being an astronaut but decided to be an explorer. He could make his ears wiggle. Lorna insisted on seeing evidence of that, and he obliged.

He was a sweet and innocent kid. She vaguely remembered being sweet and innocent. Kristen was her best friend.

Until she wasn't.

Then Callie was her best friend.

Until she wasn't.

The cookies were gone, and Bean was working on his second glass of milk when there was a knock at Lorna's door. Agnes hopped to her feet and began to bark. Bean raced for the door, Agnes on his heels, Lorna trying to get off her stool and beat them there. She was too late—Bean threw open the door like he thought it might be Santa calling a little early. "Hi, Dad!"

"Hey, buddy. What are you doing here?" the man asked, ruffling his son's hair.

"I forgot my key."

"Again?"

Lorna reached the door and stood behind Bean, blocking his dad's view into her apartment. It was one thing to reveal her weirdness to a kid, quite another to reveal it to an adult. Especially one who smiled like he did. And he kept smiling, like he didn't see anything wrong. Like he didn't see anything wrong with her, which was . . . nice. "Hey, thanks so much. Sorry about Bean. I think we should introduce ourselves since this keeps happening. I'm Seth. Seth Rooney." He held out his hand.

Lorna considered it. Her palms were probably sweaty, but to ignore it would appear rude. She took his hand and gave it a good hard shake before quickly letting go. "I'm Lorna Lott. And that's Agnes."

"I've heard a lot about Agnes," Seth said.

Remarkably, he was still smiling. It made Lorna feel strangely warm. Which in turn sprouted a tiny bit of panic in her. She didn't know what to do with that warmth. Except gawk. She was so rusty when it came to exchanging pleasantries.

Bean ducked under her arm to grab his things, leaving at least a portion of her apartment exposed. "He's too young to be a latchkey kid," she blurted, the words tumbling out of her mouth before she could stop herself. It made her curl into a ball on the inside. She didn't want to be unlikable. She wanted Seth to like her. She expected shock. Indignation. At the very least, a retort to keep her nose to herself.

But Seth Rooney, by all outward appearances, was not offended. He actually chuckled. "I couldn't agree more," he said genially. "This was never the original plan, but we're doing our best. We're working on remembering important things, like our key. Right, Bean?"

"Right, Dad. Bye, Aggie!" Bean dipped down to rub Agnes behind her ears.

"Lorna, thanks so much," Seth said. "I don't know what I'd do without such good neighbors. I'm lucky to have found this place."

He was right, he *was* lucky. She was the unlucky one here—he was living in her house.

"Nice to meet you officially," he said, and put a hand on Bean's shoulder, pushing him across the hall.

"Thanks," Lorna said, like a dolt.

"Bye, Lorna!" Bean called. And then he turned to his dad and began to talk a blue streak as his dad opened their door. "Dad, she's got all these little *people* in her room. Like, *thousands*."

Not thousands, Lorna wanted to shout, to clear up any misconception that she was off her rocker.

She shut the door. Agnes whimpered.

"You're really starting to hurt my feelings, you know."

Agnes wagged her knob of a tail.

Lorna went into the kitchen and cleaned up the milk (spilled) and cookie crumbs (everywhere). She made herself a frozen dinner while Agnes dined on kibble. Her Precious Moments figurines stared at her while she ate at the bar. There really were a lot.

She put down her fork and glared back at the figurines. What *liars* they were. No one had moments like what they portrayed. They were all just someone's sick idea of a happy fantasy.

Lorna suddenly hated them. She hated herself for having them.

She thought of Bean. He was six when his mother died. None of the mother-son figurines were true for him. She was thirty-eight when her mother died. None of the mother-daughter figurines were true for her either.

She thought of herself at six and had an overwhelming urge to cry. *Again*.

Good Lord, what was with the tears lately?

Chapter 5

Lorna Is Six

THE SUMMER SHE IS SIX AND KRISTEN IS TEN, LORNA'S PARents decide to take them to Mustang Island for the week. They share their plans over hot dogs and fries one night, and Kristen does cartwheels around the kitchen until her mother shouts at her to stop.

Lorna has never been to the beach. She doesn't know what a beach is. When they are at Nana's the next weekend, Nana shows them pictures from *Encyclopaedia Britannica*: white sand, blue water, palm trees. "This is where all the fish live, and you can swim there," she says.

"Sharks and whales swim there too," Kristen says ominously.

Lorna has seen sharks and whales on the television. "I don't want to swim there."

"You're a baby," Kristen says. "We can make them our pets."

"You won't be swimming with sharks and whales, Lolo," her grandmother assures her, although Lorna doesn't believe her. "And, Kristen, you won't be making any of them your pet."

Kristen shrugs. "I bet I can."

Nana takes them to buy pails and shovels for the beach. "This is how you build sand forts and castles," she explains. "You dig the sand and put it in the pail and pack it down. It will make towers. Then pile up the towers until you have walls." She finds pictures of sandcastles and shows them. Lorna is entranced by all the pictures of things that can be made from sand—even mermaids and puppies. The castles intrigue her the most. She imagines the one she wants to build—just like her princess castle that Papa erected in the backyard.

Later, Mommy brings home bathing suits for them. "Look what I found today!" she says happily, pulling them out of the plastic bag. "Aren't they adorable?"

"Yes!" Lorna says. They are pink with little blue whales frolicking around and three blue ruffles on each hip.

"I hate it," Kristen says.

"Kristen," her mother says wearily. "You can't hate it—you haven't even seen it on."

That afternoon, Kristen gets a pair of scissors and cuts off the ruffles, then cuts a hole in the belly of her suit to make it look like a two-piece. When Mommy sees what she's done, she shouts at Kristen. "That cost fifteen dollars! You're going to pay me back every cent."

Kristen says she is sorry, but she isn't really. She giggles when Mommy leaves the room and admires herself in the mirror in her butchered bathing suit.

They set off from Austin very early one morning, Lorna and Kristen in the back seat, their parents in the front. Mommy is upset with Daddy because he doesn't go the way she said he should and shouts at him that he never listens, that he always has all the answers. From that moment on, Lorna believes that her father has all the answers.

Kristen makes Lorna play a game where she has to find all the letters of the alphabet on the license plates of cars on the highway, but the cars go by too fast, and Lorna can't find letters. She tires of the game that Kristen keeps winning, and when she refuses to play anymore, Kristen calls her a baby. Lorna pouts. She hates being called a baby. She gets out the bag of candy that is supposed to last for the week. She eats too much of it and begins to feel sick.

"Mommy, something is wrong with Lorna," Kristen says.

"What's the matter, Lolo?" her mother asks without turning to look. Lorna doesn't answer. She's scared if she opens her mouth, the candy will come back up. Kristen leans over to look at her, her brows furrowed, then turns her gaze to all the candy wrappers on the seat between them. She frowns at Lorna but takes all the candy wrappers and stuffs them in her socks so Mommy won't see. "Mommy, Lorna is going to puke."

Her mother whips around, a cigarette dangling from her mouth, her sunglasses covering most of her face. "Puke?"

Lorna folds her arms over her belly to contain the sudden and urgent need to vomit.

"Pull over!" her mother shouts.

"I'm not pulling over—we're in the middle of a highway," her father bellows.

Kristen sticks an empty potato chip bag under Lorna's chin, and she promptly vomits into it. "Gross," Kristen says, grimacing.

Lorna vomits again.

"For Pete's sake!" her father bellows.

"Did you eat all that candy? Is that what you did, you little piggy?" her mother snaps, her gaze laser sharp.

Lorna doesn't dare look at Kristen. She shakes her head.

"What the hell is the matter with her?" her father demands as he maneuvers to the right lane.

"Motion sickness," her mother says, her gaze softening a tiny bit. "For goodness' sake, Dave, pull over! Will you do anything I ask?"

"I do everything you ask," he says curtly as he coasts onto the shoulder. "Because you won't get off my back." The car rolls to a halt. Lorna vomits again in rivers of pink, green, and blue.

It seems hours upon hours pass before they are at last close to the beach, but Lorna wants to go home. She is hot and sticky from being candy sick. The smell of it fills the car. Even with the windows down, they can't get rid of it.

"It stinks so bad," Kristen complains. "How much longer?"

"Pipe down back there," her dad snaps.

It's dark when they reach their rented beach condo. Lorna doesn't remember much about their arrival, just that she was hustled into a bathroom where her face was cleaned roughly with a wash rag and she was made to brush her teeth.

An unfamiliar sound, something like wind, but not wind, wakes her up the next morning. She rolls over to look at the other bed in the room and it's empty. She sees Kristen on the balcony, leaning over the railing, her blond hair streaming behind her like a kite. Lorna gets up and goes out onto the balcony too. The sound is coming from the ocean. It's the waves rushing onto the beach and then rushing out again. She and Kristen stand together in silence, watching the vast body of water move in and out.

"I'm hungry," Kristen finally announces, and leaves the balcony. Lorna follows her because she always follows Kristen. Wherever Kristen goes is often exciting.

In the kitchen, Kristen finds a box of cereal. She opens all the cabinet doors until she locates bowls, takes two, and fills them to the brim with milk and Honey Nut Cheerios. They sit at the bar and watch *Inspector Gadget* on the TV while the ocean moves back and forth outside, calling them.

Lorna gradually becomes aware of raised voices on the other

side of the living room wall. The voices belong to her parents, and she looks in that direction.

"Don't listen to them," Kristen says. "I'm sick of cartoons. Let's go outside."

They leave their cereal bowls on the bar and Lorna dutifully follows her big sister onto the balcony again. The ocean smells like the fish market. She can taste salt in the air, and her hair feels tight. Kristen laughs at her. "You look like Little Orphan Annie," she crows, and laughs loud and long, pointing at Lorna's bushy brown hair.

Their parents' voices grow louder. Lorna cringes. She wants to hide. "I hate when they do that," she says.

"Me too. Come on, let's go swimming," Kristen says, and runs through the open door, disappearing down the hall.

"Wait!" Lorna cries, running after her. "Did Mommy say we could?"

"Of course, stupid. That's why we're here, to swim in the ocean. Get your bathing suit and a towel, and I'll pack a lunch."

By the time Lorna has struggled into her one-piece—it's hard without her mother's arms to hang on to—Kristen is packing their lunch. On the other side of the living room wall, Lorna can hear her mother's sobs and her dad shouting, "I'm sick of your bullshit, Mindy!"

"Lunch is packed," Kristen announces. She is wearing her cut bathing suit, which is misshapen now, one side of it rising dangerously high on her chest. "Let's go."

"Wait," Lorna says. "We forgot our pails."

"And the towels. Go grab them. Hurry," Kristen says. She's already headed for the door, the lunch bag slung over her shoulder. Lorna is afraid to be left behind, so she races to get the buckets and towels and then to catch up to her sister.

Kristen leads the way around the house to the pool, then

around the pool on decking so hot that Lorna's bare feet feel like they are burning. Then through a wooden gate and down a beach path that weaves through the dunes. It is all sand, and it feels strange squishing in between Lorna's toes. Overhead, the seagulls are cawing at them.

The beach doesn't look very big, and there is dead green stuff lying around. Joggers go past. Old people stroll along, occasionally stopping to bend over and examine something in the sand.

"Let's sit here and wait for the water to go back," Kristen says.

"It's going to go back into the ocean?" Lorna asks.

"Yep. It's the tide. There is high tide and low tide. Remember? Nana told us."

Lorna doesn't remember. They sit on the dunes with the lunch basket between them, watching the water. Lorna likes being with Kristen, just the two of them. A police buggy comes by and the officer yells at them to get off the dunes. They pick up their things and trudge down to the beach. It's getting bigger.

It's hot, and sand is everywhere, gritty between Lorna's toes and rubbing uncomfortably under her bathing suit. The wind is blowing, but she can feel the sun baking her skin. She suddenly gasps with alarm. "We forgot our hats! Mommy said to wear them. Can we go get them?"

"We'll be fine," Kristen says. She tugs down her uneven bathing suit. "Let's have lunch." She uses the bottom of her foot to even a place in the sand and sets down the insulated bag. She kneels and opens it with a broad smile, pleased with her efforts.

Lorna peers inside—there are Cheetos, a big jar of peanut butter, and four cans. Lorna pulls one of the cans out. It's Daddy's beer. "We're not supposed to have these," Lorna says disapprovingly.

"Stop being a baby," Kristen admonishes. She takes one and opens it, and it spews everywhere. They laugh. When it stops foaming, Kristen tastes it. She screws up her face. *"Gross."*

"Let me try," Lorna says, reaching for the can. Lorna drinks. She promptly spits it out. "It tastes like dirty feet," she complains.

"How do you know what dirty feet taste like? Have you been licking your feet?" Kristen laughs at herself and takes the can from Lorna.

They munch on Cheetos and leave the peanut butter. Kristen drinks from the can. Lorna picks up her pail and shovel. "I'm going to build a castle."

She walks down the beach a little way and settles on a spot where there isn't any seaweed but lots of shells nearby. Nana said she would need shells to decorate her castle. She drops to her knees and uses her shovel to fill her pail, then turns the pail upside down for her first tower. It falls apart.

She tries again, creating two more mounds of sand. They look nothing like the pictures Nana showed her.

A man stops to watch. Lorna instinctively looks for Kristen, but her sister is nowhere in sight. The man smells like sweat. "You're doing it wrong," he says.

Lorna doesn't speak.

He squats down beside her and takes her pail without asking. Lorna scooches back and away from him, afraid.

"You have to pack the sand," he says. He fills the pail, mashing down the sand as he goes. He turns it over and taps the pail, and it comes away, leaving a tower. "You see?"

Lorna nods.

He sets the pail down and walks away.

Before long, she has ten castle towers in a circle. She pauses to consider the empty middle of the circle. It needs a bigger tower. Or maybe some shells. She notices that her skin feels like fire. So does the top of her head. What can she put in the middle? She stands up to look for shells. That's when she sees the boys.

There are three of them. They're not grown-ups, but they're

bigger than Kristen. They're laughing at Lorna's castle. Her belly twists with fear. She wishes her mother were here. She looks for Kristen once more but doesn't see her.

One of them, the biggest one, jogs closer to her castle. "What's this supposed to be?"

"A castle," Lorna says.

"That's a stupid-looking castle," the kid says. He studies it a moment, then draws his leg back and kicks one of the towers like he's kicking a soccer ball.

Lorna gasps. "Stop!" she screams, and runs forward, pushing the boy as hard as she can. He hardly moves. The other boys laugh hysterically. The boy pushes Lorna, hard, and she flies backward, her head bouncing off the sand, the skin on her back feeling like it has ripped open. She watches helplessly as he draws his leg back again, meaning to kick the next one.

"Get away from her!" Kristen suddenly flies into their midst, launching herself at the boy. She slams into his chest. "Get out of here!" She is swaying on her feet, flailing her arms. The boys are laughing at her now. "Are you drunk?" one of them cries, and they howl.

Kristen flies at that one, but he knocks her off him as if she were nothing more than a bothersome cat. The third boy is backing away. "Let's get out of here," he says. "Come on, guys." The boys go, kicking sand as they walk, still laughing.

Lorna remains on her back, blinking away tears. She doesn't know how much time has passed before Kristen gets up and comes over to where she is. She stands with her legs braced apart, scrutinizing Lorna. "You look okay. Come on, let's go."

"I'm not finished building my sandcastle."

"You can build another one tomorrow. Let's go." The fight has gone out of Kristen. Her eyes look red and like glass.

They gather their things and trudge back to the beach house.

Kristen leads Lorna straight to the bathroom. She takes out the enormous bottle of aloe vera Mommy brought and begins to slather thick globs of it on Lorna's burned skin. She has finished Lorna's shoulders when Mommy comes to the bathroom door and stares at the two of them. Her face turns dark. "What in the hell?" she demands. "Kristen? You smell like a brewery. What have you been doing?"

"Nothing," Kristen says defensively.

Mommy's eyes go wide. She backs out of the bathroom. "Dave? Dave, come here. Kristen's been *drinking*."

Kristen sighs. She continues rubbing aloe gel on Lorna until her father thunders in. He catches Kristen by the arm and yanks her out of the bathroom, forcing her down the hall, yelling at her. Mommy follows them, shouting at Kristen.

Her parents don't notice Lorna's burned skin. Or how much pain she is in. Lorna slinks to her and Kristen's bedroom and peels off the bathing suit, whimpering as she does. The fabric brushing against her skin is so painful.

She falls asleep to the fighting.

Chapter 6

Lorna Now

WITH ALL THOSE HAPPY FIGURINES STARING AT HER, LORNA had lost her appetite. Did she want to change? Well, yes, Micah, she did. She hated what she had become. Who would want to be this sad, lonely woman? At what point had she decided this small life of hers was enough? How had she settled for using Precious Moments figurines as a substitute for living? Did she really think she could make up what she'd lost in life with porcelain?

She threw away her half-eaten frozen dinner, then went to her bedroom to change. Agnes followed, finding her bed and circling four or five times before settling in. She let out a loud sigh.

"Oh, sure," Lorna said, reaching down to pet her. "All that rolling over for attention and belly rubs must have really worn you out, huh? I feel like I don't even know you. You could have at least told me you knew how to roll over." She sniffed with indignation and stood.

Agnes yawned and rolled onto her side.

Lorna changed into pajama shorts and an old Red Hot Chili Peppers T-shirt. She'd gone to see the band many years ago. With Mike, her boyfriend of several months until he told her he couldn't deal with the constant Kristen drama. He'd bought her the T-shirt, so at least she had that. That was fifteen years ago, when she used to date. Never very successfully, but enough that she couldn't be considered a total spinster.

She could hardly recall Mike now. He had shaggy hair and was a chemist at a large manufacturing firm. Nice guy, but . . . but Lorna didn't remember much specifically, other than it had ended because of Kristen. Like everything else, it was so hard to recall who she'd been before she closed and locked the door to her internal bomb shelter.

She piled her hair on top of her head, then walked over to her small dresser and opened the bottom drawer, where she kept her important documents. In the back of the drawer, behind many papers, was a file. She pulled it out. Labeled simply *Mom*, it was all the paperwork that had been necessary to record her mother's death and settle her estate.

Lorna took the file to the living room, settled into her favorite chair (a happy yellow, with flowers and butterflies woven into the upholstery), and put the file on her lap. She wasn't sure what she intended to do, but inside this file, among many other things, was the paperwork from her mother's trust. Lorna hadn't looked at it since she'd shoved it into that drawer more than four years ago, right after she'd met with the estate attorney who told her that her mother had made her the sole beneficiary of her estate, and anything left after paying creditors belonged to her . . . on the condition she addressed her anger.

"You're kidding," Lorna had said.

"Nope. Not kidding," Tyrone, the estate attorney, confirmed. "She left a list of things she wanted you to address." He'd looked at the list. "Interesting." He'd shown her the list then, and Lorna recognized the items instantly—they were all the things she accused Kristen and her mother of ruining for her. All the things she angrily spelled out to her mother one terrible night shortly before she died.

She had turned away, not wanting to read more.

Tyrone was a no-nonsense type and unemotional as he folded the list and put it with the trust paperwork. Usually Lorna very much appreciated that in a person, but in this instance, she could have used a little *This is outrageous* attitude on her behalf. Of course, Tyrone had no way of knowing that her mother had dedicated the last few years of her life to Al-Anon and the tenants of the program. That she saw herself as a leader in the work of forgiving addicts and learning to set boundaries. And that she had this annoying idea that if Lorna took stock of her personal inventory of grievances and made a list of the people she'd hurt and why, and then made amends or apologized or did whatever she needed to do to stop obsessing about the past, then maybe she could forgive herself, stop being angry, and get on with the business of living a long and happy life.

"Forgive myself for what?" Lorna had demanded when her mother first presented this wonky idea.

Her mother averted her gaze. "For not having saved your sister. For not being the sister you think Kristen needs."

Lorna was taken aback. "Excuse me? I'm not the sister *Kristen* needs? What about the sister I need, Mom? I don't need to forgive myself; I need to figure out if I can ever forgive Kristen, because I've tried, and I can't."

That conversation, like many that would follow, had gone from bad to worse. It had constantly amazed Lorna that Kristen could break every promise she ever made, and her mother would still seek ways to forgive her. There had to be an end point, didn't there?

Anyway, that argument happened before her mother knew she was sick. After her diagnosis, she turned up the volume on her wish/hope/demand that Lorna reconcile her regrets for the sake of peace. "Think of it this way," she said as she refilled a glass of wine that Lorna was pretty sure she wasn't supposed to be drinking with all the medicine she was taking. "If you could let go of the things you can't change, maybe you wouldn't be so angry anymore. You'd be able to move on from the hand that life dealt you. You need to do it before it's too late, Lolo."

Lorna had been incredulous. "It's already too late, Mom." She'd had enough of Kristen. What she could not understand was why her mother hadn't.

Her mother doggedly continued her nonsensical argument until the day she died. Lorna had ignored it then, and she kept on ignoring it after her mother was gone. And after Kristen moved to Florida. She would have forgotten it all had it not been for the matter of her grandmother's house. With the house soon up for sale, she needed whatever money was in her mother's trust.

She remembered a Sunday afternoon in the garage apartment they'd lived in behind Peggy Shane's house. Her mother was lying on a single bed, her face etched with pain. Most of her hair was gone, and what remained had turned stark white from the chemo and the stress. She was so thin, she looked like a living skeleton.

A breeze coming through the open windows kept the apartment comfortable, but her mother was covered with a thick blanket. Lorna had been infuriated with Kristen that afternoon. She was supposed to have been there with Mom, but as usual, she wasn't.

It was becoming increasingly difficult to remember a time she hadn't been angry with Kristen.

"Oh, Lorna, I worry about you so," her mother had croaked after Lorna unleashed her opinion of Kristen skipping out on her one responsibility.

"Don't worry about me, Mom. I'm fine," Lorna snapped. But

she'd regretted her tone instantly. It wasn't her mother's fault that Kristen had bailed on caretaking responsibilities, disappearing into thin air without telling anyone. Kristen didn't have a job, but Lorna did. Kristen didn't have to pay rent, but Lorna did.

Her anger wasn't really directed at her mother, but where else would she vent her frustration? Even when she caught herself, when she knew she was being unfair to her ailing mother, it came bubbling out because she didn't have the strength to contain it. Fury seemed to ooze from every pore.

"Well, you don't look fine to me," her mother said hoarsely. "You hold so much regret and guilt, Lolo. It's not good for you."

Regret? Guilt? What she was holding on to was fury. At her mother for dying, at Kristen for leaving her to deal with her mother's death on her own. At the world in general for always dumping on her.

"I wish you would consider joining Al-Anon. It's made such a huge difference for me. If you'd just address your issues—"

"Stop," Lorna said.

"I'm trying to help you."

Lorna's pulse was pounding, her head on the verge of exploding. "Stop, Mom."

"You don't need to live with guilt. You can free yourself of it."

"Stop!" Lorna cried. "I don't need to free myself from anything. You're the one dying—not me." The moment those words flew out of her mouth, she tried to claw them back. "I'm sorry," she said. "I'm so sorry."

Her mother, who once would have used that remark as a jumping-off point for a massive argument, smiled weakly. "Well, you're not wrong about that, Lolo. So maybe give me the benefit of my deathbed insight, will you?"

Lorna had not given her mother the benefit of that insight.

She'd grown impossibly angrier and said things she truly, deeply regretted. So much so that now she was choking with regret. Her mother had been right about that, at least.

She could hardly bear thinking of her mother's last few weeks on this earth. Every memory felt like a gut punch. She missed her terribly.

She even missed Kristen, although she was hard-pressed to say why.

Lorna looked at the stack of unsent letters to Kristen and the unopened ones from her stepmother. She looked around at her apartment. This was the space where Nana helped her and Kristen make Christmas ornaments. They would sit around the coffee table with their yarn and glitter and felt and construction paper, listening to Nana tell stories about when she was a girl while they made snowflakes and Santas and stars. This was the space where they created dance routines or, on the hottest days of summer, read their books under an enormous ceiling fan. This was where Lorna had lived her happiest life. Nana made meals for them—full meals, never microwaved. She helped them wash their hair, and at bedtime she would hug them tight and tell them she loved them to the moon and back.

Mr. Contreras had chopped up all those memories. Now she was isolated in this space, her inability to trust anyone a thick coat of armor keeping her away from people and from life.

Keeping her lonely.

She stared down at the file. She couldn't open it. She knew what was contained in those pages by heart; she'd practically written the thing herself that night she'd let out all her frustration and disappointment with her family on her dying mother.

She mentally flipped through her catalog of intact memories, and even those that were fractured confirmed what she always knew. Everything—the good and the bad—had always started and ended with Kristen.

The truth, which Lorna was very good at ignoring, was that she was terribly tired of being herself. She was exhausted from being so angry and distrustful. She wanted friends. She wanted to go for drinks and get invited to parties and know how to have casual conversations. She wanted camaraderie with her co-workers and to laugh and go on vacations. She wanted men like Seth not only to smile at her but to *like* her. She did not want to be called King Kong. She wanted to be called Lolo.

Micah had urged her to open herself to the process. She was afraid of his process, because she had the feeling he meant to open the door to her bomb shelter. She was afraid of what she might say or do, things she could never take back. How much more of her could she risk? It felt like there was hardly anything left of her as it was.

Without looking at the papers inside, she took the file back to her dresser, opened the bottom drawer, and put it away.

She didn't know where to go from here. She was usually so practical, so set in her decisions about how to move forward. But tonight she felt like she was tumbling through space, thrown for a loop.

Micah had said it wouldn't hurt her to try.

She guessed she'd try. But she wasn't going to like it one bit.

> Well, thanks a lot again, Kristen. I've been sentenced to a "wellness" program because I am uptight and still mad about you and all I want to do is get away from you, and all my new life coach wants to do is talk about you. So great! I can't wait to relive everything! It was so much fun the first time through! All this because Mom thought I was the problem, that I needed

to let go of the past and all the things you made me do. This is all YOUR FAULT. It's always your fault. You will probably argue it can't be your fault because you're not here, but that's just it—you're ALWAYS here. You. Are. Always. Here. I don't want you living in my head anymore.

But I don't know how to get you out.

Chapter 7

Lorna Now

MONTREAL WAS WAITING FOR LORNA IN THE LOBBY OF THE Bodhi Tao Bliss Retreat and Spa. "How are you?" he asked, then pressed his hands together in a prayer pose and bowed.

Lorna did not make prayer hands or bow, but she conceded she was giving this program her best shot by saying, "I'm wearing yoga pants." As a rule, she did not like to wear yoga pants in public. She had standards of dress for different occasions: suits to the office, dresses for shopping, cargo shorts for gardening, athletic wear for exercise. Yoga pants were reserved for rainy Saturdays or Sundays spent at home.

But, as the saying went, if you can't beat them, join them.

"Will you look at that," he said. "Well done."

He probably already hated her. He was probably already complaining to Micah. *That tall lady with the hair . . . she's the worst. It's like she needs an amendment to the Constitution before she'll wear proper spa clothing.*

But he was all pleasantries as he escorted her to the gym for morning meditation. He talked about how great the weather had been (and he wasn't wrong). He handed her a mat and said, "I'll be back for you," then smiled warmly.

At the very least, she was pleased that she was able to sit cross-legged like everyone else. She even went the full mile by touching her thumbs and middle fingers to create a circle, the purpose of which she had no clue, and resting her hands like that against her knees, palms up, like everyone else. When in Rome.

Unfortunately, she couldn't keep her thoughts from wandering when the meditation leader invited her to clear her mind and get in touch with her deeper self. *Deeper self. What does that even mean? Was it necessary for the person next to me to put his mat so close to mine? It's weird. Who is snoring? Someone is snoring. Do these people have jobs? How does everyone have the time to sit around and smile like loons at each other? I feel like I should stretch.*

And then the meditation practice was over.

Montreal came to get her. "How did it go today?" he asked as they made their way down the long white corridor toward Micah's office.

She did not excel at small talk and debated how honest she ought to be. Should she tell him she was terrified of what Micah might find repulsive about her? Probably not. "Okay, I guess, given the circumstances. At least I was more comfortable."

Montreal looked at her curiously. "Is everything okay?"

"Not really. I should be in my office making sales. But I'm here trying to meditate, and let me tell you something, Montreal, meditation is impossible. I don't believe anyone can clear their mind of all thoughts. Do you believe it?"

"I do," he said. "But I will grant you it is a learned skill that must be practiced. I think you will find the longer you are in the Leaves of Change program, the easier meditation might become. I hope so, because meditation is a great tool for centering yourself. When you're centered, you will eventually feel yourself begin to expand and shift. Let it happen."

She was dubious. She preferred to have empirical evidence or, at the very least, the word of someone who had gone through the shenanigans she feared she was about to go through. "Do you know if anyone who has gone through this program says they are better for it? Leaves of Change, I mean. Like hard data?"

His kind, light brown eyes locked with hers. "Hard data on people's feelings is difficult to obtain. But you should ask Micah." Speaking of which, they had reached Micah's door. Montreal knocked, opened it, and said, "Lorna is here." And then to Lorna, he said, "Great first step with the yoga pants. Lean into them." He glided away.

News flash, Montreal. One couldn't lean into yoga pants, as they were specifically made to give. You could lean in them, but not *into* them.

Lorna squared her shoulders and entered the office.

Micah was already seated on a beanbag. She did not understand the insistence on beanbags when there was a perfectly good white couch across the room. He was wearing sweatpants cut off just below the knees and a T-shirt with a peace symbol painted on the chest. A checkered Arab headdress wrapped around his shoulders, and a small elephant carved from jade hung from a leather string around his neck. His hair was piled on top of his head just like Lorna wore hers in the bath.

"Lorna, so good to see you again," he said. "I made some tea. You prefer lavender, correct?"

He remembered. "Thanks."

He gestured toward the other beanbag. "Care to sit?"

"I don't care to at all," she said, but eased herself down and sat facing him. "But in the spirit of getting through another hour of interrogation, I will do it. I haven't sat cross-legged so much since kindergarten."

He laughed like he thought she was joking, proving once again that she had no sense for what was funny anymore. "I'm sorry you saw it as an interrogation, but I've been thinking a lot about our conversation," he said as he handed her a cup of tea. "I've got some ideas."

"Great. Can't wait."

"You might try for at least a little bit of enthusiasm," he suggested with a smile.

She winced. She hated being this person, but she couldn't seem to get out of it—and what's more, she was a little afraid to. If she was intentionally crusty, she hypothesized, she could better accept how others would inevitably feel about her. Of course they didn't like her. Look how crusty she was! "Sorry. I don't have much enthusiasm . . . but I've got a little."

"That's all I ask. Have you ever had a sound bath?"

Lorna's cup of tea halted midway to her mouth. "A what?"

"A sound bath."

"I have no idea what that is."

"It's a different sort of meditation."

"Oh boy," she muttered.

"But we use singing bowls, gongs, et cetera to create a sound capable of releasing energies and allowing our minds to see deeper into ourselves. To see things maybe we haven't seen before."

That deeper-into-self business again. And why the plural? Was this a group project? Who was "we"?

"You may have seen the singing bowls around. Big white ones, small brass ones."

Lorna had seen those bowls in the meditation room. She thought they were for making lunch for the masses.

"The sound and vibrations help with relaxation by affecting your brain waves."

"That sounds . . ." She tried to think of an inoffensive word.

"Relaxing?"

"Bananas."

Micah chuckled. He was completely unruffled by her. "It's actually a fascinating area of study and practice."

"I'm sorry, but it doesn't sound even remotely real, singing bowls and brain waves. And anyway, I'm relaxed."

"Right, yes, you're fine, as you've said more than once," he said. "But I've never had anyone say no to more relaxation. Are you telling me you are completely relaxed?"

"Well, no. Because now I have to do a sound bath."

He laughed again, because apparently, he thought she was all jokes. She was not. The very thought of being subjected to a sound bath made her feel exposed. Like someone was going to jump out of the curtains and laugh at her. It sounded like a terrible prank. And what could she possibly see inside herself that she didn't already know?

"You might enjoy it," he suggested.

"Nope," Lorna said firmly.

"I understand," Micah said. "Change and opening yourself to new experiences and ideas can be hard, right?"

She hesitated. It was hard, and she didn't like it, but where was her resolve to try? She'd promised herself she would. What was she so afraid of? She sighed. "Yes," she mumbled.

"But that's why you're here, isn't it?"

"Trick question," she said, pointing at him. "I'm here because I did something stupid. You know that."

"I know what the referral said. But I'm interested in the precipitating event or events that got you to that point. I want to know how Lorna Lott became the woman I see before me. She is attractive, she's fit, she's smart . . . and avoidant. She is terrified of letting me see too much."

Wow. How did he know that? She didn't know about the attractive, fit, or smart part, but the terror? Somehow he'd figured out how to look inside her bomb shelter. Even she didn't know how to do that. "Not true," she argued. "I'm not avoidant, I'm safe. I just don't think you need to see too much."

"What does safe mean to you?"

"What do you mean, what does it mean?" She could feel a bubble of anger beginning to grow in her. The rage at being asked to explain her complicated thoughts and feelings, mostly because she didn't know how to explain them. "It means I am safe from idiots and hurt and disappointment and any number of things."

He nodded.

Oh, she was going to find something sharp and rip this beanbag into pieces. "I'm not a people person, Micah. I haven't been since . . ." She cut herself off before she said too much.

"Since the pandemic? A lot of people found it hard to reenter society after so much isolation."

"Not that."

"Then what? Because I see how you don't make eye contact easily. Your posture is that of someone who is afraid to move because they're sitting on a bed of nails. And you don't want to know about the possibilities here, much less consider them. If it were me and I had a month off work completely paid for, and all I had to do was explore some options to make myself a better person, I'd be all over it. But you seem anxious about what you might find."

Nailed it. And she didn't know if this was intentional, but he was making it clear that she would not be able to escape her current reality either physically or spiritually. She looked down at her teacup and the string of the tea bag floating serenely on the surface, oblivious to how cold the water had gone. *Try.*

"Once, when I was a kid, I saw an old, beat-up dog at a gas station. He just sort of appeared while my dad was getting gas." She pictured the golden dog, one ear half gone, scars on his body, a foot that didn't land right. "There were two kids who were trying to get him to come with them. 'Come on,' they said, 'you can live with us.' They were holding out a hot dog to entice him. The dog got closer and closer, and when he got close enough, one of the kids tried to grab him by his scruff," she said, gesturing to the back of her neck. "But the dog snatched the hot dog and broke free. He trotted back into the woods, his nose and tail high, like he was proud of himself."

"That's really sad," Micah said.

Lorna blinked. "Sad? No, you don't get it. It was liberating. That dog didn't need anyone. He didn't need two kids who were going to betray him like that. He didn't need a house or a family. He needed food, and once he got it, he was perfectly fine on his own. Fewer entanglements. Fewer disappointments. No one to mistreat him. That's where I am. That's how I stay safe."

Micah said nothing for a moment. "But you do know that dogs are pack animals, and a lot of those that get rescued at gas stations may start out reluctant, but then find they really like having people around. That dog might have had a cushy life if the kids had caught him, instead of the hard life of a street dog, all alone with no one to lean on."

Something roiled lightly in her chest. She shrugged. "Maybe. Maybe not. Maybe life with those kids would have been worse." She shifted on her beanbag. This was getting too, too close to the door of her bomb shelter. "So anyway, you want to know how Lorna Lott got here. It started a long time ago."

Micah leaned forward. "How long ago?"

"Thirty-five years? More? And my sister was . . ." She clamped her mouth shut. Why was Kristen the first thing, the first person, she mentioned?

"An addict," Micah said.

Lorna eyed him warily.

"Your sister was an addict," he said calmly. "That must have been very difficult for you and your family. Can you tell me how it affected you?"

"Why do you even want to know?" The heat or her ire was beginning to build. "Anyway, I doubt you have the next year free," she added flippantly. But she recognized what she was doing and groaned. She held up a hand. "I'm sorry," she said wearily. "I don't know why I can't seem to take a beat before I speak. I get so angry out of nowhere. Honestly, Micah, I can't even begin to list the many ways her addiction affected me without feeling the rage, you know? If you read addiction literature, it will tell you that using drugs affects your relationships, your work, and every aspect of your life. But it never tells you how your addiction casts a long shadow and wraps like a rope around the necks of everyone else in your life."

"That sounds suffocating," Micah said.

"Suffocating, enraging. Kristen's drug use made it impossible for me to have friends. When they came over, she was high or just weird. And try being the sister of the girl who got arrested on school grounds not once, but twice. Just imagine all the fighting at home about the drug use and the arrests and her just disappearing, sometimes for a few hours, sometimes for a few days. Even when you move out as an adult, it doesn't end. You end up missing work because of some crisis or doctor's appointment or some big worry." She paused, considering how often her mother had worried over Kristen's whereabouts.

"I can't imagine," Micah said.

"You couldn't possibly unless you lived it," she said flatly. "I hope you never do. I have never been free of Kristen. I could never just carry on with my life without waiting for loads of shoes to drop, because they always dropped, usually when I was least expecting it. I could never just accept who she was. I kept getting angrier."

And then everyone was gone. Nana. Her mother. Her sister. Her dad, if he ever really counted. She shook her head. She'd said enough.

Micah didn't seem surprised or disgusted by her confession. "An addict in the family takes up a lot of time and attention and emotional energy."

"Yep," Lorna said, and put aside her teacup. "It made me invisible in my family."

"How young were you when the trouble began?"

She looked at the window, at the way the leaves on the tree just outside moved on the fall breeze. The same way the trees used to move outside the window of Nana's house. "Six. That's the first time I can remember her using something, anyway. It was during a trip to the beach. She was only ten."

And just like that, the story of her life came tumbling out before she could stop herself. She talked about how her family, who she thought had known happiness early on, became increasingly ruled by her sister's addiction issues through the years. How she had always loved Kristen, still did, or at least she thought she did, or maybe she told herself she did, and really, she wasn't even sure if she did. But she had once considered her the best of big sisters. And now she didn't want to be near her. She talked about how long she had begged and hoped for Kristen to change, and how she still had trouble accepting that this was Kristen's life.

She told Micah that she believed Kristen's struggles ruined her parents' marriage and stole so many moments—moments that Lorna could never get back.

She told him about her grandmother's house, where she and Kristen and her mother went to live after her parents' divorce, that place of so much childhood happiness. How she thought they would be so happy there, and how they were for a while, and how she loved that house. But when her grandmother died, her mother sold it to pay for Kristen's longest stint in treatment. And when her mother got sick with cancer, Lorna had to caretake on top of a full-time job because Kristen couldn't be trusted to follow through on doctor's appointments, or not to steal her mother's pain pills, or money from her purse. She told Micah that two relationships she'd had with men had crumbled under the weight of caring for her mother and her sister.

And then she told him that her mother left her estate in trust for Lorna, but with untenable conditions, because her mother had decided Lorna was the one who needed to change.

Micah listened to all of it, his face conveying his empathy. He filled her teacup when she admitted to having the gut-wrenching regrets and suffocating guilt her mother had tried so hard to get her to acknowledge.

She told him she hated herself for believing all the lies Kristen told her and believing that she would change when she promised. She hated herself for believing that Kristen would stop using drugs, that she would get a job, that she would be part of the family again. She'd wanted so badly to believe her and was let down over and over.

"Addiction is a cruel master," Micah said. "You love the person and hate the disease."

"That's too trite," Lorna said. "I mean, sure, it's true, obviously, but sometimes . . . well, really, a *lot* of times . . . I hated Kristen. I hated her," she said again. "She was so impossible to love, no matter how hard I tried. Like, it's not her fault she's an addict, so you're supposed to overlook that like you would if she had cancer, so they say, even while she is tearing you and your family apart." Lorna had never been good at articulating how she felt about Kristen's disease. Much less grasping her feelings fully—they were so damn complicated. "I tried to save her," she said quietly. "But it was pointless. Kristen didn't want to be saved."

"That is indeed a very personal decision," Micah said. "To be sober or not. You said your sister is in Florida?"

"With my dad."

"Do you see her or speak to her?"

She could feel the door of her bomb shelter swinging closed. She shook her head. "We're on a break. It's been almost two years." Her eyes were beginning to fill with tears. Of fury? Of sadness? It was hard to know anymore.

Micah slid the box of tissues across the floor to her.

"I haven't had any contact with her. I've hardly spoken to my dad either. My stepmother sends me a couple of letters every month. But I don't read them."

"Why not?" Micah asked.

Because she was afraid of what was in the letters. She couldn't bear the blame or the guilt or the pleas for help. "They'll just make me mad." She took a tissue from the box. "All I know is that every time I get a pink envelope, I feel like crying. I know it will be about Kristen."

"Ah," Micah said.

Ah. Lorna heard that as Micah not understanding. Could she blame him? How ridiculous was it that she wouldn't open a letter and read it? How could she explain she would rather just leave it like an unexploded mine in her apartment? If she didn't know what was in them, she didn't know what there was to be upset about. *Avoidant*, he'd called her. Maybe she was.

"I know this has been difficult, but thank you for sharing. I think it will help us set some goals for your wellness program. Let's start with what you hope to achieve?"

What sort of question was that? She wanted to keep her job. She wanted to be liked. She wanted her grandmother's house. "I want to go back to work and have a normal life. That's it."

"And what does a normal life look like to you?"

Use your context clues, Micah. "Just a normal life. Not having to talk about my sister. Not having to pretend I had a normal childhood. Just being happy in my grandmother's house like I used to be."

"For the record, normal is a myth. But it's very interesting to me that you equate having a normal life with not talking about your sister. Clearly, your trust has been destroyed many times."

Damn it, the tears would not stop welling. She hated to be vulnerable. She'd said more today than she'd said in years, and she was already regretting it. "It's not just that I don't trust people. People don't trust me either. Deb can't trust me not to say the wrong thing. And I'm not trying to say the wrong thing; it just happens. My mother put conditions on her trust because she didn't trust me to be the daughter she wanted." It all seemed perfectly obvious to her.

"But is that true, Lorna?" Micah asked kindly and handed her another tissue. "Seems to me the evidence would suggest otherwise. You were there for her. When your sister wasn't, you were there. What's upsetting you?"

"Oh, let's see—that my mom had a list of things she wanted me to do to somehow forgive Kristen? Or understand her? Or accept her as she is? But her list is all about *my* regrets. So . . . not helpful, Mom. I was the good daughter. I did what I was supposed to do. And she wanted me to do more."

"That must have been frustrating," Micah agreed. "Let me offer a different perspective."

"No," Lorna said before he could say more.

"I'm just wondering if—"

"No. I've already wondered enough. I've wondered so much my head hurts. I don't need to wonder anymore. I'm not doing it." She felt her feet encased in concrete when it came to that damn trust codicil. She resented it so much she could hardly think of it without wanting to scream.

"Isn't it possible your mother understood that sometimes you must face your demons in order to move forward? The past has a way of sucking us in and holding us there. And if you can address those things that hold you back—the things that put you on this beanbag—don't you want to at least try? Don't you want to change, Lorna?"

A minute ago, she'd thought that kind of thinking was smart. A minute ago, she was still all for trying. But now she did not like the direction this conversation was going. "Do you really think visiting past regrets—some of them from childhood, I might add—is going to show me the way to a better life? I don't want to revisit them. They are regrets, water under the bridge, which essentially means I don't want to talk about them."

"Okay. But can you see any disadvantages to letting go of those things that make you feel so angry?"

Lorna felt a quake so deep she feared she would explode in his office. Those emotions, those thoughts around her so-called regrets, and her mother, and Kristen, were packed tightly away, and she didn't think it was a good idea to get them out.

"Lorna?"

She frowned. "I have let go of the past, Micah. I never think about it." *That's a lie*, a little voice inside told her immediately. She slammed her bomb-shelter door shut on her conscience. "But I'll consider exploring it." She was not going to explore it. Get out of here with that "opening herself up" crap. Every time she did, something terrible happened.

Micah smiled. "I think we've made progress."

"I'm not making any promises, so don't get too excited."

"I understand." He looked almost smug, like he'd won something.

"I might not even come back to this stupid place," she added.

"Not even for a sound bath?"

"Especially not for a sound bath."

"I'll schedule one for you after our next session. It should help you down the path of reframing all your negative thinking and self-talk," he said with cheerful confidence.

"You seem awfully sure there is going to be a next session," Lorna said, and rolled off the damn beanbag onto all fours. "And for your information, I feel like an idiot sitting on beanbags."

"Thanks for the feedback."

She made it to her feet, but her yoga pants felt twisted around her legs. She started for the door, pausing there to look back at him.

"See you tomorrow," he said.

"Don't be so sure," she said, and went out the door, nearly colliding with Montreal in her haste to get out of there.

Chapter 8

Lorna Now

WELL, NOW SHE FELT BAD. WHEN SHE REVIEWED HER TONE and demeanor in Micah's office on the drive home, she could see she'd been very prickly. That damn codicil was going to be the death of her.

The rage she'd felt leaving Bodhi had dissipated, and now she felt sheepish for leaving in a snit and flouncing out of Micah's office. He was just trying to help her. Why couldn't she have left in a dignified manner? Despite the beanbag, things had been going well. Until he brought up that "face yourself" business and defended her mother's motives.

Everything about that trust and her mother was mixed in a thick, tar-like morass of feelings that she'd quit trying to sort out a long time ago. She couldn't just pull out a few bad feelings, have a look at them, and think, *Okay, everything's probably fine now*. It didn't work that way, so she'd just allowed the toxic brew of feelings to simmer deep in the pit of her.

She probably owed Micah an apology. Too bad Deb wasn't here to confirm. She sincerely wished Deb were here—somewhere along the way she'd lost the ability to gauge when she was being obnoxious. Deb was just . . . comforting. A solid person.

She took the third slot in the gravel patch. The new guy's

massive truck was missing, but it looked like everyone else was home. Fabulous. Lorna's head was pounding with tension and Martin probably had a marching band coming over later to stomp around overhead.

She got out of her car and went inside. She paused at the mail table. Something felt off. She realized that she'd usually hear music coming out of Martin's apartment, but the lobby was strangely silent.

She picked up the mail someone had stacked for her and went to her apartment door, expecting to hear Agnes whimpering on the other side. She heard nothing.

Inside her apartment, she dropped her purse and mail on the console and whistled for her dog. Agnes did not come. She walked to the back of her apartment, where she could hear voices slipping in from the dog door into the backyard. Agnes was with the boy, of course. They'd probably dug tunnels to go with their massive hole or built a spaceship out of the wooden fence. It would cost her a small fortune to return the backyard to an oasis when she owned the house.

She opened her back door and stepped onto her small landing and, surprisingly, saw a crowd gathered—Martin and Mrs. Foster had joined Bean. Agnes was on her back, her legs in the air, and Martin was rubbing her belly.

"Hi, Lorna!" Bean waved at her from his spot between the adults. Mrs. Foster and Martin looked up, both smiling. "Oh, hey," Mrs. Foster said with a wave of her own. "Come join us!"

Lorna almost checked behind her to see if someone had followed her out, but no, they were clearly speaking to her. She moved hesitantly toward the edge of her landing, unconvinced they really wanted her to join them. "What's going on?"

"We found some cool rocks," Bean said. "Want to see?"

Lorna spotted a pile of seemingly ordinary rocks. Heaven only knew where they'd come from—probably shoring up the corner of the house. She walked down the three steps into the yard, and Agnes, having finally turned from the sea of adoring faces, trotted over. At least that was an improvement from other times Lorna had found her with Bean. But after touching her snout to Lorna and accepting a head scratch, she trotted right back to the group of fun people.

Even her dog was choosing other people over her.

Bean hopped up and carried a rock in each hand to meet her halfway. "This one is metmorsit," he said, holding up a striated rock.

"Metamorphic," Martin corrected.

"Yeah, that's what I meant," Bean said. "And this one is sedentary."

Mrs. Foster and Martin laughed. "Sedimentary," Martin said.

Lorna looked at the rocks Bean held out to her. They were rocks all right.

"Martin knows how to tell all rocks apart," Bean said excitedly.

"He does?"

"I'm a geologist," Martin said.

Lorna's gaze snapped to Martin to see if he was joking.

Martin smiled a little. "Did you think I was a rapper or something?"

Lorna knew better than to answer that, but she did think he was some sort of musician. What was she supposed to think? He was always wearing the over-the-ear headphones and turning up the volume of his music. "No," she said, unconvincingly.

"Oh my God, you did," Martin said, and laughed with amazement.

"Well, I didn't know he was a geologist until today either,"

Mrs. Foster trilled. "The rocks are very interesting when you hear him talk about them. It's hard to imagine the thousands of years that have gone into making them."

"Miss Liz said I will learn about rocks in the fifth grade," Bean said. "She's a teacher."

"Was," Mrs. Foster said. "I'm retired now."

And all this time, Lorna had thought she worked at a home and garden center. She was always dressed in capri pants and Crocs, with her gray hair pulled back into a ponytail. How had this happened? How was it that faceless neighbors Lorna had lived next to for nearly two years were only now becoming known to her? Also, did Bean know everyone?

"Did you get your letter from Mr. Contreras?" Mrs. Foster asked.

"A letter? No." Unless it had come today—she hadn't gone through her pile of mail.

"Rent is going up," Martin said. "We're thinking about banding together to fight it."

"Another two hundred and fifty dollars a month," Mrs. Foster said, looking slightly traumatized.

Lorna was surprised to hear it. It wasn't as if their current rent was affordable—she already thought it was overvalued by 20 percent. "Two hundred and fifty a month is outrageous," she said.

"Right?" Martin said. "He shouldn't be charging what we're paying now. There are so many things in disrepair."

"Right!" Lorna emphatically agreed. Maybe she and the geologist had more in common than she'd perceived.

"Then you'll help us fight?" Mrs. Foster asked.

Whoa. "Fight? I think he should just sell it."

Mrs. Foster gaped at her as if she'd just blasphemed the Almighty. "But if he sells it, we'll be out."

"Maybe we shouldn't be living here."

"Look!" Bean said. "Martin gave me a geode." He held up a rock.

"Hold on, bud," Martin said, and looked at Lorna. "What are you saying?"

"Nothing, really." Why hadn't she kept her mouth shut? She'd just revealed herself. "I just think this should be a house. A family house."

"But it's an apartment building."

"But it was a house before that."

Martin and Mrs. Foster were staring at her so intently that Lorna almost confessed her scheme.

"What kind is this one, Martin?" Bean asked. He was holding up another rock, clearly oblivious to the adult conversation.

"Metamorphic," Martin answered. "Sure, it was a house," he continued to Lorna, "back when there were horses and buggies. But now it's four separate apartments, and it would take a lot of money to put it back together. No one is going to do that. Because no one could afford a house this size in the middle of Austin. The property taxes alone would be more than some people pay for an entire house. Which is why it's been split into apartments. But it should be affordable apartments, because this ain't the Ritz."

"No, it is not," Mrs. Foster agreed. "He still hasn't fixed the leak in my bathroom."

Lorna made a mental note to complain about the leak in that bathroom to Mr. Contreras. This house had enough problems without adding mold to the list.

"But I understand where you're coming from," Mrs. Foster said.

"You do?" Lorna asked, surprised.

"Sure!" Mrs. Foster continued. "It clearly needs some work, but it's a beautiful old house. Unfortunately, I think that time has passed. Martin's right—it would be cost prohibitive to make this into a family home again. I think we should at least talk about working together to stop such a sharp rent increase."

Lorna didn't know what to say. Her headache squeezed like a vise, and she rubbed at one temple. She understood what they were saying. She felt bad for her neighbors—no one liked to be priced out of their home. And yet, as inexplicable as it was to anyone but her inner self, Lorna had to have this house. They would never understand that it was almost a matter of life and death to her. Metaphorically speaking, anyway. She had this crazy notion that she would have the normal life she craved if only she had this house. All she had to do was go back to the way life was and redo the last thirty years.

She looked at her dog, who was now nosing around the rocks, knocking over the piles that Bean was busily putting up again. "Aggie!" he admonished her, then followed that up by petting her as he reset his piles.

"Maybe we should wait until Seth is available later this afternoon so we can all come to some agreement," Mrs. Foster said.

"My dad and I are going to Ranger Explorers tonight," Bean said. "I'm getting a new badge for LEGOs. I have a whole box of badges."

"Sometime this week?" Martin asked, shifting his gaze between Lorna and Mrs. Foster.

"Ah . . ." Lorna tried to think a way out of this. "I'd like to call Mr. Contreras and talk to him first."

"Oh, would you?" Mrs. Foster asked, and let out a breath. "That would be so helpful. Could you do that today or tomorrow? Then we can talk about what you learned and decide how to proceed. Is there anything you need from us before you talk to him?"

"Umm . . . no, I don't think so." Lorna rubbed her temple again. She could now add queasiness to her headache. She was going to call Mr. Contreras, but not about the rent hike. "I should run," she said, pointing to her door. "Agnes, are you coming?"

"She likes Aggie better," Bean said. "I did an experiment."

Agnes began to wag her stub of a tail.

Lorna sighed. "Okay." She was fighting a war on too many fronts. "Come on, Aggie."

Her traitorous dog reluctantly followed her.

"Bye, Aggie! Bye, Lorna! Martin, look at *this* rock!" Bean said, and he and Martin and Mrs. Foster turned back to rock gazing.

Once inside, Lorna made sure Agnes had water, then went directly to her mail. She flipped through the flyers for window replacements, bath resurfacing, and cell phone deals until she found the letter from Mr. Contreras. She ripped it open and read it. Effective in three months' time, rent would go up two hundred and fifty dollars. *Like hell it will.* She tossed the letter down and picked up her phone.

Mr. Contreras answered on the third ring with a gruff "Yo."

"Mr. Contreras? It's Lorna Lott at—"

"I know who you are. What's up?"

"It's about the rent increase," she said crisply.

"I figured. What about it?" He made a sound like he was puffing on a cigar. "Too rich for your blood?"

She bristled. "Well, it is a lot of money. Practically robbery when you get a load of the place."

"Hey."

"I'm sorry, Mr. Contreras, but I feel like you are taking advantage of us. I would like to discuss a sale again."

"Lorna," he said, and sighed wearily, like she called him all the time to talk about a sale. "Why are you so stuck on that idea?"

"I'm not stuck." Wow, her head was killing her. "I want to buy this property from you."

"Yeah, I know. Look, I already told you—it's going to cost too much. I can only sell that heap of bricks to deep pockets. You a millionaire?"

"That's none of your business. I've done the math and I—"

"The upkeep alone is going to kill you. Why do you think I'm going up on rent? I'm not making a dime off that property. I got problems with the foundation, the plumbing will have to be redone, there may even be some wood rot."

"And the roof needs to be replaced," Lorna added.

"My point exactly. You're not ready for this."

"Mr. Contreras, you can't possibly know what I am ready for."

Mr. Contreras clucked his tongue. "Feisty, aren't you?"

Lorna's hand curled into a fist. "Not feisty so much as I'm full of rage."

Mr. Contreras chuckled. "Now, no need to get upset. It's just a house. Look, tell you what. If we can come to terms, I'll sell it to you. But I'm not going to drag this out. You want it, you've got a month to come up with a plan for purchase. In three months, I'm getting more rent or I'm selling. Who knows—I might do both."

Lorna bit her bottom lip. She was ready . . . but a month was quick. She didn't have the down payment together just yet.

Her silence caused him to chuckle again. "I thought you said you were ready, sweetheart."

She *was* ready. Emotionally. Maybe not quite financially. "You have a deal, Mr. Contreras. And I am not your sweetheart."

Mr. Contreras snorted.

"You think I can't do it," she said.

"Babe, I know you can't."

"A month from tomorrow," she said. "And don't call me *babe*."

"Whatever you say, sweetheart."

Lorna hung up on him. She stood a moment, her breath coming in furious bursts like she was a huffing and puffing cartoon character. That had been happening a lot lately. She walked into her bedroom, went to the small dresser, and took out the file labeled *Mom*.

This time, she took the papers to her kitchen table and spread everything out. She picked up a white legal envelope and took out the two pages inside. The first one was a typed letter, instructions from Tyrone, her estate attorney. The second page was a handwritten note from her mother. Her handwriting was shaky in the end but still elegant.

> You will find the list with my trustee, Peggy. I asked Tyrone to leave it in her capable hands because I feared you would burn it, eat it, or wrap it around a rock and throw it at your sister.

"Probably would have," Lorna muttered. The shame for the last months of her mother's life was gutting. It was impossible to feel any lower than she did about that. She'd been so angry with useless Kristen. She'd come from a very bad day at work, expecting to find Kristen there making sure her mother had taken her meds and was getting enough to drink and eating what she could, only to find Kristen had taken the little bit of cash her mother had for groceries and left her alone in the apartment for hours with no food.

When Lorna expressed her disappointment in Kristen, her mother defended Kristen by arguing that she was in the grip of an illness as bad as her own. That argument caused Lorna to reach her limit more than once. "You coddle her, Mom. You let her get away with *so much*."

Her mother argued that she'd tried everything she could think of to help Kristen. "What do you want me to do? I tried for years to force her into sobriety, because nothing is harder than watching my once-bright daughter with everything going for her waste away in addiction. It wasn't until I started attending Al-Anon that I realized trying to force her is the wrong approach. She has to come to the conclusion she needs help on her own, Lolo, and until then, all we can do is love her."

What her mother never seemed to remember was that Lorna had suffered Kristen's addiction, too, right alongside her. And when she tried to press home all the wrongs Kristen had inflicted on them (the loss of friends, family, and confidence, to name a few), her mother argued it was up to Lorna to right those wrongs now, and Lorna—

Well. Lorna had lost her mind, that was what.

And now, after so much time had passed, Lorna had to consider that maybe her mother was right. Maybe it was time to address the wrongs she'd blamed on Kristen. To own up to them, to get the monkey off her back, so to speak. To stop living in the past.

Starting way back when.

If she wanted this house, she was going to have to do it. Because without the trust money, she didn't have a chance of buying back her happiness.

Chapter 9

Lorna Is Nine

THEY MOVE IN WITH NANA ONE SUMMER WHEN THE HONEYbees are buzzing around the honeysuckle and the sprinklers run every morning. The wisteria in the backyard has gone wild, and purple blooms are everywhere, vines curling around fences and one dead tree.

"We get our own bedrooms," Kristen says. "We'll be next to each other so I can come in whenever I want." Her tone is both menacing and loving.

Lorna loves her bedroom. It has a padded bench just below windows that crank open. The boughs of an enormous oak tree brush against the side of the house when the wind blows. The closet is dark and deep, and in the back, a little trapdoor leads to the attic. "You should lock your closet at night so the ghosts don't get in," Kristen says soberly.

"There are no ghosts, Kristen," her mother snaps. "Stop scaring your sister."

But Lorna isn't scared—she wants to see ghosts.

There are built-in corner bookshelves and thick crown molding. The carpet is worn but plush. It feels bouncy under her feet. "It smells like cat piss in here," Kristen says. Her room is an exact copy of Lorna's, but with three windows instead of two, and no attic door.

"No, it doesn't," Mom says. "Don't let Nana hear you say that." She takes out a cigarette and lights it. She sits on the padded window seat and blows smoke through an open window. She looks like she is staring at something in the neighbor's backyard.

She looks sad.

Lorna knows her parents are divorcing. They didn't tell her, but Kristen did. "It's about time," Kristen said when she informed Lorna. "They hate each other."

"They do?"

"Haven't you noticed?" Kristen asked as she put on the lipstick she'd stolen from Mom's purse.

Lorna doesn't know what divorce means in practice, other than her dad is not going to live with them anymore. He promises her he will see her every week. She hasn't seen him in at least two.

Lorna and Kristen have spent many nights in this house before, usually without their parents. Her mom's presence makes it feel different. A little less fun, because Nana spends a lot of time with Mom.

She likes to sit at the top of the stairs where she can overhear Mom and Nana talking downstairs.

"He's been running around with some bitch from work," Mom says.

Lorna knows that word is bad. Why would her dad be running around with a bad person?

"That's so typical of men," Nana says, and Lorna hears liquid being poured over ice in a glass. She knows it is the stuff in the ice-blue bottle that Nana keeps on top of the fridge. Nana has been drinking a lot of it.

Kristen finds her and pulls her downstairs. She yells at Mom that they are going outside. The backyard is overgrown since Papa died.

"Watch out for snakes!" their mother shouts from the kitchen door.

"Ooh, let's find some snakes," Kristen says, excited. They wander down to the fence to look for them, but there aren't any. Beyond the chain-link fence is a small creek with water running through. The gate is overrun with wisteria and jasmine vines, so they can't open it. "We have to figure out a way to break out," Kristen says.

Break out? Why would they want to leave this house? Lorna thinks it is wonderful. It's big and rambling, with a lot of creaks and moans and weird things, like niches in the walls. She can't believe she gets to live here all the time now.

"This is the best thing that's ever happened to us, you know that, right?" Kristen adds as an afterthought, as if she is reading Lorna's mind. She gives the gate one last tug. It won't budge. "At least we don't have to listen to them fighting anymore."

"I hate when they fight," Lorna says. Her parents yell so loud, and her mom throws things. Sometimes she and Kristen crawl into the same bed and pull the covers over their heads to hide from the shouting until Kristen says she is hot and throws the covers off.

Kristen doesn't find a way to break out, at least not that day.

That summer, Lorna and Kristen find new life at Nana's. They play in the sprinklers. Mom lets them walk to the corner store for popsicles. They watch TV, endless hours of cartoons and old sitcoms.

Eventually, Kristen befriends two girls who live down the street, Mary and Tanya. They are a grade below Kristen. Kristen is tanned and blond and has a body like in the magazines. Everyone likes her. Tanya's brother Todd really likes her. Lorna is tall and pasty-skinned with a mess of hair Nana says came from their crazy great-grandfather. No one seems to notice Lorna when they are outside with the kids on the street. But everyone notices Kristen.

Their new friends come over to watch TV on very hot afternoons. Mary is quiet and doesn't say much. Tanya is the opposite—she talks all the time and copies everything Kristen does. She wants to be like Kristen. Lorna knows this because she does too. Tanya looks at Lorna and sneers. "Does she have to be here?"

Kristen looks at her sister, then at Tanya. "She has to be here because she is my sister. But you don't have to be here, Tanya."

Tanya sinks down onto the couch and pouts.

She tries to exclude Lorna all summer, but Kristen won't allow it. Kristen decides who stays and who goes. Lorna is allowed to watch TV with them, and she sits next to Kristen so Tanya can't. But Kristen explains to her that thirteen-year-olds don't want to hang out with nine-year-olds, so she can't do everything with them. Lorna is grateful for anything she gets.

When school starts, there are too many kids at Lorna's new school, but she does not go unnoticed in her class, especially without Kristen's bright light to shield her. Lorna is in the fourth grade and stands nearly as tall as her diminutive teacher. One boy accuses her of being in the sixth grade because of her height.

She hates school. No one likes her. She tries to make friends on the playground, but no one lets her join in. Sometimes she comes home in the afternoon to Mom screaming at Dad on the telephone about money. Nana is always in the kitchen, always happy. But Lorna has begun to notice the scent of her grandmother. It smells a little like beer, but not exactly beer.

Nana makes pastries and bread for the girls, and they are so good. Mom says Lorna is eating too much and will get fat. Kristen says to leave Lorna alone. Mom never mentions food to Kristen, who remains slender and pretty no matter what.

Kristen has a radio in her room. At night, when they are supposed to be doing their homework, Kristen teaches Lorna all the latest dances. They perform them for Mom and Nana, who always applaud. Once, Mom tried to do the dance with them, and they all laughed until tears were sliding down their faces.

When Kristen's friends come over—and there are more and more of them—she kicks Lorna out. But she always comes looking for her the next day.

One night, Kristen comes to her room, bored. Mom is on the phone fighting with Dad. She says Nana is passed out in her chair. She glances out Lorna's window. "Let's jump to that limb and climb down. Everyone is at the park tonight."

"Who is everyone?"

"My friends. Come on, don't be a chicken." Kristen opens Lorna's window and climbs out onto the ledge. She jumps, fearless. She almost misses the limb but manages to catch it and haul herself up. She assesses her options and begins to shimmy down, using the long, twisting boughs as a stepladder. "Come on, Lolo!" she shout-whispers. But Lorna is afraid she will fall. She won't do it.

"You're never going to do anything fun if you're a chicken," Kristen says, and disappears into the night.

Lorna falls asleep. Sometime in the night, Kristen comes home. She crawls into bed with Lorna and tucks Lorna's favorite stuffed animal in with them. She smells like Nana. She is gone when Lorna wakes up the next morning.

The next afternoon, two police officers come to the house, looking for Kristen. She's with her friend. The officers say some kids broke into a house down the street.

Mom and Nana are appalled. Mom is angry that the police

have come to their door and insists her daughter had nothing to do with it.

"She was upstairs with her sister all night. Wasn't she, Lorna?" she asks.

The police officers look at Lorna. She doesn't know what to do. She thinks she should tell the truth, but what would they do to Kristen?

"Don't let them scare you—just tell them," her mother says again, sounding annoyed.

"Yes," Lorna says.

After the police are gone, Kristen finally comes home, and Mom confronts her. "Did you sneak out? Did you break into someone's house with your delinquent friends?"

"Not a whole house. Just the screened-in porch."

Mom shouts, Nana cries. Kristen claims it was Todd's idea and they all went along with it.

"So if Todd said to jump off a cliff, would you do that too?"

Kristen laughs. "Maybe."

"Help me understand, Kristen. Were you drinking?" Mom asks coldly.

"No," Kristen says, and sounds offended. But Lorna knows she was—she smelled it.

Her mother believes Kristen. She turns to argue with Nana about who was supposed to be watching who, and why didn't she get the alarms like Mom asked? Kristen winks at Lorna. Then she puts her hand in her shorts pocket and slowly pulls it out. Behind Mom's back, she shows Lorna what looks like one of Mom's cigarettes, but without the filter. Lorna doesn't know what it is, but she knows it's bad.

Mom calls Dad about the police. He is coming over to give Kristen a "talking-to."

"No," Kristen groans. "Call him back and tell him not to come. I won't do it again, I promise."

When Dad arrives, he and Mom argue. Mom says they will probably charge Kristen with trespassing. Dad says she will have to make amends. He asks where Mom was when her daughter was out joyriding. Mom turns red in the face and asks where he was. They argue about whose fault it is that Kristen is like this.

Kristen and Lorna slip upstairs. "It's not that big of a deal," Kristen says. "They're the ones making it into a big deal." She opens Lorna's window and then pulls the cigarette and lighter from her pocket. She lights it, and Lorna knows the smell. She's smelled it in the park before.

"Was the door to the other house open?" Lorna asks.

"Nah. We had to cut the screen to get in."

Lorna watches her sister for a moment. "Why?" she finally asks.

Kristen shrugs. "I don't know. I guess because we could."

"Kristen, get down here!" her mother bellows up the stairs.

Kristen puts out her cigarette and sticks it back in her pocket. "You should let your room air out for a little bit. Don't let Mom in here, or she'll freak." She tousles Lorna's hair as she goes out. "Stay up here. It's probably going to get loud."

Lorna sits at the top of the stairs. She listens to everyone yell at everyone else. Mom is the loudest, Dad is biting, Kristen is screechy about how no one ever lets her do anything. Nana is crying.

After some time, Lorna gets bored. She goes to her room and shuts the door. She changes into her nightclothes and crawls into bed. She is so hungry. No one made supper.

Chapter 10

Lorna Now

LORNA TURNED ONTO THE STREET WHERE HER MOTHER last lived. It was a few blocks east from where she lived now, sandwiched between the old Mueller airport redevelopment and the trendier Hyde Park. Here the homes were modest and overshadowed by pricier real estate.

Lorna pulled up in front of a redbrick ranch-style house. The yard was cluttered with bird feeders and yard art, just like it had been when her mother lived here. It also contained plastic pink flamingos, metal flowers, two concrete birdbaths, and, bizarrely, something new: a red, blue, and green metal rooster that stood about five feet tall.

Lorna knew that in the backyard she'd find more yard ornaments and bird feeders, a large patio, an old tire swing hanging from one of the oak trees, and two plastic life-size longhorn cows. At the end of the drive was a two-car garage, and above that, a garage apartment with two small bedrooms, one bath, a tiny kitchen, and a living area.

Her mother had moved them into that apartment after she'd sold Nana's house. She'd needed the money from the sale to put Kristen into long-term drug treatment.

Living in the garage apartment had been a bit like living in a tree house. The tops of the live oaks were visible outside the windows, and they never lost all their leaves. For another family, it might have been charming. To Lorna, that small apartment felt like prison. It had put her too close to Kristen when she was at her worst and too close to her mother when she was at her sickest.

Lorna hadn't been here since she'd cleaned out the apartment after her mother died. Of course she'd been the one to settle all the details of her mother's estate, with no help. She couldn't even remember where Kristen had been at that time. In jail? With a boyfriend?

She sat in her car, staring at her past, until she began to feel hot. "For heaven's sake, Lorna," she muttered. "Don't be such a chicken. Just do it." Still, it took a moment for the command to travel from her brain to her body to *move*. At last, she got out of her car and walked up the path to the front door and knocked. She waited a minute or two, and when no one came to the door, she walked a rock path around to the side of the house, taking care not to get her pant legs caught in the pinwheels turning in the spring breeze along the path. She rounded the corner into the backyard and spotted a toddler's car, the red-and-yellow sort driven by their feet. There was also a doll lying face down on the path.

The back gate was tall, made of redwood, with lattice work up top. There was a small porcelain medallion hanging next to the latch that read WELCOME. Behind the gate, she could hear water running and someone humming. She knocked and opened the gate, poking her head just inside. "Peggy?"

She startled the older woman, who clumsily whipped around and almost lost her footing. But when she saw Lorna, her face broke into a warm wreath of smiles. That, in turn, startled Lorna—she was not used to people looking so pleased to see her.

"Lolo! Oh my goodness, what a sight for sore eyes! Wait, wait, don't go anywhere!" She dropped the hose she was holding and hurried to turn off the spigot. She wiped her hands on the apron Lorna had never seen her without and came quickly to the gate, her arms cast wide.

Lorna sheepishly slipped inside the gate. Peggy kept advancing, holding out her arms, until she had them firmly around Lorna, who stiffened—she was quite unaccustomed to human touch. Certainly to hugs.

After a moment, she began to soften. This reminded her of something. Of Nana. Nana used to hug her so tight when the family would come to visit.

She felt a little guilty, showing up like this after all this time. Peggy was exactly where Lorna knew she'd be, tending to her plants. She owned the house and the garage apartment and had been their landlord. She was always available, taking care of issues immediately and, probably most important, being her mother's dear friend. Mom and Peggy had spent a lot of time on this patio, drinking wine and reminiscing about the good ol' days. And when her mother was sick, Peggy was there to help.

It made sense that Mom had made Peggy her trustee.

Peggy finally let go and stood back to examine Lorna from head to toe. "Look at you, look at *you*. You finally figured out how to tame that hair, I see."

"Um . . . no. I just put it in a bun. Less trouble that way," Lorna said self-consciously.

"Well, you look great," Peggy said. "So professional!"

Lorna was wearing what she considered her casual clothes. Black slacks, a blue linen blouse. Peggy, who must be in her seventies now, looked a bit heavier than the last time Lorna had seen her. But her hair was still a halo of tight silver curls around her plump face. She was wearing support stockings and Crocs and a smile that took Lorna back in time. Peggy had always been so kind to them. Lorna had no idea why—there'd been nothing but death and drama in the years the Lott ladies had occupied that garage apartment.

"I'm so happy to see you, you can't imagine. Don't just stand there—come in!" she said, and grabbed Lorna's wrist, pulling her into the yard.

Lorna allowed herself to be dragged. It was nice to be with someone who liked her. "Thanks, Peggy. It's good to see you too." It truly was. But of course, as usual, her warm, fuzzy feelings had to be accompanied by something sour. This time it was a wave of remorse that suddenly washed over her. She should have come after her mother was gone. Peggy had been so good to them, especially Mom. After Mom died, Peggy had made sure Lorna was eating, and Lorna had been so . . . Well, she didn't know what. Not exactly angry. Shell-shocked? And probably very gruff.

All she knew was that she had retreated into her bomb shelter and slammed the door shut.

"I've got a fresh batch of iced tea. Let's sit on the patio, and I want to hear about all that you've been up to. Do you still like cookies? You're so trim, Lorna! How did you manage it? I should take a page out of your book. You sit here, and I'll be right back."

There was no page in Lorna's weight-loss book other than the one about stress. She'd figured out a long time ago that she was a Big Girl and had stopped trying to fit the mold of what society considered beautiful. That was Kristen's job—she'd been the beauty. For a while, anyway.

Peggy was back in a few minutes with her plastic pineapple-print serving tray. She had two large glasses of tea, a caddy of sugars, and a plate of cookies. Lorna took a cookie. *Peanut butter. To die for.* "I noticed you've got some kids here now," Lorna said as she munched on the cookie. "Grandkids?"

"Heavens, no. My son is just as recalcitrant about relationships as he ever was and refuses to give me grandchildren. He lives in London now. Isn't that wonderful? Imagine, driving by Buckingham Palace on your way to work every day. But never mind him. How are you, Lolo?"

"Umm . . ." Lorna put down her half-eaten cookie and wiped her hands quite rudely on her pants. She didn't know how to answer Peggy's question. Or rather, where to start. "I'm . . . fine," she said tentatively. "I'm . . ." Her voice trailed off—she wanted to express herself but didn't really know how.

"You know," Peggy said, "I always knew you'd come."

Lorna's eyes widened in surprise. "Really?"

"Oh, sure," Peggy said with a determined nod. "I didn't know when, but I knew you'd be here. These things, you know, they take as long as they take."

Lorna wondered what "these things" meant to Peggy. She was only now working out what they were for herself.

"Your mother loved you so much, Lolo."

"Oh. Okay, we're going straight there," Lorna said, feeling suddenly uneasy. She'd never questioned her mother's love for her. But she had questioned how much her mother *liked* her. There had been times it felt as though she didn't like Lorna at all.

"She might not have always made the right decisions, but she tried to do her best before she left this earth," Peggy continued. "That's what mothers do. They make the hard decisions for their kids."

Why was she telling her this? "Okay," Lorna said, trying to

sound light. But then she felt the terrible trickle of a tear sliding down her cheek.

"She wanted you to be happy, and I know how she worried that regrets would eat you alive. She really wanted to help you let go of those regrets."

Yeah, yeah. She'd heard it all from Mom. "I know," Lorna said, and shakily wiped a finger beneath her eye.

"Good heavens, listen to me, going on about something you've obviously thought long and hard about. You wouldn't be here if you hadn't, would you?"

Lorna sniffed and tried desperately to will away more tears. She wouldn't be here if she didn't need the trust money. She hadn't come to admit her mother was right about anything. "I guess?" she said, because it would be great if they could get this over with.

"Wonderful." Peggy brightened a little. "How is Kristen?"

Lorna's belly did the sickly little ripple she felt anytime someone mentioned her sister. "I'm not sure," she answered truthfully. "She's in Florida with my dad."

Peggy nodded. Curiosity was practically oozing out of her.

"We're not speaking."

"Oh, I hate to hear that," Peggy said. "You two were once so close."

"A very long time ago."

"Well, I'm glad your father finally stepped up to the plate."

"I wouldn't say that," Lorna said. "It was more like he didn't have a choice this time. I mean, with Mom gone."

"It's all been so hard for you, Lolo," Peggy said kindly.

Another tear slipped from captivity. "Nope. Not hard." She'd been happy to let her father take on the burden of Kristen for once. Hadn't she? Hadn't she been relieved when they'd left

Austin, taking all the family dysfunction with them at long last? She glanced away, checked out the four birdhouses hanging from a tree limb, and swiped under her eyes again. The birdhouses looked unused.

"It's all right," Peggy said, and leaned forward to pat Lorna's knee. "I know how hard it is for you to do emotion."

Do emotion? What did that mean? She did emotion. She did it all the time. She was doing it this very second. She was a walking cauldron of boiling emotions, a gristmill, a factory, a cargo hold full of emotion. She just didn't show it on the outside because she had too much of it, and if she showed how she really felt, she'd come across like a monster. Probably people would consider calling the cops. Primal screams didn't go over well in public. "I don't . . . know what to say to that."

"You don't have to say anything, hon. I'm simply acknowledging your difficulties." She smiled as if they had talked about this before and were on the same page about her "difficulties." But they never had. And they never would, if Lorna had anything to do with it. It was bad enough she'd spilled her guts and more to Micah.

This conversation was exactly why she built her internal bomb shelter. Look what happened when she came out of it—people started guessing what was wrong with her, and she came close to wanting to rip the roof right off Peggy's house.

The best thing to do was tackle the reason for her visit in the hopes of speeding things along and getting the hell out of here before Peggy started to talk about what a wonderful mother Mindy Lott had been. Before Lorna did or said something she would regret. She did not want to add to the list. "Peggy, I've come—"

"About the trust. I gathered. Hand to heaven, I told Mindy not to make me the trustee. I said, 'Surely there is someone in your family who should do it?' But she assured me she had no one. I said to her, 'What do I know about wills and that sort of thing?'

My son has taken care of mine. But Mindy insisted, and she said I was the best for it and that I knew almost everything."

Well, that was disconcerting to hear.

"My son said I shouldn't involve myself."

Because he was a smart man and knew trouble when he saw it.

"But I decided it was simple enough, and Mindy really needed my help."

"Is it?" Lorna asked curiously. "Simple?"

"Well, sure," Peggy said cheerfully, as if the entire world knew how simple it was. Lorna had no idea.

"What do I have to do to prove that I've, you know, done the things Mom wanted from me?"

"Oh, Lolo. That's where you've got it all wrong. Your mother didn't want them. *You* did."

False. Lorna had most certainly not wanted to address her regrets, thank you very much, but for the sake of ending this conversation, she said, "What I wanted, then. How will you know I've, like, made my apologies or whatever?"

Peggy shrugged and reached for a cookie. "Just tell me."

Lorna stared at her. "What do you mean, just tell you? How will you know I'm not lying? What will the courts say?"

"Courts? There's no court. As it was explained to me, if I agree that you've done what your mother wanted, that's all that is required. And I don't need anything fancy, honey. You be the judge of whether you've done what you needed to do and just let me know. And I know you. You won't lie. You're too honest."

She had to be kidding. Mom had gone to all this trouble, and now Peggy was going to be loosey-goosey about it? "It can't be that simple," Lorna argued. "There should be some proof."

Peggy smiled. "What would you like your proof to be?"

Maybe she didn't understand. "Peggy, there has to be something that proves—"

"Not in this trust. You could come here tomorrow and tell me you've addressed them all and I will sign off."

Lorna sat back and tried to make sense of it. She had avoided this for four years, and all she had to do was announce she'd done everything in the codicil? What was to stop her from doing exactly as Peggy suggested and declaring tomorrow that she was done with it? But Peggy was right—she was too honest.

This was precisely the sort of thing that led to people thinking she did not "do emotion." Because right now she appeared calm on the outside, but on the inside, she wanted to body slam that very large rooster in the front yard to the ground and pummel it.

"Stay here," Peggy said, hopping up and going into her house. She returned in a few minutes with a yellowed envelope. "This is the codicil."

Lorna took it. It felt heavy. Full of history. She knew what those pages contained and didn't want to look at them. Unfortunately, she'd come this far and she was going to have to see her plan through and decide which of her mother's list items to tackle first. "Thanks, Peggy."

"Just curious . . . what made you change your mind? About the trust, I mean."

Lorna was reluctant to admit she wanted the money to buy her grandmother's house. Peggy would probably disapprove of such a base motivation. She probably wanted something deep and meaningful, some reflection on how it had taken Lorna four years to realize what an inspiration her mother was. Then again, maybe Peggy would understand. She seemed the understanding sort.

But Lorna decided to speak with caution and not reveal herself, as usual. Instead, she parroted Micah. "It came down to wanting to know where I'm going with my life. And I have to know where I've been to figure that out."

Peggy's brown eyes sparkled like Christmas lights. "That's *wonderful*, Lolo. How *astute* of you. How *proud* Mindy would be."

Yeah, well, Mindy would be proud of Micah. Lorna suddenly felt exhausted. She honestly didn't know what her mother would think of her now. Of the forlorn, terminally single, awkward daughter she'd become.

"Just know that I am here for you."

That was one thing Lorna could believe. Peggy would be there for her. Remarkably, she'd been there for Lorna and her family for several years. It defied logic. Her family had done nothing to deserve such devotion from a good person like Peggy.

She thanked Peggy again, promising to see her soon, and as she dragged herself out to her car, she paused to kick the giant rooster. It did nothing for her other than hurt her foot.

She went home with her mother's wishes burning a hole in her pants pocket.

Chapter 11

Lorna Now

LORNA LET HERSELF IN THROUGH THE FRONT DOOR OF THE house and spotted Bean sitting in the hallway with Agnes. He was leaning against his door, legs outstretched, flipping through the pages of a book. Agnes had her head in his lap and was snoozing. Lorna glanced at her watch; it was ten past four. He'd forgotten his key again. If he were her kid, she would have fixed this forgotten key problem in a day.

As much as it annoyed her, a part of her was also glad he'd forgotten his key. Something about the boy and the dog made her feel... something. Nostalgic, maybe? But looking at him was a little like looking at a work of art that spoke to her. She liked Bean, which, if she thought too long about it, would make her question her mental state, because since when did she have any affinity for eight-year-old boys? But lately, she'd talked more to Bean than anyone else. He didn't make her feel awkward; she was surprisingly free of awkwardness with him. Free to be herself. He didn't judge her. Or at least not that she could tell. It was entirely possible he was going home and telling stories about the weird lady across the hall. Except she didn't think so—she had the impression that Bean liked her too.

"Excuse me?" Lorna said. "How did Agnes get in here?"

Bean looked up. "Hi, Lorna! Miss Liz let her in from the backyard."

That back door from the main hall was supposed to always remain locked. Lorna sighed with exasperation. "Is no one concerned about home security?" she complained as she moved forward.

"Don't worry, I wouldn't let anyone snatch her," Bean said, parroting her concern from the first time she'd found him in the hall.

"I know *you* wouldn't, but what about the rest of the people in this house?" She slid down the wall and sat beside him on the floor. He eyed her with surprise. "I know," she said. "I'm not the type to sit on the floor. But honestly? This week I've been on the floor a lot."

"I like the floor," Bean said.

"I'm starting to hate it less. You forgot your key again, didn't you?"

"Yep. That means I have to wash dishes after supper because there are conskences. But I don't mind because I like all the suds. Yesterday I made this huge tower, then—*bam*—I knocked it down," he said, demonstrating how he'd swung his fist through weightless bubbles.

She wondered what he'd do with a giant metal yard rooster. "What are you looking at?"

"It's a book about desserts. I'm going to get my baking badge. But I have to decide what to bake. Do you like cake?"

"Only idiots don't like cake."

He grinned. "Is it your favorite?"

"Probably, although I could be persuaded to like pie or ice cream or cookies just as much. What's your favorite?" she asked as she eyed a key lime pie on the open pages of his book.

"Umm . . . I don't know. My dad doesn't let me have sugar."

"What? That's appalling. What is the point of life if you

can't have a sugary dessert occasionally? In fact, it ought to be a law."

Bean glanced at her sidelong, clearly afraid to agree with such a bold statement.

"Come in, and I'll see what I've got with sugar."

"Dad said not to bother people," Bean said.

"You're not bothering me."

"Can Aggie come, too, or does she have to go outside?"

"Of course she comes too."

The two of them leveraged themselves up to standing with about the same amount of grace. "Come on, Aggie," Bean said, and headed for Lorna's door.

Once Lorna opened the door, Bean and Aggie rushed toward the kitchen. She paused to put the codicil on her desk next to the stacks of envelopes. In doing so, she had to step over a white envelope on the floor that had been pushed under the door, sealed with a red heart sticker. She picked it up and flipped it over. *Liz Foster, 2B.* Inside was a handwritten note:

> *I would love to hear if you made any progress with our landlord. Feel free to knock anytime, 2B.*

On the bottom she'd added, *Aggie is welcome!* Lorna peered at her dog, who had trotted back to see if the envelope might be bearing treats. "I guess your name really is Aggie now," she said.

Aggie's butt swished back and forth in her tailless version of a wag. "Hey, Bean . . . didn't you say Mrs. Foster had a cat?" Lorna called into the kitchen.

"Yes. His name is Garfield."

Of course. "Let me guess—he's fat, orange, and stupid."

Bean was startled enough to come back into the living area. "Garfield isn't stupid. He and Aggie are friends."

"Friends! How do you know that?"

"Because sometimes Miss Liz brings Garfield to the backyard, and they play."

"No way." Lorna thought Aggie hated cats. She barked at them on their walks. Then again, she barked at bushes and bicycles lying in yards and kids bouncing basketballs.

Bean nodded. "They're best friends. Even Miss Liz thinks so. Diego's my best friend. But he's moving to California."

"That sucks." Lorna opened her pantry door. "When?"

"I don't know. My dad says he can come for a sleepover before he moves. And that maybe we can go visit him in California."

"California is not all it's cracked up to be," Lorna said. She didn't have any cookies or cereal bars, but she spotted a box of brownie mix from the time she was going to bring brownies to the office for Deb's birthday. But then she'd found out the team was treating Deb to lunch. Without her.

"Have you been there?" Bean asked. "Diego said you can see the ocean from California."

"Yes, I've been there, and you can definitely see the ocean from California." One of the treatment centers Kristen flamed out of was in California, and Lorna and her mom had spent a week searching for her in downtown Los Angeles. "Want to make brownies?"

Bean gasped. "*Can* we?"

She slapped the box down on the bar so he could see it. "We can." She sent Bean to leave a note on his door so his father would know where he was, and while he was gone, she found one apron for him and one large dish towel. When he returned, she tied the apron around his chest and then tucked the dish towel in the neck of her blouse and into her pants, effectively covering her front.

She set Bean up with a bowl and had him turn on the oven

to preheat, which, he informed her, he did at home all the time. As she gathered the ingredients, Bean began to talk. He told her how Diego had an oven *just for pizza* on his porch and he also had a pool. He informed her he'd spent the night once at Diego's birthday party and Trey Wheeler had vomited into the bushes. "It was yellow," he said.

"Thanks for the details," Lorna said.

He talked about all the badges he had, which included skating, coin collecting, first aid, camping, astronomy, weather, rocks, art, canoeing, and some others he couldn't remember and not necessarily in that order. And then he listed all the badges he was eager to get, including inventing, cooking, baking, fishing, fire starting, helping, and Texas lore. Diego didn't have as many badges as he did, but he was working on them, and Bean shared his badges with Diego. Lorna failed to understand how that could possibly work, but okay. Bean said he was going to get a blue vest like the other Rangers and put his badges on it.

When they had the ingredients in a bowl, he paused in his running monologue and looked at Lorna as she greased a pan for the brownies. "Do you have a best friend?"

He might as well have shot that question at her from a cannon, because it hit her just as hard. People needed to warn her before they asked personal questions. At least give her time to suit up in her personal armor. "Well . . . not right now."

"Why not?" he asked, still stirring.

She put down the pan and studied the kid. She didn't know how to describe the agony of having a sister as a best friend, only to have her continually lie and let you down. Or explain how, when you had the good luck to find a new best friend, you could screw it up royally. She decided to stick to the basics. "It's hard for me to make friends."

"Why?"

Oh, because she was afraid of trusting people. And she was afraid of what they might think if they knew about Kristen. She was afraid of so many things, really. Being used. Being lied to. Being tricked. Being generally unlikable. And continuing to grow more awkward the longer she lived. "I'm kind of weird," Lorna admitted.

"Like when you said Garfield was stupid?" Bean asked helpfully.

"Exactly." She paused. "Seriously, I thought everyone knew that orange cats are stupid."

Bean didn't look convinced. "Dad says you never know how smart or dumb someone is just by looking at them."

Well, good for Seth and his ability to be nonjudgmental. Except when it came to sugar, obviously. "The bottom line is that I find it really hard to trust people." She shrugged.

"What does *trust* mean?"

"It's like . . . you know how you can tell your dad anything?"

Bean nodded.

"And you know he won't tell anyone? He'll keep any secret you ask him to."

"He will," Bean said eagerly. "Like, I told him that Diego likes Molly, and Diego told me not to tell anyone, but I told Dad, and he hasn't told a single person." Bean's eyes were starry, as though he were completely amazed by his father's feat of secret-keeping. Meanwhile, she was apparently now the second person Bean had told Diego's secret to.

"That's exactly what I mean. I don't really have anyone to tell secrets to."

Bean seemed to take this in, stirring the batter. "You can tell me secrets."

Given the news on Diego, she didn't know if that was wise. She smiled. "Thanks, Bean."

He turned to the task at hand. "And I'll be your friend if you want."

Her smile got bigger. She could feel it crackle all the way to her toes and spark in her chest. "That is so sweet of you, Bean. But I'm not sure you'd like it. I'm kind of boring."

"Yes, I would. Because I like you. That's what friends are—people who like each other. Your eyes are leaking again."

"Damn it," she said, and reached for a tissue.

It was ridiculous that her eyes should well because of his offer to be her friend. This kid would be friends with an alien from outer space, which, if she thought about it, was perfect for an eight-year-old boy. Still, she was moved. Maybe because no one had offered her friendship in years. *This kid, man.* "Thank you, Bean. I would really like that."

"Okay."

And just like that, the deal was done.

He continued mixing the batter, then looked at her again. "But did you *ever* have a best friend?"

Read the room, kid. She didn't want to keep talking about it. She couldn't help but think of Callie. The thought was still painful, like a hand squeezing her heart. After all these years, she still missed her. Still wanted to talk to her. "I did. When I was thirteen."

"Did she *die?*" Bean asked in a whisper.

"I don't think so. I feel sure someone would have told me if she had." Maybe, but who? The thought of Callie being gone from this world squeezed her heart even more. She remembered her so clearly: long red braids, blue eyes, and too many freckles for two young girls to count without laughing. Free spirited and kind and so accepting of Lorna and her terrible homelife. They were both outcasts from the popular circles at school, which made them a merry band of two.

She shook off the memory. "I'm sure she's fine," she said.

"Diego is funny. We play *Interspace Zombies*, and one time Diego blew up a space monster and it turned into marshmallows."

"Sounds sticky."

"And then the marshmallows swallowed all our chickens and made them glitch."

She had no idea what he was talking about. "Keep stirring until you don't have any chunks."

"I'm supposed to have a notebook," he said.

"For what?"

"For field notes. That's how you get a badge—you show them your field notes."

"Hang on." Lorna left him on his knees on a barstool, stirring the batter. She went to her writing desk and opened a drawer. She had several notebooks from various functions and stationery stores and found one from a sales conference a few years back. It was emblazoned with *Driskill Workflow Solutions* above the company logo. She returned to the kitchen with it. "Here you go—a notebook. It's yours now."

"Thanks!" Bean said.

She found a pencil in her catchall drawer. "I'll pour this batter into the pan while you make some notes."

Bean picked up the pencil and bent over the notebook. After a moment, he said, "I don't know what to write."

"Write down *Brownies*. And then you can rank them on a scale to get a score."

"Huh?"

"Like on a scale of one to ten, ten is the hardest, how easy are they to bake?"

Bean looked at the pan with the batter. "Um . . . a seven."

A *seven*? She would have gone with two. But as she was not trying to earn a badge, she said, "Okay, seven it is. When they're baked, we'll taste them and give them a score for taste. And then another one for presentation, because that's a big thing with desserts. You've seen decorated cakes, right?"

Bean blinked.

"We'll take the scores and add them together, divide by three, and you'll have an average score for your dessert."

"Divide?" Bean repeated uncertainly.

It occurred to Lorna that she didn't know what sort of math skills eight-year-olds possessed. "Why don't you just give it a number between one and ten based on how much you enjoyed making and eating the brownies overall." He would never make it at Driskill, where data was king.

"Diego is going to get his fishing badge. After my baking badge, I'm going to get one too. But Dad works a lot, and my grandpa had a stroke."

"I'm sorry to hear that," Lorna said.

"Why?"

"I mean I'm sorry your grandpa is sick."

"Do you know my grandpa?"

"Nope."

"I'm going to visit him on the weekend. Grandma is going to cut my hair. Diego's mom takes him to a barbershop, but Grandma cuts mine. What was your best friend's name?"

He was not going to let it go. She could almost believe Peggy or Micah had put him up to this line of questioning. She averted her gaze. "Callie," she said, and opened the oven door.

"Why did you stop being best friends?" he asked. "I would never stop being best friends with Diego."

"Well . . . life kind of got in the way."

"What does that mean?"

"It means I might have done something stupid."

"Like an orange cat," Bean said.

"Exactly like that."

"Dad says you have to make sure you're being a good friend. But I don't have to try with Diego. We like all the same things. Red is my favorite color and it's his, too, and we both like cars, and we both play *Interspace Zombies*. Did you and Callie have the same favorite color?"

Lorna and Callie had been close like that and had shared everything. Until Lorna blew it. "I don't remember."

"You could ask her if she's not dead," Bean suggested.

Lorna stuck the pan of brownies into the oven. She felt kind of sick. Like she'd lost something all over again. Like a laser beam was scoring her heart.

She set the timer for the brownies to bake. While they waited, they took turns with two spoons, scraping the last of the batter from the bowl. Then, at Bean's insistence, they perused her Precious Moments figurines. He arranged his favorites in a village of sorts on the hearth while Aggie slept under the desk. But then he noticed the stacks of pink and white envelopes.

"What's that? Are you having a party?"

He reached for one, but Lorna caught him before he could pick them up. "They're just some letters."

"But why—?"

Lorna was saved from any interrogation about them by a knock on the door.

"I'll get it!" Bean shouted, racing to yank open the door. His father was standing on the other side.

"Something smells good," Seth said.

"We're making brownies," Bean said. "And Lorna gave me a notebook for my field notes."

"Ah. Did you say thank you?"

Bean whipped around to Lorna. "Thank you," he said dutifully.

"You're very welcome." Lorna couldn't quite make eye contact with Seth. Had he noticed her apartment? Her fixation with Precious Moments? Had he picked up on the lonely spinster life she was living in here? Because she really didn't want him to see her that way. She wanted him to see her as a capable professional, a normal woman, someone worthy of his attention. And that desire was a little discombobulating. It made her feel anxious near him. "The brownies are almost done. I can bring him home when they're finished."

"No, Dad, come in," Bean said. "Remember all the little people I told you about? I want to show you my favorites."

Lorna noticed Seth's gaze slide past her and into her living area, and she felt shame creeping up her neck as he took in her figurines. Bean had already grabbed some to show his dad—the one depicting the dog and a boy, and one of a boy with a fishing pole. "Wait," she said weakly, but it was too late.

"These are my favorites," Bean said, holding them up for Seth to see.

"Yeah, I can see why those would be your favorites," Seth said, but his gaze strayed to the hundreds more. He looked at Lorna curiously. "Are you an art collector?"

Sweet of him to pretend this was art. She was more of an emotions collector. "Sort of." She wanted to die. All she really knew about this man was that he cried a lot and slept through *Gunsmoke*, that he was handsome and kind to her, and that she didn't want him to think she was pathetic. Now she felt entirely conspicuous, like a troll living under a bridge with her stupid collection. Thank heaven for the oven, which beeped and saved her the utter humiliation of explaining her collection. *It's like I try to find scenes that I wish I'd had in my life but didn't because I'm a stone-cold loser with a wildly dysfunctional family. Hope you don't mind that your son and I are hanging out, because of course, there's nothing weird about that.* "Excuse me." She hurried into the kitchen before Seth noticed the flame in her cheeks. What had ever made her buy so many of the damn things?

"Look!" she heard Bean say. "This is my notebook."

"That's a good one," Seth said.

Lorna took the brownies out of the oven and put them on a rack. *Please hurry the hell up and cool*, she silently begged them. Then she could stuff a brownie in their hands and send Bean and Seth on their way. Probably she'd stuff the rest into her mouth to bury her shame.

"I'm really sorry," Seth said.

Her head snapped up. "What?" She braced herself, expecting him to tell her that his son couldn't be in this weird apartment wearing an apron, surrounded by her obsession with happy little scenes from life. "I'm supposed to get off work at three, but we've been having some issues lately."

Thank goodness. "Oh. Yeah, it seems like you're late a lot." Her brain tried to claw back the words her mouth had issued, but it was too late. "Not . . . not that I . . . I noticed, that's all. Not because I know when you work or anything, but . . . ."

"But because Bean is always with your dog," he said, helping her out.

"Yes," she said, grateful to him for that small kindness.

"I know. I had a babysitter lined up, but she flaked on me. I'm trying to find after-school care for Bean."

Lorna looked at the kid. His tongue was sticking out the corner of his mouth as he made notes in his new notebook.

"If Bean could just remember his key, it would help a lot," Seth added, his eyes narrowing on his son, who, as far as Lorna could tell, was not paying his father the slightest heed.

"Maybe that's asking a lot of a kid," Lorna opined. And then inwardly groaned. "I'm sorry," she said, and held up a hand before he could ask her where she got off. "There I go again.

I have a terrible habit of stating opinions without being asked for them, but believe me, I know that uninformed opinions are the worst."

"They kind of are," he agreed. But he was smiling. He was *amused*—not offended. That only made her care even more about whether he thought she was a loser.

But then Bean chimed in, "It's hard for Lorna to make friends."

"Bean!" his father exclaimed and apologized profusely to Lorna.

"No, it's all right—I told him that," Lorna admitted, her gaze on the brownies. "Just going through a bit of a rough patch on that front." *Shut up. Shut up shut up shut up.* She was making herself come off like a psycho now. She had utterly forgotten how to talk to a man. She was more like herself with Bean around—or at least herself as she remembered herself—and she didn't want to lose that. She liked this kid a lot.

She liked Seth a lot.

"So, about Bean," she said.

"Yeah, I'm sorry to have imposed. I promise, I'm working on it," Seth said. "I know no one wants a kid hanging around." He laughed and self-consciously dragged his fingers through his hair.

"But I do." She realized how creepy that sounded and felt her face heating again. "Gosh, I'm making a mess of this," she said sheepishly. "But I'm on a sabbatical from work—temporarily." Lest he think she'd been fired for something unacceptable. At least she hadn't been yet.

He seemed confused. "Why, are you studying something?"

"Oh. No. It's more like . . ." She hesitated. There was no way to make her reasons for being home sound logical. "It's for . . . self-improvement." Which sounded like she was on the verge of being fired. "It's a thirty-day break. Sort of. The point is, I'm usually home in the afternoons and will be for the next month. If you like, I could watch Bean. I mean, until you get it sorted out. I'm not trying to steal him or anything."

Seth's eyes rounded.

Oh Lord, please stop talking. "Bad joke!" she said too loudly. "Of course I'm not. I'm just . . . I can help. That's all."

Seth's expression morphed into a mix of surprise and healthy skepticism. "I'm not sure what is happening just now, but . . ." He appraised her. "Are you offering to babysit?"

"In exchange for Bean walking Aggie."

Bean's head came up at that and Aggie leaped to her feet, sensing something was about to happen. "I can walk Aggie?" Aggie's bread loaf butt began to wag. "How far can I walk her? Like a mile? Two miles? *Five* miles?"

"Ah . . . around the block?" Lorna offered.

"I can walk her around the *entire block*?" Bean cried. "Aggie, did you hear that? We can walk around the entire block!"

"Hold up there, buddy." Seth put his hand on his son's shoulder and turned back to Lorna. "I really appreciate the offer, but I don't think it's a good idea."

Of course he didn't. He'd have to be crazy to leave his kid with her and these creepy figurines. Especially after her lame joke about stealing him. "I understand," Lorna said, deflated. "I'm actually very safe with kids, but I understand."

Seth squinted at her. "What? It's not that I think you're not safe. I didn't mean that at all."

"Oh." *What a relief.* But then . . . "What did you mean?" she asked, even though she was pretty sure she didn't want to know.

"Dad, please. Please please please please," Bean begged. "I can get my badge for helping an old person."

"Hey!" Lorna protested. "I'm not that old."

"You're not?" Bean asked in all innocence.

"Benjamin," his father said. But he turned his inquisitive gaze back to Lorna, as if he, too, thought she was old.

"I keep completely to myself. I'm harmless, really, just a cat lady. But with a dog. I live right here, and Bean would be a help with Aggie."

"Why?" Seth asked.

"Why . . . would he be a help?"

He blinked. "No, why are you a cat lady who keeps to herself?"

Why had she said anything at all? "I . . ." She paused, searching for the right words. "It's a long story. It's . . ." What? Self-preservation? A yearslong shame spiral? "I don't know, to be honest." She smiled sheepishly. "It's weird, right?"

"No," Seth said. "For what it's worth, you do not come across as a lonely cat lady. And for the record, I said it wasn't a good idea because I don't think it's right to impose on neighbors. This would be a big imposition."

Yes, it would be a huge imposition to most. "Not to me." She hoped that was true. She hoped she wasn't making a huge mistake that would scar Bean for life.

"Well . . . thank you," Seth said, giving an incredulous laugh. "Honestly? It would be a great help to me if you could do just this week. Until I line up a babysitter. I'm working on it."

Lorna grinned. He said yes! "Sure," she said. "There is one small thing, though. Bean said you wouldn't let him have sugar, but we're on a quest to find the dessert he wants to try to bake. If you don't mind making an exception, I promise not to overdo it."

"I won't let him have sugar?"

"We never have any sugar, Dad," Bean said.

"Because I don't buy it. But, bro, you have plenty of sugar. You ate an entire bag of gummies yesterday, remember?"

"Oh yeah," Bean said.

Seth turned back to Lorna. "He can have sugar. I mean, within reason. I wouldn't want him eating an entire cake."

"No, of course not," she said. "Whew! That's a relief, because I honestly can't abide people who are holier-than-thou about sugar."

Seth and Bean both laughed, like they thought she was joking. She wasn't.

"Lorna, are you really sure about this?" Seth asked again. "It's awfully generous of you. And I am grateful. But I hope you're not offering because I seem desperate."

He didn't seem desperate; he seemed very sure of himself. "Aggie loves him, and I—" She caught herself just in time. She'd almost said she loved him too. "I think it will be fine. Fun. It could be fun. Shall we cut the brownies?"

"Yay!" Bean shouted.

She cut them and put three squares on three small plates. They agreed the brownies looked good—not too fluffy, not too flat. And they tasted very good. "I'm giving them a ten!" Bean declared, and wrote it down in his notebook.

"Thanks, Lorna," Seth said as he moved his son along toward the door. "You're the best."

She was the best? Lorna could feel the gigantic smile forming on her lips.

He paused with Bean at the threshold of her apartment. "You've got a bit of chocolate on your cheek."

She put her hand to her cheek.

"Other one," he said, and smiled so warmly that it practically melted that chocolate right off her face.

Chapter 12

Lorna Now

LORNA WAS BEGINNING TO REALIZE SHE DIDN'T HAVE A lot of "casual" clothes. Her clothing had somehow become her shield. She was not the most fashionable woman—never had been—but she wouldn't mind having a bit more flair. Her confidence to do that had deserted her somewhere during the pandemic. She didn't have the body type for frilly dresses or the sophistication for slender capris. Suits hid a multitude of physical flaws. So said the salesperson at Dillard's.

At one point in her life, she'd worn a lot of dresses. Her favorite one, an egg-yolk yellow, had been ruined when Kristen vomited on her. Now she associated that style of dress with being too soft. To be successful in sales, according to her books, you had to project an air of authority.

But she wasn't projecting anything while on leave and didn't know how to dress for every day. It would have been super helpful if she could ask Kristen what to wear. There was a time Kristen had been very stylish. Even when she was disgusting.

Today, Lorna pulled her hair into a low, tight pony. She chose a simple black skirt that came to her knees. Stockings, of course—no one needed to see sun-damaged skin. A lavender pullover sweater that Deb had once said made her blue eyes pop.

Sensible flats with arch support. No sense being distracted by aching feet shoved into heels.

She cut up the last of the brownies she and Bean had made and put them on a plastic tray decorated with dancing Christmas trees, a holdover from the last Christmas party she'd attended some six years ago at her coworker Sheldon's house. She hadn't been invited back, and it was probably her own dumb fault—she'd decided to debate some drunk dude on whether marijuana ought to be legalized. She tended toward firm opinions and, as Deb said, could be weirdly adamant about topics most people didn't feel so strongly about. "Opinions about legalizing marijuana are just part of the zeitgeist."

Deb made a fair point. Lorna didn't care about a lot of things in the zeitgeist—like sports or politics or road improvement projects. She knew people who could talk for days about any of those topics.

But she did care about drug use. She was adamantly against it.

She was arranging the few squares on the tray when she heard a knock on her door that roused Aggie from her nap. She wiped her hands and went to the door, opening it only a crack.

"Hi!" Mrs. Foster said cheerfully, peering through the crack.

"Umm . . . hi," Lorna said, surprised.

"Liz. From upstairs?"

"Yes." Did she really think Lorna didn't know who she was?

Liz from upstairs tried to peer into Lorna's apartment, so Lorna made the crack a tiny bit smaller, which somehow only made Aggie's sniffing at the door louder.

"I was wondering if you'd had a chance to speak to Mr. Contreras?"

"Oh. Yes, I—" She realized her response was going to be too long to relay through a tiny crack in the door. "Actually . . . could I come up to you in a minute? I was just finishing up here."

"Not a problem. 2B!" Mrs. Foster reminded her.

"Got it." Lorna shut the door. Then she used the breathing techniques she'd learned at Bodhi to keep from hyperventilating. Those damn Precious Moments!

"Bring Aggie!" Mrs. Foster shouted from the other side of the door, startling her.

She was not bringing Aggie. She had enough trouble managing small talk, much less trying to corral her dog in the event Bean had misread the friend situation between Aggie and Garfield. She gave Aggie a biscuit and scratched her head, made empty promises to be home soon, and then made her way upstairs with the brownies.

Mrs. Foster answered right away, swinging the door open onto a scene from Lorna's childhood, but with all the wrong furniture. Lorna stood frozen for a moment, staring into the room that looked exactly like what she remembered—but also completely different.

Mrs. Foster was dressed in shorts and an old baggy T-shirt. Lorna, on the other hand, was dressed as though she might be headed to a funeral. The dumb orange cat was wrapping around Mrs. Foster's legs.

"Thank you for coming!" She looked at the brownies. "Oh."

"Bean made them," Lorna said, pushing the tray into Mrs. Foster's hands.

"Well, thank you! I've noticed you're home a lot these days. Vacation?"

She hadn't had a vacation in two years. "No, I'm taking some time off to . . . to work on myself," Lorna said.

She expected a litany of follow-up questions, but Mrs. Foster said only, "That's great! Everyone should." She took a bite of a brownie. "Yummy! Come in!"

Lorna did. Reluctantly. And walked right into a bubble of childhood nostalgia. Her eyes began to feel a little misty. *For heaven's sake, not now.* "I love what you've done with the place, Mrs. Foster," she said, and turned her head slightly, dipping a knuckle under her lashes to catch a tear that felt like it might fall.

"Oh please, call me Liz," Mrs. Foster said.

"Liz. Got it." Lorna glanced toward the door that led into what had been her bedroom all those years ago. She could see the corner of a poster bed.

"And maybe I can call you Lorna? Do you go by Lorna?" Liz asked. "No need to be so formal here."

"What?" Lorna looked away from her old bedroom. Her skin began to itch. She shouldn't be here. She didn't know how to be here. *What am I doing? This is Nana's house. Why did she take down the wood blinds? They were perfect for this room. We built our Barbie dream towns in here. This was our playroom. But wait . . . didn't Nana die in here? Yes, this is the room where Nana died. Should I tell her?*

She became aware that Liz was watching her, waiting for a response. "Oh. Yes. Lorna. I'm Lorna." She smiled. And now her nerves were launching a full-on assault. She felt like a beacon for disapproval—wrong clothes, wrong attitude, her mind wandering off. She could feel a bead of perspiration on her nape.

Liz ate another brownie. "These are so good. I'm going to get a glass of water." She put the brownies on a coffee table.

Lorna watched her walk into what had once been a front bedroom. She and Kristen had carved their initials into the windowsill. Nana had thrown a fit and had her handyman sand them out and repaint the sill. Then Kristen had carved KL + CD in the same spot, because she had a crush on Casey Dell. She claimed she could see his bedroom from that window. She couldn't—Casey Dell lived blocks away. But then again, Kristen lied about everything. Lorna had known it then, but she'd always wanted so desperately to believe Kristen.

There had been a piano in this room, although no one ever

played it. Mom had made them take lessons, but neither of them had any love of the piano, and once the lessons had ended, the piano sat unused.

On the doorframe to Lorna's old room, there had been pen markings to track the girls' height. Red for Lorna, blue for Kristen. From the time she was twelve, Lorna was taller than Kristen. But the marks had been painted over.

"Would you like some water?" Liz called from the kitchen.

"Pardon?" Lorna asked, shaking off the memories. "Oh, no thanks."

A moment later, Liz returned. She gestured to her couch. "Make yourself at home."

She *was* at home. But she was standing in the middle of the room with her hands clasped tightly in front of her. Something felt off. These rooms belonged to her and her happy memories. And yet there was something not quite right about that. Like the memories were flawed. She turned slightly and suddenly had a vision of her grandmother sitting in a chair near the window, her head lolling on her chest, passed out again from too much gin. *No no no no . . .* this was the playroom. They had played here. It had been filled with books and toys. Not drunk old women.

"Are you okay, Lorna?"

"What?" She had to stop acting like she was having an episode or whatever this was. "Oh, I'm fine. Just looking around." She forced a smile.

Liz plopped down on the couch. "I do my best with decor. I'm not a natural. Feel free to let your hair down."

Lorna carefully lowered herself to sit. When she did, she watched a run in her stocking begin its path down her leg.

"You were going to tell me about your conversation with the landlord," Liz reminded her.

"Right."

"Let me tell you, I've never had such a bad landlord," Liz began. She had a long list and was determined to enumerate each item on it. The run in Lorna's stocking took off every time she moved. Her perspiration reached a code-red level, and she wished she'd taken that offer of water.

Liz's complaints were all legitimate, of course. There were so many items on the list for repair: leaks, holes, nonworking appliances and lights. But somehow Lorna went from adamantly agreeing that things needed to be done to explaining possible reasons Mr. Contreras hadn't done them. She pointed out that the house was expensive and costly repairs would result in costly rent. "It's simple math."

"Well, sure," Liz said. "Big repairs are going to cost. But we should see some repairs before we start paying more in rent. Like, the more immediate problems. If we pay more rent before they are fixed, we run the risk they will never be fixed."

Lorna couldn't disagree.

"So what did he say when you called him?" Liz asked eagerly.

"Umm . . ." She surreptitiously wiped a bit of perspiration from her temple. "That he wants to sell the house. But if he can't, he's going up on rent because he's hardly breaking even."

Liz snorted. "Did he at least seem like he might be willing to work something out?"

"I didn't ask him, to be honest. I agreed with him that this is a money pit."

Liz was silent for a moment. "Excuse me? You did what?"

Too blunt! "I agreed that he should probably sell it, because that is the only way he might get back what he put into it. That's what I would do. And really, it should be a single home."

"Oh hon," Liz said, and smiled sadly at Lorna, as if she pitied her. "But it's not a single-family home. Not anymore."

"Okay, but hear me out," Lorna said hesitantly. "It makes sense to me because he's only got four units. He could go up a thousand dollars a month on each unit and probably still wouldn't be able to collect what he needs to make major repairs on top of paying taxes and upkeep. The house never should have been split up."

"Yes, but again, that train has left the station," Liz said. "And we've all made this our home. If he really intends to sell it, we should have enough time to find other living arrangements. A serious amount of time, too, because there is hardly anything affordable in Austin anymore. And what about Bean? He already lost his mother, and now he'll have to change schools?" Liz shook her head.

Lorna winced. If anything would make her give up her idea, an appeal to Bean's best interests might be it. But then again, she couldn't be such a softy about this. She'd been planning this a long time. It was her turn now. She deserved it. *She deserved it.*

"I don't want to move," Liz insisted. "This house is the perfect location. It's central to everything." She looked at Lorna. "Do *you* want to move?"

"No! I belong here."

"Exactly," Liz said.

Lorna's palms were perspiring now, and she quickly debated telling Liz the truth. She swallowed down her guilt and fear and the overpowering need to have this house. It was inexplicable. *She* was inexplicable. So there was no sense in even trying to explain it.

They were interrupted by a knock at the door. Liz hopped up and went to open it. "Martin!" she said cheerfully.

"Hi, Liz. Oh, hi, Lorna."

"She brought brownies," Liz said, hurrying to fetch the tray. She held it up to Martin, who took one and bit into it.

"That's dope," he said.

"Bean made them," Lorna said, and stood. "I have to run. I'm watching Bean today."

"No worries!" Liz said brightly. "I'll fill Martin in. Thank you for coming up. Come anytime! I'm always here."

Lorna nodded and slipped out past Martin as he took another brownie. "He should be a baker, that kid," he said as the door closed behind her.

Lorna ran downstairs. Maybe one day she would tell them. She didn't even know the words she would use, but one day, she might say it. Maybe she'd go up to Liz's apartment for an afternoon just to hang out, like women did, and tell her.

Then again, maybe not.

Once she was safe in her apartment, she looked down at herself. The run in her stocking now disappeared into her shoe. Her skirt was covered in cat hair. She was still perspiring, and she felt like a gargoyle. She felt entirely at odds with herself, like pieces of her were not fitting together.

Later that night, after Bean had gone home, Lorna and Aggie were in bed, nestled against the pillows. Lorna wore a conditioning cream on her hair, covered in plastic. The ad had promised it would make her hair smooth and silky. She hoped so. She intended to sue if it didn't.

Aggie was asleep, twitching now and then, snoring softly, and Lorna was flipping through a photo album, trying to confirm her memories of the playroom. The photos were mostly taken in the years before they had lived here with Nana. Before Kristen was the worst sort of problem. She was annoyed with herself, at her inability to tell her neighbors why this house meant so much to her. That this house, and all it represented, was the only thing she had left of her family. Of her life, really. But she feared her reasoning wouldn't be good enough, that they'd tell her she was wrong. That they would resent her or shame her or dislike her.

She couldn't bear to experience that.

There were pictures of her and Kristen, their arms around each other, laughing, their tongues stained dark red by candy or juice. One of Nana in her ever-present homemade blouses, smiling with love at the two of them. There were pictures of them swinging in the backyard and looking at the kittens a neighborhood cat had birthed under the house. Pictures of her entire family, smiling happily, hiding the turmoil that engulfed them.

Another set of pictures showed Kristen braiding Lorna's hair, then putting makeup on her. Lorna remembered it was for a birthday party she'd been invited to. In another, teenage Kristen looked beautiful and happy. And then there was one of Kristen asleep on the couch, her hair covering her face. Passed out.

There were pictures of their bedrooms in this house, decorated for Christmas. Mom had let them each have a tree, and Kristen had let Lorna pick her ornaments first. Then the two of them, laughing in matching Christmas pajamas. Nana helping Kristen and Lorna make Christmas cookies.

Lorna had been happy here once upon a time. They'd made a happy family here. Once upon a time.

Sometimes she fretted what would become of her if she didn't find happiness. She was afraid of dying alone.

She picked up her laptop and opened a blank document. She began to type.

Hello Kristen,

> I visited a neighbor today. Shocker. I wore a skirt and hose like I was going to give a presentation and looked like a jackass. You probably think that's funny. When

did I lose the ability to dress myself appropriately for the right occasion? It's a confidence thing. I don't have any, you know. Except in software sales. No one can touch me there. But out in the world, with others involved, I lose all confidence and worse, I start to sweat. Or tear up. Like, literally, what the hell is that?

You know Mom sold Nana's house to pay for your last stint in treatment. Or did you forget because you were high all the time? Anyway, fat lot of good it did for her to sell it, obviously. I hope I don't have to remind you of all the things that happened after we moved. I still can't believe that you made us lose everything. Sometimes I wake up and think, *Oh yeah, we lost everything because Kristen couldn't stop using*. I know I'm supposed to be compassionate because you have a disease, and I am, I really am. I can't imagine what it must be like to live in your skin. Especially now. But losing the house pissed me off. You knew how much it meant to me.

I'm going to buy it. I know it's crazy, and it will cost a fortune, but all I do is work. I will be okay.

Speaking of okay, I hope you are. I've been meaning to tell you that I'm sorry. I'm really sorry. I think you know why.

Lolo

She printed the letter, put it in an envelope, and stuck an address label on it, then padded into the main living area. She added this letter to the stack. When she returned to bed, she noticed the envelope Peggy had given her on her bedside table. She still hadn't opened it, was almost afraid to pick it up for fear of releasing mayhem into her life. But this was ridiculous. If someone on her staff was taking so much time to complete a project, she would have had a few choice things to say about it. She had never understood why people didn't just get on with the task of doing what they were supposed to do.

Yet here she was, not doing what she was supposed to do, paralyzed with indecision and fear. Either she was going to do what she must to have her house back, or she was going to start looking for another apartment. "For heaven's sake," she said angrily, and, in a moment of decisiveness, swiped up the envelope, breaking the seal.

She withdrew a folded piece of standard notebook paper, which had yellowed slightly over the last four years. On the outside was scrawled *Lorna* in her mother's handwriting. She drew a breath and unfolded it.

There it was, in black and white: the apologies Lorna needed to make because of her crazy family. They were her own words thrown back at her. It was surprisingly difficult to look at the list and not feel the pain associated with the things that had created it to begin with. She wasn't sure how addressing these things now was going to work. It was entirely possible this exercise would send her deeper into her bomb shelter, where she was safe.

Too safe.

But she didn't want to be alone anymore. She didn't want to cling to old hurts. She didn't want to be this person. And if she wanted things to be different, she needed to start somewhere.

The sight of her mother's handwriting unleashed a wave of longing.

Start with Callie. You were so close. She was so important to you.

Lorna's eyes began to well again, damn it.

You didn't have to end things. She would have understood. Reach out to her. Tell her you love her. She will welcome you because she loved you too. I heard she is in Pflugerville.

Lorna blinked. How could her mother have known where she was? And anyway, she didn't believe for a moment that Callie would welcome her reaching out. Lorna would never forget the last time she saw her, that lethal mix of disappointment and fury in her eyes. "She hates me," Lorna murmured. She reached for the laptop and typed *Callie Ann Kleberg* in the search bar.

A few Callies popped up. One was in Pflugerville. She was a teacher, according to the link that led her to a news article about a middle school teacher. *Callie Kleberg, girls' coach, world history, geography.* That was Callie, all right. She'd always wanted to be a teacher. Lorna navigated to the school's website and found an email listed for her. She let her fingers hover over the keyboard. But she couldn't bring herself to click the link. *Coward.*

She slammed the laptop shut and picked up her mother's note. *Forgive your father, Lolo.*

Lorna gaped at the notebook paper. "Never," she whispered. *He handled things poorly, but he didn't mean to hurt you.*

"But he did, Mom."

You didn't know any better either.

Mom hated Dad. Why was she defending him? And why was she defending Lorna, for that matter? Lorna had betrayed her too.

There was more written, but Lorna had read enough for one evening. She recalled the way her mother had lain in bed in the garage apartment, so frail, the few remaining tufts of her white hair sticking up every which way. "You'll understand one day, I hope," she'd said, her face filled with a cadaverous smile. "When you have children of your own."

It was too late for children of her own. All she had left of her family was this house.

She reopened her laptop, went to Facebook, and found Callie there. She didn't want to ruin Callie's whole day at work with an email. She clicked on the message icon.

Chapter 13

Lorna Is Thirteen

TWO YEARS AGO, RIGHT AROUND CHRISTMAS, DAD MARRIED Trish. Thenceforth, according to Mom, every Christmas has been ruined. Between drags off her cigarette, she likes to say he married Trish because he knocked her up.

It doesn't matter anymore, Lorna thinks, because Mom is right—Christmas is ruined because Mom can't stop hating Dad.

She was so looking forward to this Christmas morning. She has asked every way she knows how for a portable CD player and the new Bon Jovi CD. She and her best friend, Callie, have created a dance routine to the latest hit, "This Ain't a Love Song."

They've been practicing for weeks. From her spot on Lorna's bed, Kristen has lazily directed them, and when Callie goes home, Kristen confirms to Lorna that she is the better dancer. "You could be in music videos," she says proudly.

Given Lorna's height and general clumsiness, this praise is a Big Deal. She trusts Kristen's opinion on pretty much everything except drugs and alcohol.

Christmas morning, she wakes to heavy rain. She rouses Kristen from her room and they race downstairs. The scent of fresh-baked cinnamon rolls hits her the moment she is in the grand hallway, and she and Kristen head to the main salon.

Mom is curled up in a chair, smoking, staring out the window at the gray, rainy day.

"Come on, girls," Nana says. "Come open your presents." She hands them each a cinnamon roll on a plate as they enter.

Lorna and Kristen put aside the rolls and begin opening the presents while Nana watches with delight. Mom seems to have forgotten what day it is. "They had that baby six months after they married," she says as Lorna tears the wrapping paper from a gift. "That tells you all you need to know."

Contrary to what her mother says, that doesn't tell Lorna anything she needs to know; she still has a lot of questions. She wants to ask Dad, but he's been kind of scarce lately. Kristen tells her not to worry about it, that people break up and move on. "It happens all the time in high school," she says as the oracle into a mysterious world Lorna will enter next year.

"And now they've got another one on the way," Mom adds, angrily snuffing out the butt of her cigarette on a saucer.

"Another baby?" Kristen holds up a gold sweater and laughs. "The joke is on Dad, then."

Lorna opens the gift from her mother. It's a doll, the Winter Sports Barbie, with skis. She looks at it with dismay. She doesn't play with dolls. She hasn't in some time.

"How come he gets to go on with his life and I don't?" Mom asks of no one in particular.

"Mindy, honey, we're opening gifts," Nana reminds her.

"Yeah, that I bought," Mom says. "What did he get them?" But she stops staring out the window and seems to notice the pile of wrapping paper. "Lolo, do you like the Barbie? It's so cute."

Lorna hates that doll, but she says, "Yes."

"No, she doesn't," Kristen says. Now she is holding a gold bracelet up to the light to admire it. "She's too old for dolls. What are these numbers?" she asks, examining her bracelet. Lorna can see a few small beads.

"It's a sobriety bracelet," her mother says proudly. "You count the days you've been sober. You turn it every day and watch the days add up. Isn't that clever?"

Kristen glares at her mother. "Seriously? You're going to ride my ass on Christmas?"

"Watch your language," Mom says sharply. "I thought it was a great idea."

"You make me sound like a loser, Mom. I'm not an addict. I don't need to count anything. I smoke weed because I *like* it." Kristen tosses the bracelet aside and gets up. "You think Dad ruins everything? *You* ruin everything." She flounces out of the room.

Lorna's mother turns her wide eyes on Lorna. She is obviously shocked that Kristen didn't love the gift. Lorna clutches her stupid doll to her chest. "I love it, Mom."

"You're a good kid, Lolo," she says, and turns her attention to the window again. She has adopted that faraway look, like she has stomped out of the room with Kristen.

Lorna opens another present. This one is from Kristen, and it's a hit—a Rubik's Cube. Everyone wants a Rubik's Cube. She can't wait to show Callie. She immediately starts to work it.

Mom lights another cigarette. Nana gets up and goes into the kitchen. Lorna can hear her taking the bottle off the top of the fridge.

Lorna searches under the tree. She gives her mother a gift from her—she made it in ceramics class. It's an ashtray shaped like a frog. Her mother sets it aside and doesn't open it. Lorna finds another gift for herself. It's from Kristen. She opens it—and sees the new Bon Jovi CD, *These Days*. "I got the CD!" she exclaims as Nana comes back into the room with a coffee tumbler. Lorna can't see the booze, but by now she recognizes the scent.

"That's wonderful!" Nana says dreamily and sits in her recliner.

Lorna searches under the tree for the CD player. It must be here. There is another gift for Kristen from Mom, but nothing for Lorna. She sinks back on her heels in disappointment.

Later, Lorna is in her room, staring out at the rain. She's already lost interest in the Rubik's Cube. It's too hard to figure out. She still can't believe she didn't get a portable CD player. Everyone has one but her.

She hears voices and glances toward her door. That's her mother, shouting again. She gets up and cracks open the door. Mom and Kristen are fighting. They fight all the time now. Every time Lorna hears them, she feels nauseous, like she's the one who has done something wrong.

"Don't lie to me!" Mom shouts. "I know what this is, Kristen. It is forbidden in this house! And with your sister just next door."

"She's fine," Kristen shouts back. "Can you just stay out of my room? You have no right to go through my things!"

"That is not your room!" her mother bellows. "You are borrowing it!"

Lorna crawls into bed with the Rubik's Cube and tries to distract herself from the scene unraveling in the hall. It doesn't work. Sometime later, she hears the front door slam and knows Kristen is gone.

They haven't had Christmas dinner yet.

That night, Kristen comes home after everyone has gone to sleep. She sneaks into Lorna's room and sits on the edge of her bed. She smells like weed and beer. Lorna hates being around Kristen when she's been drinking; she can be mean. "Hey, let me see the Rubik's Cube."

Lorna fell asleep with it in her bed and hands it now to her sister. Kristen tries to solve it a few times, then tosses it aside. She reaches into her pocket and pulls out the bracelet. "This is for you."

Lorna stares at the bracelet. "That's yours. I can't take it."

"Sure you can. It's mine, and I want you to have it. The Barbie was lame."

It was lame, all right. Lorna looks at the sobriety bracelet. She suspects a joke, a prank. But Kristen holds it out to her. "Take it. Ignore the numbers. Or count something you want to count. Or better yet, sell the damn thing and get a CD player."

Lorna puts the bracelet on her wrist and admires it. It's pretty; gold, with crystal beads between the numbered beads.

Kristen pulls out a joint from her jacket and holds it up. "Want to try?"

"No," Lorna says instantly.

"Come on, it's not so bad." Kristen smiles. "You're listening to Mom too much. She doesn't know what she's talking about. It's harmless. You can't get addicted to pot."

"I'm not listening to Mom," Lorna says defensively. She's listening to her gut. There is no part of her that wants to try. She associates that cigarette and that smell with trouble.

"Mom makes pot sound like heroin, and they're not even remotely the same. This will help you sleep." She produces a lighter and fires it up, taking a long drag. She blows the smoke toward the ceiling, then holds the cigarette out to Lorna. "Just try it. Don't be such a chicken. When you go to high school, people will think you're a nerd if you don't try things."

That's what does it, the threat of being labeled a nerd before she's even graduated eighth grade. She's got enough strikes against her—taller than everyone, clumsy, some god-awful hair. She reluctantly takes the cigarette, inhales, and then coughs violently. Her throat burns.

"Keep it down," Kristen warns. "If Mom hears you, she'll be in here in a minute."

Lorna tries again. This time she swallows her cough. She holds her breath as Kristen instructs her and feels a lightness overcome her. It's a weird feeling, like she's floating, but her body is heavy. She doesn't like it. She doesn't feel like she has control. She hears a sound outside the window and gasps.

"Calm down," Kristen warns her. "You're such a nervous Nellie." She smokes more of the joint and then lies back on Lorna's bed.

"I hear something," Lorna whispers. "Is it the police?"

"The police? Are you crazy? Remind me never to let you smoke weed again," Kristen says and giggles uncontrollably. "You're acting so paranoid."

Lorna never does smoke weed again. But Kristen will smoke enough for them both.

She wakes the next morning to the sound of Mom and Kristen fighting.

Chapter 14

Lorna Is Thirteen

JUST BEFORE NEW YEAR'S EVE, LORNA'S DAD COMES TO TAKE them to dinner. He's brought Christmas gifts—hair clips and earrings for Kristen, a cardigan sweater and a deck of playing cards for Lorna. Why do her parents think she's a kid?

Kristen is sullen during dinner. When Dad asks what's wrong, she accuses him of not caring about her and Lorna. She tells him she fights with Mom all the time. Dad tries to defend himself, but Kristen is in a mood and calls him stupid.

Lorna loses her appetite at the Spaghetti Warehouse, a first in her lifetime.

When Dad drops them off, Kristen goes in with a curt "See you," but Lorna hangs back, standing between the car and house.

"Dad, can I ask a favor?"

"Sure, Lolo. Anything. You know that."

She doesn't know that. He's hardly ever around. She doesn't quite know how to ask.

Dad is bundling her gifts and leftovers to hand to her. "What is it?"

"Can I come live with you and Trish?"

Something comes over Dad's face. Like he suddenly doesn't feel well. "What?" He lets out a forced laugh. "Why do you . . . Why?"

"Because Mom and Kristen really do fight all the time. Kristen runs away a lot, and she got kicked out of school again."

"Again? No one told me that." He frowns in the direction of Nana's house, as if he's trying to decide whether he should go in and say something about that.

"I just think I would be happier if I lived with you. I hate all the fighting."

Dad turns his attention back to her. He looks stricken, like she imagines people look when they are having a heart attack. "Oh, Lolo," he says after a moment. "Oh, baby . . . that's not a good idea."

"Why not?" she asks, but her heart is already sinking. Maybe she hasn't explained it enough. "I won't bother you, I promise. And I'll keep my room clean."

"You would never bother me, Lolo, but we have Baby Allison now."

Lorna panics. "I can help with Allison!" She grabs his hand.

"And another baby on the way. It's not that I don't think you would help, it's just that . . . So let me talk to your mother and see if we can't make things better here."

"No!" Lorna cries. She feels sick, like she's made a terrible, terrible mistake. "She'll be mad."

He doesn't argue. He squeezes her hand. "Why don't we revisit this when you're older?"

"What does age have to do with it?"

He peels her hand off his. "Lolo, you know I would take you in a heartbeat if I could."

"But you can, Dad. Why won't you?"

"You're misunderstanding my situation. Look, I'll call you tomorrow, and we'll talk," he says.

He won't call her. He never does. "Dad, please—you don't know what it's like."

"Listen, honey, whatever it is, it will pass. You're young and sometimes problems feel much bigger than they are. I have to go now. I'll call you. Love you!"

He is walking backward. He opens the car door and waves at her over the top, then drives away.

He doesn't love her. If he loved her, he would save her from this nightmare.

She stands there long after his taillights have disappeared. She looks down and realizes he somehow managed to shove her gifts and leftovers into her hand. She feels like she might fall. Like the slightest breeze would send her toppling down the street like a tumbleweed. She feels dumb and weird and completely unlovable.

• • •

The last day of Christmas break, Mom and Kristen have such a huge fight that Kristen throws a chair at Mom. She misses her, but Mom says she's calling the police. Kristen tells her not to bother. She grabs a backpack and takes off.

Lorna slips away to Callie's house, where she's been spending as much time as she can without it seeming odd. She loves Callie's house—it's warm and smells like supper, and everyone is always laughing. The Klebergs are a big family, full of love and fun. Mrs. Kleberg always gives her a big hug when she comes in. Today she says, "Happy New Year!"

"Happy New Year," Lorna mumbles in return.

She's brought her Rubik's Cube. Callie got one for Christmas too. They spend the afternoon watching TV, working on their Rubik's Cubes, and fending off the stealth pinch attacks from Callie's little brothers.

Callie says she has a secret to tell her. "You're my best friend in the whole world, Lorna."

"I know," Lorna says. She looks up. "That's not a secret." She looks down again, because she is so close to solving her Rubik's Cube.

"It's something else."

The blue tiles are the ones that always ruin everything and won't line up. Lorna tosses the cube aside and looks at Callie. "What is it?"

Callie looks nervous. She is twisting her T-shirt into a knot. At first, Lorna thinks she is going to tell her she is dying. "What is it?" she asks, and leans forward. She feels a little panicky. What would she do if she lost Callie?

Callie looks like she is going to throw up, and Lorna knows she must be dying and says, *"Callie!"* at the same time Callie says, "I like girls."

Lorna is so relieved Callie is not dying that she sinks back, disappointed the secret isn't something bigger. "I already know that."

Callie looks confused. "You do? How?"

"Easy. You never like boys. You always talk about girls. And I've seen the way you look at Mandy Harper." A thought suddenly occurs to her, and she gasps. "Are you going to *kiss* a girl?"

"Maybe," Callie says.

"Yuck," Lorna says, and giggles.

"Are you going to kiss a boy?" Callie shoots back.

"Maybe," Lorna says.

"Yuck," Callie says emphatically. They stare at each other for a moment, then burst into laughter. They laugh so hard they fall over on her bed. That's the way it's always been with her and Callie—they understand each other completely.

Callie's mom comes in and asks what all the laughter is about. Callie says nothing. Her mom asks Callie to help with laundry, and Callie groans but goes off to do it. Mrs. Kleberg sits down with a basket of clothes to fold and asks Lorna how her week has been.

Lorna does not want to be reminded of the hellscape that occurred between Christmas and New Year's in her house. Just thinking about it makes her feel queasy. "It was okay, I guess."

"Did you get a lot of nice presents?"

She is reminded of the Barbie doll and shrugs.

Mrs. Kleberg frowns. "Is something wrong, sweetheart?"

In that precise moment, Lorna makes a decision that will change her life. An idea pops into her head, and she latches onto it with no regard for the consequences. She blurts it out before she can even consider what she's doing. "Can I come live with you and Callie?"

At first Mrs. Kleberg laughs, but then she sees that Lorna is serious. "Lorna, honey." She affectionately squeezes her knee. "What would make you ask such a thing?"

That's a loaded question, and while Lorna clearly has not thought this through, she opts for the obvious answer. "Callie and I have been best friends since the sixth grade. We're like sisters."

"Well, I know, but you aren't really sisters. You have your own sister. Callie has her brothers. Girls should live with their families."

Lorna has said the wrong thing and feels a twinge of desperation. "But your family is different, and it's really nice here."

Mrs. Kleberg looks concerned. "Is something going on at home that you'd like to talk about?"

Lorna doesn't really want to talk about it because it's so embarrassing. But she trusts Mrs. Kleberg. And she knows she must make her case. Her experience with her father taught her that just wanting something isn't enough. She nods slowly.

"You can tell me."

So Lorna does. She tells Mrs. Kleberg about Kristen's drug use and truancy. How her grandmother drinks until she passes out. How her mother and Kristen fight all the time and then Kristen runs away and stays out all night and doesn't go to school. How her dad doesn't want Lorna to live with him. How everything is getting worse, and no one seems to remember she's even there.

When she has said it all, told every dark secret, Mrs. Kleberg wraps Lorna in a tight hug. She smells like caramel and vanilla.

Callie bounces back into the room with another load of laundry and looks curiously at the two of them. "What are y'all talking about?"

Her mom smiles at Lorna. "Lorna was just telling me about her house."

"Did she tell you that her sister knows how to sneak out?" Callie asks with a giggle.

Mrs. Kleberg smooths Lorna's unruly hair with her hand.

Later, when it's time for Lorna to go home, Mrs. Kleberg hugs her and says things will get better, and in the meantime, she will think about what to do. Lorna takes that to mean she's going to let her live here and practically skips home, planning how she will tell her mother. She will present it as an opportunity to focus entirely on Kristen. Or as one less mouth to feed—her mother complains about the cost of groceries a lot. She really thinks her mother won't mind at all.

The next day, the spring semester begins. It's a good day for the most part, but when Lorna comes home, she sees a police car and another unfamiliar car in front of her house. Last year, Kristen was arrested for shoplifting. Lorna feels a rush of panic and assumes she's been arrested again. She hurries inside.

A police officer is with two people in suits who look like detectives on a cop show. Mom, Kristen, and Nana are all sitting on the couch. They look too relaxed, like they are having tea.

Kristen doesn't seem to be in trouble—there would be a lot of shouting and finger pointing if she were. So why are they here?

The two people—a man and a woman—introduce themselves to Lorna. They say they are from child protective services. "What's that?" Lorna asks.

Her mother holds her cigarette over the frog ashtray Lorna made and then snuffs it out so hard Lorna fears she will crack the ceramic in two. "Have you been talking about us, Lorna?" she asks, her voice silvery smooth like it gets when she's angry.

Fear creeps through Lorna. She doesn't know what is happening right now, but she knows what she said to Mrs. Kleberg. "Umm..."

"Because someone out there seems to think that we are brawling and drinking in here every day." Her mother doesn't try to contain her anger, or Kristen her smirk, or Nana her embarrassment.

Lorna's heart sinks. She trusted Mrs. Kleberg to help her. She is shaking with fear. Not of the police—of her mother.

"Mrs. Lott, please," the suit-wearing woman says. "Lorna, may we speak to you privately?"

No one waits for Lorna to answer. She is taken into the dining room and made to sit. "You're probably wondering why we are here," the woman says.

"Yes," Lorna says. "Something is messed up."

"What's messed up, Lorna?" the man asks.

"Huh?"

"You told a trusted adult about some things that have us concerned," the lady says. "Has anyone hurt you? Or touched you inappropriately?"

"*What?*" Lorna is mortified. She never said anything like that. She feels like she might throw up. All she wanted was to be happy. Now she feels sick to her stomach and very much afraid. "No."

"What is the trouble at home that prompted you to speak up? Whatever you say is safe with us."

She doesn't believe that. Nothing is safe anymore. Nothing will ever be safe again. Mom and Dad will be furious. Lorna tried to escape this house, but all she's done is made things worse. The Klebergs are probably laughing at her. She's humiliated—she can never go there again. She chokes when she thinks of Callie. They can't be friends anymore. How could she even look at her? Mrs. Kleberg told the *police*. She probably won't allow Callie to be her friend.

Lorna feels something harden in her. She knows in that moment she can never trust anyone again.

"Lorna . . . are you safe here?" the woman asks, leaning so close that Lorna can see the red in the whites of her eyes.

"Yes! I'm safe. I just wanted to spend the night with my friend." A tear slides out of her eye and down her face.

"Just the night?"

She can tell the lady doesn't believe her. Lorna's face is flaming. The internal shiver is getting worse, but her arms and legs aren't moving. She wants to flee to her room, to cover her face with her pillow, to scream. "Just the night," she insists.

They keep asking questions, keep trying to make her say something else. Lorna puts her head down on her arms and tries to sink into the table.

Finally, they leave. They tell Mom they will be checking back in the next few weeks.

Mom watches until they drive away, then turns on Lorna. "What the hell did you *do*?"

Lorna tries to deny it, but she is no match for her angry mother. She finally confesses that she asked Mrs. Kleberg if she could live there.

Her mother looks stunned. Confused. "Why?"

"Because you and Kristen are always fighting," Lorna says.

Her mother blinks. "And so you betray me? What a stupid, childish, moronic thing to do, Lorna," her mother says coarsely. "I can never show my face in this town again."

"It's your fault," Kristen snaps at her mother.

"Oh sure, my fault that you're running the streets," her mother says. She picks up her phone. "I'm calling your father."

"Great," Kristen says. "That's helpful. What will he do, say he can't come over right now, that he's burping his kid or something?" She points at Lorna. "Thanks for all the drama. Now we have to listen to one of Dad's dumb lectures."

Mom gets off the couch and goes into another room to call Dad and yell at him. Kristen grabs her backpack. "I hate this place," she says, and goes out, the door slamming shut behind her.

Nana puts her arm around Lorna. She smells of booze. "It will be okay, honey."

How can it be? This is a complete disaster. Her envy of Callie and her family has been revealed and rejected. How can she go to school now? Everyone will know the very lame thing she did.

Her shame is so great that Lorna stops being friends with Callie. She avoids her at school because she can't bear to look her in the eye. It is surprisingly easy to do—Callie is avoiding her too.

Chapter 15

Lorna Now

LORNA WASN'T READY TO ADMIT IT TO MONTREAL, BUT SHE was beginning to appreciate the morning meditation practice, especially since they added yoga flow to it to "fire up her nervous system." She didn't know about that, but she was managing to silence her wild pinging thoughts and follow instructions to look inward. She could imagine her breath sliding over organs and down to her toes, then slowly sliding out of her and into the universe, carrying all the stress and worries of the day.

Of course, that ended the moment the gong sounded and she was herself again. The thoughts would recommence their pinging. She was suspicious of those around her, and especially the lady who offered to take her mat. Why would anyone offer to take another person's mat and put it away? Nevertheless, this morning she felt optimistic. She'd finally done something. She'd unlatched the door of her bomb shelter. She hadn't opened it, just cracked it, but knowing that it could be opened was sort of amazing.

Micah whooped when she showed him the codicil list and reported she'd reached out to Callie. "Lorna! This is epic!" He jumped up from his beanbag and onto his haunches, like he was going to leapfrog around the room. She sincerely hoped he did not.

"You're going to hurt yourself," she warned him. "Anyway, it's not *epic*. It was just a Facebook message. No one even uses Facebook anymore. She'll probably never see it, and if she does, she'll ignore it. It was pretty stupid if you think about it."

Micah was still grinning as he waited a beat. "Are you done?"

Lorna thought about it. "One more—I probably have the wrong Callie."

"Glad we got the negativity out of the way," he said jovially. "But you are missing the point, as usual."

"As *usual*?"

"As usual. You're a master at missing the point. This is great progress, Lorna. This is a step in moving past your fears."

Lorna rolled her eyes. "I haven't moved past anything—in fact, I'm even more afraid now. What if she emails back and says she hates me? Worse, what if she wants to see me and then *sees* me? What do you think that is going to do for my fragile self-esteem?"

Micah was unfazed. "Let's look at those two possibilities. If she hates you, well . . . that's her problem, isn't it? You can't control another person's emotions or thoughts, right?"

Lorna stared at him.

"Right?" he said again.

"Right," she grudgingly admitted. She sank down onto her elbow and stretched her long legs off the beanbag.

"But you did what you set out to do, to help *you*, to make *your* life better. It is a giant step toward freeing yourself of this major roadblock."

It wasn't a roadblock, exactly. That implied she could get past it. This was more like a Go to Jail, Go Directly to Jail card.

"And two, if she wants to see you . . . isn't that what you want? To make amends?"

"On paper," Lorna said. "But in real life?" She winced. "I don't know. It scares me."

"What exactly do you fear?"

She thought that was obvious. "That she'll hate me to my face, like everyone else." She imagined the expression on Callie's face, and it made her insides twist. What could be worse than the one person who had meant so much to her eyeing her with disdain? "She already hated me once. I don't know if I could go through it again."

"Because if she hated you, you would . . . ?" Micah gestured for her to fill in the blank.

"Be heartbroken."

"And?"

"And? Isn't it enough to be heartbroken? How about die? Do you like that? I might die."

"You *wouldn't* die."

"Not literally," she said with a scoff. "But, you know." In other words, she may not physically die, but she might as well. Sure, she hadn't been friends with Callie since middle school. But Callie was just one of those people in life who, when you met them, you knew you'd be connected to for more than just a season. Their friendship was supposed to endure a lifetime. She'd only felt that a couple of times. With Callie. And with Kristen.

She would be truly devastated if Callie didn't feel the same about her, and the chance of that being the case was quite high. It had been thirty years! It was wildly absurd to think there was any hope of a reunion after so much time had passed. But in a tiny way, even if there was no hope, that would also be freeing. To no longer have that what-if hanging over her head.

"It's all out of your control, Lorna. The only thing you can control, the only thing that will free you, is your ability to rectify the wrong in a way that feels right to you. That's your goal. Nothing else."

That wasn't entirely true. She could control everything from the comfort of her bomb shelter and had been doing so for a long time. She might be friendless in there, but at least she wasn't hurting.

Micah seemed to be reading her mind. "Do you like living with the past?"

"Of course not."

"There's an old saying by a French philosopher that goes something like, 'Whoever fears suffering is already suffering what he fears.' In other words, the outcome can't be any worse than you fear."

"Easy for you to say," she muttered.

He smiled and eased himself down on his beanbag. "I feel hopeful. We're getting somewhere."

The door opened and Montreal stuck his head inside. "Ready for your sound bath, Lorna?"

She had almost forgotten about that. She'd never in her life heard of anything more froufrou. She was going to have a long list of comments for Deb about the company's new wellness program when she was done here. That is, if she survived it, which was not a given. "I will never be ready for a sound bath, guys."

"You will never know the benefit of different things if you don't try," Micah said cheerfully. "Just allow yourself to exist in the moment. Can you do that?" he asked as Lorna rolled onto her knees to get up from the beanbag.

Did this guy's optimism ever fade, even for a moment? She stood up and straightened her shirt. "Highly doubtful, Micah.

But I'll do it if you will check *sound bath* off so I can get back to work."

He laughed. "Good work today, Lorna. Very good work."

"I didn't do anything but roll off your dumb beanbag," she said, and followed Montreal.

He led her down a new hallway to another all-white, cavernous room where people were rolling out their mats and taking seats on them.

Lorna had this part down now and sat, legs crossed, reminding herself to exist in the moment as the class started. It was impossible to do at first—and she resisted it in the usual ways. *Who is giggling? What's so damn funny? Also, someone should really crack open a new bar of Irish Spring. What is that thing in the corner? Is it a spiderweb? ARE THERE SPIDERS?*

The instructor asked them all to put themselves on their backs, shoulder blades flat against the floor, and to do a mental scan of their bodies, releasing any tension. "Begin with your toes. Your feet. Your ankles . . . ," she whispered melodiously.

Lorna felt too vulnerable flat on her back, her eyes closed. Anyone could come right up and kick her and she wouldn't see them coming. And when the sound started, it startled her almost to a comfortable seated position. She opened one eye to see three people dressed in white using wooden mallets to ring the bowls. She closed that eye and listened to the dozen Tibetan singing bowls of various shapes and sizes reverberating through the room.

After a few minutes, she could feel the sound reverberating in her, just as the instructor had said she would.

She didn't know how, or at what point, she was able to stop worrying and let herself exist in the moment. But it happened. She concentrated on the vibrations and felt herself grow light of being, like she was floating away from herself. Her mind filled with images of sun-drenched mountain valleys. Of butterflies and trees and flowers and puppies. She felt drowsy, like she was hovering between sleep and lucidity. It was peaceful. Maybe as peaceful as she'd felt in a long while.

"You are invited to reach deep into the vault of negative thoughts and take hold of one to release. Feel it sliding up and away. When you are ready, release it into the ether," the instructor whispered, and the Tibetan bowls sang.

Lorna drew a long breath. She took hold of the most prominent negative thought, felt it sliding up and away, floating like a bubble to the top of her head, and when she was ready, she announced to one and all, "I hate myself." She realized, of course, the moment she said it, that it was not supposed to be said out loud.

"Are you okay, hon?" A cold hand slid onto her arm, and Lorna startled up, clumsily putting herself into a cross-legged position. An older woman next to her smiled kindly.

"I thought . . . I understood we were to release the thought," Lorna whispered.

"You were," the lady confirmed. "But silently."

Lorna nodded and settled onto her back and closed her eyes again. The bowls continued singing, but the moment was lost for her. She sat up once more on her mat, her mind racing, her mortification climbing up her neck and into her scalp. Did she really hate herself? The thought had come from somewhere so deep that it had seemed like more than an occasional annoyance. It startled her. Unnerved her. She didn't want to hate herself. She wanted to like herself. Because if she didn't, what was the point to anything? What was she trying to save herself for?

When Montreal came for her, he cocked his head to one side and looked her up and down. "You look . . . different."

"Really? Maybe because I just made a fool of myself."

"No, you look as if the sound bath was relaxing. Was it?"

"Not exactly. I followed instructions and let myself go in the moment and caused a stir."

Montreal smiled. "Interesting."

Lorna snorted. "I'll say."

"You're definitely leaning into those yoga pants, girl."

"Don't get your hopes up."

"Oh, Lorna," Montreal said with a grin. "You should know by now that hope is always sky-high around here."

Chapter 16

Lorna Now

BEAN WAS NOT HIS USUAL CHEERFUL SELF WHEN HE ARRIVED home from school that afternoon. He dragged in through the door looking like someone had kicked his puppy. He went down on his knees and wrapped his arms around Aggie, burying his face in her fur. It alarmed Lorna.

"What's wrong?" she asked. "You look terrible. Are you sick?"

Bean shook his head. "I just remembered today that my best friend Diego is moving."

She'd forgotten too. "That really sucks, Bean."

"It feels like someone stabbed me in the stomach," he said, and enacted the motion, then fell over onto his back, arms spread wide in death. "I forget sometimes, but then I remember. I don't want him to move. I won't have any friends then."

"Of course you will. I'm your friend and Aggie is your friend."

"Yeah, but I mean at school."

Lorna was still clad in her yoga pants and came almost effortlessly to sit beside him on the floor. Cross-legged, of course. "The cool thing about that is you get to make new friends."

Bean sat up, idly stroking Aggie. "Did you make new friends?"

The memory of that year without Callie hit her hard. "Well . . . I was a bit older, and, um . . ." She didn't know how to explain to this kid that making new friends when you were sure everyone was talking about you, and if not you, your addict sister, was harder than it looked. "Hey, wanna make some cupcakes?" she asked.

Bean brightened. "Yes!" He pounced on his backpack and withdrew his notebook for his field notes.

They went into the kitchen, and she gave Bean some apple slices to munch while she got out the cake mix and a can of frosting she'd bought today.

When Bean had finished his snack, she gave him a bowl and the ingredients to mix the batter for the cupcakes.

"You can get a new best friend," he suggested, like they were still talking about it. "You could even be friends with your old best friend now, maybe! Dad says Diego and I might be best friends all our lives if we call each other on the phone."

"Funny you should mention it. I'm trying to find her," Lorna admitted. "I want to tell her I'm sorry for something."

"Dad says sometimes friends say things they wish they didn't say. And sometimes it's hard to be a friend when someone says something mean to you. And sometimes maybe you weren't meant to be friends."

It sounded like maybe Seth had been hanging out with Micah. "And sometimes it's hard to admit you were wrong," she added. "Callie was the best friend I've ever had." Oh how she regretted her cowardice now. She'd been so embarrassed, so humiliated. *I hate myself.* "She might not want to be friends, you know."

There was that negative thought again, dancing around her, daring her to banish it.

What was odd was that her mother seemed to regret her cowardice too. Why else would she have put Callie on the list? Had she not been just as humiliated as Lorna? Whatever her reason, her mother was right to list Callie. At the very least,

Lorna wanted to apologize for putting Callie's family in that position. She needed to, so that she could forgive her thirteen-year-old self.

"She will," Bean said confidently.

Ah, to be eight again and believe the best of everything.

The cupcakes turned out okay, but there were a couple of lumps of batter that had not been completely mixed. Bean made his notes and gave the effort a six. They were more of a one for Lorna, but she kept that opinion to herself. When Seth showed up to fetch Bean, she shoved the cupcakes at him.

"You didn't have to do that," he said. "You're really too kind."

Lorna stiffened a little. *Kind* was not a word she would ever ascribe to herself. "It's nothing," she said, her gaze on the cupcakes.

"Well, it's something to Bean. It's something to me." Seth glanced over his shoulder at his kid, who was leaning up against their apartment door. When his gaze settled back on her, she could see the regard in his eyes. She couldn't remember the last time someone had looked at her like that. "Thanks again, Lorna. You've been a lifesaver. Same time tomorrow?"

"Yep." She shut the door. And then opened it. "Aggie," she said, and her dog trotted back from Bean's side to her. Seth lifted his hand in a bit of a wave. Lorna did too. And she was smiling.

She wasn't hungry after the taste testing. She pulled out her laptop to stalk Deb and see what was going on at work. But when she opened it, a message from Callie popped up, and her heart seized.

Hi, Lorna. Surprised to hear from you after all this time. What's up?

Lorna slammed her laptop shut and gulped air. She hadn't expected Callie to respond. She'd expected Callie to ignore the message, to roll her eyes and tell whoever she was with now that some crazy chick from the eighth grade was reaching out. But Callie had answered her.

She gingerly opened the laptop again. It was still there, the message from Callie, with a little green dot that indicated Callie was using the app. Did the tone sound accusatory? *After all this time*. Was she making a dig? Or did she simply mean it had been a long time?

"No," Lorna said to herself. She refused to allow herself to spiral into an epic level of self-doubt. Before she lost her nerve, she fired back, *I would like to see you again*. That was it, the whole truth.

Callie immediately replied. *Why?*

That sounded resistant. If she were open to it, Callie would have said *I would love that* or *When?* But Lorna had come this far, and if she didn't continue, she would hyperventilate her way into dry heaves and then a never-ending litany of whys and what-ifs. What should she say? That she missed her? That she wanted to apologize? That she was trying to right her little ship before it completely capsized, and to do that, she had to apologize for having been a terrible friend? What was it Deb always said? *Short, sweet, and straightforward.*

I'm not asking for anything other than a quick meeting. I need to tell you something.

You can't tell me now? Callie responded.

Did Callie hate her? She did, didn't she? Lorna could feel it. Okay, but even if that was true, the purpose of this was not to stop Callie from hating her. It was to lift a burden Lorna had put on herself for thirty damn years. *I'd rather say it in person, if that works for you. I promise not to keep you or get all weird.*

She hits Send and then waited. The moments ticked by. She pictured thirteen-year-old Callie, her red hair spilling around her shoulders, her brow furrowed in thought, considering if she wanted to see Lorna Lott again. And Lorna felt seventeen again, like she was standing in the wings of the gym, waiting to see if she made the volleyball team, her entire life worth riding on it.

Okay, Callie wrote back. *But it has to be tomorrow. We're going on vacation the day after.*

Tomorrow! Tomorrow? Lorna barely had time to get her thoughts together, to decide what to wear, what to say. Where the hell was Kristen when she really needed her?

Thank you. Where should I meet you?

Are you still in Austin? Come to the house after work tomorrow, Callie wrote, and sent her the address in Pflugerville.

Come to her house. *Come to her house.* Either she was going to shoot her and bury her in the backyard, or she wasn't as angry as Lorna had imagined. Either way, Lorna would not sleep a wink tonight.

She typed, *Is 6 okay?*

Yep. CU then.

Chapter 17

Lorna Now

BEAN ARRIVED HOME FROM SCHOOL THE NEXT AFTERNOON in a red-and-white-striped T-shirt and brown cargo shorts, like some cartoon character. The only thing missing was a beanie with the propeller on top. It was a sad fact the boy had no mother to gently guide him into dressing less like a caricature.

Not that Lorna had any idea how to guide him, given her own problem with selecting clothes. She'd spent the better part of the day fretting about this evening and trying on different outfits. No matter what she put on, she looked ridiculous, like a nineteenth-century nanny come to drag a child away to boarding school.

She finally settled on black slacks and a white shirt. She put her hair in a low messy bun and tied a scarf around her neck. She thought maybe it looked jaunty and not stuffy. No sartorial magic was going to transform her wardrobe or hair on such short notice.

Bean was full of news about Aiden, a kid in his class who liked to wear silly hats to school and then make the teachers chase him. "He had to go to the principal's office," Bean reported with wide eyes.

Lorna, with one of her own eyes on the clock as it slowly

ticked its way to five, said, "He sounds like a delinquent in the making."

"What's that?"

"Someone who is always going to be trouble."

Bean laughed. "Aiden is *always* in trouble."

"Guess what, Bean?" Lorna finally blurted, unable to contain her news another moment. "My friend said I could come over today."

Bean gasped and clapped his hands over his mouth. "Your *best* friend?"

"Yes, Callie."

"She wants to be friends again?"

"I don't know yet. She may want to tell me to my face that she hates me. But at least I'll know, right?"

"Right," Bean emphatically agreed.

Lorna pressed a hand to her belly and laughed self-consciously. "I'm so nervous. Is that crazy?"

"Dad says if I'm nervous, then probably my friends are nervous, too, so she's probably nervous too."

Seth was a gold mine of advice, apparently. She wondered if Callie was nervous. Lorna imagined her looking the same, maybe her hair in braids, with cannons in her windows to blast Lorna out of her life once and for all. Which was an absurd thing to imagine. Callie was a grown woman. "She may be nervous, but I bet she doesn't feel queasy like I do."

"Okay, if you feel like you're going to throw up in the car, open your door and lean over," Bean instructed her. "I had to do that once after Grandpa took me to SeaWorld. He said I ate too much junk. Did you eat too much junk today?"

Lorna shook her head. She swallowed down another swell of nausea. She should not have mentioned it, because now she felt like she might throw up. What were these nerves? Why was she such a wreck? This wasn't a broken marriage or a broken law. She made sales pitches to bigwigs and head honchos all the time and never felt anything but annoyed that they'd kept her waiting. This was a childhood friend she wanted to apologize to. There should not be so much anxiety about it. And yet she was filled with it. She pressed both hands against her belly.

"You can always tell if you're sad or scared because something hurts," Bean informed her. "But if you're happy, you feel kind of floaty, and nothing hurts. So be happy."

It took a moment for the words to sink in, but she took her eyes off the clock, which had just hit five, and looked at Bean. "What are you, like, a miniature Eckhart Tolle or something?"

Bean's brow wrinkled. "Is that a candy bar? I'm not a candy bar. But if I *were* a candy bar, I'd want to be a KitKat."

"Smart," she agreed.

Her phone rang, startling them both. She picked it up. "Hello?"

"Lorna, hi. It's Seth."

Seth, she noticed, sounded breathless and her anxiety ratcheted. Breathless on the phone was never good. "I'm so sorry," he said. "I'm going to be late—"

"No, no," Lorna interrupted before he could finish. "You can't be late today! I have an appointment at six with someone. *In Pflugerville.* I should be leaving now, Seth. This is really important."

"Oh gosh, I'm so sorry," Seth said again. "We've had a system failure, and I need at least another hour. Maybe Liz—"

"I'll take him with me," Lorna said abruptly, and looked at Bean for approval. He nodded enthusiastically and then started to jiggle his hips like he was dancing. Or running. She wasn't sure.

"Take him? No, I don't think that is a good idea. I don't know where you're going or who you'll be with. I'd rather you give me a minute to track down Liz and ask her to look after him."

"I don't have time for you to track her down and I can't miss this meeting. I've been waiting for it for thirty years."

"What? I don't—"

"Thirty years, Seth!" she said, louder. "It will be fine, really. It's a house. An old friend. No drugs, no parties, no guns." She sincerely hoped that was true.

There was a pause. She sounded crazed, and not in a good way. "I'm not sure what any of that means, but . . . but let me talk to Bean, okay?"

"Make it quick." She handed the phone to the kid.

Bean listened as his dad presumably explained his predicament. Lorna could only hear Bean's answers, which were "Yes," "Yes," "Uh-huh," and then "It's her best friend, Dad," as if that were an obvious fact being overlooked. And then he listened. For what seemed forever to Lorna, but at last he said, "Okay," and handed the phone back to her.

Lorna put the phone to her ear. "Seth?"

"Okay," he said. "He can go. I'm so sorry, Lorna. I know this is a huge imposition, but I'm between a rock and a hard place here."

Lorna glanced at the clock. "No offense, but can you give me your apologies later? We've got to go. I can't be late."

"Sure, and tha—"

Lorna clicked off in a mild state of alarm. She had enough to deal with just in her own head—her terror at being rejected by Callie, her sudden and vicious determination that her memories were all wrong, the uncertainty of what she would say and if she could say it without pissing anyone off—and she had not counted on a kid tagging along. But she would not miss this shot. "Okay, dude, we gotta jet, and you're riding shotgun," she said. "Bathroom?"

"Nope."

"Aggie needs a treat."

"On it," he said, and headed for the pantry.

"Okay." Was she missing anything? She was too worked up now to think clearly, especially with a literal clock ticking next to her head. It had taken a monumental effort for her to get here, so the idea that a slight ripple to her plans could knock her off course was not only unfathomable but unacceptable. She remembered something and hurried to the desk with the stack of unopened letters. She pulled open a drawer and grabbed a small homemade bracelet, put it in her purse, and said to Bean, "Ready?"

"I have to get my Ranger Explorer backpack. Then I'll be super ready," he assured her, as if they were off to save the world.

Chapter 18

Lorna Now

THE ADDRESS CALLIE HAD PROVIDED LED THEM TO A SOLIDLY middle-class neighborhood in the bedroom community of Austin. The houses here were mid-century ranch, and US flags flew from many of them, interspersed with the ubiquitous burnt-orange flags of the University of Texas and, occasionally, the maroon flags of Texas A&M.

Callie's house was on a corner lot. It flew a rainbow flag. The house was green with black shutters and was surrounded by a wood and wire fence. There was a Little Free Library tucked into the corner of her lot, where big oak trees shaded a manicured lawn. A playscape dominated the right half, and two bikes had been discarded next to the walk. This looked like a happy home. A family home. Just like the house Callie had grown up in. A wave of happy nostalgia hit Lorna so hard she gulped a breath. And then another. "You wouldn't happen to have a paper bag, would you?" she asked Bean.

Bean opened his Ranger Explorer backpack and rummaged around. He withdrew his first aid kit and opened it, studying the contents. "No. But I have this." He produced a flattened-out gum wrapper.

"Nope, won't work. I need a paper bag to hyperventilate into."

"What's that mean?" Bean asked.

"It means I'm about to panic."

Bean turned in his seat and put his hand on Lorna's. "It's okay if she doesn't want to be your friend," he assured her. "Because I'll always be your friend."

Lorna looked at his small hand on hers. She'd never wanted to hug someone so bad in her life. A tear slid from the corner of her eye. "You're not just saying that? You promise?"

"Promise." He handed her the gum wrapper and she dabbed at the tear with it.

Just then, the door of the house opened and five kids swarmed out, ranging in age from about five to fifteen and with a variety of skin colors. "They're like a kid rainbow!" Bean said, and opened the door before Lorna could pull him back. He hopped out, forgetting to shut the door, and ran to the fence. "Hi!"

Lorna got out as quickly as she could in case Bean was about to be swarmed. But the kids just stood in a clump and eyed him warily. Bean was not fazed. "Guess what? I have a geode." He pulled out a rock from his pocket. Where had he gotten that? Should she be checking his pockets daily?

"Hey, I wanna see," one of the kids said. "Did you break it open yet?"

"No, I've been saving it for the perfect time. I'm getting my rock collection badge."

The kids had all inched forward to see the rock he held in his hand. One of them, a taller one, looked at Lorna with suspicion. *You're right to be suspicious, kiddo. Stranger danger and all that.* She felt suddenly conspicuous and backed up, hiding under the mulberry tree like a criminal. One of the kids opened the gate, and Bean went through without a care, holding out his rock so they could see.

The front door of the house opened again, and this time a woman wearing a T-shirt with flowers on it, cut-off jeans, and sandals walked outside. Lorna's heart immediately skipped a beat. She would know Callie Kleberg anywhere. The long red hair was gone—cut short and dyed black now—but even from a distance, Lorna could see the smattering of freckles, the wide blue eyes. Callie was fit, her legs shapely.

She walked off the porch, her gaze on Bean, and then, as she walked across the yard, she scanned the property line, her eyes landing on Lorna after a moment.

Well, she'd been discovered. She could stand here like an idiot, or she could get this over with. Make her apologies and hightail it out of there. So she hitched up her King Kong panties and stepped forward. Not all the way out of the safety of the mulberry tree, but enough that Callie could see her.

Callie came to a halt a few feet away from her on the other side of the fence, put her hands on her hips, and looked Lorna up and down. "Well, hello, Lorna."

"Hi, Callie." Tears sprang to her eyes, and two of them fell before she could squeeze them back in. *She thinks I'm a freak. Probably thinks I'm damaged from all the family drama, and she is obviously not wrong, because who cries when seeing their best friend from middle school? Why are my emotions so complicated? Why can't I just be like other people and send a Christmas card or something? Why do I want to take a swing at this tree? Why do I miss Callie so damn much? It's not natural. It's weird.*

"Are you okay?" Callie asked, interrupting her wild gallop of thoughts. "You look like you're going to be sick."

"She needs a paper bag," Bean said, suddenly popping up in Lorna's field of vision with a slew of kids behind him. "She's about to panic."

Callie looked curiously at Bean. "Is this your mom?"

"No, my mom's dead," Bean said. "Lorna is my friend. But we're not best friends because you're her best friend."

Callie shifted her gaze to Lorna.

"Mom, can we break the geode?" one of Callie's kids asked.

"Sure, if it's okay with . . . What's your name?"

"My name is Benjamin. My mom used to call me Benny, but my dad calls me Bean, and now everyone calls me Bean."

"Okay, Bean," Callie said. "Is it okay to break your rock?"

"Sure!" he said cheerfully.

"You can do it on the porch," she said, and Bean raced off, shouting that they needed another rock to break the geode. The kids followed him.

Callie turned back to Lorna, but before she could speak, Lorna blurted, "You're not my best friend. I mean, not now. I told him you were my best friend a long time ago. I don't want you to think that I'm walking around thinking we're still best friends. I know that's not true. Is this making sense?"

"Not a lot," Callie said, and unexpectedly smiled.

Lorna sucked in a breath. "This is exactly what I was afraid of."

"What?"

"Terrible misunderstandings."

Callie squinted a little, like she was trying to suss out whether Lorna was going to do something they'd all regret. "For what it's worth, I think I understand everything that's been said. But I don't understand who the kid is to you."

"Oh." Lorna caught a glimpse of Bean on the porch with the other kids. One of them had found a hammer. "He's . . ." Something squeezed around her heart, the sensation not at all unpleasant. "He's my friend. He's also a neighbor kid I watch sometimes. It's a long story. Are these your kids?"

She nodded. "Foster kids." She glanced up to the porch,

watching the kids break open the geode. She turned back, about to speak, but at that moment, something hot landed on top of Lorna's head. She reached her hand up, probing, and her fingers found the splat of bird poop.

"Are you kidding me right now?" she murmured.

It had hit her shirt, too, which Callie noticed also. She glanced at the stain, then at Lorna's head, and laughed. "I'm sorry," she said instantly, still laughing. "But what are the odds?"

Probably pretty good when it came to her. "This is not at all how I thought any of this would go. I really think that was Mom."

"Mom?"

"Joke."

Callie was still smiling as her gaze slid over Lorna again. "You don't look like you're about to panic. You look like you always did, only older. You'd better come in. At least move out from beneath the tree. The doves love it there."

"Thanks," Lorna said, and stepped forward, trying to keep her head high but finding it remarkably difficult to do.

Callie opened the gate for her and called up to the kids. "Tate, take the kids to the playroom and keep an eye on them, would you?"

A tall, lanky boy with an Afro nodded and began to usher the kids inside. Bean went along like he was one of them.

Callie closed the gate behind Lorna. "You look good, Lorna. I wouldn't have guessed you to be a flight attendant. I hope that bird shit comes out of your uniform."

Great. She had dressed like a flight attendant. She would be sure to complain about this to Kristen later. "I actually work in software sales."

"Oh," Callie said, her jaw slackening a little and eyes widening, as if she was mystified by this declaration. "I don't think I would have guessed that either. Come in."

Lorna followed Callie into her house. They walked past discarded toys on the lawn, past a bench in the foyer with shoes crammed into cubby holes. Backpacks were strewn across the entry floor. She could hear a TV on in some room, kids loudly talking. A cat was curled on top of a mound of books on a side table. Lorna could see through to the living area and the backyard where there was another play set and sandbox. A pair of big dogs lie panting on the patio.

It was chaotic, just like Callie's house had been when they were kids, and Lorna felt homesick.

Callie showed her to a small hall bath, handed her some paper towels, and then said she'd be in the kitchen, pointing it out. Lorna stepped into the half bath with the paper towels and eyed herself in the mirror. She didn't look like a flight attendant. She looked like someone who was trying way too hard. She yanked the scarf from her neck and her hair from its bun and watched her curls spring into a mess.

When she had cleaned herself as best she could, leaving a patch of wet in her hair that matched the ginormous wet patch on her shirt, she went into the kitchen. It smelled like soap and something sweet. Dishes were piled in the sink, and a coloring book had been discarded on the kitchen table. "I hope you don't mind, but I need to finish the cake I've baked," Callie said, moving to the other side of the kitchen bar.

Lorna stood in the middle of the kitchen, her hands fisted by her sides. She felt odd in her skin. She didn't fit in this room. She didn't fit in Callie's life. It felt so strange not to fall back into the friendship they'd had, even now. This was like walking onto a movie set where everything was make-believe. But it wasn't make-believe; it was Callie's life.

The life that Lorna had always wanted.

Callie picked up a can of icing and began to spread it on the sheet cake with a knife. "So? How are you?" she asked. "I mean besides the unfortunate incident with the bird."

"Fine. I'm fine." *Probably.* Her eyes wandered around the room as her mind searched for words. "And you?" she asked after a moment.

Callie glanced up at her. "Great! Life has been good. Okay, I can't wait another moment—what's up?"

"Right." Lorna was thankful for the task of explaining herself. It was better than standing and watching Callie ice a cake while her imagination ran amok. "This must be really strange."

Callie paused icing the cake. "Not really. Other than wondering why now. Why not ten years ago, or twenty years ago, or hell, even thirty years ago?" She fell silent then, waiting for an answer.

Lorna swallowed. She didn't know how to tell Callie she'd been carrying the guilt like a rock in her gut for all these years.

"Wait . . . you don't need money or a kidney or something, do you?"

Lorna gaped at her. "What? Callie—no."

"I was just kidding. Sort of," Callie said, and resumed the icing of the cake. "I mean, the last time I really spoke to you was to remind you not to forget your Rubik's Cube." She chuckled.

Lorna gripped her hands together in front of her so she wouldn't tremble. "About that. I want to apologize."

"For forgetting your Rubik's Cube?" Callie asked mildly without looking up from her cake.

The words Lorna had tried to rehearse earlier did not come. So she went the chicken route and said, "I think you know, right?"

Callie glanced up. "Umm . . . no? I don't think so. Unless it's . . ." She paused, wiped the back of her hand across her forehead. "Well. It was a long time ago." She put the knife down, braced herself against the bar, and locked gazes with Lorna. "Go ahead."

"I totally understand if you're still angry," Lorna said. "And I don't blame you. I would be too. I'm angry at myself. I'm angry with myself all the time. And I hate myself for what happened."

"Wow, okay. I'm not angry, Lorna, but I don't know what you're talking about. Whatever happened . . . we were thirteen. We were just girls. It's pretty hard to hold a grudge that long."

"Unfortunately, it's not hard to hold a regret that long," Lorna muttered. She sighed and shoved her fingers through her hair, probably making it worse.

"Listen," Callie said softly, gesturing to the cake. "We're leaving tomorrow for Red River, and I've got a million things to do. I appreciate you coming to see me, but—"

She was going to blow this chance. "Okay, I sincerely apologize for asking your mom if I could come live with you," she blurted.

"Huh?"

"I honestly never anticipated that it would cause such a mess. And I regret more than anything that I didn't just tell you then what I'd done. But I was so ashamed and so certain everyone at school knew, and I was a coward."

Callie looked even more confused. "What?"

"I should have just talked to you, Callie, I know that. But I was in a bad way. I don't remember if I told you that my dad had just rejected me—and I couldn't take my house anymore, which I'm sure you do remember—and so I came up with this plan to move in with you. So I could be like you. So I could be a Kleberg and not a Lott. I had it all mapped out. But I shouldn't have assumed we were so close that I could just . . . just *be* you. Especially without talking to you first."

Callie stared at her like she was speaking another language.

Lorna's heart sank. She wasn't responding. Maybe she did still hate her. "I'm so sorry, Callie. I loved being at your house, you know that. I was there all the time. And there was so much warmth and laughter. Oh my God, the laughter," she said wistfully, remembering the Kleberg family dinners. "You can't imagine how alluring your family was to me. We weren't laughing much at my house in those days, and I really wanted to be a part of your family. In my teenage brain, I couldn't see why not."

Callie remained silent, but her hands were on her waist and she was looking heavenward, her mouth slightly open.

"But then, you know, your mom reported me to CPS, and they came, and I was absolutely mortified that your family didn't want me, and I could imagine the whole school hearing about it and knowing what a loser I was. So . . . so I panicked, I guess. I was a coward. I couldn't face you because I couldn't bear to see the disgust or hate in your eyes. I avoided you. And I've regretted it every waking day since."

Callie looked around the kitchen, as if she was trying to find something. Her cannon, maybe.

"You probably had no idea how important you were to me, but you truly were the one person in my life I could trust then. You were the only person who cared about me, I think. My whole life has been about Kristen, and I get it now—I get that I was making you fill a void that you shouldn't have had to fill, and didn't even know you were filling. I'm working on all that, and part of the work is to say what I should have said then: I loved you, and I never would have done anything to intentionally hurt you, and I'm so, so sorry I didn't have the courage to face you after it got so messy. I'm just so sorry, Callie. I hope you can forgive me."

There. She'd gotten it all out. Not as eloquently as she'd hoped—it was a bit of a word salad, actually—but she felt confident there was nothing left to say. She was depleted. Limp. But all the dread and fear of seeing Callie again after all this time had evaporated. The hard part was done.

Callie was still staring at her like she was talking gibberish. "Wait a minute," she said. "Are you talking about that week between Christmas and New Year's? Eighth grade? I'm talking about the time you left my house, like a day or two before school started again, and you never spoke to me again. Are we talking about the same thing?"

Lorna nodded.

Callie suddenly planted both hands on the countertop and leaned so far over her cake that her shirt brushed against the icing. "What the hell, Lorna? You're saying my mom called child protective services? When did she do that? What do you mean you asked if you could live with us?"

Wait a minute. Lorna could not have this wrong. How could she? Her heart started to race as she tried to understand. To *remember*. Could she have been so wrong about what happened? All these years she'd been walking around feeling horrible about herself, and Callie didn't even know. "You must remember," she insisted. "Because . . . because you didn't talk to me either. You hated me for it, remember? Almost as much as I hated me for it."

Callie was shaking her head. "This is wild. No, that's not what happened. I mean, it is, in a way, because I did hate you, Lorna. For a little while, I did. But not for that. I didn't even know that! Are you sure it was my mom?"

"I'm pretty sure," Lorna said. "They said a trusted adult, and she was the only one I talked to about my life."

Callie rubbed her face with her hands. "I suppose it's possible. My mom cared a lot about you, and it was no secret that your family was a total trainwreck."

"That's putting it mildly," Lorna said, trying to process this. "But if your mom didn't tell you, then why did you hate me?"

Callie sighed. "You really don't know?"

"I really don't."

"Because I was gay, remember?"

That made no sense. "Yes, you were gay. You told me. But even if you hadn't, I knew it."

"Lorna!" Callie exclaimed, as if she was being intentionally obtuse. "You were the first person I ever told! You were my best friend, and I confided in you. I *trusted* you. And you just disappeared on me."

"Wait, wait, wait," Lorna said as puzzle pieces slowly started to fall into place. She remembered the way Callie would look at her across a classroom. It wasn't anger in her eyes; it was hurt. "Oh my God, Callie . . . you thought I didn't talk to you because you were gay?"

"Well, yes! What was I supposed to think? All I know is that I told you my deep, dark, shameful secret, and you never spoke to me again. My mom would call your mom and ask if you could come over, and your mom said no, that you weren't feeling well, or you were at your dad's, or you were busy. I knew why, Lorna. Do you even know what happened to me that year? How Leslie Pratt spread rumors about me? Do you have any idea the names they called me? Did you know that two girls tried to jump me, and if it hadn't been for my brothers intervening, they could have killed me?"

Lorna was stunned. How could she have known that? She'd been living in her own nightmare. "No," she said softly. "I didn't know any of that." Her mother had never told her about Mrs. Kleberg's calls. And Lorna had hidden herself from everyone, afraid her terrible homelife would be discovered and she would be humiliated. "Your sexual orientation was never a thing to me, Callie. I'd always known it—it was just who you were." She'd been so mired in her own mortification that she'd turned into a hermit that year and hadn't really come out of her self-imposed prison until later in high school, when Mr. Sanders, the choir teacher, took notice of her.

"Yeah, I'm getting that now," Callie said. "But at the time, I thought the worst." She picked up the knife and shrugged. "Well, it's water under the bridge now, right? It's okay, Lorna. Whatever I thought, I got over it a long time ago." She carried on with the icing.

Of all the things Lorna had expected, this scenario never entered her mind. Because Callie, and whatever she might have been dealing with, had never entered her mind. She couldn't remember ever considering how hard it must have been for Callie to come out at that age. She could never see past her own despair.

Lorna never wanted to be that girl again, the one who was so locked in her own misery she failed to see what was happening to people she cared about. Except she was still that girl in many respects. "Wow. This is really . . . not what I expected," she said. "I'm so sorry, Callie. I really had no idea. All this time I thought it was because I tried to insert myself into your family without even telling you. I was too wrapped up in my own drama to think of how hard things must have been for you. I hope you can forgive me."

Callie smiled and waved the knife in the air. "Don't sweat it. I already have. Don't look so sad—it doesn't really matter now, does it?"

It matters. To me, to my life, to my ability to crawl out of this damn bomb shelter. "I wish I could make it up to you."

"How? I'm out and I'm proud, as the saying goes." She suddenly laughed. "I really did hate you for the longest time," she said, giggling.

Lorna nodded. Her self-loathing was still zipping along at a clip, but she didn't feel like she was carrying the weight of that lost friendship exactly. She felt . . . she felt . . . lighter? All was not lost, and in that place where the weight had been, hope was now released in her; she could feel it churning, and before she even knew what was happening, she burst into tears. "Oh my God!" she exclaimed, swiping at the sudden deluge of tears.

"Lorna!" Callie grabbed some tissues from a box and came hurrying around the kitchen bar. "Why are you crying? I don't hate you now. What is this?"

"What, you mean this?" She gestured lamely at her tears. "Just something that keeps happening to me. Don't mind me." She slid down onto her haunches, burying her face in several tissues. "I suddenly have all these emotions bubbling up."

"It's kind of hard not to mind you." Callie squatted next to her. "Are you okay? Should I call someone?"

"No, no. I'm fine." As if her mortification could run any deeper, Callie thought she was having a nervous breakdown.

"Hey!" Another woman was suddenly on the floor beside her. "What's going on? Are you okay?"

"I think we're okay," Callie said. "She's just having a moment."

Lorna forced herself to her feet and, in doing so, accidentally pushed Callie and the other woman trying to help her. "Sorry." She managed to stop crying and attempted a smile as she dabbed at her face with the tissues. "So sorry." She risked a look at the other woman. She was tall and slender and had a long, sleek, blond ponytail. She looked like she'd just come from the gym.

The woman's gaze darted between Callie and Lorna. "Wow. I guess you're the famous Lorna Lott I've heard so much about. I'm Kate—Callie's wife."

Lorna stuck out her hand. "That's me, Lorna Lott. The worst friend ever."

Kate laughed. "Callie has talked so much about you. Are you okay? Would you like some water?"

"No, thank you," Lorna said. "I'm really okay."

"I'm going to get you some water," Kate said, and went to the other side of the kitchen bar. "Let me ask you something, Lorna," she said as she filled a glass. "Did you really jump off the patio roof onto a trampoline?"

A sparkly memory suddenly erupted in Lorna's head. They'd all gathered around, Callie and her brothers, a couple of neighborhood kids. She couldn't help her smile. "I had to. Her stupid brothers dared me. I almost died because of them."

Callie laughed. "You almost died because of my dad, who was going to kill you. You're so lucky you didn't break your fool neck."

Kate smiled fondly at Callie and came around the kitchen bar. She handed the glass of water to Lorna, then slipped her arm around Callie's waist and kissed her. They looked happy. They looked so happy that an ache sprouted in Lorna's chest all over again. "Where are the kids?" Kate asked.

"Playroom."

"I'll be back," Kate said. "You two can finish doing whatever this is," she said, making a swirling motion with one finger.

Lorna watched her go, then looked back to see Callie eyeing her curiously. "What?"

"Not sure. I don't know what's going on with you, although it looks like it might require medication, if I'm being honest. For the record, you were not the worst friend ever. You were the best friend ever, Lorna. We had a misunderstanding, like all thirteen-year-old girls throughout history. I'm just sorry we didn't get to do high school together."

"Me too," Lorna said. "I've been agonizing about it for years. Literally, years. I'm in a wellness program now, trying to stop agonizing about things that happened in the past. That's kind of why I'm here."

Callie nodded. A corner of her mouth tipped up. She went back to the cake, got a different knife, and cut a slice. "Did Mom really call CPS?"

"I'm positive it was her. I didn't confide in anyone else. And they came the day after I talked to your mom. You could ask her."

"Can't. She has Alzheimer's."

"Oh, wow. I'm so sorry, Callie. I loved your mom as much as my own mother. Sometimes more."

"I know. Don't say more, because then we'll both be crying. What about your mom?"

"Dead. Cancer got her."

"Sorry," Callie said softly. "And Kristen? Is she, like . . . alive? Still using? Living in a crack house?"

Lorna took no offense at the question, but a knot formed in her belly. She glanced at the window. "She's alive. Living in Florida now, very near my dad. Not using, presumably." She shifted her gaze back to Callie. "So part of this wellness thing is that I . . . Well, it's hard to explain," she said, and rubbed her forehead. She hardly understood it herself. "Is there any way I can make it up to you?"

Before Callie could answer, Kate returned with the whole crew, all of them chanting, "Cake! Cake! Cake!"

"Can we have cake?" one of the girls asked.

"Before dinner?" Callie asked, pretending to be shocked.

"Yes, before dinner," Kate said, raising her fist and encouraging the kids to do the same.

Bean gasped and turned to Lorna. "Can I?" Lorna glanced at Callie.

"Are you kidding?" Callie asked. "Of course."

"Okay," Lorna said to Bean.

"My field notes are in the car!" Bean sprinted out of the

kitchen, slamming the front door on his way to Lorna's car. Kate and Callie didn't even seem to notice.

"What does he mean?" Kate asked curiously.

"He's conducting a completely scientific study in search of the best dessert with the hope of baking it for a badge."

"Ice cream," one of the kids said, ignoring the baking part.

"No, cupcakes," another argued.

A full-blown debate had erupted by the time Bean returned with his Driskill Workflow Solutions notebook.

Later, Callie walked Lorna to her car. Bean was already in the passenger seat, his head bent over his notes. He'd had two pieces of cake. "Cute kid," Callie said. "A little odd, like you." She smiled.

Lorna could feel her affection for that odd little kid blossom in her chest.

"And until you figure out what to do with your hair, you probably always will be." Callie smiled.

Lorna put her hand to her head, felt the unruliness of it. "What are you saying? The high-dollar smoothing cream I bought isn't working?"

Callie laughed.

Lorna glanced at Callie's short hair. "Why did you go black? I always loved your brilliant red hair."

"You were the only one. I got sick of my brothers calling me Pippi Longstocking."

Lorna surprised herself with a bark of laughter. "They weren't wrong."

Callie gasped, then laughed roundly. "It's good to see you, Lolo."

"You too, Callie. You have no idea."

Callie reached out and touched Lorna's cheek, then dropped her hand. "Okay, so listen. I don't know if I have the time or patience for your wellness program. I mean, between Mom and the kids . . . it's a lot. And we're going to be gone for a couple of weeks. But maybe we can get together when we get back and catch up." She leaned forward and hugged Lorna tightly.

Lorna wanted to cry. Two hugs in a week. She'd had no idea how badly she needed them. Especially from Callie. She'd never dreamed this would happen—never considered that Callie was still the same girl who had meant so much to her, with a heart as big as the sun. She felt foolish for having spent so much time convinced Callie hated her for something she never even knew about.

Callie let go and said, "I'm really glad you came. You're the same old Lorna, but now with panic attacks." She grinned and, with a wink, turned back and walked into her house.

Lorna watched until the door shut behind her. She felt giddy and relieved and like a two-ton weight had been lifted from her. Callie might not be all in, and even if she was, they might not recapture the friendship they'd had. But Lorna had made her apology, and now she was filled with hope they might find those two teen girls again. Micah would be beside himself.

You were right, Mom. You must love to hear me say that. Too bad you're not here to say "I told you so." I know you would enjoy that.

• • •

Bean was asleep in his seat when Lorna turned on the street where she had lived with her mother and sister in a garage apartment. It was getting late, but the lights were still on in Peggy's house. Lorna walked up the path to the door, giving the rooster a happy slap to the side of its head on her way. She knocked on the door.

Peggy answered, dressed in a robe and pajamas. "Lolo!" she said delightedly. "I wasn't expecting you."

"I'm sorry for showing up so late." What time was it? Eight or so? She'd lost track. "I need to give you something." She took a friendship bracelet from her purse. One cold winter day, she and Callie had made dozens of them in Lorna's room, sifting through the beads, hoping to give them to people they wanted to be friends with. Mostly people who would never be friends with them.

They'd made a best friend version for each other. Lorna had kept the one Callie made for her. The string was yellowed, and a couple of beads had somehow gone missing. She handed the bracelet to Peggy, pressing it into her palm.

"What's this?"

"It's my proof that I took care of my first item on the list. I apologized to my best friend." Just saying those words out loud, she could feel herself smile. *Really* smile.

And it felt amazing.

> Hey K, guess who I saw today? Callie Kleberg. She looks great. You always said she would be really pretty if she tried. I don't know if she is trying, but she is really pretty. She thought I was a flight attendant because of the way I was dressed. Still hitting it out of the sartorial park over here. Get this—she doesn't hate me. Not anymore, anyway. But the most interesting thing is that the end of our friendship was not your fault. Can you believe it? Me either. Turns out, the reason she never spoke to me again was because I was a shitty friend. That's it. I didn't hear her. It wasn't because you were making my life miserable or because I tried to become a Kleberg. It was because I wasn't listening. But don't get it twisted—I wasn't listening because you were making my life miserable then.

This was before your first go in treatment. Remember how impossible you were?

I remember that treatment didn't last long. I remember you showed up at my concert so stoned or high or drunk or whatever with that stupid, gross guy. What was his name? It doesn't matter. That was the most humiliating moment of my entire life in a long list of humiliating moments. I always wondered, did a switch go off in your head? I'm just trying to understand how you were clean for so long and then one day—*poof*—it was all gone. I always tried to understand, Kristen. Well, except in the end.

Speaking of the end, I'm so sorry about that. You have no idea. I can't even talk about it right now.

Chapter 19

Lorna Is Sixteen

KRISTEN COMES HOME AFTER THREE MONTHS IN A RESIdential drug treatment program. Nana and Lorna have made a cake—well, Lorna made it while Nana drank. She has written *Welcome Home* on it. It's chocolate—Kristen's favorite.

There are circles under Kristen's eyes. She has skinny arms, but her beauty is coming back. She's so thin. Except for her stomach. Her stomach is too big, like she's malnourished. She says the food was terrible in prison. She means rehab.

Kristen seems flat and lifeless, not excited to be home. She keeps her arms folded over her body, and her eyes dart around the rooms she is in, like she expects someone to jump out from the curtains and haul her off. Maybe because that's how Mom and Dad got her into treatment—strangers came to the house and took her.

Kristen says thanks for the cake. She eats a piece, says she can't eat anything else, and goes to her room to lie down.

As the first week home unfurls, Kristen mopes around the house. She tells Lorna it's because she's bored. "I have nothing to do. Mom won't let me get a job because I have all these stupid meetings to go to."

"Do you want me to go with you?" Lorna asks, although she has no idea what kind of meetings Kristen means.

Kristen plays with Lorna's long hair, twisting it around her fingers, making corkscrew curls. "No. Then both of us would be bored."

Mom finally relents and tells Kristen she can get a job. Kristen is happy and begins to look but quickly discovers there are not many options for a twenty-year-old woman with a record of petty theft.

"That doesn't sound right," Mom says when Kristen complains about it.

"Are you kidding?" Kristen snaps. "No one wants someone with a record, Mom. I told you."

Kristen's mood gets darker as the days roll on. "I hate being sober," she confides in Lorna. "I hate who I am when I'm sober."

"Buy why?" Lorna asks. "You're funny and smart, and I really like you like this."

Kristen smiles at Lorna like she's a stupid little kid. Maybe she is. "It's hard to understand, I know. Sometimes I don't understand it myself. It's not like I want to be like this. But I am, and I'm sick of trying to be someone I'm not."

Lorna doesn't understand what "this" is. "But you're not going to do drugs or anything, are you?" she asks.

"Are you kidding? And risk going back to that hell pit known as treatment? I'm not going to use, Lorna. Or drink. Or steal Nana's pills. Trust me."

Lorna is relieved to hear this. She doesn't think she can survive another year like the one before Kristen went. "Do you promise?"

"Of course I promise," Kristen says, and hugs her. "Besides, you need me. Who else is going to listen to you practice your songs?"

Lorna has been spending as much time as she can at school.

She made choir this year, and they are preparing for the all-state spring choir contests. She is not the best singer, but she tries harder than anyone. That's what her choir teacher, Mr. Sanders, says. He tells the entire choir that if they had even half the work ethic Lorna has, their group would be in first place. The kids look at Lorna like she's trying to make their lives miserable. Mr. Sanders tells her to ignore them. He works with her after school, trying to help her find her voice and use her diaphragm to support her breath. Lorna goes home and practices with Kristen, who tells her when she is sharp or when she is flat, even though she says the songs are dumb.

One month before the contest, Mr. Sanders hands out solos and duet assignments. He tells the choir that Mr. Collins, his college buddy and chief rival, who is now the choir director at another local high school, has beat Mr. Sanders and his choirs four years in a row. He rouses the choir into believing this will be the year they win—and they will do it with Jamie McCorkle, the best singer in the choir. Everyone cheers when he points to Jamie.

Mr. Sanders asks Lorna to come to all the rehearsals for soloists, duets, and ensembles to help. She remains in the chorus, but she is thrilled to be part of the more intense rehearsals. She hands out music, then picks it up after rehearsal. All the singers work hard. Kristen says it's a waste of time, it's only a dumb high school choir contest. But she is there to pick up Lorna every day.

A week before the contests are to begin, something terrible happens. Jamie McCorkle comes down with bacterial meningitis after a volleyball tournament. Mr. Sanders looks slightly sick when he calls Lorna into his office and tells her she will be doing one of Jamie's solos.

"What?" Lorna says, unable to absorb the news. It makes her frantic. But excited.

"You're the only other person who knows that solo. We'll work every day, make sure you're ready," Mr. Sanders says. He takes her by the shoulders. "You can do this, Lorna."

"I can do this," Lorna repeats.

When Lorna comes home with her news, Kristen is on the couch, eating from a bag of chips. She's been working at a fast-food burger joint. She talks about how fat she is getting, how she hates the job, how the place is bogus.

Lorna suggests she go back to school and get a degree. "You always loved art," she reminds her.

Kristen laughs. "Did I?" She laughs again. "I don't want to do art. I want to direct movies. Maybe even star in them." She suddenly leaps up from the couch and does what Lorna thinks is supposed to be a pirouette, but she stumbles and falls back on the couch. She laughs uproariously.

It's odd.

But Lorna is bursting with her own news and ignores that tiny little alarm. She tells Kristen what happened at school, how she is now a soloist with only one week to prepare. "There is no time to waste," Kristen says. "You need to practice. I'll help." And she does. She tries to coach Lorna on pitch, although hers is no better. But she is helpful when it comes to presentation.

As the weekend and the contest approach, Lorna's nerves begin to take on a life of their own. In full rehearsals, she feels strange to be the one to step forward. She imagines a Jewish golem taking a giant step, and the audience and choir staring at her in shock and dismay. She tugs on her shirt, tries to smooth her hair. Mr. Sanders tells her not to fidget.

Two days before the contest, Kristen doesn't come home from her shift.

"Here we go again," her mother says wearily.

"What?" Lorna asks.

Her mother grimaces. She glances at Nana, who is asleep in her chair. "You know what that means," she says ominously.

Maybe Lorna knows, but she doesn't want to hear her mother say it.

Her mother does anyway. "She's at it again."

"Don't say that," Lorna snaps as they head to the car. "She's not, Mom. She promised me. She's been helping me with my solo."

Her mother stops and looks at Lorna. Then she laughs. But it's not a pleasant laugh; it's dark, and it makes Lorna feel stupid. "Why are you laughing?"

"Let me tell you something, honey. Addicts never tell the truth. Never. They will lie to your face till the day they die."

Lorna is shocked. "That's not true. You always say she's trying."

"But I'm not a fool," her mother says.

Lorna is furious with her mother's lack of faith in Kristen. She pushes aside any niggling doubts and refuses to argue. She goes to practice and works with Mr. Sanders. He tries so hard to look happy when she does the solo, but Lorna can tell he wishes Jamie McCorkle was well.

Saturday morning, Lorna is so nervous she feels sick. She refuses breakfast. "You have practiced and practiced," her mother says. "You will do fine. I wish I could be there to see it, but I have to work." Her mother recently took a job at a dress shop to help make ends meet.

"I'll be there," Kristen says from her place at the table.

"Where's that?" Nana asks sleepily.

"Nowhere, Nana," Kristen says. But she looks at Lorna. "I wouldn't miss it."

Lorna is relieved. Someone on her side.

"Lolo, you look like you're going to pass out," Kristen says. She gets up from the table and comes forward. "Has anyone ever worked as hard as you at anything? No. It's going to be fine. And you know what? After it's over, you and I can go for pizza."

"That would be great," Lorna says.

"I don't think that's a good idea," Mom says.

Kristen rolls her eyes. "Stay out of it, Mom." She smiles at Lorna, then pushes some of her hair back into the bun she's supposed to wear. "Remember, look at the back wall. If you don't see them, they can't see you. And project," she says, tapping Lorna's belly. "You're going to do great."

"Don't get her too hyped up," Mom says.

Kristen whips around. "Why can't you be supportive?" she shouts.

"I'm not going to pretend she's Pavarotti when she's not," Mom shouts back, and they begin to argue. Lorna goes outside to wait for Mom. She's thankful for Kristen's pep talk, but she fears Mom is right—she's not that good.

After Mom drops her off at the school, Mr. Sanders runs through the music one more time. Then they board a school bus to go to the neighboring district's performing arts center for the contest. There, they stand in a circle holding hands before heading onstage. "We are here because we have Knight pride. We are going to win. We will beat Westwood and stand victorious!" They all begin to chant, "Go, Knights! Go, Knights! Go, Knights!" Lorna swallows down a swell of nausea and nerves.

They file onstage. Lorna is shocked to see the auditorium is full. There are other choirs from other local high schools. Parents, teachers, and who knows who else. She is so jittery she can hardly stand. She takes deep breaths like Mr. Sanders taught her.

When it comes time for her solo, she moves to the front of the stage. *The golem is in place.* The music begins, and she opens her mouth, and the first notes come out of her, clear and loud enough. But just then, there is a terrible commotion in the audience. Lorna takes her gaze off the back wall and looks down to see Kristen and some guy tripping over people to get in the front row. They are giggling and loose-limbed and shushing each other too loudly. She knows instantly that Kristen has been using something. Kristen looks up and sees Lorna, waves, and then slides down in her seat, telling the guy to be quiet, saying loud enough for Lorna to hear, *"That's my sister."*

Lorna's stomach churns. Mr. Sanders starts the song over. Lorna begins to sing, but she can't take her eyes off Kristen and that boy. He is looking around, like he wants something, speaking to people behind him. Kristen slaps his arm hard, and he barks at her. Lorna is still singing, her voice wobbling, her pitch breathy—she can hear she is off-key. The chaos unfolding in front of her causes acid to churn in her belly. When the boy begins to laugh, Lorna's anxiety reaches a sickening threshold she can't contain. She takes a step, intending to flee before the unthinkable happens, but it is too late. She vomits on the stage. The crowd cries out. The contest is disrupted and she flees, choking on tears and mortification and another swell of nausea. How can life be so cruel?

She doesn't know what happened after. How the vomit was cleaned up. How the choir continued. How the contest ended. Even who won. On the bus back to school, no one will speak to her. Someone says she stinks like vomit. Jake Nucci finally takes pity on her and tells her Mr. Sanders sang her part and they came in third overall.

Lorna doesn't know what is more disappointing—that she lost control and cost them the win? Or that Kristen is using again?

Chapter 20

Lorna Now

MR. SANDERS WAS SURPRISINGLY EASY TO FIND. HE HAD TO be in his seventies now, maybe even his eighties, but he was active on social media. He was no longer a teacher, of course, but he was a church youth director at one of the megachurches in town, and he had his own website. It announced he was putting on a musical, and rehearsals for *The Curse of the Moneylenders* (which, the website noted, was written and scored by Mr. Sanders himself) were happening from five to seven every night this week.

Lorna couldn't wait to tell Bean. After their visit to Pflugerville, she'd told him there was something else she regretted and someone else she should probably apologize to. Bean was quite excited about the prospect of a choir. "I don't have my singing badge yet," he said.

There was a badge for everything, she guessed.

Bean wasn't due to come over after school today as he had a Ranger Explorer meeting, and Seth was picking him up. When Lorna heard the truck on the gravel patch, she went to the door, hoping to catch him.

The front door squeaked open (Mr. Contreras really needed to oil a few hinges) at the same time she opened her apartment door and stuck out her head. Bean didn't see her—he slammed the front door on Seth, then stalked toward his apartment without looking right or left. He took out a key and shoved it into the lock, opened the door, went inside, and slammed it too.

Lorna was stunned. She'd never seen Bean like that.

"Hey."

She hadn't even noticed Seth slipping into the house. She stepped out of her door and waited for an explanation.

Seth smiled sheepishly. "Sorry about that. Bean's pretty upset with me."

"Why?"

"It was his turn to bring snacks to the Rangers and I forgot to pick them up. And I haven't managed to find a blue vest for his badges. Apparently, he is the only kid without one."

Lorna blinked. She almost said out loud that was unacceptable but managed to hold her tongue. Surely Seth knew there was nothing worse than being the only one who didn't have what the other kids had. Like a happy family, for example. "That sucks," she said flatly, unable to let her indignation for Bean go.

"Yep. So I've heard," Seth said.

"Sorry," Lorna muttered.

"Don't be. The condemnation is deserved." He shifted his gaze to his door. "I guess I'd better go deal with my child's bitter disappointment." He gave Lorna a sort of two-finger salute and went into his apartment.

Lorna remained standing in her partially opened doorway. Poor Bean. She knew what it was like to be the odd one out. She shut the door and went to her small bathroom, where she dragged a brush through her hair and straightened out her sensible blouse. Then she went to rouse Aggie from her bed. "Come on, girl," she said. "Bean needs you."

Aggie leaped up from bed, her nub of a tail wagging at just

the mention of Bean's name. Lorna took her across the hall and knocked on 1B. Moments later, Seth answered the door. He'd removed his outer shirt and was wearing a T-shirt and some joggers. Lorna was momentarily struck by the size of his biceps. She hadn't seen biceps like that up close and personal in a very long time, and they sent a tiny shiver up her spine and froze her brain. "Umm . . ."

Seth didn't seem to notice her gawking; he was watching Aggie walk right past him like this was her house and disappear into the apartment. He turned back to Lorna, curious.

"I thought she might help soothe hurt feelings. She always does for me."

"You know what? That's a great idea. Thank you." He opened the door a little wider. "Come in."

"Oh no. I don't want to intrude." Or bore him to death while she tried to make small talk, which was more likely.

"Please, I could use the company. If you have time, that is."

She had nothing but time. "Well. Okay. But I'm horrible at small talk."

"I know." He smiled, and his eyes twinkled in the low light.

Lorna resisted the urge to put her hand to her throat. She didn't feel like herself—her limbs were jittery, her blood sparkly.

"Just come in, Lorna. I'm not exactly a master at small talk either, but I think we can manage."

"Okay." She took a tentative step inside. She could hear Bean speaking low to Aggie, the sound coming from the direction of what would have been Nana's room. She and Seth were in the old den. If Lorna kept her gaze directly in front of her, she could imagine her mother in a chair, smoking a cigarette, flipping through the pages of a magazine. Or maybe, if she was lucky, she could imagine Nana knitting, like she used to do in the early days, when Lorna and Kristen would lie on the floor at her feet and cut out houses and people from magazines for their storybooks. Before Nana was drunk all the time. When exactly had that started happening?

"Would you like a beer?"

She jerked her gaze to Seth. She debated telling him she didn't really drink, but that, on top of no small talk, seemed too much. How insufferable could one person be? "Sure. Thanks."

"Coming right up." He walked into what used to be a large bath. She didn't know where the bath was in this apartment now.

She looked around while he got the beers. His furniture was standard, without a lot of character, one of those purchase-an-entire-room packages. She shifted her weight, uncertain how to fit her body in this familiar yet not familiar space. She felt stiff, like a robot. Why could she not relax? It had been years since she lived with her family here. So many people gone, so many things changed. In fact, she had a sudden memory of her last time in this room. Her mother was shouting at her to stop her damn crying.

"I've got some low-carb beer," Seth said. "Hope that's okay. It's a thing now, I guess."

Lorna didn't know if it was a thing or not and said nothing as she took the beer he handed her. She looked at the label.

"No good?" he asked.

"Umm . . . I haven't tasted it."

"Well, you can trust me that it won't be great," he said with a chuckle. "I failed to mention that it's also budget beer."

Lorna smiled. She liked his honesty. She hated beer, truth be told. But she sipped it, and it wasn't terrible. "It's okay," she said, noting the surprise in her voice.

He laughed. "Shocker, I know. Want to sit?" He gestured for her to have a seat on the sofa, then moved papers and Bean's backpack off a chair for himself. Lorna sat on the edge of the couch, her back straight. Seth had some darkness under his eyes and the beginning of a beard on his face and chin. She wondered how he slept, if he heard Martin's marching band practice at night like she did.

He glanced up to see her staring at him, and Lorna quickly averted her gaze. *Great.* Her awkward self was not going to let her be. Her gaze happened to land on the windowsill and one of her Precious Moments figurines. *Oh, hello, how did you get here?* Had Bean taken it without asking? Surely Seth didn't collect them too. She leaned slightly forward. The figurine was of a woman in a sun hat and a boy with a puppy.

"I must look like crap," Seth said, drawing her attention back to him. "I've been working a lot. Too much." He took a long swig of beer. "I'm having trouble keeping my hours down. I'd offer you a snack, but the cupboard is bare. Turns out, I suck at the single-parenting thing."

"I'm sure that's not true," Lorna said.

Seth sighed and shoved his fingers through his hair. "You know, Bean's mom and I struggled to make ends meet when he was a baby. There was always something, right? But then I got this great promotion at the university—I work in IT—and for once, things were looking up. It was longer hours, but we were both okay with that. It meant more money, more freedom. She got a better job, too, and Bean was in school. We had plans, we were doing things on weekends, we were planning trips and talking about the future, and I thought I had it made. Then—*wham*—she gets hit by a bus."

Lorna managed to hide her surprise at his bluntness with a cough.

"Sorry. I thought you knew."

"Bean mentioned it."

"The bus was coming out of a garage, and I guess Jill wasn't looking where she was going. I don't know. I've never been able to figure out how she didn't see a whole damn bus. She was on a bike—she had to notice something so much bigger than her coming out of that garage." He shook his head. "Anyway." He took another swig of beer, then picked at the label. "She was really into fitness. Cycling in particular. She'd ride for miles around town." He glanced off, toward the window with the figurine on the sill. "I told her it was too dangerous to ride around Austin. We have one of the highest bike fatality rates in the country. But she insisted I shouldn't worry, that everything was fine. Well, it wasn't fine."

Lorna gulped down a swallow of beer, surprised he was telling her this. "I'm so sorry," she said. "You must be furious about that."

Seth slowly turned his head back to her. "What?"

"You know, when you love someone and you want them to take care of themselves, but you can't control what they do. I mean me—I feel that way."

He looked down. But when he looked back up, he opened his mouth to speak, then paused. He squinted. "Lorna . . . are you crying?"

"What? Am I?" She put her fingers to her face. "Oh my God," she said, horrified by the notion that tears could just fling themselves out of her eyes without her noticing. Her cheeks heated with shame. She wiped away the tears. "I really need to see someone about that. I'm fine, I really am. I'm just sorry for you. I know about loss. My mom died about four years ago, and my sister . . . well, we don't speak anymore. I realize that's not the same as losing a spouse, but I know what it's like to want so desperately for someone to be safe. That's all I meant." She had to look away in case more tears fell. She felt so sorry for Seth and

Bean and hated that either of them had to feel anything close to the loss she'd felt. Probably even worse.

"I'm sorry you have experienced this kind of loss," Seth said. He stood up, went to an end table, and brought back a box of tissues for her, then took a seat next to her on the couch. So close that their legs touched. It was oddly comforting. "How did your mother die? And please don't tell me she was hit by a bus, too, because that would be such a coincidence I would have to laugh." He smiled.

Amazingly, Lorna did too, but she shook her head. "She had cancer. It was slow and long."

"Ah." He nodded thoughtfully. "Yep, I think I prefer quick and shocking to long and painful. I'm sorry. That must have been tough."

He really didn't know the many ways, up and down and all around, that it had been tough for her. But he knew something similar, and that was a connection she hadn't expected. Sometimes Lorna would marvel that she'd managed to come out of that period of her life still a sort of functioning human. She'd lost her family in short order—Nana, Mom, Kristen.

He drummed his fingers on the beer bottle. "Are you alone too? I mean, without a partner?"

The question surprised her, and she must have looked it, because he held up a hand. "Sorry. That was bad form. I just haven't seen anyone come and go, and I wondered."

"There's no one," she said. "It's not in the cards right now." Or probably ever, given that she was not particularly attractive as a mate, either literally or figuratively.

"What do you do for a living?" he asked.

"I sell workflow software. We help determine how a company's work flows best, then design a system around it. Boring. Which is why I like it, I think. Nothing to get too worked up about." She considered what she'd just shared. "I don't . . . You must think I'm so weird."

He gave her a funny frown. "I think you're interesting. You said you're on sabbatical?"

"Yes." She looked away again, unwilling to explain her sabbatical to him because she feared how it would look. Even weirder than she was, and she really didn't want Seth to think she was weird. Of all the people in this house, she didn't want him to think it. Like, Martin could think it all day if he was so inclined, but Seth? She really cared about his opinion of her. He was sitting so close that she could feel his energy wrap around her, and she wanted to bore into that energy. That strength. Just crawl up his shirt and build a nest.

She looked off before she gave herself away, and her gaze landed on the Precious Moments figurine again.

"By the way, thank you for that," he said, having noticed where her attention was focused. "It reminds Bean of his mother."

Of course. She hadn't given it to Bean, but she didn't mind that he'd taken it. She didn't have to worry about him seeing a promise in that figurine that didn't really exist. The poor kid was light-years ahead of her—he already knew the Precious Moments were lying to him.

She drank one long glug from her beer and decided it wasn't half bad. "Umm . . . do you still need help with Bean after school? Because I like having him around. He's such a great kid. He's . . . he's been helping me on my little apology tour."

"Your what?"

"That's what I'm calling it. I'm working to let some things go from my past. Things I feel bad about, things I wish I had done differently."

Seth's gaze moved over her face, settling on her eyes. His eyes looked so blue in this light, and the way they were locked on her made her heart skip around in her chest.

"Not for murder or anything," she quickly added.

"Damn, Lorna, I should hope not."

"I mean, nothing illegal or bad. Just, you know . . . things that I wish I'd handled differently." Part of her wanted to tell him, to admit what had happened, why she had this time, why it was important to address these regrets. But she feared it would make her sound slightly nutty, and she did not want to talk so much that she somehow confessed her plans to buy this house. Or worse, gave him any reason to think Bean shouldn't hang out with her. "It's called self-actualization," she added. Micah had said that just today when he sent her off to make a vision board.

Seth nodded, like he knew what that meant.

"Anyway, Bean is helping me, and he does love Aggie, and Aggie loves him."

"Yeah," Seth said. "If it's okay with you, it's okay with me. He's going to miss that dog more than anything when we move."

Her heart stopped at the mention of it. She didn't want Bean—or Seth—to move.

"Mr. Contreras told me he has a buyer," he added. "Maybe even two."

"Oh." Lorna resisted the urge to squirm. "Well . . . maybe you can get Bean a dog if you move."

"I don't think so," Seth said. "I can hardly take care of him right now, much less a dog. Between you and me, it's a whole lot easier if he can just borrow one." He grinned and nudged her with his elbow. "I hope you don't mind that I am totally using you and Aggie."

"Interestingly, I don't." She sort of liked that Aggie was needed, and by association so was she.

She took another sip of the beer and set it aside. This was nice. It was so nice it made her nervous. What would happen if she revealed too much of herself? Micah would have a field day with that fear. She abruptly stood.

Seth seemed surprised and awkwardly came to his feet. "You're going?"

"Yes. I need to, ah . . . do some things." Like order a blue Ranger Explorer vest.

"Oh. Okay. I was enjoying the chat."

Lorna swallowed. "Me too."

He looked slightly confused and put down his beer. "I'll get your dog."

"Bring her back in the morning. She can sleep with Bean if it's all right with you."

"Ah . . . sure," Seth said, frowning. He glanced toward Bean's bedroom. "Are you sure?"

She wasn't sure at all. Aggie was a huge comfort to her too. They hadn't been separated since she picked her up as a young pup at the shelter. But she said she was fine with it and walked to the apartment door before she changed her mind.

Seth opened the door for her, but he didn't move out of the way. He stood so close that Lorna had to look up at him. "Thanks, Lorna. You have been a tremendous help to me and Bean these last few days. I don't know what I would do without you."

She could feel herself blushing, and worse, she could feel tears building. "No problem," she said, and skirted out, her heart beating wildly.

> Hey K. Tonight I went across the hall and hung out with Bean's dad. You don't know him, and I'm glad you don't, because you would probably try to hit him up for something. You used to make me so nervous

around my friends. Anyway, their apartment is where Nana's bedroom and the den were. Remember when you'd sneak in there and find bottles under her bed? You thought it was so hilarious that she was a drunk. Why was addiction always so funny to you? Well, I guess you're not laughing so much now. The last time I was in those rooms, I cried like a giant baby because we were packing up the house. Mom yelled at me to stop, like I wasn't allowed to have those feelings. I wonder if you have any idea how hard it was for me to leave. You were so selfish, Kristen. I know I'm not supposed to say that, because addiction is not your fault and yada yada. But you were.

Still, I take no comfort in the fact that you are having to put up with Dad now. Sorry about that.

Chapter 21

Lorna Now

"WHAT DO YOU THINK?" LORNA ASKED BEAN, MODELING the skirt, blazer, and flat shoes she intended to wear to show Mr. Sanders she was not a loser, despite the evidence he might have to the contrary.

"Umm . . ." Bean studied her hard. Too hard. "You look like a principal."

"Okay," she said uncertainly. "Is that bad or good?"

"I'm scared of my principal," Bean said.

Lorna groaned. "Ugh."

While she changed into something less scary, Bean used Lorna's phone to type in the address of the Community Celebration Church. He was wearing a giant compass around his neck; she supposed in case Google Maps didn't work. But the geographic charting and compassing aside, it wasn't necessary—Lorna knew exactly where the church was. It was a huge monolith on MoPac Expressway that attracted people from Austin and surrounding towns. She remembered that at one point, Kristen had gone there in hopes of spiritual healing. She wondered what happened with that. She knew only that it was a short-lived effort.

When she and Bean arrived, people were exiting out of the

church doors, dispersing to cars in the parking lot. The rehearsal appeared to be over for the day. "Ready?" she asked Bean.

"Ready," he said solemnly.

They made their way to the large sanctuary. With all the lighting and sound systems suspended from the ceiling, it looked more like a civic auditorium. People were picking up their things from the seats and heading for the exits. Two men remained onstage, and from where Lorna stood, it looked like they were having an argument. One of them was Mr. Sanders. He looked almost the same as he had when she was a teenager, dressed in his trademark newsboy cap and a gray button-up vest.

"This church is big," Bean said, looking around him. "Do you think they have a Christmas tree that goes all the way to the ceiling?"

"If they don't, they should," Lorna said as she watched the man Mr. Sanders was talking to come off the stage. He turned back and said something, then, with a dismissive wave of his hand, walked up the aisle to the exit.

Mr. Sanders remained onstage, his hands on his hips, staring after the man who disappeared into the foyer. "Okay," she whispered to herself. "Okay. Here we go."

"Remember to slow down if you talk too fast," Bean said. He pressed a tissue into her hand.

"Thanks." She made herself move.

Mr. Sanders didn't seem to think anything of a woman and boy moving down the aisle to him when everyone else had left. He was still standing with his hands on his hips, staring at the door the other man had gone through. When they reached the apron of the stage, Lorna cleared her throat.

Mr. Sanders turned his head to look at her. "Yes?"

"Mr. Sanders? Do you recognize me?"

He frowned. "Should I?"

"She threw up onstage in front of a bunch of people," Bean said. "It went *everywhere*. I don't know what color it was, though. When Trey threw up in the bushes, it was yellow."

"Pardon?" Mr. Sanders asked.

"I'm Lorna Lott. In high school, I had a solo at a choir competition, and unfortunately, I threw up onstage."

Something clicked in Mr. Sanders's eyes. "Ah." He nodded slowly. "Lorna Lott. That was a day. What can I do for you?"

She didn't like standing below him. "Do you mind if I come up?"

He gestured for them to come onstage. There were stairs immediately to their left, and she walked up, Bean on her heels, and came eye to eye with her former teacher. She'd remembered Mr. Sanders being a tall man, but either he had shrunk or she had gained yet another inch in her late teens. "How are you?" she asked.

"I'm well. What brings you here?"

Lorna's palms began to sweat. She felt a little more confident than she had been speaking to Callie . . . but the whisper of doubt that was her constant companion was getting louder. *What am I doing here? He doesn't even remember me.* "Umm . . . so I came here to apologize."

"For what?" He looked quite serious. Quite unsure.

"For the mess I made of the choir contest."

"Why?" He folded his arms. "Is this one of those new age things I hear about? Some TikTok fad?"

"Well . . . probably," she admitted. "I'm addressing some events from my past that happened because of my sister. I regret them and would like to apologize."

"I don't know why I'm included in that." He turned slightly, like he meant to walk away. He clearly had no patience for her apology tour. She felt on the verge of giving up, of excusing herself for bothering him. But then Bean touched her leg. He was watching every moment of this exchange, and she realized that, because she'd invited him to be her wingman, he was invested in this. "My sister," Lorna repeated. "She was there that night, she and some guy she'd met. They were in the front row causing a scene."

Mr. Sanders's frown deepened. "I don't know what you're talking about. I remember you getting sick, but I also remember you were a ball of nerves. That was probably my fault, making it a bigger deal than it needed to be."

"We had a chance to win first place," she reminded him. "And you would have beaten your college friend."

"My college friend," he repeated slowly. "Are you talking about Charles Collins?"

Memories were beginning to jumble, just like in Nana's house. She'd thought she remembered so clearly but now wondered if she was wrong. Still, she was sure there had been a rivalry, someone Mr. Sanders wanted to beat. She had not pulled that from thin air.

"Ms. Lott, that was nothing," Mr. Sanders said. "I said that every year to my classes to encourage them to perform at their highest level. We lost the contest before we ever walked onstage."

"How?" Had she done something to doom them?

"Oh, that girl. Beautiful voice. Can't remember her name, but she got sick—"

"Jamie McCorkle," she said automatically.

"That's it," he said, pointing at her. "I hope she went on to do something with that instrument of hers. You don't get many students who can sing like that, believe me. But when she got sick, we lost any chance we had. We weren't good enough. And you were . . . well, what I recall is that you were very earnest in wanting to help, but you didn't have a lot of talent. It was your hard work that led to you standing up there." He smiled, like she ought to be pleased with his assessment. "I felt a little sorry for you, to be honest. I put too much pressure on you. Kids get sick when they have a lot of anxiety."

She'd been filled to the top with anxiety. But he wasn't remembering correctly. "But my sister—"

"I don't know anything about a sister," he said, shaking his head.

How was that possible? Hadn't everyone seen Kristen and the guy? It had seemed to Lorna that they were moments away from an audience uproar over their antics. Had she imagined it? She couldn't have—she saw them making a scene. *But wait . . .* She'd been a pity backup singer? And he hadn't really cared how they did in the contest?

She was suddenly struck with the realization that he had not been harmed by her. He hadn't even *noticed* Kristen. For years she had lived with the shame of what she'd done to the one teacher she thought believed in her.

"If you need me to accept your apology, consider it accepted," he said. "Good to see you," he added, and turned as if to go.

"Lorna!" Bean said. "You have to make it up to him."

"What?" Mr. Sanders asked.

"He's right." Lorna nodded. "I came here to make amends. It's part of my . . . therapy," she said, uttering that word out loud for the first time. "I am addressing old wounds. For my sake, this time."

Mr. Sanders looked confused. He rubbed the nape of his neck. "This touchy-feely new age business baffles me."

"Me too, Mr. Sanders. I just know I need to do this. It's helping somehow." She couldn't explain how important it was to erase this mark from her slate. He might not have noticed Kristen, but she had, and she was certain she had not imagined what happened. "There must be something I can do for you."

"I can't think of—" Mr. Sanders suddenly stopped talking, then turned back to look at her. "Okay," he said.

"Okay!" she said, relieved. "What can I do?"

"Our youth group is putting on a musical this weekend. It's a fundraiser to send them to Guatemala to help build schools."

A worthy cause! That was precisely the sort of amends she wanted to make. *This* was the kind of thing she wanted to achieve. She'd do something noble to atone for what happened, to erase her mistake from the universe. She and Bean beamed at each other. "I can help," she said quickly, before Mr. Sanders changed his mind. She could man booths or hand out flyers along with the best of them.

"Well, good. Because my moneylender can't perform Friday night."

She nodded, awaiting her instructions.

"So I need a moneylender."

She was pretty sure he didn't mean she should literally lend money.

"It's only one line," Mr. Sanders continued. "You come in, sing the line, then the townspeople attack and kill you." He cast his arms out wide, as if it was the simplest thing in the world.

"They kill me?" Lorna repeated uncertainly.

"Sure. You're a hated moneylender."

"That's cool!" Bean said enthusiastically. "You get to *die*."

"There's a mattress to fall on if that's what you're worried about," Mr. Sanders said, and pointed to the back of the stage. There, under a black cloth, she could see a lump that she supposed was the mattress.

"Can I try?" Bean asked, already headed for the mattress.

"One of the kids' dads was set to play the moneylender, but he claims to have something for work on Friday that he has to attend," Mr. Sanders said, rolling his eyes. "I ask that they commit to the monthlong preparation and program—that's it. You wouldn't believe how many times they say, 'You bet, we'll be there,' and then bail at the last minute." He sighed. But then he looked at Lorna again. "Perfect. You solve all my problems."

"Lorna, watch me die!" Bean shouted, then threw himself onto the mattress with a guttural moan of death.

"See?" Mr. Sanders said. "Your kid gets it."

"Can I come?" Bean asked.

"Sure," Mr. Sanders said.

"Wait," Lorna said, panicking slightly. "There are only three days until Friday. I couldn't possibly learn the part. And you forget, I vomited the last time I was onstage."

"That was a long time ago. And the part is easy." He pivoted and walked to a piano at the corner of the stage. He played some basic chords and sang her line. "'I will lend you the money for your troubles, but you must return it doubled.' You sing the line, the kids attack, and you fall on the mattress. Easy. So?"

What could she say? She'd made her stand, had said how important making amends was to her. But just the thought of returning to a stage, of ruining his performance again, made her feel nauseous. She had not considered that her amends would involve something like this.

"Okay," she said weakly.

"Yay!" Bean said. "I'll help you practice!"

"You do that, young man," Mr. Sanders said. "Let's do a quick robe check on you, but I'm pretty sure it will fit." He walked briskly offstage, and while he was gone, Bean flung himself on the mattress again. Dissatisfied with that fall, he tried again. "You have to do it like this." He clutched his chest, shouted, "*Aaauuugh*," dramatically, and fell back on the mattress.

By the time Mr. Sanders returned with what was essentially a choir robe and a wig, Bean had died about ten times.

Bean chattered about the musical all the way home. He was terribly excited about her role. "You'll do really, really good if you practice," he assured her. "But make sure Aggie isn't sleeping on the bed when you do, because if you landed on her, you would smash her."

Lorna's belly was twisting with anxiety. She imagined walking on that stage and making a mess of the small role.

The next day at Bodhi, Lorna told Micah about Mr. Sanders and her return to the stage.

"This is amazing, Lorna," Micah said.

"How so? Back then he gave me a pity role and I didn't pick up on it. I'm not sure my apology tour is accomplishing anything other than pointing out what a fool I've been all these years."

"I think the bigger takeaway is that you were not responsible for the chaos in your life. You were not responsible for Kristen's actions, or Mr. Sanders's for that matter. You weren't even responsible for the nerves that made you sick. You did the best you knew how, and so did he. And you are both still doing that. So what have you learned about yourself so far in your journey?"

She thought about it. "That I'm a glutton for punishment?"

"Besides that."

"That maybe I wasn't as unlikable as I thought."

Micah grinned. "Anything else?"

She squirmed on her beanbag. She was wearing her one pair of shorts today, and her legs stuck to the vinyl. "That as I work on getting myself out of my bomb shelter, I need to practice giving myself some credit."

"You're doing great," Micah said, beaming. "You're changing, and that is excellent progress. Do you know how hard it is to change? You have to really want it." He leaned closer. "You really want it, Lorna Lott."

"Not so fast. I haven't gone onstage yet. What if I throw up again?"

Micah shrugged. "You'll clean it up, make your apologies, and go on with your life. But don't use that as a reason to close yourself off to the world. No one is perfect. No one expects anyone to be perfect. Except, well, you seem to expect it of yourself. So!" He clapped his hands together. "How was the vision-board process?"

Lorna groaned. "It's hard to imagine your ideal world when you haven't actually seen the world in a while. But I've got a house on my board. And pictures of Paris."

"Keep imagining your life after the bomb shelter. Now, are you ready for your float?"

She threw her head back with a long sigh. "Is it necessary?" The float, so to speak, involved her, naked, in a pod filled with a high concentration of salt water so she would float effortlessly, without sound or light, for an hour. Sensory-deprivation therapy during which she was supposedly going to gain clarity on her life.

"It is," Micah said. He stood, offering her a hand to help her up. "I hope you will dig a little deeper into your negative thoughts. Maybe start to think about the real reasons why you don't like yourself and whether they are fair reasons."

"Great! This ought to be totally relaxing. That should be your slogan for this program—focus on the negative."

"I think our current slogans are pretty good," he said, and walked to his office door and opened it, handing her off to Montreal.

At first, Lorna was too worried about who might walk in on her, floating naked in salt water with no lights or sound, to focus on her negative thoughts. But as the minutes ticked by in the tank—she imagined them ticking, as there was no sound but the screaming cacophony of her thoughts—she began to worry less about being found and more about why she didn't like herself.

She had always thought it was because she was not pretty in a conventional way, or because she didn't have a good girl's personality. Plus the many familial issues she was saddled with made her undesirable as a friend or a girlfriend. But even as those things had gone away over the years, she still found herself unbearable. *Why?* What had she ever done to deserve her own disdain? The only thing she knew with certainty was that there was no one who would be there just for her. No one. Well, except for Bean. But she felt immeasurable sorrow for the girl she'd been, who could count on no one, and the woman she'd become, who was so afraid to count on anyone for fear of being disappointed that she'd built a barrier so no one could even know her. Was *that* it? Was she so afraid to be vulnerable that she couldn't even face herself?

Whatever it was, it made her feel terribly sad in the dark space where there was no up or down.

She cried so much she was convinced the water level rose a bit. She cried until she felt there were no more tears in her body and no resources to manufacture more. She was going to count that as a win.

Chapter 22

Lorna Now

DESPITE ALL THE PRACTICE AND BEAN'S ENCOURAGEMENT, on the night of the musical, Lorna was nervous and still a little nauseated. Nothing like she'd been in high school, thank heaven. But she felt like she'd eaten something that didn't sit well with her.

Bean had come, of course. He'd insisted on it as her coach. Plus, he thought he might find a way to get a theater badge. Seth had come, too, much to Lorna's horror.

"You don't want to come to this," she tried to convince him. "It's just this dumb thing I have to do. Trust me when I say life is too short for you to be there."

"Really? It feels like life has been tedious lately and anything but short. I could use some entertainment. I haven't been out of the house on a Friday night in so long, I don't remember what it's like." He grinned.

But even with Bean in her corner, and Seth unfortunately looking on, Lorna felt terribly exposed. Like everyone in the audience (there weren't many, to be honest) had gone to high school the year of her Big Blow. Yet here she was. And Mr. Sanders did seem genuinely grateful.

Bean and Seth took seats in the front row, just like Kristen and that guy had years ago. She'd begged them to sit at the back and make a quick getaway to avoid the crowd.

"First of all, this is hardly a crowd," Seth replied. "And second, are you kidding? I've never known the star of the show."

"I am so not the star," Lorna scoffed.

"You are, Lorna!" Bean said proudly. "I want to sit in front so you can hear me clap."

Before the musical began, Mr. Sanders had her fall three times in quick succession to make sure she had it right, especially with little kids falling on top of her. The kids seemed to really like the idea of landing on her. She was already feeling a little beaten up come showtime.

When her time came, she stepped out onstage, looked at the back of the auditorium as Kristen had once instructed her to do, and sang her line. "'I will lend you the money for your troubles, but you must return it doubled.'" Her voice warbled, and she was pretty sure she wasn't even near the key—not that she could hear a key, with the blood of sheer panic rushing in her ears. But she managed to deliver the line without vomiting. She took two steps toward the mattress as she was supposed to do, but her foot caught on her robe and she stumbled, falling onto the stage just short of the mattress. And then the children threw all their acting chops along with their bodies on top of her. And *then* (and Mr. Sanders had failed to mention this) three parents performed a pratfall on her too. The worst part of it was that she saw Seth cringe when she went down with a thud, and Bean's fists raised victoriously in the air, as if all the training had paid off.

When the whole thing was done, Bean came out of his seat and clapped and cheered louder than anyone. Quite a bit louder. She wondered if there was a badge for training someone to fake a death in the badge catalog.

Seth and Bean met her at the door to the wings after the cast had taken its bows. Lorna smiled sheepishly. "That was one for the ages, I suppose. I am happy to announce I will not be pursuing a career in theater."

"You did great," Bean insisted, and looked at his dad.

"Yeah," Seth said immediately. "You were . . . different." He smiled.

Lorna laughed.

"You tried so hard," Bean added. "That's the important thing. You have to try your best really *hard*. Right, Dad?"

"Right, son." Seth was still smiling. "Lorna tried so hard I say we go for ice cream to celebrate."

"Yes!" Bean shouted. "I want sprinkles. Can I have sprinkles, Dad?"

"Let's ask Lorna," Seth said, and looked at her. "Is that an appropriate amount of sugar?"

"All I know is, I'm not going if there aren't sprinkles."

"Yay! See, Dad? Let's go!" Bean cried happily, grabbing Lorna's hand.

She listened to Bean list all the ice cream flavors he wanted to try as he pulled her along. She glanced over her shoulder at Seth, who was looking at them with such fondness she could feel it lighting up her chest. She, too, was smiling. She felt surprisingly light with these two.

But there was another, deeper feeling in her. Something was shifting. Opening. For the first time in her life, she sensed the real possibility of shedding the burden of her past.

Chapter 23

Lorna Now

IT WAS SETH'S IDEA TO MEET AT CENTRAL MARKET, WHERE they could get gelato and sit on the deck while Bean played on the massive playscape or chased ducks. Lorna met them there, and when she arrived, Bean was well into a cup of gelato, making field notes in his ever-present Driskill notebook. When he'd finished with his cup, he announced the gelato was a "twelve out of ten!" and then skipped off to the massive playscape.

"I don't know if he has figured out you can't really bake ice cream," Lorna remarked.

"We've gone well past the baking badge. He's so proud of his field notebook, he's making notes about everything," Seth said. He collected Bean's empty cup as Lorna dug into the chocolate gelato Seth had purchased for her. He'd insisted, said as she'd provided the entertainment, it was only fair that he provide the ice cream.

"I don't know," Lorna had said. "We're not really friends like that."

"Nonsense," Seth said easily. "We are friends exactly like that. And for real, Lorna, are you always so hard on everyone?"

"You know what? I think I am."

He laughed. "Okay, well, maybe try not to be so hard on me? Just accept that we are friends. Got it?"

"Got it." She was ridiculously pleased with this banter. It made her feel like a living, breathing woman. Not a King Kong.

When they were seated on the deck under the tree canopy, Seth said, "So Mr. Sanders was a teacher? The musical was good."

Lorna snorted with a mouthful of ice cream and said thickly, "No, it wasn't."

Seth grinned. "Yeah, I can't lie. It was subpar, and you were sort of terrible."

"Terrible!" she agreed. "Thank you for not trying to gaslight me."

"Oh, I don't think I could," Seth said. "Too many witnesses."

She laughed. She was amazed by it, this hearty laugh coming from her chest. She'd been crying for so long—this felt good.

"I am curious, however," Seth said. "What is this all about? I mean, really."

For a moment, Lorna was confused and thought he meant her reluctance to join the fight to save the house. "I just think it's really a house and not four shitty apartments."

"Not that," Seth said. "While I agree they are indeed four shitty apartments, I'm talking about the apology tour. I don't get it. And honestly, I guess I'm asking about your friendship with my son."

Lorna froze. The pleasure she'd just been feeling began to fade away. This was exactly what she'd feared, so why was she surprised he would find something wrong with her?

"Don't get me wrong," Seth said quickly. "I'm grateful for it. Bean misses his mother and he's lonely. He considers you and Aggie his friends. But it's different when you think of a grown woman hanging out with a kid she's not related to."

Lorna felt her soul curling into a ball. She put down her ice cream. Here is where he would tell her that it was too odd, that she couldn't hang out with Bean, that it just didn't make sense. She thought of the blue vest she'd ordered that had arrived today. Would he at least allow her to sew on the badges?

Seth's face crinkled into a frown. "I think I'm making a mess of this. I'm curious, that's all."

"No, no, I get it," Lorna said. "You're getting an ick vibe."

"No, that's not—"

"But Bean is the first friend I've had in a very long time." There, she said it.

"Oh." He looked even more alarmed now.

"I didn't mean that to sound like I'm sure it does. I just mean that Bean accepts me as I am. It's nice."

Seth's gaze shifted to the playground, and to Bean, who was organizing a small army of younger children. "I don't think there's anything strange going on, if that's what you think," he said. "I know my kid is pretty remarkable."

"He really is," Lorna said quietly. She wished she had words to explain that no one had been able to crack open her bomb shelter for years, but Bean had managed to do it without even trying. "As to what this is?" She thought of herself in the float tank and wondered if she ought to make herself more vulnerable. She didn't want to do anything that would cause her to lose Seth as a friend, and she didn't think she could bear to lose Bean as one. "I had some trauma early on in my life."

"I'm so sorry."

"My sister was an addict. Like, a *serious* addict. You know, the kind you see on documentaries about drug use in America."

"Wow," Seth said, clearly startled.

"Don't worry, she's in Florida and therefore unable to be a poor influence on anyone around here."

"I see." He relaxed a little. "Still, that sounds pretty heavy."

"It is. Or was. Most of my life, friends were not easy to come by. Or relationships, for that matter. I'd find someone who sort of got me, but then my family drama would creep in and make it unworkable. And then my mom got sick, and I had to take care of her and my sister, and, you know, life can be too much sometimes." *Stop talking. He'll think you're one big pity party if he doesn't already. No one wants to hear your tale of woe. No one wants to be friends with someone who has that kind of drama lurking in the background.* "Anyhoo!" She slapped her hands on her knees like she'd just said she was thinking of buying a car, or she had some work to do when she got home. No biggie.

But Seth's expression made her feel like he was seeing a lot more than she'd intended, and ever the one to close the door before anyone could see too much of her, she said, "In other words, a lot of stuff happened and now I'm kind of a loner, but I'm working on it. Like, working on getting out of my shell. Or in my case, a bomb shelter." *Ha ha ha, you're so funny, Lorna! For heaven's sake, shut UP.* But her mouth wouldn't stop. "Inside joke," she said. "I guess what I'm trying to say is that I have some unresolved issues."

"Right," Seth said. "The apology tour."

"Yes! And Bean has been my friend and helper. But I would never, you know, expose him to anything, like . . . *bad.*" She smiled, but she could tell it wasn't a real smile. It was a smile of worry, of fear. She couldn't peel her eyes from Seth, silently willing him not to take her friend. Silently begging him to still like her, to want to be her friend.

"I don't know," Seth said, wincing. "What about the musical?"

Lorna blinked. And then she laughed. She really *laughed*. "Correction—nothing as bad as that."

He leaned forward and put his hand on the table between them, almost as if he was reaching for her. "I can understand, in a way," he said. "Not like what you're talking about, but how addiction can affect a family."

"Really?" she asked.

"My wife, Jill, was addicted to exercise. Or maybe that's OCD, I'm not sure. But it was a problem."

Lorna didn't know what to say.

"I'm not trying to equate my wife to your sister. I'm just saying I understand what it's like to live in the shadow of someone else's obsession. It can take over everything. Especially everything that was good."

Hello. She had the insane urge to hug him right now. "Exactly," she said quietly. She'd never met anyone who knew the hell it was to live with an addict. She wasn't sure Seth truly knew either, but what mattered was that he understood her. Or was trying to. He was relating to her experience. And she liked that feeling.

She liked it so much.

"So can Bean still be my friend?" Lorna asked.

Seth frowned. "Are you kidding? He needs your friendship, Lorna. It's not like kids are lining up around the block to be his friend. I have to insist on it."

A warm, fizzy feeling shot through her. Her face cracked with what she could tell was one of those crazy, *too-too-much* smiles. But hearing him say Bean needed her had just blown out a few more windows in her internal bomb shelter, and sunlight was streaming in.

The talk turned to whatever it was Bean had organized the kids to do. Which turned out to be a choreographed show of sliding skills. A half hour later, Seth said it was time to go.

"Thanks for this," Lorna said.

Seth smiled and put his hand on her arm. "You're welcome. Bean and I are just happy to be a part of your tour." He moved his hand down to her elbow and gave it a soft squeeze before letting go.

She waved to them and got into her car. And then she headed in a different direction than her apartment.

When she arrived at Peggy's house, she could see the blue glow of the TV through the windows. She slapped the metal rooster on her way to the door... but it was a friendly slap, a *Pleased to see you* slap. The rooster didn't make her angry anymore.

Peggy opened the door in a robe and with curlers in her hair under an old-fashioned net. "I knew it was you," she said with much cheer.

"I'm sorry to come so late," Lorna said.

"Oh, that's all right, Lolo. I'm always happy to see you. Come in!"

Lorna stepped through the door and handed Peggy the crumpled church musical program.

Peggy frowned as she perused it. "You went to church?"

"Sort of. I was in Mr. Sanders's play. He was my choir teacher. You know, the choir concert—"

Peggy gasped with delight. "Of course I remember! From the list."

Lorna nodded. "My name isn't on the program because it was sort of last minute. But the point is, I apologized. And I made it up to him."

"Wonderful!" Peggy turned and went to her recliner. On the end table next to it was a notebook, which she picked up, opened, and made a mark in. "That's two. Only three to go!"

"Three?" Lorna frowned, trying to remember.

Peggy looked at her notes. "I have the boyfriend, Mrs. Tracy, and Mr. Cho."

The boyfriend. She'd forgotten about Brett Miller. She'd forgotten she'd told her mother about Brett.

"And then you're done!" Peggy chirped. "I can release the trust to you."

"Yes." Lorna tucked her hair behind her ear. Funny, she did not feel excited by the prospect of having the money she needed to buy Nana's house. She felt a bit ambivalent about it. That trust . . . something felt very wonky about it.

Maybe it was because there was an unanswered call sitting on her phone from Mr. Contreras. He'd phoned yesterday, but she and Bean had been practicing her fall, and she hadn't called him back. She had a good idea what he wanted—he struck her as the kind of guy who, once he had some sort of deal, was relentless. She didn't understand why she felt so reluctant to call him.

Maybe it was because she didn't want to hurt Seth and Bean, and she could feel that coming.

Chapter 24

Lorna Now

"HEY THERE, BIG SPENDER," MR. CONTRERAS SAID THE NEXT morning when Lorna made herself return his call. "How's that offer coming along? I got a developer knocking at my door."

Already? "It's coming, Mr. Contreras."

"Yeah, this guy, he's going to raze the house and build an eight-unit condo complex. He can make bank with that."

A spark of rage shot through Lorna. She couldn't trust the man to tell her the truth. "There's not enough room for that on this lot."

"Sure there is. You squeeze them in and up. But if you don't like that idea, get me that offer, sweetheart."

She hated that he called her that. He seemed to delight in making her uneasy. "You will have it," she said firmly.

"When?"

She glanced at the clock, as if that would tell her anything. She would just have to speed up her apology tour. "Two weeks," she said.

"Sooner's better," he said, and hung up.

Jerk. Lorna looked at the codicil list. Mr. Cho, her first employer, was next. He'd owned Cho's Drugstore, where Lorna had worked when she was seventeen. Brett Miller was listed after that, but those two regrets had technically happened at the same time. She figured Mr. Cho was the more complicated apology for a lot of reasons, and Brett was . . . Well, Brett was the easy one.

In Lorna's junior year of high school, she'd had her first boyfriend. Not Brett. If she was being honest, she probably wouldn't have looked at Brett had it not been for Luke Brown. Luke was her first love, the senior Lorna believed would be the last guy in all of Austin to fall for her. She was as tall as he was. She was not popular and was considered too brusque by some. Luke had blond hair, a dimpled smile, and a baseball physique. All the girls drooled around him.

"He's totally into you," Lorna's friend Mariah had whispered one day, her voice full of surprise.

"Why me?" Lorna had asked nervously, not knowing what to do with this information. It defied all teenage logic. But Mariah was right—Luke kept coming around and flirting, suggesting they go to her house after school.

It hardly took any persuading for her to take him home. She reasoned it was safe enough—the house was big, and the chances of him running into Nana were almost nonexistent since she rarely left her rooms those days. Mom was working. Kristen had been recently discharged from county jail, which she'd been sentenced to for public intoxication, but was rarely home. And when she was, she kept to her room.

Or so Lorna had thought. Because Kristen did manage to slink around when Luke was with her, sliding into a room like a cat. She liked to make fun of the "lovebirds" or tell Luke he should comb his hair. Luke would say she should comb her hair (he was not the best with clapbacks), and they would continue to banter back and forth until Kristen slid out again, on her way to a job or to meet yet another guy.

In the heady three months that Lorna and Luke were an "item" (at least according to Mariah), Lorna believed things were finally turning around for her. While it was true Luke avoided her at school—he said he had to hang out with his friends or they'd be mad—he came to her house almost every day. In her mind, that made him her boyfriend. That year, she had Luke, she got a job at Cho's Drugstore, and she made the volleyball team. All was right with her world.

But then Nana died. They found her in her chair, stone-cold, an unopened bottle of vodka at her feet.

"Wow," Kristen had said, her voice full of shock. "She died before she got to drink it." Only Kristen would see that as the tragedy.

After Nana's death, which was probably more shocking than it should have been, given her health trajectory, Lorna had moved in something of a fog. She went to school, went to work, laughed with friends, hung out with Luke, pretended like nothing had happened. In a way, it felt like nothing had happened. She'd mourned the loss of Nana long before her death—in the last two years of Nana's life, she was usually too drunk to be present for her grandchildren.

Lorna tended to stay away from home when Luke wasn't there, and especially when Kristen was around, because Kristen and Mom still argued all the time.

Kristen took Nana's death the hardest. Lorna remembered Kristen cleaning out the front salon for the memorial. She vacuumed and polished the furniture and brought in flowers and displayed framed pictures of Nana as a young woman and a young wife. There were other pictures, too, photos of the family from a happier time. Kristen, Lorna, and Nana under the oak tree in the backyard. Kristen and Lorna doing gymnastics on the lawn while Nana proudly looked on. Mom, Nana,

Kristen, and Lorna arranged on the stairs, dressed in their Easter finery. The four of them again, but with Dad, too, gathered for Christmas around a dining table that was groaning with ham, potatoes, cranberries, and green bean casserole. Lorna as a toddler being held by Nana and beaming up at Kristen.

The house had filled with people paying their respects. Lorna didn't know any of them—most seemed to be people who had known Nana when she was a university man's wife, or people who knew Lorna's mother. Lorna had stood stiffly as people passed her by and commented, "My, you're tall, aren't you?" and "So sorry for your loss, young lady," and "Where is your sister? She was so pretty."

Where *was* her sister? The question had eventually penetrated Lorna's brain fog, and she'd gone in search of poor, grieving Kristen.

She found her, all right, and in so doing, the occasion of Nana's death became known as the time Lorna discovered that Luke had used her. Because there he and Kristen were, making out in Kristen's room, the smell of pot so thick it was a wonder the entire bereavement party hadn't come upstairs to investigate. It became apparent, in the arguing that followed over the next few days, that not only had Luke used Lorna to get to Kristen, but Kristen had allowed it.

"I didn't even like him," Kristen insisted one day when she had Lorna wrapped in a bear hug, trying to make her listen. "He's a dick, Lolo, no good for you and no great loss, okay?"

Except that it was a great loss to Lorna. Of her first boyfriend, of her pride, and even of the naive belief that people were who they showed you they were. It wasn't up to Kristen to decide that for her. "If you didn't like him, then why did you do it?"

Kristen let go of Lorna. She shrugged and looked away. "He had money to get some weed," she said simply.

That was it. Money for weed was all it took for Kristen to betray her.

The pain had been terrible. Gut-wrenching. Lorna hated Luke for what he'd done. But she owed an apology to Brett Miller, who had come after Luke.

Brett was a guy who was even lower on the school social ladder than she was. He had a weird sense of humor that was off-putting to other kids. But he seemed to truly like Lorna. And she had strung him along, pretending she liked him, then treating him poorly, inventing hoops just for the sake of watching him jump through them, then taking him back. She'd kept that up until the shame she felt for treating him the same way Kristen had treated Luke drowned out her shame for having been used by Luke and betrayed by her sister. The feeling of control she'd craved had not come without harm. So she dumped him.

Brett had seemed crushed, because Brett was a nice guy.

She owed him an apology. She was not a mean person, contrary to what they said at Driskill.

One morning she googled Brett and found he was the owner of Miller Tire Barn in nearby Round Rock.

Lorna called the number listed on the website and asked for Brett. The woman who answered told her he'd be in at noon. "That ulcer is acting up again, so he's at the doctor's."

At half past noon, Lorna walked into the front lobby of Miller Tire Barn. Through a glass door she could see the auto bay and cars up on risers. Tires were stacked in and around the bay, and the scent of rubber and grease was heavy. There seemed to be a coat of dust on everything. Lorna glimpsed a woman's head behind the counter. "Excuse me . . . may I speak to Brett?"

The woman behind the counter hardly looked up. "Brett! Customer wants to see you!" she shouted.

A moment later, a man with a paunch, wearing a sweat-stained shirt emblazoned with the Miller Tire Barn logo, walked out of a back office. He was smiling, wiping his hands on a paper towel, like she'd caught him in the middle of lunch. "How can I help you?" he asked, but the moment the words had left his lips, the spark of recognition shone in his eyes. "*Lorna?*"

"Yep. It's me," she said nervously, and gave him a nerdy little wave. "Hi, Brett."

He tossed the paper towel aside and came forward, his hand extended to shake. "How the heck are you?" She reluctantly took it, noticing his wedding ring. He was grinning, still the happy galumph he'd been in high school, only bigger.

"I'm okay. How about you?"

"Doing good." He looked past her, presumably for her car. "You need tires?"

"No, I came here hoping to talk to you."

"Oh. Why?" He let out a laugh. "We don't have a love child out there, do we?"

Lorna was so startled she gaped.

"Kidding," he said.

The woman behind the counter was suddenly all ears. Brett noticed her interest too. "Just joking around, Teresa. This is Lorna. She was the love of my life."

Lorna's mouth dropped even more.

"Kidding!" he said again.

"Still a jokester," she said, pressing a hand to her belly. "Maybe we can go in your office?"

"What's the matter?" Brett asked, sobering. "Did someone die? Was it John Turweiler? I heard he had cancer or something."

"No. I mean, I don't know anything about John. I don't know anyone who has died. This will be quick—nothing bad."

Brett looked over his shoulder into his office. "I guess. It's kind of a mess."

"Kind of?" Teresa muttered.

"Come on," Brett said, and ushered Lorna into the office.

He moved some papers off a red leather chair and gestured for her to sit. Lorna didn't want to sit on that chair, but she also didn't want to be rude. She perched on the edge of it. Brett leaned against a desk that was stacked with even more papers, a small tire, some framed photos that faced away from Lorna, several used coffee cups, and some tubing. The room smelled of sweat, coffee, and rubber.

"What's going on?" Brett asked. "I feel like I'm about to be punked."

"No, it's nothing like that. I came to apologize for the way I treated you."

Brett said nothing, but he frowned uncertainly. "Okay." He rubbed his chin. It looked like the gesture of a man who was trying to recall.

"Do you remember?"

"Oh, I remember all of it," he said. "You really hurt my feelings."

Lorna swallowed. She knew she had, but to hear him say it made her feel queasy. "I'm really sorry, Brett."

"Are you?"

"Yes. That's why I'm here—I'm trying to understand things about myself, about why I did things."

"That was a long time ago."

"I know," she said. "But you didn't deserve that. I used you."

He snorted derisively. "Yeah, I got that," he said impatiently. "But why? I really liked you."

Lorna's queasiness turned to acid. "The why was my sister. She and Luke Brown betrayed me in the worst way, and I was lashing out. At least that's what I think I was doing. I'm so, so sorry, Brett. I was awful to you."

He looked at her a moment, then shifted his gaze to his feet, crossed before him. "I hope you're sorry, because you ruined my life. You're the reason I'm selling tires instead of doing something like accounting."

Lorna's heart skipped a beat. "What?"

"You broke my heart, Lorna. I couldn't get it together to apply for college. Hell, I couldn't even make myself get a job after high school. I had no confidence."

"Oh my God." She felt sick. "Brett, I—"

He suddenly laughed. "Just kidding."

Lorna's anger gauge began to flicker. She had come here with a sincere apology. Maybe it wasn't fair of her to expect him to take it, but he didn't have to make her feel worse than she did.

Brett's smile faded as he studied her. "Come on, it was a joke. Don't you remember how I used to tease you back then? You used to be so much fun."

And just like that, the anger left her. She'd been fun? "No one has ever told me that."

"Seriously? You were a lot of fun. We laughed all the time. Why do you think I had such a crush on you?"

She smiled sheepishly. "I've been trying to figure that out."

"So, whatever happened to Kristen, anyway? I saw her once, you know. I got popped for a DUI in Georgetown, and there she was in court with the female inmates. She kind of waved at me. I mean, as much as she could, because she was shackled. But she acknowledged me. I was surprised she remembered me." He seemed pleased that she had.

"She's in Florida now."

"Awesome. Don't take this the wrong way, but I'm kind of surprised she's not dead. She was one risky chick."

"I'm surprised too," Lorna said. "So listen, Brett. I'd love to make it up to you somehow."

"What, like a twelve-step program?"

"Not exactly, but—"

"If you really want to make it up to me, I guess we could bang it out."

Lorna's mouth gaped again. That was decidedly not what she had in mind. "I don't know if—"

"Kidding!" He laughed uproariously at her shock. "Girl, I'm married."

She inwardly breathed a sigh of relief. Because she wasn't sure what she would have done had he insisted. "There must be something I can do."

It happened that Brett did have an idea for how she could make her amends. She left with a new set of tires. When they were installed, he walked her out to her car. "Who are you going to apologize to now?"

"Mr. Cho."

"The pharmacy dude? We used to get milkshakes there, remember?"

"I do," she said, and smiled fondly at the memory. "Take care of yourself, Brett."

"You too, Lorna." He turned and walked back to the lobby of Miller's Tire Barn.

And Lorna drove to Peggy's house with her receipt for new tires.

Chapter 25

Lorna Is Seventeen

MR. CHO IS THE FIRST PERSON TO TRUST LORNA TO DO A job. She applied for dozens before he hired her, and she has worked for him for six months now. She comes in after school and always asks for weekend shifts. The more she is at work, and not at home, the better.

Mr. Cho likes an industrious student. He is half her size and thin as a pencil. He has a loyal fan base for his eclectic Cho's Drugstore. It has everything—it's a pharmacy but also a kids' toy store, a hardware store, and a bookstore. The crown jewel is the soda fountain with the Formica bar top and the five red leather stools mounted to the ground. Mr. Cho allows all employees to have an ice cream cone at the end of their shift.

Lorna loves working here. She loves the people who come in every day. She loves stocking shelves (it's oddly satisfying to see a tidy row of products). She mostly loves chatting with Mr. Cho. He is an immigrant, and he says he came to America with only ten dollars in his pocket. He gives her life advice: Obey all traffic laws. Always be kind. Don't let others create expectations for your life, because this is the only life you'll have. Work hard and play hard. Always leave some money in the bank.

He likes to ask her about her future. Where will she go to college? What will she study? He seems genuinely interested in her when Lorna can't seem to interest anyone at home.

But then again, there is only her mother and sister to be interested now, and how could they find the time? Kristen has been in and out of treatment. The last go was bookended by two arrests, one for possession of marijuana and the other for vandalism. She is sober now, having promised Lorna once again that she has stopped for good. She is working in a fast-food chicken restaurant and comes home from her shift smelling like fried chicken. Lorna thinks Kristen has worked at every fast-food joint in town.

Mom's office administration job pays for Kristen's bail and court fines. When she's not working, she is arguing with Kristen. Mom thinks Kristen should go back to school. Kristen has only a GED, and Mom says she'll never have a life outside of minimum-wage jobs without a better education.

"Maybe I will go back," Kristen says. "I always wanted to be a lawyer."

News to Lorna. Kristen has wanted to be, in no particular order, a dancer, an actor, a movie director, a teacher, a police officer.

"Are you ridiculing me with that?" Mom asks. She looks tired all the time now. Dark circles are a permanent part of her eyes.

"How is that ridicule?" Kristen asks.

"Because you will never be a lawyer, Kristen. You have to have a college degree for that, a law degree—"

"So what? That's what I want to do!" Kristen shouts.

"Stop it," Mom snaps. "Just go get a trade certificate so you at least make enough to live on your own."

Kristen digs in. Kristen always digs in. "No thanks. I think I'll stick to chicken. You obviously don't think I'm capable of much else."

"Well, are you? Because the only thing I've ever seen you determined to do is get high. You sure don't help with any bills around here."

"How am I supposed to do that with a minimum-wage job?"

And round they go.

Mr. Cho fills a void in Lorna—he is the parent she wishes she had. He encourages her, and he applauds her. He gave her a full week off with pay when Nana died. When she came back to work, he had convinced the other staff to chip in and buy her flowers. She put them on the small bar behind the soda counter and grinned at them all day.

It's not long before Mr. Cho begins to trust Lorna to close up at night. After he's finished all the accounting and paperwork, he leaves Lorna to sweep the floors and restock the toilet paper in the bathrooms and put items abandoned at the cashier counter back where they belong. She clocks out on her own and leaves through the front door, always careful to lock it. If she ever forgets, Mr. Cho says, she should not worry. He has a camera and his daughter, Candy, lives two blocks away. She monitors it. If Lorna ever needs anything, Candy will be there within a few minutes.

One night when Lorna is working late, Mom sends Kristen to pick her up. Kristen has been hanging around Lorna lately. She says she is "totally sober" and "totally bored." Lorna knows enough to know that "sober" and "not using" are two different things to Kristen, and while she believes Kristen when she says she isn't using—she always wants to believe her—she doesn't know if she's truly sober. That is, if she's truly committed to it.

But Kristen does seem different to Lorna. More like the Kristen of old, the sister she laughed with, who would fix her hair, who would help her choose the right clothes to wear. "You would dress like a caveman if I weren't here to help you," Kristen likes to say.

Lorna thinks she's probably right.

They talk about work and the people they work with. They make up superlatives for them. "Most Likely to Marry for Money," Kristen says of a coworker. "Most Likely to Call Off Work," Lorna says of her coworker. They giggle over TV dinners and choose more superlatives for everyone on the street.

Lorna enjoys Kristen's company again. It feels like it has been forever since they were just sisters without extenuating issues, and they fall easily into the habit of being together.

Kristen has been on her best behavior, coming home after work, not disappearing. Even trying to get along with Mom.

Mr. Cho has a rule that no friends are allowed in the store after hours, but he never said anything about sisters. Kristen sits on a red stool, twirling around, talking on the phone to someone about her favorite ice cream flavors while Lorna sweeps. When Lorna goes into the bathrooms to replenish the toilet paper, she can hear Kristen still talking to someone, and when she comes out, Kristen is still on the red stool. "Let's drive through Whataburger," she says. "I'm starving."

"Okay," Lorna says. "I just have to clock out and turn off the lights." She makes one last sweep of the aisles and goes to the back and clocks out, then turns out the lights as she heads to the front glass doors. Kristen trails behind her. But as Lorna reaches the door, she sees someone walking up. It's a police officer.

"Shit," Kristen says. "Are there cameras?"

"What?" Lorna asks, confused by her question.

Kristen bumps into her, knocking against her purse. She grabs Lorna's arm and squeezes. "Listen, Lolo, if they pop me, I'll go back to jail. I'll lose my probation. You're a minor."

"*What?*" Lorna's brain is not working, other than to sound alarms. She can't understand why the cop is reaching for the door, gesturing for her to open it, or why Kristen is talking about jail.

"Just be cool," Kristen says.

Lorna opens the door and the cop walks in. She sees two more cops walking up to the door behind him. "What's wrong?" she asks.

"You tell me," the cop says. "Empty the contents of your purses. Both of you."

Lorna does, of course, because she is a rule follower. She dumps everything right there on the checkout counter. And then everything happens so fast. She watches with amazement as makeup and jewelry with tags on them spill out of her purse.

"Oh my God, Lorna. What were you thinking?" Kristen says behind her. Nothing falls out of Kristen's purse but some cigarettes and some wadded-up dollar bills.

"Wait," Lorna says, trying desperately to make sense of this. But by the time she pieces it together, the cuffs are on her and she's been arrested for shoplifting.

Later, she is released on her own recognizance, and Kristen is waiting for her on the street, smoking a cigarette. When she sees Lorna, she drops it and grinds it out with her heel. "Don't be mad," she says, reaching for Lorna. "I could have done time for that."

Lorna twists out of her reach. She is in such a full-on rage she can't even speak.

"It's not that big of a deal," Kristen says. "When you turn eighteen, it will fall off your record. No one cares—everyone shoplifts as a teen."

"No, Kristen, not everyone," Lorna bites out, her voice shaking. "And I care. *I* care, Kristen!"

It is a huge deal, of course. Lorna is fired from her job by a very weary-looking Mr. Cho. His daughter had called the police after seeing something on the camera. Lorna tries to explain she didn't do it, but the camera angle was not great, and the items were in her purse. She is kicked off the volleyball team before the tournament season even begins. She is assessed fines, which means all the money she has saved working is now going to a court.

At home, Kristen is contrite and keeps reminding Lorna that it could have been worse, that it was just a Class C misdemeanor, which will fall off her record when she turns eighteen. When Lorna does not tell Kristen it's okay, it's fine, Kristen gets angry. "This is no big deal, Lorna," she snaps. "It's only a problem because *you* are making it a problem."

Lorna is stunned. "Are you kidding me right now? I let down the one person in my life who believes in me."

"Who?" Kristen asks. "Mom? Believe me, she thinks her precious Lolo can do no harm."

"Not Mom. Mr. Cho."

Kristen rolls her eyes. "Dramatic much?"

"You are unbelievable," Lorna says, and she goes to her room and slams the door. And then she does something she has never done in her whole life: She puts her fist through the Sheetrock and breaks her little finger in the process.

Chapter 26

Lorna Now

ONE LATE AFTERNOON WHEN SETH RETURNED FROM WORK, he found Lorna in the backyard with Bean and Aggie. She was sewing Bean's accomplishment badges crookedly onto the blue vest she'd ordered. Bean and Aggie were working on the hole, making it bigger for a reason that Bean had explained in detail, but Lorna had lost the thread of his logic. Remarkably, she didn't care. She cared only that Seth had come out to join her, putting his hand on her shoulder as he moved past her to take a seat.

They sat on the steps outside the main back door, the length of their legs touching. "Those look familiar," he said, nodding at the vest. "Unless you've been earning badges, those must be Bean's."

"I hope you don't mind," Lorna said. "It just seemed like a real need. The only problem is that I'm not very good at sewing." She held it up and showed him. Some of the badges were crooked. Some were not.

Seth studied it a moment. "I think you're amazing at sewing, Lorna, and far better than me. Thank you."

"No need," she said crisply. "It's my pleasure." Surprisingly, it did give her pleasure. She could think of nothing more worthwhile to do with her time.

Bean had been arranging her Precious Moments figurines into different villages. Each village had its own rules for entrance. If a figurine couldn't meet the requirements, it was put in a box until Bean could decide what to do with it. His method had the surprising effect of clearing out her apartment. Which was a good thing, as her apartment had looked more like a museum of broken dreams than a home. She at least owed him the vest.

"I have a question for you," she said to Seth.

"Shoot."

"I'd like to take Bean to visit Cho's Drugstore. I worked there as a teen."

"Mm," Seth said. "Apology tour?"

"Yep."

"What did you do there?"

"I mostly stocked and swept. But sometimes I was lucky enough to get to make ice cream cones when it was busy. The ice cream there is amazing. So are the baked goods. I thought I might treat Bean to homemade pecan pie, if that's okay with you. You know, for his fieldwork. I'm not sure I'm the person to help him bake a whole pie if he chooses that, but he should at least know about the option, right?"

Seth frowned. "I don't know . . . sounds like a lot of sugar. Tell you what—I'll allow it if you will allow me to treat you and Bean to pizza. Strictly to counterbalance the sugar with cheese, you understand."

Lorna grinned. "A proven scientific fact. But, as you know, I'm not very social."

"Not at all," he agreed.

"So, it would be kind of hard for me to just, like, take a slice of pizza."

"Sorry, that's the deal. You want Bean as a ride along, you need to commit to pizza."

Lorna's smile widened a little. Was this flirting? It felt a little like flirting. "Wow. Well, the pecan pie at Cho's is amazing, so . . . I guess I will make the sacrifice."

Seth grinned. "Thank you for your service." He nudged her shoulder with his, and when she glanced up, he was smiling at her. Their gazes held for a long moment, until Lorna could feel her blush turning hot.

She was the first to look away, of course, because she was a pansy. But she was feeling less cowardly every day. They sat companionably for another hour or so, watching Bean and Aggie play and talking about little things. This and that. Nothing important, just . . . talk. Lorna knew this sort of activity existed, the sharing of one's daily thoughts with a friend. She couldn't say she'd ever actually experienced it. But that early fall evening, she did. She felt relaxed. She felt social and, dare she think it, likable.

She felt like a person, a woman, capable of having friends, of being less awkward. She didn't think once about her hair or what she was wearing, or fret about every word that came out of her mouth.

That's what she told Micah the next day.

"Wow," Micah said, nodding solemnly. "This is amazing, Lorna. I hope you appreciate how much you are opening yourself up and how far you've come. Everything starts with a little introspection, and then a release of negativity, and then, before you know it, you are living in the moment and not in the past."

"I don't actually live in the past; I live in a bomb shelter," Lorna corrected him.

"Ta-may-toe, ta-mah-toe, the past," Micah said breezily. "Now the trick is to keep opening yourself up. You've got more work to do on your vision board," he said, consulting his notes. "And we'd like to get you started on body meridian work this week."

"Body what?"

Micah sighed. "Do you ever read the materials I send home with you?"

"No."

"We're going to do a little acupuncture and release some of the good chi in you. And then we'll talk about attainable goals for beyond your wellness sabbatical. Sound good?"

"You know . . . it kind of does," Lorna admitted.

Micah grinned. "Montreal will take you to the studio for your body meridian assessment." He rang a little bell, and the next moment, Montreal entered the office.

Lorna hopped out of the beanbag—wearing appropriate clothing to Bodhi did seem to help her mobility—said goodbye to Micah, and followed Montreal out. "Have you ever done acupuncture, Montreal?"

"Many times," he said cheerfully.

"For what?"

"Anxiety. Same as you." He smiled at her. "I see that you braided your hair today."

"So?"

"So, first came the yoga pants. Then the braid instead of the bun. I don't know, Lorna, I think you're loosening up and letting go. After this assessment, I predict you will really let go."

"That sounds ominous."

"My advice? Go with the flow," Montreal said, and practically shoved her into the body meridian studio.

The "assessment" was conducted by an overweight woman

with gray hair who remained mostly silent as she probed Lorna's body through a thin cotton robe. When she'd finished probing, she made several notes, then announced, without preamble, "You have a lot of bad energy."

"I do?"

"You're very tense," she said with a grimace. "It will require a *lot* of needles."

"I don't think I like that," Lorna said, alarmed.

"You'll be fine. Sign here, here, and here," the woman added, pointing to three places on the white iPad.

Lorna hesitated.

"Sign," the woman said firmly. "Trust me, you need this treatment."

"Okay, fine," Lorna said. She signed with the rubber-tipped pen.

Every time the woman—Sarah, she finally said—inserted a needle, Lorna yelped. Sarah was right. She was tense. And every time Lorna yelped, Sarah sighed as if she was being intentionally squeamish. Lorna fully intended to report her to Montreal for being less than sympathetic about this treatment.

But forty-five minutes later, when Montreal came to get her for her vision boarding, Lorna felt as easy and free as the wind. "How was it?" he asked.

Lorna laughed at the question.

Montreal's brows rose with surprise. "We have a winner," he said.

"We're all winners, Montreal."

"Okay," he said. "This is a new side of you. She wasn't serving drinks in there, was she?"

Lorna laughed again.

Amazingly, by the time she made it home, she was still feeling light and breezy. Like something heavy had been lifted from her. She wasn't entirely sure where the lightness came from, but honestly, she didn't care. The feeling was too good to question.

She walked Aggie around the block and then tossed a ball for her until Bean came home. She told him where they were going, emphasizing the pecan pie.

But Bean was confused. "Was the drugstore mad at you?" He was moving some Precious Moments figurines to their correct villages.

"Not the store, but the owner, Mr. Cho, was. Unfortunately, he died."

Bean's eyes widened. "Was he murdered?"

"Murdered! No, it was a heart attack or something. Why do you go straight to murder?"

Bean shrugged. "But if he's dead, how are you going to apologize?"

"I'm going to apologize to his daughter. She runs the drugstore now." Or she had, the last Lorna heard.

Bean frowned. "Does that count? Maybe you could apologize to his ghost." He gasped. "What if he's a ghost? Ja-nay's grandmother is a ghost, and she haunts their house!"

"Yikes. I think I would move."

"I'd make friends with a ghost. Is his daughter mad at you too?"

"Well, she was. I don't think she likes me much."

"Yeah," Bean said, nodding, as if that was a given. He was a quick learner.

"But I'm still going to apologize. And get some pecan pie while we're at it."

"Okay," Bean said. "I have to go to my room and get my compass." But he paused on his way there and turned back. "What did you do?"

"Huh?"

"What is your apology for?"

"Oh. That." Lorna bit her lip. She didn't want Bean to be disappointed in her. "It's sort of a long story. I'll tell you on the way."

"Okay!"

When Bean had his compass, his ranger backpack with necessary supplies, and his new addition—an explorer's hat—they gave Aggie a chew stick and set off for the fifteen-minute ride across town. As she drove, Lorna filled him in on the night her sister took some things that didn't belong to her and put them in Lorna's purse. She didn't get to the part where she was arrested, because Bean had a lot of questions about what she'd taken and why she didn't give everything back. "My dad says if you do something wrong, you should try and make it right. And if you take something that doesn't belong to you, you should give it back."

"Your dad is . . ." Lorna didn't finish her thought. She lost the thought altogether when she realized Cho's Drugstore was not where it should have been.

She was confused—in the place where Mr. Cho's had stood was a massive construction project. It looked like a high-rise was going up. "*What?*" she murmured and scrambled out of the car, staring over the hood at the spot where the drugstore had stood. She could feel the old familiar thrum of rage. Would she be denied her quest because she had waited too long to make amends? How could this have happened? How could she not have known this? How would she apologize now?

Bean got out the other side of the car and tilted his head toward the sky, his explorer hat sliding off and onto his back. He had a disposable camera and took a picture. "It's really tall," he said. "Where is the drugstore?"

"That's what I'd like to know," Lorna said through gritted teeth.

"But . . . what about the pie?"

"Exactly," Lorna said. "What about the pie?" She glared at the construction.

"That lady is waving at us." Lorna followed Bean's pointed finger. There was indeed a woman in a hard hat waving at them. In one hand, she held a clipboard. The other was free to wave them away. She began to advance toward them, teetering on very high heels. Lorna was no sartorial expert, but she couldn't imagine the thought process that would bring any woman to this construction site in high heels. Until the woman came closer, which was when Lorna understood. Well, she still didn't know why the heels, but she knew who was wearing them. That was Candy Cho.

"Get out!" Candy shouted at them.

"Candy! It's me, Lorna Lott!" Lorna said, coming around the front of her car.

"Get out! You're trespassing! You're not welcome here. Don't you see the sign? No trespassing!"

"But she came to say she was sorry," Bean said.

Candy drew up short and stared down at Bean. "Who the hell are you?"

"Hey," Lorna said.

"I'm her friend," Bean said, unperturbed.

"Hold on," Lorna said, putting herself between Bean and Candy. Her anger was ratcheting, pushing against all the light-and-breezy feelings she'd been having lately.

"Why are you here, wasting my time?" Candy demanded of Lorna.

She'd forgotten that Candy was a bit of a ballbuster. "He's right. I came to say I'm sorry."

"Sorry! For breaking my father's heart?"

"Yes. Exactly that."

"You broke his heart?" Bean asked, sounding distressed.

Candy scoffed at that. "She stole from him, that's what she did, and got arrested for it."

Bean gasped.

"Okay, Candy," Lorna said, a little breathlessly. "It was a long time ago. How long are you going to hold the grudge?"

"As long as I want," she snapped. "My father loved you and you betrayed him, and he's not here to tell you himself."

"Well, I loved him too, and I didn't betray him. I told you then and I'll tell you now—I didn't know my sister had stolen anything. I was devastated she had. Can you at least hear me out?"

"No," Candy said. "Now get off my property."

"But she hasn't apologized yet," Bean said, frantic.

"Please let me apologize," Lorna added. "I'm sorry for what happened, Candy."

Candy laughed. "Apology not accepted. What is the point after all this time? You should have come before Dad died. Go away and leave us alone, Lorna. If you don't, I'm calling the cops again." She turned on her wobbly heels and hobbled off. Only then did Lorna notice the sign: Cho Construction.

Lorna was dejected. She'd tried, and that was all she could do. But her effort didn't feel right this time. It didn't feel like enough. "Come on, Bean," she said.

She and Bean were back in the car, and she was staring straight ahead, her mind whirling. The apologies felt so imperative now. How did she walk away from this? Damn it, she felt wetness on her cheeks. She hadn't cried since float therapy.

"Did you really get arrested?" Bean asked in a whisper.

Bean. She had to pull herself together for his sake. She used the tips of her fingers to swipe the tears from her face. The rage—or sadness (which one was it? It was so hard to tell them apart now)—would consume her if she let it. "Yes."

Bean reached into his backpack and pulled out a tissue. He twisted in his seat and pressed it into her hand. "Did you go to *prison*? Did you try and break out?"

"No and no. I had to pay a fine and do some community service. I had to help clean up some roadways for a while." She looked out the window at Candy, who was back with two men in hard hats, one holding blueprints. "I don't know what to do, Bean."

"You apologized, though," he said.

"But she didn't accept it."

"But she's not Mr. Cho."

"Mr. Cho is dead. How do I make amends if she won't let me?"

"Maybe Mr. Cho's ghost will let you," Bean suggested. "Sometimes Dad tells me to think of what Mommy would say. What would Mr. Cho say?"

Lorna blinked. This kid, with his earnest little face, sitting here with his explorer hat crookedly perched on his head, was brilliant. "Are you sure you're not some AI creation?"

"Huh?"

"Lemme think," she said, rubbing her temples. "Mr. Cho was very giving. He would probably tell me I didn't need to make amends, and then I would insist, and then he would say, 'Well, if you feel you need to do something, you should do something kind for someone else.'" A thought clicked into place. "The soup kitchen!"

"Yay!" Bean cried.

"He went every Sunday morning to the one on Cesar Chavez and helped hand out meals. I could do that. I could make amends by doing community service in his honor."

"I could get my community service badge!" Bean said.

"Oh. We'll have to ask your dad about that." She imagined Seth might draw the line at a soup kitchen.

"Okay," Bean said agreeably. "Hey, what about pecan pie?"

"Hmm . . . The pie at Cho's Drugstore was the best, but I know a close second." They drove to Upper Crust Bakery where she bought an entire pecan pie for them to try at home.

Chapter 27

Lorna Now

THEY ARRIVED BACK AT THE APARTMENTS AT THE SAME TIME as Seth, who was reaching into the bed of his truck. He withdrew a stack of pizza boxes and waited for Lorna and Bean to get out of her car. "I'm getting a community service badge!" Bean shouted as he raced ahead. "Can I let Aggie out?" He was already inside before Lorna could answer.

Lorna eyed Seth's pizza boxes. "Are you hungry? Or do you think I can eat a whole pizza on my own? Because if pressed, I will own up to it."

"I hope you don't mind, but I invited Martin and Liz," he said. "I think we should talk about the apartments again. I spoke to Mr. Contreras today. He says he has a pair of buyers and thinks he'll have a decent offer in a week or so. We need to be realistic about what's going to happen here."

Lorna's mood began to crumble. "Yes," she said tightly. She looked at Nana's house. She couldn't imagine it not being here. She couldn't imagine that she would never be in Nana's room again or sit in the window seat in what was once her mother's room and watch the birds at the feeder just outside. She couldn't imagine where all her memories would go, both good and bad.

But she couldn't imagine being in this house alone now.

They decided to have the pizza in the backyard. Martin and Bean tossed a Frisbee for Aggie. Liz puttered around, making sure food and drinks (she'd brought a pitcher of tea) were covered. Seth brought out some old lawn furniture from the shed and dusted it off.

When they gathered to eat the pizza, Bean told his dad about their trip to a drugstore that wasn't there anymore and the mean lady who was building something in its place. "She didn't like Lorna," he said.

The three adults looked at Lorna. She shrugged. "It happens."

"It certainly does. You can't please everyone all the time," Liz said. "But we like you, Lorna."

"Oh," she said, happy with Liz's proclamation.

"Lorna was arrested because she stole some stuff," Bean said.

"Oh, okay," Lorna said, sitting up taller. "We're going there, are we?" She put down her pizza.

"Is that true?" Seth asked.

"Yes. But there were extenuating circumstances. I was seventeen, and it was my sister who did the shoplifting. She made me take the fall."

"Take the fall? That sounds like you were part of an organized crime network," Martin said with a chuckle.

"While that sounds like a lot of fun, I am not and have never been part of an organized crime network," Lorna confirmed.

"Goodness," Liz said. "That's horrible for your sister to do that."

"It certainly was," Lorna agreed. "I lost my job at the drugstore because of it, and I never got to tell Mr. Cho how sorry I was."

"Wait," Martin said. "Cho's Drugstore? My mom used to take us there when we were kids."

"It was a great place," Lorna agreed. "Bean and I went there today so I could apologize. But I found out the drugstore has been torn down."

"They did that two years ago," Martin said. "They're ripping out old Austin everywhere."

"You went there to apologize for what happened when you were seventeen?" Liz asked curiously.

"I did." Lorna resisted the urge to squirm in her lawn chair. "I'm attempting to, you know, make amends for a few things in my past that I'm not proud of."

"Huh," Martin said, eyeing her closely. "I like that."

"We're going to work at a soup kitchen," Bean said.

"Excuse me?" Seth asked.

"Well—I am," Lorna said. "Mr. Cho used to work in a soup kitchen on Sunday mornings. You know, the one on Cesar Chavez? I thought I would honor his memory by volunteering."

"Can I, Dad?" Bean asked. "I can get my community service badge."

"Not unless I'm there," he said firmly. "I don't like the idea of the two of you in a soup kitchen without me there."

"I'll go," Martin offered.

Lorna looked at him with surprise. "You will?"

"Sure, why not? Sounds like a worthy cause."

"I'll go too!" Liz said. "I've got aprons."

Seth looked at Lorna. "Well? Can we help?"

"I . . . *yes*," she said. She'd expected judgment, but no one was judging her. It was remarkable—they didn't look appalled or confused. They looked like they were with her.

"That must have been very difficult for you," Liz said, looking off. "My sister is the one person I can always depend on to have my back. I can't imagine a betrayal like that."

Oh, if she only knew. "It was terrible at the time," Lorna admitted. "But in some ways, it feels even harder now." She wished she had done this years ago, when she had the chance to make it up to Mr. Cho in person. Why had it taken her so long?

Martin pulled out his phone and looked up the soup kitchen. "They have volunteer spots open on Sunday. Shall I schedule us in?"

Lorna couldn't quite believe this was happening, but they all agreed that he should, and when that was done, Seth raised the issue of the house.

"I spoke to Mr. Contreras," Seth said. "He's got two buyers and expects to get final offers within the next several days. Guys, I'm going to be honest. I don't think it matters what we say—he's going to sell it."

Liz sighed wearily and put aside her pizza. "Figures."

"I knew he'd sell us out," Martin said.

"One option is to try to buy the place ourselves," Seth suggested.

Lorna's pulse ticked up. They had just accepted her, had offered to help her with her apology tour, at least in part. Should she tell them? Should she confess that all this time she was one of the buyers and then watch the goodwill they'd extended disappear before her very eyes? Or should she simply say she was interested in buying?

"Another option is the condos going up on Burnet," Seth added before she could think it through. "I drove by there the other day and checked into them. They're basic but affordable. The community is gated, and there will be a pool and an amenity center."

Of course! All they needed was an alternative to this house. She could help them find it. Sure, it would sting a little, and no one liked to move, but they would be in a new space with new appliances and *amenities*.

"I don't want to move," Liz said.

"So maybe we pool our resources and make an offer?" Seth asked. "I don't know how it would work legally, but my brother-in-law is an attorney, and maybe he could help us."

No. No, no, no. Lorna gripped the arms of her lawn chair. She'd been feeling so good, so accepted, like she was finally getting somewhere. And now she felt . . . not rage. No, this was different. This was confusion. Her grandmother's house, her goal, her North Star, was within reach. And Seth, of all people, was throwing a wrench into everything. And her feelings about it had her terribly bewildered.

She wasn't sure what she wanted anymore.

> I saw Candy Cho today. She's still mean. And she still hates me, so thank you for that. She would not accept my apology. Can you imagine someone trying to apologize to you, and you just refusing it? You're probably thinking that I never accepted your apology either, but that was different. You didn't deserve to have your apology accepted. I deserve to have my apology accepted. I still can't believe you framed me, Kristen. What a horrible, selfish thing to do to your little sister. But you know what's weird? I'm not as angry as I was. After all these years, I'm tired of thinking about it. I just want to be, as Micah says. Did I tell you about Micah? He's my life coach. He says I need to let go of the past to live in the future. So I guess I'm going to accept your apology for that night and let it go. You're welcome.
>
> Did you get the sweater I had sent to you? I hope pink is still your favorite color.

Chapter 28

Lorna Now

A LINE OF VOLUNTEERS WERE WAITING AT THE SOUP KITCHEN Sunday morning. They were given assignments by a cheerful woman with hair braided into tight cornrows. Seth and Martin were tasked with setting up tables and chairs. Liz was assigned to the bread-and-butter line. Lorna was to keep plates, utensils, and napkins flowing.

"And you," the lady said to Bean. "Do you think you can clear plates?"

"My teacher says I'm the most helpful."

"I bet you are. This boy here will show you what to do." She pulled a lanky kid forward and sent Bean off in his company.

When the doors opened, people flocked in. Men and women. Families. Older citizens who made Lorna's heart ache. Others so young that Lorna fretted about how they would survive. The kitchen was busy, but the people who needed the breakfast were patient and grateful. She could see why Mr. Cho had been drawn to this endeavor. It felt good to help.

Lorna was so busy that she didn't see Candy Cho until she almost stepped on her when she went to the back for more supplies.

Candy was wearing a red apron and had her long black hair

pulled back in a net. "What are you doing here?" she demanded. "Are you stalking me?"

"*Stalking* you?" Lorna repeated impatiently. "Do you honestly think I'd wait fifteen years to do that? I'm volunteering, like you. I mean, I assume you're volunteering."

"Yes, I am. I have been for years. But I've never seen you here, and now I've seen you twice this week."

"That's right, it's my first time volunteering. I told you I wanted to make it up to Mr. Cho, but you wouldn't accept my apology. So I had to think of a way to make amends on my own. I didn't know you'd be here."

Candy's brows knit into an even tighter frown. "What are you talking about, Lorna? You can't make it up to him—he's dead."

Lorna suddenly glimpsed herself in Candy. Candy was angry. Maybe at Lorna, maybe at her dad for dying. At everything in general. Lorna's anger was about Kristen's addiction and her mother dying before Lorna could apologize. She realized, in that very moment, that some of the anger had left her. She really was getting better. Which made her feel quite sorry for Candy. "I understand," she said. "I understand the anger."

Candy opened her mouth as if she was going to retort, but she hesitated and eyed Lorna curiously. "I don't know what you're talking about."

"I have it too," Lorna said. "I had no idea how much anger had seeped into me, going all the way through until it became part of me. Kind of alarming that you can get so mad and not even know it." She leaned her back against the wall, thinking about that. After a moment, Candy did, too, her head reaching Lorna's shoulder. The fight seemed to have gone out of her.

"My neck is stiff," Candy said, rubbing hard at her nape.

"You should get your body meridians assessed for tension. It can help."

"Ridiculous," Candy said with a roll of her eyes.

"I've found acupuncture to be very helpful. But I also know a couple of yoga moves you might try."

Candy looked terribly exasperated. "You don't know anything."

"Try this," Lorna said, doing a couple of neck rolls side to side, backward and forward.

After a moment's hesitation, Candy did try. More than once. Then she sighed, closed her eyes, and rested her head against the wall. "I'm not going to forgive you, you know. My dad was crushed by what you did."

That was hard to hear, even after all this time. "I know. I was crushed by what my sister did."

"Well . . . weirdly, I appreciate this," Candy continued. "This was super important to him. And you even brought your friends."

"They're not . . ." Lorna stopped herself from denying they were friends. She glanced over Candy's head at the crew from Nana's house. Wasn't this what friends did? Help each other out? Have each other's backs? Even if they weren't technically friends, they were the closest thing to it Lorna had had in a very long time. "They wanted to help too."

"The kid is cute," Candy observed.

"Yeah." Lorna could feel her smile to the tips of her toes. Bean was talking to an older gentleman, his hands moving in the air as he sketched something. Bean was a special kid. Person. Friend. Bean was special, period.

"Okay," Candy said, pushing away from the wall. She eyed Lorna once more. "If you're going to make a habit of this, you should get here earlier. All the good assignments go first."

"Noted," Lorna said. "Thanks, Candy."

"Don't thank me. I didn't forgive you or anything." She gave Lorna the barest hint of a smile, then turned and walked away.

Lorna watched her disappear into the kitchen. She felt good. Better than she had in a long time. She pulled out her phone and booked volunteer time for the following weekend.

When she went back to the dining hall, she found Bean and took a selfie of them with their official paper soup-kitchen aprons.

Later that afternoon, Lorna put Aggie in her car and drove to Peggy's house. While Aggie explored the backyard, Lorna showed Peggy the picture of her and Bean and explained where she'd been.

Peggy fetched her small notebook and marked off another item. "Only one more," she said, beaming at Lorna. "Your mother would be so proud."

Lorna wondered if that was true. She hoped it was. But her relationship with her mother had been so hard at the end she truly didn't know how her mother had felt about her.

"What does it say here?" Peggy asked, squinting at her notes. "Oh, that's right. Mrs. Tracy."

Lorna felt an immediate roil in her belly. Mrs. Tracy was the worst one yet. The memory was so disturbing that on the way out, Lorna kicked the metal rooster so hard that Aggie yelped.

Chapter 29

Lorna Is Twenty-Two

LORNA WAS STILL IN COLLEGE WHEN MOM SOLD NANA'S house and moved them into a small, two-bedroom garage apartment. Lorna didn't want her to sell, but Mom said it was the only way she could afford to get Kristen out of jail and into long-term treatment. This time, when Kristen was arrested for petty theft, she was found with cocaine in her possession. Seeking treatment was part of her release agreement. "Insurance only covers so much," her mother said wearily.

There was no money for anything. Lorna was working two jobs to help with the bills and her college expenses, which made her college career a longer slog than it should have been.

"She's twenty-six," Lorna argued. "Let her suffer the consequences, Mom. She's making the choice to steal and use drugs."

"So you think I should let my daughter end up on the street? She's not thinking clearly, Lorna. Have some compassion."

Compassion? Lorna has been asked to have compassion so many times she ought to get an award for it. But at what point does compassion give way to hard truths?

When Kristen is released from nine months of treatment, Mom brings her home to live with them in the tiny apartment. Kristen is her old self—funny, easy to be with. Supportive of

Lorna. She registers for general education classes at a local community college (that Mom pays for). She gets a job as a cashier in a grocery store.

"I knew she would eventually turn it around," Mom says proudly. "Not everyone is as goal oriented as you, Lolo. Sometimes people need time to find their way."

Lorna does not consider herself particularly goal oriented. But she has been desperate to get out of the house the last few years. And as for people finding their own way, well . . . Kristen has found her own way. But her way is steadily destroying her.

Still, in this new phase, Kristen is never surly. Lorna has learned over the years that surliness is the first sign she's using again. The two sisters spend their free time talking about everything: life, their parents, how much they miss Nana and Nana's house, what they want to be and where they want to go. They play their superlative game again, assigning titles to people Kristen works with.

Kristen encourages Lorna to finish her last semester of school. "You could be the one to break free of this family," she says.

Kristen is full of ambition and hope now that she is sober. She's going to get a degree, she says. "I'm going to go into fashion design. You can be my model."

Lorna laughs. "I don't think anyone wants to look at this."

"Are you kidding?" Kristen says. "You have a perfect figure. And we'll figure out what to do with your hair." They laugh.

Kristen advises Lorna about what to wear when she goes out. She's always shaking her head at whatever Lorna picks, then rearranging the clothing pieces and accessories in a way that makes Lorna look so much better. She doesn't know how Kristen does it, but she is eternally grateful that she does. Having Kristen home is nice. It's more than nice—Lorna is happier than she's been in a while.

While Kristen and Lorna are hanging out, Mom is with their landlord, Peggy Shane. They have become the best of friends. They sit on the back patio with their wine and cackle about Lord only knows what. Peggy strikes Lorna as a lonely soul; it's a blessing that her mother is too. She wants to believe the two women found each other when they needed each other most.

Lorna studies for class and Kristen keeps the apartment clean. Lorna believes Kristen when she says she feels great and that she is never using drugs again. She believes that Kristen has grown up, that months in treatment have worked. "Look what drugs did to my life," Kristen says, wincing. "Look at what they did to me. I have a lot of catching up to do."

"And you look so much better now," Lorna adds. "Beautiful." Kristen *is* beautiful. Her skin and hair are revitalized and she's at a healthy weight.

"Thank you," Kristen says. "It's amazing how much happier I am now."

When Lorna graduates from college, Mom, Kristen, and Peggy come to watch her walk. Dad comes, too, with his wife and two preteen daughters. They sit on opposite ends of the stadium. After the ceremony, Dad hugs Lorna and then hands her an envelope full of cash. "I didn't know what to get you, but I'm so proud of you." Not proud enough to put aside his differences with Mom and go to dinner with them. But proud enough to hand her twenty-five hundred dollars. "Use it to start your life," he advises.

"Twenty-five hundred dollars?" Kristen says sourly when they get home. "Wow. I guess he's not as broke as he's been telling me."

Something tickles Lorna's brain. Kristen has been talking to Dad about money? She feels a little sick, but she pushes the feeling off, tucks it away. This is her day and she's not going to worry about something she probably misunderstood.

That weekend, Lorna prepares to go to a graduation party. She is trying to decide what to wear when Kristen asks if she can go too. "Come on, Lolo, I'm so bored. I'm always by myself. And I've been good—you can't deny that I have. I deserve this. I promise I won't drink."

Kristen has been good, but her insistence that she has seems off. Something doesn't feel right again.

"You think I'm going to get drugs, don't you?" Kristen asks. Her eyes well with tears. "How long are you going to punish me?"

Lorna gapes with surprise. "I'm punishing you?"

"Yes! It's on your face every day. I can see it in your eyes. You don't trust me. You will never trust me. I could be Mother Teresa, and you wouldn't trust me."

"That's not true," Lorna insists. But deep down, she thinks maybe it is true. She has believed Kristen's claim of sobriety, but in the back of her mind, she knows she can't fully trust her.

"You make me feel so bad about myself," Kristen says petulantly. "I'm sorry, okay? I am so sorry for using drugs, but I'm not using anymore. I swear to you, I won't do anything at your party."

Lorna is so confused. How has she made Kristen feel bad about herself? She thought they were getting along so well. "Okay," Lorna says, because she feels guilty, like somehow she has become Kristen's jailer. "Okay."

Kristen squeals with delight, then takes forever to get ready. But to the party they eventually go. Lorna with her hair in a low braid, wearing jeans that Kristen says make her ass look sexy and a cute top. And her gorgeous, gregarious sister with loose blond hair, wearing a tube top that showcases her flat belly and jeans so tight that Lorna worries she'll somehow manage to split them.

The house where the party is being held is packed. The

night turns into a blur. Lorna is in a celebratory mood and uncharacteristically drinks too much. She loses track of Kristen, but that's okay because the last she saw her, she was drinking water and laughing with a couple of guys. And anyway, Kristen promised she wouldn't do anything at this party. And Lorna desperately needs to believe her.

It is close to midnight, Lorna thinks, when Kristen finds her and tells her she is leaving with two of Lorna's college classmates. Nicole and Anna are together, laughing, loose-limbed, clumsy. They've been drinking, but Kristen looks as sober as a judge. "Where are you going?" Lorna asks.

"Don't know," Kristen says. "We're just gonna ride around. Anna says she has a pool. We may go there."

Lorna's gaze darts to Nicole and Anna again. She has a bad feeling. Kristen grabs her arm and forces Lorna to look at her. "Why are you being like this? I'm fine. Everything is fine. We're just going to hang out. You're so like Mom sometimes," she snaps.

It's the surliness that ratchets Lorna's fear. But she doesn't say anything to stop her friends or Kristen. They are grown women, and Lorna is not her sister's zookeeper. And anyway, what would she say? *My sister hasn't had anything to drink, but she is a recovering addict, and we should not trust her?* Lorna doesn't say it. She goes back to the party. She doesn't even see them leave.

It is sometime early in the morning when her mother wakes up Lorna, panic-stricken. She says Kristen has been in an accident. Lorna dresses quickly and they drive to the hospital. Her heart thumps painfully the entire way.

Kristen is okay, just banged up. Anna has a broken leg and will have surgery later. Nicole, though . . .

Nicole.

Nicole didn't make it.

Kristen talks wildly on the way home about how she was sitting in the back and didn't see the car coming. She seems jittery and fearful, but then again, she's just been in a terrible accident in which the driver lost her life.

Several days later, Lorna learns from her mother that Nicole had meth in her system. *Meth?* Lorna didn't know Nicole that well, but she knows what a meth head is like. She looks at Kristen.

"What?" Kristen asks defiantly. Guiltily, to Lorna's eye. "You think I had something to do with it?"

Of course she did. "Nicole didn't use drugs," Lorna says, her voice full of rage.

Kristen shrugs and averts her gaze. "I guess she did that night." She walks out of the room.

In the days that follow, Kristen says over and over it wasn't her fault. But wasn't it? Where else would Nicole have gotten meth? Why did they leave the party, anyway? Why didn't Lorna warn Nicole and Anna about hanging out with Kristen? She tries to see Anna, but Anna is still in the hospital and is too distraught for visitors.

A few days after the funeral, Mom finds drugs in Kristen's purse.

"Yes, I have some drugs, okay?" Kristen shouts at her mother. "I almost lost my life in a car accident, Mom! How am I supposed to cope with that?"

Lorna's guilt at not having warned her classmates about Kristen is massive, pushing all the air from her lungs on a daily basis. She wishes she could somehow apologize to their families for her failure. She wishes she had never believed Kristen could or would change.

Lorna gets her first professional job at a tech company and is saving to move out. Living with Mom is cheap, but living with Kristen is impossible. Mom allows Kristen to come and go, even though she is using again. Sometimes Kristen goes a few days without being high. But then she'll disappear for a few days. Sometimes money and things of value go missing.

And then on rare occasions, when things are quiet and Kristen is clean, she will quietly admit she wishes she knew how to get out from under the rule of addiction. "Have you ever wished you were someone else?" she whispers to Lorna one night.

"All the time," Lorna says flatly.

"Yeah," Kristen says, and sighs wearily. "Me too. Just . . . anyone else."

Lorna stays in that apartment another year because she feels responsible for her mother, who worries endlessly about Kristen. She has always felt a crushing responsibility to be the good daughter, a role she took on at the age of six. But she finally reaches her limit when Kristen brings home a guy who is obviously stoned, and Mom responds to Lorna's complaints by saying, "At least she's not out on the street."

Frankly, Lorna would rather be on the street than here.

She moves out soon after. She feels a true liberation from the roller coaster that was her life. She pours herself into work, trusting no one. Or maybe what she trusts is that any person she meets could take it all away from her.

Lorna knows she isolates herself and that it is happening with alarming frequency. But she tells herself that everything is probably fine.

But then Mom is diagnosed with cancer.

Chapter 30

Lorna Now

AT THE START OF LORNA'S LAST WEEK AT THE BODHI TAO Bliss Retreat and Spa, Xandra handed her a piece of paper. On it was a catalog of how she'd spent her time there, listing the required hours and the number Lorna had completed. She was surprised to see she was ahead of schedule. It was true that in the last week, she'd been spending longer hours here. At Micah's suggestion, she'd added art therapy, where she was encouraged to get in touch with the deepest level of her mind and express it in an art medium of her choice, including dance, music, drawing, or writing. Lorna stuck to drawing and was guided into uncovering some difficult emotions and releasing them into her so-called art. Micah was right—it was the perfect companion to her meditation practice. She was uncovering a lot of old beliefs that didn't have a place in her world now.

Micah also sent her for more sound baths and float therapy, which had helped reduce not only her negative self-talk but also her fear. Her body seemed to be expelling all of that through her tears.

She'd continued work on her vision board, adding anything and everything that could possibly make her feel happy or fulfilled. She told Micah that if her future turned out to be anywhere near as pretty or colorful as her board, she would be happy.

"I'm holding you to that," he'd said.

Of course she'd had more sessions with the acupuncturist. She loved the very concept of body meridians and the opening of her chi. She left feeling lighter in being each time. Like she was a person who could be liked and was worth knowing. She had value.

Armed with the accounting of her time, Lorna went to her meeting with Micah and showed him how much she'd progressed. He was wearing silk joggers, a woven hoodie, and torn ribbons in his graying hair. Yet his look did not annoy Lorna in the least, which she considered a mark of great progress.

"That's right," Micah said, looking at her paper. "You're coming to the end of your time with us. That is, the time required by your employer. You are, of course, free to carry on with us."

"I don't think so," Lorna said. "I saw the rates on your brochure." And yet, the idea of carrying on *without* Micah and Montreal to guide her was more disturbing than she ever would have dreamed possible. She had come to depend on this place. She even looked forward to coming.

Micah laughed. "Inner peace is not cheap. Nevertheless, I can confidently say we're down to a few tweaks before we sign off and I send you back to your employer."

"Tweaks," she repeated. She'd been coming here long enough to know that when he said things like that, she was not going to like whatever followed. "Like what?"

"Maintenance skills," he said. "You've done a great job of learning to recognize and rid yourself of negative thoughts. And you are opening yourself up to examining your resentments and letting them go. You are learning to live in the moment and not the past. So now we want to make sure you have the skills necessary to keep that up and to move forward on your own. In our last few sessions, we'll focus on how to maintain your positive outlook when you go back to work."

She hadn't thought about work in weeks. She shifted uncomfortably on her beanbag.

"Let's begin by talking about your staff."

"Let's not," Lorna said.

Micah ignored her, as he'd learned to do. "I've got a list here from your employer," he said, and reached over to his desk to grab it.

"I'm not ready to talk about them." She didn't want to remember how they felt about her, how they made her feel about herself. It would ruin everything she'd worked hard to achieve these last few weeks.

"Suzanne," he said stubbornly. "Tell me about her."

She has a punchable face. Lorna grimaced, recalling the way she'd so bitterly written that to Kristen. Suzanne was an attractive woman. Why had she ever thought that? "I don't know. She's . . ." Oh, how she hated this exercise. "She's a little rough around the edges."

Micah's brows rose.

"What?" Lorna asked defensively. "Oh, I get it. That's the pot calling the kettle black, right?"

"I didn't say that."

"I can say it. She's just like me, and that's not exactly a good thing."

"Why isn't it? You're a top-notch salesperson. You're in charge. I would think she'd want to emulate you."

But her staff hated her. She'd earned their hate too. She felt uncomfortable, like her skin didn't fit right or her head was on crooked. Very uncomfortable. She breathed in, looked for the negative thought. "I don't think I can do this, Micah. I don't want to like them."

He laughed with surprise. "Why not?"

She closed her eyes, reaching for the truth. "Isn't it obvious? If I like them, they will leave in one way or another."

Micah set aside the paper that had their names written on it. "Like everyone else in your life."

She opened her eyes. That thought felt toxic and sour. "Yes, Mr. Freud. Not exactly a breakthrough. If they get to know me, if I get to know them, they won't stick around. No one ever does."

"That is demonstrably untrue," Micah said. "What about Bean and his father?"

"Come on. He's a kid. And they live across the hall. My staff won't know what to do with me if I come back like this, all free to be me. I am not currently the Lorna they know. I can't waltz in and say, 'Hey, everyone, welcome to my bomb shelter! I've opened the doors, so let's order pizza!'"

Micah shifted onto his elbow. "Why can't you say that?"

"Because they will leave. Or do something that means I have to leave. What are you not getting? I'm still not a likable person. Maybe I don't hate myself, but that doesn't mean others don't hate me. I'm closed off, I can't trust them, I second-guess everything."

He tapped a finger to his lips for a moment. "Question: Have any of your neighbors left?"

"Of course not," she said irritably. "They don't have anywhere to go."

"Sure they do. They may not want to, but any one of them could leave tomorrow to get away from you. And yet, they haven't. You've had pizza with them. They volunteered with you. Are they giving off an *I hate Lorna* vibe?"

"No," she said slowly. Pizza in the backyard with them had

been one of the better days of her adult life. "But they don't really know me or understand me."

"Maybe," he said with a shrug. "But if you really believe that, you should help them know you. If your theory is that anyone who really knows you will not like you and will leave, then test it."

She frowned. "How am I supposed to do that?"

"You could start by telling them the truth. That you intend to buy the house and why."

Lorna glared at him. "I am obviously not going to tell them that. They would really hate me then. Even Bean might hate me, and I couldn't bear that. Also, Micah, you are ruining the good vibe I had from my sound bath earlier."

Micah smiled a little. "I told you you'd love it. Look, Lorna. This idea that you are unlikable, unlovable, is a narrative you've created. But it's not true. Maybe you feel that way because you've been too afraid to let anyone close to you. You've been so sure history would repeat itself that you've locked yourself down. No admittance. And you've told yourself that no one is banging on the door because you are so unlikable. None of that is true. If you're ever going to find peace, you need to rid yourself of the fear that whoever knows you will leave you. That's letting the past rule you."

She could feel the truth in that, but it felt too dangerous to let go of everything she'd clung to. "The past does rule me, Micah. The past shows me exactly what I can expect." She popped up from the beanbag, annoyed with him without really understanding why. "I'm supposed to have my astrological chart read today. Can you buzz Montreal?"

"You're kidding yourself," Micah said calmly. "Just think about what I'm saying." He stood up and hit the little button on his desk. "What do you have planned for this weekend?"

He asked in a manner that made Lorna think he didn't really care but was looking for something to fill the awkward silence until Montreal came. Lorna stared at her hand. "Actually, I'm paying a visit to someone who is *really* grieving. Someone who lost her daughter in a car accident."

"How tragic," Micah said sincerely. "Is this Mrs. Tracy from your list?"

This guy with the ribbons in his hair had a mind like a steel trap. "Yes, as a matter of fact."

"Were you in the car?"

Where was Montreal? "No." She glanced to the door. "But Kristen was. She escaped with some bruises, is all."

"I'm curious why this woman is on your list if you weren't involved."

Lorna shook her head. Why was it so hard for her to explain it was all her fault? "No one should have been in the car. I could have stopped them, but I didn't. Where is Montreal, anyway?"

"I know *you* know that you can't hold yourself responsible for the choices anyone made during that tragedy. You didn't physically put anyone in a car, did you? You are not guilty by association."

"I *know*," she said irritably. But she didn't know, not really. She thought her guilt by association was terribly damning.

"For what it's worth, I understand your thinking. Grief is hard work," he said sympathetically. "It's true what they say—the only way out is through. If you're going to visit the girl's mother, just make sure you know what you need from that visit for your own grief work."

"My grief work?" Her gaze snapped back to him. "Since when have I been doing grief work?"

"Since the moment you came into the program. You've been grieving your past and your family for a very long time."

Lorna was appalled. She didn't understand why his proclamation should annoy her so completely, but it did. She glowered at him. She'd been feeling good about things, about herself, and he was ruining it all. "I'm here to learn how to be a better person, remember? You can't just switch everything up on me at the last minute."

"I didn't mean to switch it up. To me, it's all part and parcel of the unique Lorna Lott. Whether you realize it or not, you're doing the work of others who have grieved a loss. The tears, the rage . . . they are all signs of it."

Now she was feeling defensive. "I haven't cried in a week."

"And that is great progress. Here is Montreal," he said.

Lorna hadn't even noticed that the door had opened. She was still glaring at Micah, who returned her gaze with absolute serenity. She was indignant—she'd been sold a bait and switch. "Have a good session," he said, as if nothing had happened.

Chapter 31

Lorna Now

GRIEF WORK.

She had never wanted to rip out someone's ribbons like she did the moment Micah said that. Just when she was wondering how she'd carry on without Micah's help, he had to go say that. Who did he think he was kidding? Lorna had been to therapists, she had talked about her mother's death, she was versed in the basic tenets of depression and grief and so on and on and on. Grief was not her problem. Grief implied she had lost something, but really, she was getting herself back.

Then why did his proclamation make her so angry? Was that proof she was grieving? Why else would she fill with rage?

She shook her head. She was going to get Nana's house back, and when she did, she would be whole again. She would be the Lorna she was supposed to be, the Lorna she was before everything went so terribly wrong. She was not *grieving*. And she would simply ignore the alarming feeling that even having Nana's house back wouldn't be the right panacea for what was ailing her. She would not entertain the idea that her plan wasn't the right one.

Nope, she was not going to change her mind. It had been made up for too long.

Bean dragged a bucket of plastic building blocks to Lorna's apartment that afternoon. "I'm building some houses for the villages," he announced. He set up his construction zone on the living room floor, admonishing Aggie when she picked up pieces and chewed on them.

Perhaps Lorna should have been more concerned about Aggie eating small plastic pieces, but she was engrossed in the search for Mrs. Tracy.

Unfortunately, her memory was failing her. She couldn't remember Mrs. Tracy's first name anymore. There were several people with the Tracy surname scattered around town. What she could recall was that Nicole was from somewhere near Central Austin. She remembered driving by Nicole's family house in those nights after the accident, tears clouding her vision.

It was possible the family had moved, but that didn't stop her. She made a list of the Tracy addresses, putting the ones in Central Austin at the top. "Hey, Bean. Grab your explorer gear."

He looked up from his construction. "Where are we going?"

"To find a family I used to know."

"Will there be dessert? I still haven't decided what I'm going to bake."

She smiled with great fondness at the kid. "We'll find one."

Lorna fed Aggie while Bean picked up his building pieces. They left the dog with a Nylabone and headed out. Bean had his map, his compass, his explorer hat, and, today, a watch. "Dad got it for me," he explained. "It has the temperature, and also you can see how many steps you take."

The first address they drove to was a house with white siding and a green metal roof, surrounded by an overgrown lawn that sported some overturned lawn chairs. Lorna remembered a brick house and a neatly kept lawn. "This isn't it."

Bean pulled out a pair of child's binoculars from his backpack and surveyed the house and yard. "There are papers stuck in the door."

"Flyers," Lorna said. "I don't think anyone is home."

"No," Bean agreed. He took out his disposable camera and snapped a picture of the house. "I'll put this in our field notes," he said.

They headed to the second address. This one was in East Austin, in a modest neighborhood marked by redbrick houses and neatly trimmed yards. It had a porch swing, and something about that swing niggled Lorna's memory. She vaguely recalled—

"*Stop!*" Bean shrieked.

Lorna hit the brakes. "What?" she cried.

"There's a *puppy!*"

"I hit a *puppy?*" Horror sluiced through Lorna, but Bean didn't answer—he'd flung open the door and was out before she could stop him.

"Bean! Wait!" she said, but Bean was at the fence. "Can I pet your puppy?" he shouted.

Lorna got out of the car to stop him from accosting anyone and saw the woman sitting on a blanket under an oak tree. A black Lab puppy was on the edge of the blanket, gnawing on a stick.

There was Mrs. Tracy. She was probably in her seventies now, but she hopped to her feet without a problem and gestured for Bean to come through the gate. Bean eagerly went in, careful to shut the gate behind him. He spoke to Mrs. Tracy, then dipped down to meet the excited puppy. It instantly abandoned its stick in favor of the boy.

Mrs. Tracy smiled down at the pair, then looked across the yard to Lorna, whose gut turned over on itself. She tried to smile back, tried not to look like she would vomit at any moment as she walked up to the fence. "Hi," she said.

"Hello," Mrs. Tracy said. "Your son must love dogs."

"Oh, he's . . ." She didn't need to explain Bean. "Umm . . . could I come in?" she asked.

"I beg your pardon, I should have invited you," Mrs. Tracy said, and opened the gate. She was hardly looking at Lorna; her gaze was fixed on Bean and the puppy. Bean was running in circles, and the puppy was nipping at his heels, barking. Bean laughed.

"I should . . . I should introduce myself," Lorna said. How did one go about meeting the mother of the woman your sister killed? She realized she wasn't quite prepared.

Mrs. Tracy turned back. She had deep lines around her eyes and mouth. But she was still smiling.

"I'm Lorna Lott."

The name apparently didn't register, because Mrs. Tracy said, "I'm Karen Tracy. Do you live nearby?"

"No. Umm . . ." Her heart was racing. "I know who you are, Mrs. Tracy."

Mrs. Tracy's smile faltered. She looked at Bean, as if she suspected some nefarious plot to kidnap her dog.

"We're fine—*he's* fine. He's innocent. I'm Kristen Lott's sister. She was . . . with Nicole . . ."

She couldn't say it, but she didn't have to. Mrs. Tracy's expression morphed into instant grief. *That* was grief, Micah. Pure, unadulterated grief.

"I don't understand," Mrs. Tracy said.

"I would like to apologize."

"For what?"

"For my sister."

Behind Mrs. Tracy, Bean squealed with delight. He was on his back, and the wiggling, excited puppy was crawling all over him.

Mrs. Tracy was staring hard at Lorna. "What is this all about?

My daughter died years ago, and I would rather not relive it. I don't know anything about your sister."

"That's what—"

"Do you think that even after all these years, I can talk about it without feeling terrible pain? Because I can't. I think about her every day. So whatever you think you need to say, I don't want to hear it."

Mrs. Tracy's grief was rolling off her in waves that hit Lorna hard. She felt unsteady because she knew that sort of grief. She had felt it at her core. "My sister was with—"

"Then I am very sorry. But my daughter was driving and on drugs. I never knew she did drugs, not until the toxicology report came back and said she had *meth* in her blood! Nicole! On meth! That girl never did anything wrong in her life, but what do I know? What did I really know about my daughter? People don't just do meth."

Bean had stopped playing with the puppy and was watching the two of them with concern while the puppy latched onto his pant leg and began to growl and pull in a tug-of-war.

"That's what I'm trying to say, just very badly. She didn't do drugs, Mrs. Tracy; I feel confident she didn't. I knew her all through college and she never did anything like that. But my sister did. My sister is an addict, and she was in that car, and I'm certain she talked them into taking the meth. She probably talked them into driving her to get it. She might have even talked them into paying for it, because she didn't make a lot of money."

Mrs. Tracy's mouth fell open.

"I am so sorry. For your unconscionable loss and my sister's part in it. It's been eating away at me since—"

"Why did no one tell me?" Mrs. Tracy cried angrily.

"I don't . . . I don't know," Lorna lied. She hadn't because both

Mom and Kristen had told her to leave it alone, that nothing would bring Nicole back.

"But her family deserves to know," Lorna had argued.

"Are you trying to get your sister arrested?" her mother had fired back.

"I'm trying to tell the truth," Lorna had said weakly.

Mrs. Tracy suddenly burst into tears. Bean leaped to his feet and came forward. He grabbed Mrs. Tracy's hand. "Don't cry," he said.

Mrs. Tracy swiped at her face. "Is that really true?" she asked Lorna. "Or is this some sick joke?"

"No!" Lorna shook her head. "It's true. I wanted to tell you then, but my mother was worried about my sister. That she would be . . . held accountable." She swallowed down a lump of shame.

Mrs. Tracy looked heavenward. "I've always resented the two girls who lived." She dipped down, picked up the chewed plastic piece of some toy, and threw it. The puppy chased after it. "It wasn't fair that they got to live but Nicole had to die. And now you're telling me one of them *gave* her the drugs?"

"If it's any consolation, my sister never really lived after that either," Lorna said softly. It had been the beginning of the end, really. Kristen fell off her wagon and never got back on.

Mrs. Tracy snorted. "That is no consolation. It's infuriating. Because she is still alive." Her tears started again. "Why did you come here? Why did you have to bring this into my life today?" She began to sob. Bean threw his arms around her waist and pressed the side of his face to her. She bent over him, crying.

"I wanted you to know the truth."

Mrs. Tracy somehow got hold of herself and straightened up. Her face was red and puffy from sobbing. "You're a very selfish woman. I don't know what kicks you get out of this, but you've ruined my life all over again."

Two tears slipped from the corners of Lorna's eyes. She had never meant to cause such pain. She'd wanted to give Mrs. Tracy something to hold on to. "Nicole was not a drug user."

"Don't say her name," Mrs. Tracy said bitterly. "You don't deserve to say her name." She dislodged Bean from her. "Pepper!" she called. She looked at Lorna. "Never come here again." She turned, walking unevenly to her house.

The puppy raced by them, tripping over his big feet, then scrambling up the two steps to the porch behind Mrs. Tracy.

Lorna's heart was racing so wildly that she thought she might pass out. What had she done? The woman's pain gripped Lorna like a vise, making her work for every breath. What was it doing to Mrs. Tracy? Lorna had reignited a mother's deep grief, and the only thing she could hope for was that one day, Mrs. Tracy would appreciate knowing what really happened. She'd spent all those years thinking she didn't know her own daughter. Did it matter that she knew the truth now?

Did it matter that Lorna had always known the truth about the accident? It didn't change anything.

None of this had changed anything.

There was no going back.

She bent down and picked up the chewed piece of plastic. "Come on, Bean," she said quietly.

Bean slipped his hand into hers. They walked in silence to the car. In the car, Bean looked out the window to the house, as if expecting Mrs. Tracy or the puppy to come out the door. "Sometimes people just hurt too much," he said.

"Yeah," Lorna agreed. She hurt too much a lot of the time.

"I was really sad when my mom died," Bean said. "It hurt really bad."

"I was really sad when my mom died too." And she'd hurt too much when Kristen went to Florida.

Bean turned toward her. "Your sister is bad, isn't she?"

Lorna released a soft, shaky sigh. "She's not bad. She's . . ." Heaven help her if she could think of a word for what Kristen was. *Broken.* "She's damaged, I guess."

Bean looked out the window again.

Lorna wished she and her mother could have been truthful about Kristen when Nicole died, instead of being too fearful of consequences or too proud to say the truth out loud. Mom had been worried about Kristen, but it wasn't fair that Mrs. Tracy had suffered because of Mom's fear. It wasn't right.

She started the car. "Let's go get some dessert."

"I'm not hungry," Bean muttered, and he looked down at his lap.

Great. She'd reignited his grief too.

> Well, Kristen, I saw Mrs. Tracy today. Don't you dare ask me who that is. I told her that you were the one who did meth. That you had somehow convinced Nicole and Anna to give it a try. You would never admit it, but I know you did. Why did you, though? You couldn't stay sober, okay, but did you have to take them down with you? Because the pain you caused extended to people we didn't even know.
>
> Don't say you're sorry. It's too late.

Chapter 32

Lorna Now

LORNA BOUGHT CHOCOLATE CHIP COOKIE DOUGH AND SHOWED Bean when he came home from school the next day. "Have you ranked chocolate chip cookies yet?"

Bean shook his head.

"You know that chocolate chip cookies are the backbone of America, don't you?"

Bean nodded.

"I don't see how you could possibly decide what you're going to bake for your badge without a test run of cookies. Do you?" Bean shook his head.

"Then shall we make them?"

"Okay," Bean said. The life was coming back into him.

"And when they are done, maybe we can invite Martin and Liz to have some too. In the backyard." She'd begun to clear out the clutter of her Precious Moments figurines—those that did not occupy a place in Bean's villages were now stored in boxes. She didn't need them anymore. But she still had so many that she wasn't comfortable letting anyone get a glimpse of her apartment just yet.

After she helped him roll the cookie dough into balls and put them on the baking sheet, she set him to work making invitations for cookies in the backyard. She thought today would be a good time to present him with his badge vest. She'd managed to sew on all the badges he had . . . and it was completely covered. The kid was going to need a trench coat for badges at the rate he was going.

Last night, when she'd been sewing the last two badges, Mr. Contreras had called.

"Hello there, Ms. Moneybags. You getting that offer together?"

The man was the worst.

"I'm going to the bank this week."

"Well, that's good. I got an offer from a developer just this afternoon, and I'm ready to make a deal. You want to know the amount you have to beat?"

She didn't, not really, but she was going to have to know sooner or later. "Is that even ethical?"

"What, you've got some morals you need to tend to?"

She rolled her eyes. "What's the offer?"

The amount he quoted did not surprise her—Lorna had done her homework—but it did make her eyes water. "Got it," she said.

Mr. Contreras chuckled. "I just bet you do. You still going to pursue this?"

How many times would he ask her? "Yes, Mr. Contreras. I will finalize the financing and my offer by Friday."

"Well, lookee there," Mr. Contreras said smugly. "I like how confident you sound. I like that in a woman."

"Good for you. Is there anything else? I'm in the middle of something."

He chuckled. She wanted to reach through the phone and smash his smug face. "I need to hear from you by Friday, Lorna."

She drew a deep breath. "So you've said. Message received." She hung up on him.

She did not sleep well last night. Friday was just a few days away.

Bean delivered his invitations, and when the cookies were ready, Martin and Liz joined them in the backyard. Lorna had set up a table with a cloth over it and brought water in plastic bottles along with the cookies. She was branching out. Some might even call this entertaining, despite how bare bones it was.

"Wow," Liz said. "This reminds me of the way my mother used to invite friends over for tea." She took a seat. "How are you, Lorna? You're looking well rested."

"I am?" Lorna wondered when she hadn't looked well rested.

"This sabbatical must be working," Liz added with a smile.

"You know? I think it is."

"That hole is getting big," Martin said. He was watching Bean and Aggie dig. They could not come to the backyard and not dig something.

Lorna saw that he was right. How interesting that she was not annoyed by it. She was almost amused by it. Maybe she'd turn the hole into a pond. It was just a hole after all.

The three of them chatted about the news around Austin—Martin was very excited about a new Torchy's Tacos opening nearby. Lorna said she had never been to a Torchy's. Martin made a show of falling out of his chair and Lorna, Liz, and Bean laughed.

Seth arrived soon after and walked outside, still shrugging out of his jacket. "Hey," he said, and sat heavily in a lawn chair. He took three cookies, shoving one into his mouth, then seemed to realize what he was doing and blushed slightly. "Sorry. Long day."

"What's up, man?" Martin asked.

Seth shook his head. "This job is going to kill me." His gaze found Bean, and he watched as Bean brushed dirt off Aggie's coat. "When I took this promotion, I had a wife. We knew it would be longer hours, but we thought we'd handle it well enough with the two of us." He rubbed his face with one hand. "The hours aren't letting up, and the long hours are keeping me from my son."

"What are you saying?" Martin asked. "Are you going to change jobs?"

"I don't know." Seth sighed again, then bit off half another cookie. "It's just got me thinking in general." He sat up a little and shook his head, like he was shaking a clutter of thoughts. "By the way, I went back to the condos I told you about. They've got some finished models now. They're nice. They've got more square footage than any of our apartments. But they are a bit more expensive."

"How much more?" Liz asked.

"A couple hundred a month. But without a list of things that need repair."

They all took this news in. It seemed to Lorna that the four of them were silently contemplating what came next for them. She certainly was.

She was thinking about Bean and Seth, and about Martin and Liz. She was thinking about this house, and what it was like when she was a child. About the time she and Kristen found a litter of kittens under the house. About when her grandparents had a party and the next morning, bowls of candy were still out. She was thinking about what would happen to her fellow tenants. How she hadn't even thought of them in the beginning, when the only thing on her mind was getting Nana's house back. Would she regret buying this house from underneath them? It was obvious Mr. Contreras was going to sell. If not to her, then someone else. Could they blame her for being the one to buy it? Would buying their homes out from under them become another burdensome bundle of guilt? Would she be hunting them down in the years to come to apologize?

She could be their landlord, she realized. Buy the house and rent back to them. But would that change this thing between them that was feeling like friendship? She didn't want to lose that. She didn't want to be a landlord either.

She honestly didn't know what she wanted or felt about this house anymore. Her thoughts were beginning to confuse her. She looked at Bean and Aggie. "Oh, right," she said. "I have something for Bean." She got up and went into her apartment to get the vest. When she returned, she called Bean from the yard.

He and Aggie loped together to where the adults were seated, and Lorna presented the vest like a king's robe. "Ta-da!"

Bean gasped. He'd seen some progress in the beginning, but he hadn't seen it in several days. "These are all my badges!" he crowed as Lorna slipped it on him.

"Dude, you have to model it," Martin said, and made him do a walk up and down.

"Do you want to know all the badges?" Bean asked, and then began to rattle them off, pointing to each one. The list was long. "Dad!" Bean said suddenly. "I can wear this to the science fair!"

"You can," Seth said, and explained, "Bean has an entry in the science fair this week. Martin helped us. We've got a volcano."

"Now that I'd like to see," Liz said.

"You should all come," Seth offered. "Wednesday at five at the school."

As the school was a mere two blocks away, Liz immediately said she'd go.

"I'll be there too," Martin said. "Lorna?"

She couldn't believe Martin was inviting her. "Me too."

"We can walk together," Liz said.

They talked about science fairs while Bean counted his badges. Lorna realized she was going to miss this group. It wasn't like they were besties, but she cared about them.

These people had indeed become her friends.

After the cookies were eaten, Lorna leashed up Aggie and drove to Peggy's house. In her living room, Lorna presented the chewed piece of a dog toy to her.

"I don't know what this is," Peggy said, examining it.

"It's a piece of a dog toy that Mrs. Tracy threw across the lawn."

"Oh." Peggy's eyes widened.

Lorna filled her in on what happened. "I left her with the truth," she said quietly. "I don't think it makes a difference, but I wanted her to know."

"Oh, I'm sure she will appreciate knowing the truth one day," Peggy said kindly. "That must have been a hard one for you."

"The hardest yet," Lorna agreed.

Peggy reached over and patted her knee. "Well, my dear, you've done it. You've completed the list your mother left with the trust. Which means the trust is yours now. I'll go to the bank tomorrow and sign some papers, but after that, it's all yours." She walked to a buffet and picked up a blue file, which she then handed to Lorna. "She would be so proud of you, Lolo. So proud. All the information you need to access the trust is in here."

Lorna did not feel victorious. She felt like she should have done this a long time ago.

"Now promise me you will come and visit and bring that precious boy and this sweet dog," she said, bending down to pet Aggie behind the ears.

Lorna smiled. "I will. And for the record, I'm not done yet."

"Sure you are. We can get the list out and look again if you'd like."

"No, I mean, I finished Mom's list. But I haven't finished what I started here."

Peggy looked confused. "What do you mean? What did you start?"

"I . . ." Something snapped into place in Lorna. Some deep understanding she hadn't known she possessed or, moreover, could even access. "I want to finish the long process of forgiveness. It's part of my grief work."

Peggy smiled. "That sounds important."

Peggy probably thought she was referring to Kristen. But Lorna was talking about forgiving herself. And the only way to do that, to finally accept her grief and move on, was to apologize to her mother and her sister.

Chapter 33

Lorna Is Thirty-Eight

AT THE COMPANY'S ANNUAL SALES CONFERENCE, THERE IS an awards luncheon at which Lorna is named the top salesperson at Driskill for the fourth year in a row. She accepts the award shaped like a crystal mountain with an engraved snow top. She stares at the thing in her hands, wonders why it is a mountain with a snow top, then smiles at the audience and thanks the people she is supposed to thank. There is applause, but she doesn't really hear it. She was given three tickets for her table, but there is no one here for her other than Deb, who is smiling at her and applauding harder than anyone. She is here as a representative of the company.

Lorna had no one to bring. Her mother is too ill, and she didn't bother to tell Kristen about it. She didn't see the point.

Lorna takes her award to her mother's house. She waves to Peggy as she climbs up the stairs to the apartment above the garage. She opens the door and walks in . . . to find a strange man sitting on the couch, his feet propped on the coffee table, watching TV. He is heavyset, dressed in a tank top that displays his tattoo-covered arms and neck. His hair is a long, greasy ponytail. "Who are you?" he asks.

"I'm Lorna Lott. My mother lives here. Who are you?"

He shifts his gaze to the TV. "Friend of Kristen."

What a charming fellow. "And where is Kristen?"

"Ran out for something. She'll be back." His tone sounds bored, like Lorna should know this. Like she's bothering him by asking. Like he is there not to provide information to anyone but to watch the TV Lorna bought and lounge on the couch she bought after Kristen nearly burned down the cheap one that was here before.

The rage begins to build.

She stalks back to her mother's room and finds her in bed, a scarf around her head. She is propped against the pillows and watching a smaller, older TV. "How long has that guy been here?" Lorna demands.

"What guy?" her mother asks idly. She tries to sit up and grimaces. "Lolo, I can't find my pain pills. They should be right here on my nightstand. Will you look in the bathroom?"

Lorna goes into the bathroom. The countertop is covered with hair products, tooth-cleaning products, and brushes and combs. The toilet has a ring in the bowl. It doesn't look like it's been cleaned in weeks.

She can't find the medication. She goes into the kitchen and searches there, opening drawers and doors.

"Can you keep it down?" the man asks over his shoulder.

Her rage bubbles like a cauldron.

She goes to Kristen's room and stands at the threshold, feeling seasick. The floor is completely covered in clothes and shoes and empty fast-food bags and dishes. Something smells like soured milk. She can't find the pain pills here either. She picks her way to Kristen's unmade bed and lifts a sheet to look. All she finds is a pair of panties and a used condom.

"What the hell are you doing?"

Lorna drops the sheet and turns to the door. Kristen is standing there holding a plastic CVS shopping bag. She is too thin, her hair as greasy and stringy as that of the guy she's with. The T-shirt she's wearing is too big on her skeletal frame, and her collarbones are protruding.

"Looking for Mom's pain pills that have gone missing. She's hurting and I can't find them in the mess of this apartment."

Kristen holds up the bag. "They're in here. Stop searching my room. What are you, a cop?" She tosses the bag onto the bed. Lorna picks it up. There are some cigarettes, an orange pill bottle, and some Takis and gummy worms, like Kristen is twelve. Lorna takes the bottle out and notices that it contains only fifteen pills. "Why so few?"

"Because Mom lost the other ones. They wouldn't fill it up."

Lorna stares hard at her sister, who won't make eye contact. "*Mom* lost the other ones?"

"That's what I said. What's your problem?" Kristen snaps.

"Did you take Mom's meds that she is prescribed for cancer?"

Kristen colors slightly, but a hardness fills her eyes. "Could you for once not come in here accusing me of everything?"

"Could you for once not steal from Mom? You're unbelievable! She is in pain, Kristen."

Kristen jumps over the mess to her closet and takes out a duffel bag. She starts stuffing clothes into it. Off the chair, off the floor.

"What are you doing?" Lorna demands.

"Beau and I are leaving. I am so sick of you."

"Leaving? What about Mom?"

Kristen twists around to face Lorna, her face an ugly grimace. "What do you want from me? You accuse me of doing a bad job when I'm here, and when I'm not, I'm not taking care of Mom. I can't win with you!"

"You can't leave, Kristen. Mom needs help. She needs someone here."

"Peggy is here. She'll do it."

"It's not Peggy's responsibility!" Lorna shouts.

"Who made you the queen of us? Huh? It's not my responsibility either. If you don't like it, hire someone. You make good money."

Lorna gapes at her sister. "Are you kidding me? You can't hold a job, you're high most of the time, and yet you get free room and board. All you have to do is look after our mother and not steal from her. Is that so hard?"

"Yes!" Kristen shrieks. And just as suddenly, she sighs wearily. She reaches in her back pocket for a pack of cigarettes.

"Don't you dare smoke in here," Lorna snaps.

"Lorna, stop," Kristen says wearily.

Lorna can't stop. She is seething. "Stop what? Stop trying to get you to be responsible for one damn thing? Stop trying to get you to put down the crack pipe?"

"I don't smoke crack."

"Today," Lorna snaps.

"Yes," Kristen says. "Stop it. All of that. When are you going to get it through your head that you are not going to change me? This is who I am, Lorna. Why can't you accept that?"

Lorna is stunned by the question. "Because I can't accept it. Could anyone?"

"Yeah, lots of people. Because the thing is, it's not up to you. You don't get to decide my life—*I* do. You may not like who I am or what I do, but I'm fine with it."

"That's a lie."

"No, it's not."

"You're fine with drug use and no job and stealing from Mom? You're fine with how your life impacts everyone else?"

Kristen rolls her eyes. "Stop trying to change me. You harping on it all the time is not going to work. I can't be like you, Lorna.

I see the world very differently. So just stop." She hauls up the duffel and goes out the door.

"Kristen!" Lorna adds panic to rage. "You can't be serious—you can't walk out that door. What about Mom?"

"Yeah, I can walk out. Because I'm sick to death of being made to feel like I'm subhuman. Come on, Beau."

"Where to?" he asks, hauling himself up off the couch.

"I don't know. You figure it out," Kristen says.

Lorna is shocked. "Kristen—"

"Lolo, for crying out loud, go live your own life and stop worrying about mine." Kristen leaves, slamming the door behind her.

Lorna hears her and Beau begin to argue on the way down the steps. She doesn't hear her mother at first, but she feels her icy hand on her arm and turns around. Her mother looks pale and terribly thin. She eases herself into a recliner.

"Did she leave again?" her mother asks, her eyes closed as pain overtakes her.

"Yes. She's been stealing your pills again, Mom."

"Oh dear. You'll have to call the doctor and explain."

Lorna's anger is pounding in her ears. Of course she will have to. She turns around and slams her fist against the countertop, wincing with the pain it causes her.

"Don't start that," her mother says.

"Don't start what? Letting go my extreme frustration? Then how am I supposed to deal with it? Because it is filling me up, and the next best thing is taking a nosedive off the top of the garage."

Her mother opens her eyes. "Don't talk like that."

"I have a worthless sister who does nothing but float between jail and you, living off her family, and she can't even let you have your meds. It's maddening, Mom."

"Kristen can't help—"

"Don't you dare," Lorna interrupts, her voice low and dark. "Don't you dare defend her."

"I'm not defending her. I'm just saying, Lolo. Addiction is a disease. She can't help that she is in the grip of it, any more than you can help how angry you are or I can help that I have cancer. I know it's a burden—"

"Now you are putting words in my mouth."

"You don't have to say it—it's written all over your face. We are both burdens to you." She sighs. "Can you get me some water?"

Lorna goes into Kristen's room to get the medication and then to the kitchen to get water. She comes back, hands her mother a pill and the water, then sits on the couch near her. "It's not fair," she says. "I have a demanding job. Kristen lives here free without any responsibility. We should be able to rely on her."

"Kristen does her best," her mother says wearily.

The rage explodes. Tears begin to slide down her face. "You're defending her again, Mom, and I can't bear it. We've lived in the shadow of her addiction for so long that you've lost all perspective. Doesn't it matter to you that she's been ruling my life since I was a girl?"

"What does that mean?"

"Are you serious?" Lorna asks incredulously. "You've spent all your time focused on her, and I was left to fend for myself. I got an award today. But I was there by myself because there is never anyone there for me. Never! I humiliated myself and lost my best friend at thirteen because of her. I threw up onstage in front of everyone and cost my high school choir competition because of her. I treated a boyfriend terribly because of her. I was arrested because of her; my classmate died because of her! And so much more. You know this. And we just keep letting her cycle in and out of our lives like it's no big thing. It's grossly unfair."

"I never said it was fair. And there is nothing I am more aware of than how unfair it's been to you, Lolo." She reaches out her hand, forcing Lorna to take it. She weakly squeezes her fingers. "I know I was not the best mother to you. I know I wasn't there when you needed me. But Kristen has been troubled since she was a little girl, and her problems were so deep and so profound and so constant that I didn't know how to balance the two of you. And for that, I am very sorry."

Rivers of Lorna's rage stream down her face. "You could have sent her to Dad."

Her mother snorts. "She'd be dead by now."

Lorna pulls her hand free and covers her face with both hands. She thinks she hates them—her mother, her nonexistent father, and Kristen most of all. "You could have done something," she says. "You could have been my mother too. But no, you'll continue to let her crash here and use you, and you will continue to ask me to pick up the pieces."

"Oh honey, please let it go. I'm not going to turn my daughter out to the streets. But you? You're young, you have a bright future. This bitterness is going to eat you alive. You need to let the past go and be present in your life now. Think about your future. Don't think about how you've been wronged."

"If you think a few years of Al-Anon means you can start psychoanalyzing me, you're wrong," Lorna says curtly. "I've had enough therapy to last all my life, and still, nothing ever changes."

"Because the only thing you can change is the way you react, honey. Like all this dwelling on the things that happened so long ago. You could change the way you view it all. For example, Callie. You could talk to her."

"Oh my God," Lorna mutters.

"And the choir concert, well . . . things happen to all kids. If you feel so strongly about it, write your teacher a letter or something."

"You make it sound like I'm being whiny, Mom. That was traumatic."

"I'm just saying you have regrets you should find a way to let go of for the sake of your own happiness. No matter what happens with Kristen or me, your life is your choice. Your happiness is a choice. You could choose to find a way to let it go and be happy. And as for all your disappointment with your sister? You'd be happier if you let her go too. Kristen is going to do what she's going to do, and nothing is going to change that. But *you* can change if you are unhappy. You can decide now to let her go and live your life. I want you to be happy, Lolo. It's too late for me to help you, but you can help yourself."

Lorna can't stand much more of this—her rage, her grief, her inability to control a single thing in her life. "Really?" She stands. "And how is that going to work, Mom? You're going to die, and then who will be here to take care of Kristen?"

Her mother says nothing.

Lorna gets up and goes to the door. "I'll call your doctor tomorrow," she says.

"I'd appreciate it."

Lorna draws a shaky breath. "Do you have food? I'll call a service and see if they can come in a couple of times a week and check on you. Maybe do some shopping."

"Peggy will look in on me."

Lorna is seething so hard that she is shaking. "It's not Peggy's job, Mom. I'll talk to you later." She puts her hand on the doorknob, so full of rage she can hardly see.

"Lorna?"

Lorna steels herself and looks back at her frail mother.

"I always wanted to be a mother; did you know that? I never wanted to have a career; I wanted to be a mom. I wanted to be a good mother to you both, but unfortunately, I discovered I only had the capacity to be a mother to the neediest of you. That is the regret I will take to my grave."

Lorna says nothing. She leaves without speaking.

Her mother takes the regret to her grave by the end of the month.

Chapter 34

Lorna Now

THE DAY OF BEAN'S SCIENCE FAIR DEBUT WAS OVERCAST and cold. It seemed the perfect sort of weather for Lorna and Aggie to pay a visit to her mother's grave. Kristen had insisted Mom be buried instead of cremated so that they would always have a place to be near her. Lorna had been too broken to argue the practicalities or metaphysics of that, and had, of course, taken care of it. Except the coffin. Kristen had insisted on a pale pink coffin with a blue silk lining. "She's been sick for so long, I want her to be happy," she'd said.

Lorna wondered how many times Kristen had come here to be near Mom.

She brought fresh flowers with her. In the weeks and months after her mother died, Lorna came every week without fail, changing out the flowers, picking weeds until the grass grew over the grave site. But as time went on, she visited less often and moved deeper into herself. She'd told herself that her mother wasn't here, and that coming here wasn't going to bring her back, not even in spirit. She was surprised at the sense of peace she felt walking up to the grave. She did feel a little closer to her.

A church group had put plastic flowers on untended graves.

Lorna removed them from the permanent flower vase and replaced them with the flowers she'd brought. She gazed at the granite tombstone. *Mindy Ann Pearson Lott*, it read, with the dates of her mother's birth and death just below. Her mother had been sixty-eight years old when she died. *So young.*

Lorna stood with her arms crossed over her body, hugging herself. Considering who she was in this moment. She didn't feel like the same woman who had last been here with tears in her eyes and rage in her heart. She didn't feel like that lonely woman who couldn't find a way to reach out to anyone. She felt different now. Lighter. Like she was finally letting go of things she really couldn't control.

She had things she wanted to say. To the wind, she guessed. To the universe. To Mom, wherever she was now.

Aggie sniffed around the headstone, then lay down, pressing her back against the warm granite.

Lorna squatted down beside her dog. She was wearing joggers today. Bean had urged her to get some "stretchy pants" for when they sat on the floor and made buildings out of plastic blocks, and as she didn't feel comfortable bending and contorting herself in yoga pants in front of him, she'd ordered some roomier "stretchy pants" online. She liked them so much she'd gone ahead and ordered a hoodie, because Bean said his teacher wore one. The clothes were certainly versatile, but she felt like an archaeologist squatting like this in these clothes, like she was studying the artifacts of an old grave. So she sat cross-legged—why not? She'd spent the last month seated like this. She pulled a few weeds that had sprouted while she gathered her thoughts. And when she was ready and Aggie was lightly snoring, she spoke. "I hope you can hear me," she said. "Because I need to tell you something. I get it now, Mom. I needed you. I did. But now I understand why you couldn't always be there for me."

If her mother heard her, there was no indication from the universe.

Lorna suddenly flopped onto her back, draping herself across her mother's grave and gazing at the lead-gray sky above her. "The funny thing is, even though I still need you, Kristen still needs you more than me. Ironic, isn't it? You'd think I might take top billing for once, given that I was almost fired and put into a wellness program because of my rage and inability to trust anyone." She sighed. "And she still wins. But you know what? It's okay."

She squeezed her eyes shut as tears began to build. Of course they did. But they weren't tears of rage—they were tears of regret and nostalgia and grief. "First, I need to tell you that I forgive you, Mom," she said, her voice breaking. Aggie whimpered softly and shifted close to Lorna, draping her head across Lorna's belly. Lorna sank her fingers into Aggie's fur. "I'm sorry it took me so long. I'm ashamed of how long it took me to find grace in my heart for you. And the worst of it is, I hated that I felt that way. You have no idea how much I wish I could have found a way to forgive you before you died. I don't know what to say for myself, other than I was so angry that I couldn't really think for a very long time. For *years*. And as much as I regret it, it's still hard to think beyond myself. But I'm working on it. I'm opening my body meridians." She choked on a sob and a laugh at the same time. "I'll explain that some other time."

The tree canopy began to sway on a breeze. Lorna wasn't the sort to think her mother was talking to her that way—or at least she hadn't been before she went to Bodhi—but she could hope it.

"I forgive you, Mom, and I know that hardly seems fair since I was the one doing all the yelling. But I was so angry with you for dying and leaving me with Kristen. I didn't want the responsibility of her. I didn't want to spend all my energy on her. I hated her for what she'd done to us, and to you, and to me, and I need to forgive you for allowing it before I can find a way to forgive myself and the horrible way I treated you in the end. And the way I treated Kristen." She groaned with the painful memories. "Oh my, I'm so sorry, Mother. I am *so* sorry. I hope you can forgive me now. Please forgive me."

She watched the trees dance on the breeze for several moments while she stroked Aggie's fur. A sudden memory arose of Kristen standing in the door of her room, looking thin and sickly. Kristen *was* sick. She was sick in a way that had no real cure. She was as sick as Mom had been, an incurable disease that was eating away at her every day of her life, and Lorna had hated her for it.

"I miss you so much," Lorna whispered, and for a moment, she wasn't sure who she meant, Mom or Kristen. "And I want to make it up to you. I want to show you how sorry I am for the things I said and the way I acted. You didn't deserve that, not on top of everything else. Unfortunately, you're dead, so it's not going to be easy to make it up to you, you know?"

She slowly sat up and wiped the tears from her cheeks. "I'm so sick of crying. I'm not crying as much these days, because I guess the anger is slowly leaking out of me and I am learning some new coping skills. Mainly, how to get hold of my negative thoughts and turn them around." She smiled at the sky. "You would love Bodhi, Mom. It's right up your Al-Anon alley." She turned her grin to Aggie as she thought about how much her mother would have loved float therapy, specifically. But she sobered quickly, remembering her reason for being here. "I don't want to cry anymore. I want to laugh. I want to live. I want to know people, and I hope people will want to know me. You were right—once I faced those moments that had been burned into my brain because of Kristen, I could sort of see them from another angle and let go of the hate I had for myself." She sighed, brushed her hands against her legs. Aggie lifted her head and smelled the breeze. "Not *all* the hate. But I'm working hard to get there."

She turned her attention to the headstone. "You don't have to send me a celestial sign, because I already know exactly what you want me to do." She stood and picked up one of the faded plastic flowers. "And I'm going to do it, I promise. Just give me a few days." With her hand on the tombstone, she added, "I love you, Mom. I miss you." Then she dropped her hand and looked at her dog. "Okay, Aggie, let's go. I've got to get to a science fair."

Aggie hopped up obediently and trotted alongside her to the car.

Lorna drove straight to Peggy's house. She and Aggie handed her the faded plastic bloom.

Peggy knew instantly where it had come from. "Well. This wasn't on your mother's list."

"Nope. It was on mine."

Peggy nodded. She looked at Lorna and smiled tenderly. It startled Lorna to see tears in her eyes. Peggy pressed her palm against Lorna's cheek. "I'm going to guess you've got one more thing on your list."

"Yep," Lorna said, and smiled. "You're starting to sound like Mom, by the way."

"That is a huge compliment," Peggy said, leaning down to give Aggie some neck scritches.

• • •

That afternoon, Martin, Liz, and Lorna walked down to the grade school to see the science fair. It was exactly what one might expect—more parents than kids, lots of grandparents, and beaming kids. There were egg floats and clouds in a bottle. There was a 3D model of the sun. And there was a kid who had done an experiment where he took two identical plants, talked to one and not the other, and marked the difference in growth. Remarkably, the plant that had been talked to was noticeably taller than the other one.

"How does that happen?" Liz marveled.

"Easy," Martin muttered. "You go to the nursery and get a bigger one."

"Martin!"

Martin shrugged off Liz's chiding and looked around. "There are at least four volcanoes, and that's just from a cursory glance," he announced. "Shall we check out the competition?"

"Absolutely," Liz said.

"You go on," Lorna said. "I'm going to check in with the master."

Martin and Liz set off to examine the science projects. Lorna went in the opposite direction, to Bean's table. It was easy to spot—he was out front in his blue vest with his many badges and his explorer hat. She noticed he also had a flashlight attached to his belt.

She spotted Seth and waved, then pointed to the flashlight as he walked over. "Oh, that. So he can illuminate the inside of his volcano for the judges." Just then, Bean unclipped his flashlight to show two adults what was inside.

"That's a lot of mud," Lorna said, noting the construction of the volcano.

"Yep, the hole he and Aggie dug in the backyard came in handy after all," Seth said with a chuckle. "It was Martin's idea."

Lorna glanced at Seth. They exchanged a knowing smile that she felt all the way to her toes.

More parents wandered by, and Bean launched into the explanation of his experiment with each new arrival. He had rehearsed it, she knew, because he'd run it past her three times. The kid had no fear.

"Want to have a look at the other entries?" Seth asked.

"Sure."

The pair of them wandered the long hall, taking in the experiments. Lorna was impressed with the creativity. "Jill would have loved this," Seth said. "She loved all the kid stuff."

Lorna tried to imagine what the Rooney family unit must have looked like. Did they live in a house or apartment? Were there playdates and date nights and friends and holidays? "Were you going to have more kids?" Lorna asked, then immediately winced. "Sorry. None of my business."

"No, it's okay, I don't mind talking about Jill," he said. "We were considering it. But she was gearing up for a century ride."

"A what?"

"It's a hundred-mile bike ride they stage for charity. She and some of her cycling friends were planning to enter the Jalapeño 100 Bike Ride in the Valley. It requires a lot of training." He looked off. "And I'd just taken this new job with long hours, so . . . well, obviously, we never got around to it."

Lorna tried to picture Bean in that scenario. If Seth was working and Jill was riding her bike, who was playing with him? Who was helping him build his long Hot Wheels track or make houses out of blocks?

"Bean loves his vest," Seth said, looking at Lorna again. "Thank you for that. It's important to him and it means a lot to me. Honestly, that Ranger Explorer troop is the one thing he has right now. It's hard for Bean to make friends. Diego is moving in a few weeks, and he feels a little lost, I think."

"What about family?" Lorna asked. "Do you have anyone close by?"

Seth shook his head. "My mom and dad try to help, but Dad's health isn't great. Jill's parents are in New York and see Bean once or twice a year." He paused. "What about you? Any family nearby?"

She shook her head. "My mom is gone, as you know. And my sister and Dad are in Florida. We're on opposite ends of . . ." She hesitated. Opposite ends of what? Substance abuse? Self-respect? Health? There were so many things. She couldn't think of an appropriate catchall word, so she said simply, "Life."

He nodded, and maybe he understood or maybe he didn't, but Seth had a way of knowing when not to press. "What are you going to do when the apartments sell?" he asked. There was no mention of fighting it. Seth assumed they were all moving.

"Umm . . ." She could hear Micah urging her to tell the truth. She could just admit she was the buyer. Tell him about her history and the house. She could offer to let him and Bean stay. She could invite Martin and Liz to stay. They could all stay until they found other arrangements, because eventually, she wanted Nana's house to be Nana's house again.

She was 80 percent sure she did.

Then again, who was she kidding? Lorna felt something changing in her. She didn't know all the ways she was changing, or how far the changes would go. She just knew it was happening. She said truthfully, "I honestly don't know." She didn't feel as determined or cutthroat about her plans anymore. She wanted to feel like she had something, like there was a reason for her to exist. But maybe there were options.

"I wish you would look into the condos I found," Seth said. "They're opening up new units." He suddenly stopped strolling and faced her. "Bean and I would really like that, Lorna. And I'm not just saying that for Bean's sake. I would like it too."

"Oh." Lorna was stunned. She could feel a warmth creeping up her spine, a familiar swell of yearning. She could not have been more surprised if he'd announced he was an alien or running for president or a wanted criminal. She didn't even know how to respond. Part of her would very much like it too. But there was so much unfinished business for her, and there was the whole issue of her confidence and ability to trust. But she would like it. She would more than like it—she would relish it.

She glanced around them, at the happy kids, the families, the science experiments. The lives that were being lived while she lived in her past. She suddenly blurted, "I have to go to Florida."

"Umm . . ." Seth looked flustered by the abrupt change of subject.

"My sister. I have to go see my sister. And it's going to be hard, because everything with her is really hard."

"Is this part of the apology tour?"

Lorna nodded. She could feel tears building and gulped them down. "Last stop. I mean, unless something happens between now and then and I say something super offensive and have to apologize to you too."

He smiled wryly. "Let's just assume it's the last stop. Is that a good or bad thing?"

"I honestly don't know. And I'm a little scared to tell you the truth about it all."

"I can see why. Sounds like there is an awful lot of water under that bridge."

"A tsunami. But it's something I need to do before I can really think about what comes next. Do you understand?" she asked, feeling suddenly desperate. She almost wished he were Micah, who would have looked right at her and understood instantly.

"I . . . I think I do," he said uncertainly.

"And I need someone to look after Aggie. Do you think you and Bean could keep her for the week? She's good—she won't pee in your house."

"Aggie is the best," Seth agreed. "But . . ." He touched his fingers to hers, sort of playing with them, lacing into them. "I'm taking some time off. For fall break. What would you think . . . I mean, this is out of the blue, but . . . maybe Bean and I could go with you? Like travel buddies."

Lorna could feel her eyes widen with shock, to the size of small saucers, she was certain. She was amazed she wasn't crying. "Really?"

"Only if it's okay with you. Liz would look after Aggie, I'm sure of it. But I need a break, and I get the feeling you could use some moral support. Not to mention Bean could get his helping badge. You know how bad he wants his helping badge."

His fingers were still tickling hers, and she liked the feel of them. She liked the idea of Seth and Bean as her wingmen. She liked everything about this moment, and she was astounded that she wasn't afraid or being weird. She smiled. "I am acutely aware of how bad he wants his helping badge."

"What do you think?" Seth asked, and his fingers wrapped around hers in a firm hold. "Beach time for the boys, travel companions for you?"

If she agreed to this, she would have to tell him everything—she couldn't *not* tell him—but she believed it was worth the risk. "I would really like that."

Seth smiled. She did too. They stood there a minute, smiling at each other, their eyes speaking words she didn't quite grasp but knew were there, until they were interrupted by Martin and Liz.

"Earth to our neighbors!" Liz said cheerfully, startling Seth and Lorna both. "We have determined Bean has the best volcano. His spew is better than anyone's."

Of course it was.

Lorna laughed more that late afternoon than she had in a long time. She felt easier, and the knowledge that she had someone in her corner was like a warm blanket around her, holding her tight and safe. She felt great. Like she was someone and people liked her, wanted to be with her. Even King Kong had his moments.

She realized how badly she needed the support, too, because she had no idea what to expect when she saw her sister. She hadn't seen her since the night she kicked Kristen out of her apartment and told her she never wanted to see her again.

Chapter 35

Lorna Is Thirty-Nine

KRISTEN BEGS LORNA TO LET HER IN DURING THE COLDEST part of the winter. She says she's been living on the street and she's finally hit rock bottom. She says she is ready to make a change. Of course Lorna lets her into her new apartment. She is her mother's daughter after all.

In the first few weeks, Kristen behaves herself. She cleans the apartment when Lorna is at work, and she cooks dinner for Lorna when she comes home.

They watch past seasons of *The Bachelor* and groan and cringe at the same time, giggling like they did when they were girls, assigning superlatives to the contestants. "Most Likely to Spew When Drinking," Kristen anoints a tiny blond. "Most Likely to Throw Her Friend Under a Bus," Lorna adds for an ex–pageant queen.

Kristen talks about going to school for nursing, or dental school. "I just need to save for it."

Lorna is so excited that Kristen may be turning her life around, that she may have a sister again, that she says, "I'll help you pay for it."

"Really, Lolo?" Kristen asks.

"Really," Lorna assures her.

Kristen hugs her tight. "I could not have asked for a better sister. I love you, Lolo."

Lorna has noticed that Kristen has some new tattoos and a scar on her arm that she says she doesn't want to talk about, and Lorna doesn't press her. She doesn't want to think of what life has been like for Kristen. Because she's warm and funny, and when her health comes back to her, so does her beauty. She is the big sister Lorna had all those years ago, the one she so admired. The one she adored.

Kristen advises Lorna on her wardrobe again, helps her with her hair, even drags her to the gym. They make a TikTok video together—Kristen teaches her the popular dance making the rounds. They are out of sync and so bad, but it is so much fun. They laugh hard and collapse onto the floor in fits of laughter.

"It feels so good to be like this again," Kristen says to Lorna one night. "Remember when we used to dance for Nana and she would rate us?"

"Ten out of ten every time," Lorna says, laughing.

But when the weather turns warm, Kristen leaves. She's been talking to some guy and wants to "hang out" with him. Lorna doesn't know what that means, really, but she can't believe it's good.

"Don't go," she begs Kristen. "It's just going to happen all over again."

Kristen laughs. "Have a little faith! It's not going to happen again. I really like who I am when I'm sober. Do you need me to promise? I promise, I will be sober. He's sober. This is not about that."

She does not keep her promise. Again.

She comes back more times after that, and Lorna usually takes her in, just like Mom used to do. And Lorna hates herself for it just like she hated Mom for it. But she can't turn her back on her sister. She asks her dad for help, but he says he is tapped out.

"Tapped out of what?" Lorna asks. He hasn't offered emotional or financial support that she's aware of.

"Money," he says. "You think her jail fines and treatment stints are free? And I don't like the idea of her around my kids."

Lorna bristles at his characterization of his daughters as "his" kids. What does that make her and Kristen?

Lorna feels like she is on a hamster wheel. At Deb's suggestion, she starts another round of therapy, following up on the round she did after college. She attends groups for families of addicts. They talk a lot about the importance of setting firm boundaries with addicts and holding them. "You must protect your well-being and your health," the instructor insists. But no one in the group can really do it, Lorna included. She sets boundaries, and Kristen pushes past them. Lorna lets her because she is all Kristen has.

She begins to collect Precious Moments figurines, little porcelain glimpses of lives and the people she wishes they were. She gets a dog, Agnes, a cute rescue corgi, so she is not alone in this terrible battle with drugs. She feels rage every time Kristen comes around, and then guilt every time she leaves. Kristen gets odd jobs, then gets fired. She meets shady new characters, then disappears for days on end. She always has a phone—how do so many addicts who cannot support themselves have phones?

Sometimes after Kristen has been on a bender, she will swear again she is going to stay sober, that she hates being high all the time. She forgets that at times she has said she wants to be high all the time. It doesn't matter—she never keeps her promise. Never.

Lorna reaches her breaking point when Kristen steals money

from her purse and some Precious Moments figurines. Worse, when she leaves with the money and the figurines, she leaves the door open for Agnes to escape. When Lorna comes home from work, she quickly pieces together what happened. She is frantic. Hysterical, even, that she has lost Agnes. It takes her almost thirty-six hours to track down Agnes and reunite with her. When she does, she collapses with grief and anxiety.

Kristen never hits rock bottom, but Lorna finally does.

The next time Kristen comes around, Lorna has changed the locks and tells her she is no longer welcome. That Lorna can't have Kristen's chaos in her life anymore. She has set her boundary, and she is holding to it.

Kristen doesn't believe her at first, but when she understands Lorna will not allow her to crash in her house and steal from her, she loses control. She calls Lorna every name she can think of. She says she hates her, she's always hated her, and she hopes she dies. Lorna watches her sister walk to the street with no place to go. She looks broken, but Lorna is too.

A week goes by before the police contact Lorna with their Jane Doe. Lorna calls Dad, who flies immediately to Austin. Kristen, they say, has overdosed on something that was laced with fentanyl. She is lucky, they say, that it didn't kill her.

Kristen is not lucky. Lorna wishes she would have died, because Kristen has suffered irreversible brain damage. She is now in a residential facility in Florida.

The guilt and grief Lorna holds are unbearable. She tries to move on. She moves to Nana's house. She attends more therapy, takes antidepressants, tries anything there is to soothe a hurt like this, and nothing works. Nothing but her bomb shelter. She closes herself off and away so that her rage with life and the cards she was dealt festers until she almost loses her job.

She wishes she hadn't run out of compassion for Kristen, but she only had so much. She thinks only a deity could have the amount of compassion required to deal with a loved one who is a hardcore addict. She wishes her life could be different, that she could be happy. Happy like she and her whole family were early on, once upon a time.

They were happy, weren't they?

Weren't they?

Chapter 36

Lorna Now

LORNA SAT ON THE FLOOR OF HER APARTMENT WITH A glass of wine and Aggie snoozing on the couch behind her. The stacks of pink and white envelopes were in front of her, and she was casually pondering the difference in the size of the stacks. There were far more white letters than pink. She pushed the white ones to the side—she knew what they said.

But she hadn't read the pink ones. She was going to do that tonight. She was preparing for her trip to Florida, and she knew that Kristen's life there would be detailed in those letters.

Earlier that day, she'd called her dad for the first time in months.

"Lorna?" he'd said, his voice full of surprise. "I can't believe it's you. I didn't think I would ever speak to you again. Is everything okay?"

Lorna had to think about that. "It's getting better. I'm calling because there is something I need to do, and I thought you'd want to know."

"Uh-oh," he said. "I don't like the sound of that."

"I need to come see Kristen."

Her words were met with a very long pause. Lorna could feel the tension radiating through the phone. "Really?" he said at last, his voice flat. "Why now?"

"Because I'm working on letting go of the past. And I need to forgive her. And I need her to forgive me."

Dad snorted derisively. "You know she can't do that."

"I know she can't talk," Lorna said.

"She's not all there, Lolo. I don't know what you think, but she's just a shell at this point."

Lorna's chest tightened. That was exactly what she'd feared was in the pink letters that Trish kept writing.

"Still, I need to come. Is that okay?"

"Of course it's okay," he said, sounding snippy now. "I've been asking you to come to Florida for ages. I could use some help here. Text me the information and we'll pick you up."

"Thanks." She wanted to say she missed him or she loved him. But she didn't find either of those things to be true. He had ceased being a part of her life so long ago that she couldn't even remember what it felt like to have a dad, much less love one. As a result, she felt nothing for him. Family was funny that way—either you were in it or you weren't. There was no halfway. "I'll see you soon," she'd said softly.

Now she picked up the first pink letter. "Here goes nothing, Aggie," she said, breaking the seal.

Trish's handwriting was big and loopy.

Dear Lorna,

> I hope you are well. We went to see Kristen today. They have her sitting up in the dayroom, watching TV. At least it appeared she was watching. But she didn't show us any recognition.

"How could she? She never saw you either," Lorna muttered.

Kristen drew something on a piece of paper. It was just a few lines, but it was progress.

She needs underwear and socks if you'd like to help with the purchase.

They have put her on antianxiety meds because she gets agitated.

We were going to take her out for some sun, but the wheelchair we rented wouldn't fit in Dave's truck.

Kristen's hair is falling out. They think she might have an iron deficiency, but we would have to pay for that test.

And so on.

When Lorna had finished reading the pink letters, she drained the last of her wine. Then she picked up the stack of white letters and began to open them. They were all typewritten, spell-checked, and surprisingly chatty. She scanned them all, the words she'd written still ablaze in her brain. But when she read them one after another, she could see, could *feel*, the rage, the guilt, and the utter grief that dripped from each page.

It was little wonder she had locked herself away.

The true wonder was that she'd survived.

But Lorna had finally come to realize there was nothing she ever could have done to change the outcome of what happened. Of anything. Sure, she might have let Kristen stay, but there would have been a next time, and a next time, and a next time. Kristen had been on the road to this fate since she was ten years old. Maybe she'd been destined for it from the beginning. And the only person who could have stopped it, who could have changed the course of it, was Kristen. She either couldn't or, for some subconscious reason, didn't want to.

Lorna recalled what a substance abuse counselor had once told her. "Your sister likely won't change until she hits rock bottom," she'd said. "And she hasn't hit it yet. Remember, we are talking her rock bottom. Not what you think her rock bottom is. Not what *your* rock bottom is. You must make peace with loving her from afar."

Well, she guessed Kristen had finally hit her rock bottom.

She stacked the white letters next to the pink and picked up the accordion file Peggy had given her. She took out the papers and began to sort through the details of the will and the trust.

There were so many papers in that file—a death certificate, papers from probate. A certificate from the cemetery. Her mother's banking information. And then Lorna found what she'd been looking for—the information on the trust itself.

She read through it. Then read through it again. After a moment of disbelief, she burst into laughter so loud that Aggie jumped up from a dead sleep and barked. She couldn't believe what she was seeing. After all the agony of getting to this trust, there was only $7,500 in it. That was it, all her mother had left after her own illness and Kristen's continued care and the settling of her estate.

The next morning, on her way to Bodhi for the last time (unless, as Xandra said, she wanted to cough up $500 a week for services), Lorna received a text from Callie.

We are back from vacation. Our middle kid keeps asking about Bean. Maybe you could bring him and come for a glass of wine in the next couple of weeks? Do you even drink? What do you do? You were so weird when you were here I was afraid to ask.

Lorna was stunned. And ridiculously over-the-moon pleased. She quickly fired back a response. *Oh my God, I am so glad you got* in touch. Yes, I drink on occasion. And I am trying to be less weird. Feel free to point out all weirdness so I can work on it.

Callie texted back; they made a plan to meet.

Lorna had emailed Deb this morning to let her know she was attending her last session and that the program wasn't nearly as bad as she'd expected. She admitted to learning a few things about herself.

Deb almost immediately wrote back. *Great! So happy to hear it. I can't wait to have you back in the office.*

Lorna didn't believe that for a minute, but she was coming back. Just as soon as she returned from Florida.

Montreal was there to greet her on the way in. "Yoga today?"

"Absolutely," Lorna said.

Montreal smiled as he escorted her to the yoga studio. "You know, when I advised you to lean into those yoga pants, I didn't really believe it was possible. Are you going to keep up your practice?"

"*You* were surprised? Imagine my shock and awe. Yes, I am going to keep up with my practice. I pass a yoga studio on the way to work."

Montreal laughed. "Lorna, that is awesome."

After yoga and morning meditation, Lorna met Montreal so that he could escort her to Micah's office.

"I like what you're doing with your hair," he said.

"What, letting it go au naturel?"

"It's fun," he said. "Curly and wild. Kind of like you. I like it."

Lorna was far too delighted with the compliment. "Do you really think I am curly and wild?"

They had reached Micah's door. Montreal put his hand on her arm. "I think you are curly and wild and amazing." He opened the door to Micah's office.

"Lorna!" Micah called. He was in silky green lounge pants and a Bon Jovi T-shirt today, and his long locks were piled atop his head in a towering bun. He held up a cup of lavender tea for her. "Graduation day," he said.

"Yep." She took the tea and sank gracefully onto the beanbag. She'd been practicing at home with Bean. "May I say something?"

"The floor is yours."

"When you said I was grieving, I was angry with you. I didn't realize that I was grieving, but I do now."

Micah smiled. "No apology is necessary. It's not uncommon to dislike observations. And no one likes to grieve. Many people spend years denying grief. So now that you've completed your list, how do you feel about your month here?"

"That's the other thing I was going to tell you. I'm not quite done with the list."

"No?" He looked confused and took a file from his desk.

"It's not in there. I have one last stop on the apology tour. And it's a whopper."

Micah looked up. "Tell me."

"I'm going to see Kristen. And . . . I'm going so that I can forgive her. And then see if she can forgive me. If she's capable. I mean, cognitively."

"Wow," Micah said, and slowly put her file aside. "I don't think we have enough time to tackle this one."

"It's okay. I think I can handle it with my new coping skills. Although, it is entirely possible that I am being very stupid and about to undo everything I've worked for in here."

Micah chuckled. "There is a very thin line between stupidity and bravery, you know, but I'm banking on this being bravery. Just remember you've spent a month looking at the roots of your dysfunction and working to put yourself in a healthy mindset."

"My dysfunction?" Lorna smiled sheepishly. "Is that what we're calling it?"

"Well . . . your isolation and loneliness were dysfunctional, were they not? You have found ways to come out of your shell and let negative thoughts go. If you feel yourself getting tense or angry when you see your sister, remember some of those techniques to tap into your thoughts and change the trajectory."

"Right," she said.

"And remember that when you let go of the past and negative thoughts, you are open to healthier and newer experiences. The relationship you had with your sister does not have to be the relationship you have now. What she represented to you when it was a healthy relationship is still there. You might find a way forward that is new and different."

She thought of Bean. Of Seth. Of Martin and Liz, all of whom she now considered friends. And when it came to Seth, well, she hoped for more. "So . . . it's like if I can find a way to feel completely safe, even when I'm gruff and crotchety, I can let the past go."

"Something like that." He grinned. "I'm going to miss you, Lorna Lott. I hope you'll stop by and let me know how the last apology goes for you. Now . . . let's get you into some float therapy before you end for the day. Won't hurt to be in total darkness, alone with your thoughts, one last time."

Lorna sighed. "Oh, Micah. Never change."

He laughed.

She went to her last float therapy and found, as she was weightless, floating in complete darkness, that she did think about what he'd said. She thought about Bean, who accepted her from the beginning. About Seth, who never asked her uncomfortable questions and made her feel safe in his company.

She thought about Callie texting her, and seriously, was that real? Could she really be friends with Callie again?

She thought about how she was finally forgiving herself, the person in her life who needed to be forgiven the most. She thought about so many things that when Montreal eventually knocked on her door, she didn't want to get out. She had so many more things to think about.

> Hey K, so guess what? I'm coming to see you. I'm sort of glad but very scared. I don't know what to expect. Will you know me? Will you remember what happened? Will you remember how much I loved you? Will you ever forgive me?

Chapter 37

Lorna Now

LORNA'S DAD LOOKED A LOT OLDER THAN HE HAD JUST three years ago, when he came to take Kristen back to Florida. His wife, Trish, was heavily made up with not a hair out of place, like she'd always been—but even she looked a little worse for wear. Lorna knew that look. It was the stress of Kristen. She could zap the fortitude of the strongest people.

Addiction and its effects and aftermaths and consequences—all of it—was such an insidious thing, pulling apart the best of families. Lorna sincerely hoped Kristen hadn't managed to do that to Dad's second family. She wouldn't wish that agony on anyone.

It was humbling to think of Kristen's journey in this life. If she got too in her head (thanks, float therapy), Lorna couldn't help but wonder what might have been for Kristen and their family. What if Kristen had conquered her need to numb herself? What if she hadn't turned out to be an addict in the first place? Where would she be now? Where would they all be now? But the life Kristen had squandered by choosing drugs over all else was too hard to imagine.

"Lorna," Dad said, and hugged her tight. She was slightly taller than him, and it felt awkward. "It's so good to see you."

"You too, Dad," she said. But she felt nothing. Not even rage or anger or disgust. Here was a man with whom she was acquainted, who had the misfortune of being the father to a child who'd suffered brain damage. Other than that, he looked like a guy who would live in Florida.

Dad turned to Seth and Bean and said, "Oh. I wasn't expecting anyone else."

"I'm Trish," Dad's wife said, moving to greet Seth and Bean. "And this is Dave. So *nice* to meet you! We had no idea Lorna was in a relationship!"

"I'm not," Lorna said.

"We just wanted to keep her company," Seth added, smiling at Lorna. This man got her. He understood her unwillingness to give her dad and Trish a single thing, and he was going to support her in that.

She introduced them properly. Bean was dressed in his vest and explorer hat and had his Ranger Explorer backpack. On the flight over, he'd been glued to the window, making notes about what he saw, and Lorna had the chance to fill Seth in a little more about her family history. She hadn't told him all of it yet—she liked him and wanted to keep him as a friend, and she had the sense that a little went a long way. But she also knew she could confide in him. That he wouldn't judge her. She could almost hear Micah crowing, *Look at you, you're trusting someone, Lorna!*

When the introductions were made, Dad asked if she had everything. "We can swing by the facility on the way home."

"What?" Lorna was startled. She wasn't ready. She needed . . . something. Time? At least a chance to change clothes, to get her game face on. She hadn't expected to see Kristen immediately.

"It's just a few blocks from here," her dad pointed out. "Wouldn't make sense to go all the way home and then come back. Not with the price of gas what it is."

For heaven's sake, why hadn't she just rented a car? "But Seth and Bean are here. They don't want to hang out at some residential care facility."

"We can get a cab or a rideshare," Seth said. "Don't worry about us."

"Yay!" Bean said. "I've always wanted to ride in a cab!"

"You don't have to wait there," Dad said. "There's a café next door. A Starbucks on the corner. I think it makes more sense."

"Okay," Seth said reluctantly, and to Bean he said, "We'll get a cab later."

Dad turned to lead the charge to the parking garage; Seth exchanged a look with Lorna. Yep, that was her father—unwilling to consider anyone else's comfort but his own. "Are you okay?" he asked quietly.

Lorna forced a sort of smile. "I'm not *not* okay," she said. "I guess I'm just going to rip off the bandage."

Seth sort of shrugged. "May be the best way to do it."

"Are *you* okay?" she whispered.

"Don't you worry about the Rooney boys. We can survive your dad." He winked at her, and Lorna knew he could survive anything. The man was a rock.

The residential care facility was a series of buildings behind an iron fence. Lorna had searched for it on Google Maps when Kristen was admitted here and thought then that it looked more like a prison than a long-term care facility.

"I'll just pop in with you," Dad said, pulling into a parking space.

"Umm . . . if you don't mind, Dad, I'd rather go in alone," Lorna said. She was already feeling sick with nerves. The last time she'd seen Kristen was in the hospital. She'd been on a ventilator, her hair greasy and her face and arms bruised. She'd looked dead.

"Are you sure, Lolo? You don't know what ward—"

"I'll find it," she said quickly. It was one thing to face Kristen. It was quite another to do it with Dad hovering. She reached forward from her seat behind her father and put her hand on his shoulder, squeezing gently. "I need to do this on my own."

"Okay," he said, and sighed. "We'll be at the café. Just text when you're done."

"Got it," Lorna said, opening the door.

"Wait!" Bean cried. He reached into his backpack and pulled out a Precious Moments figurine. It was the mother and child with a puppy figurine she'd seen in Seth's apartment. "This is you and me," he said. "So it's kind of like I'll be there too."

Lorna studied the figurine he pressed into her hand. She thought he'd taken it because it reminded him of his mother. "*Bean*," she said, her voice full of all the emotion she was feeling. She grabbed him, hugging him tightly. "Thank you." She looked across the top of his head at Seth. She could see tears shining in his eyes, but he turned his face away, cleared his throat.

With the figurine in her pocket, she walked into the facility. There was a lot of security, and she needed to provide ample proof that she was allowed to see the patient, but she was at last escorted out of the main building, across a courtyard, and to a plain long building near the back of the complex. They went through a secure door, down a charmless corridor, and then arrived in a large dayroom with windows overlooking a waterway.

Inside were several people in various stages of presence, both mental and physical. But Lorna spotted Kristen immediately. She guessed she would never not find her sister in a crowded room.

Kristen was in a wheelchair. Her head lolled to one side. Her hair was in a high pony; it looked thick and shiny blond. She was wearing a sweatshirt that was too big for her and cotton scrub bottoms. On her feet were thick socks.

Lorna had to mentally command her feet to move, putting one foot in front of the other as she walked across the room. She was frightened of Kristen in this state, which made no sense. She wanted to hug her. She wanted to see her eyes, see that familiar gaze staring back at her.

When Lorna reached her, Kristen made no sign that she even noticed. An attendant pulled up a chair for Lorna, and she sat slowly, unsure if Kristen was capable of registering her presence. She leaned forward and put her face directly in front of Kristen's—if she could see, she could not miss Lorna looming there. It took a moment, but she swore she saw something spark in Kristen's pale blue eyes. Recognition, the sun—who knew? But something changed there.

A swell of love and grief mixed into one terrible knot in the pit of her stomach. She couldn't help herself—she burst into tears. She reached into her purse and grabbed some tissues. Then she put her hand in the pocket of her jacket and tightly gripped the figurine. She had not counted on such a great burst of emotion.

She dabbed at her eyes with the tissue and concentrated on taking several deep breaths. When she managed to pull it together, she said shakily, "Sorry. I wasn't expecting that."

Kristen's eyes were on her. They seemed quite clear now. "I don't know what to say," Lorna began. "I mean, I had something prepared and went over it and over it in my head, but I can't remember a word of it now. So I guess I'll just say that I love you, Kristen. I have always loved you so much." More tears fell. She drew another breath. "*So* much." She dropped the tissues in her lap and took Kristen's hand in hers. Amazingly, Kristen gripped her hand. "I'm so sorry," Lorna said. "I am so very sorry that this is what happened to you. That this happened to us. But I forgive you, Kristen." The words sounded like a croak, coated in shame and regret. And the compassion she'd been missing for so long. Thick globs of it, coating her words. "And I forgive myself. Probably not what you were expecting me to say, but I've really needed to do that. I realize now that I couldn't have changed you. I could not have made your choices. I could only protect myself. And now the only thing I can do is love you. And I do, Kristen."

Kristen began to squeeze her hand rhythmically. Squeeze and release. Squeeze and release. Lorna wasn't certain if it was a spasm or a sign from her sister.

"I want to ask your forgiveness," she said.

The squeezing continued.

"I've thought so long about it, about everything, and why things happened and how they happened, and I have concluded that you, me, and Mom, well . . . we did the best we knew how, didn't we? We each did the best we could."

A bit of drool began to slide out the corner of Kristen's mouth, but she kept squeezing Lorna's hand. Lorna took her tissue and wiped the drool away. She didn't say more. It didn't seem there was anything left to say. She sat with Kristen until an attendant came to get her. It was time for Kristen to go to work on some motor skills. "Motor skills?" Lorna asked.

"We try," the attendant said.

Lorna nodded. She couldn't see very clearly now, as her eyes were filled with tears. But she slid her hand free of Kristen's, then leaned over and hugged her. The antiseptic scent of her sister filled her nose. She was bone thin. But she was also familiar. Like an old teddy bear, a wistful sensation from something that had existed long ago. "I love you, Kristen," she whispered, and let her go.

Had Kristen heard her or understood her? Lorna couldn't say. She watched the attendant roll Kristen away.

And when Kristen was gone, Lorna felt a sense of peace come over her. The bomb-shelter door had been kicked off its hinges and thrown out. She felt herself coming fully into the light. She had forgiven her sister, accepted that she couldn't have changed the outcome and that her responsibility was fully to herself.

She texted her dad.

When she went outside, the sun was in her eyes, and so were tears. But they were now tears of relief. Of hope for herself. Of compassion for herself.

But her tears weren't so thick that she couldn't see Bean and Seth standing outside her father's car. Seth looked concerned. That concern was for her. Just for her. She couldn't remember when she'd ever felt someone's concern for her like she was feeling it now, and she burst into tears again. Seth immediately wrapped her in an embrace. So did Bean, throwing his arms around both their waists and pressing his face against Lorna's hip. "I'm okay," she said, and wrapped one arm around Bean. "I'm really okay."

"Just checking," Seth said gruffly.

"It's okay if you're not," Bean assured her. "We're still your friends."

Lorna could feel in her heart just how true that was.

Seth and Bean went to the beach for a couple of days. Lorna stayed with her dad and visited Kristen every day. She could never really tell if her sister knew Lorna was there for her. But Lorna knew, and she supposed that was the most important thing.

When it came time to leave, Lorna told her dad about the trust. "It's only seventy-five hundred dollars," she said. "But I'll sign it over to Kristen. I've also got some money I've been saving for a big purchase. I'm not going to need all of it. I'll call you next week with a sum after I figure out a few things."

"Thanks, Lolo," her dad said. "This has been a drain on us."

Lorna felt nothing but sadness for her father. She understood the drain. "I know, Dad," she said.

The other decision she had to make, which had been building for weeks, was much easier than she'd thought. She'd believed if she didn't buy Nana's house, she would be giving up the only home she could call hers. But Nana's house was not the home Lorna had been wanting all this time. It was only walls, and frankly, not very good walls. Home, she'd discovered, was where she felt safe and accepted for who she was. Home was with people who cared about her.

On the flight back to Texas, while Seth was gazing at his phone and Bean was once again glued to the window, Lorna studied Seth. The lines around his eyes. The stubble of beard on his face. She marveled at the forces in the universe that put him in her path at this time in her life—when she'd most needed a friend. But friends didn't keep secrets. She put her hand on his arm. He looked up from his phone and smiled.

"I have to tell you something."

"Oh. Sounds important." He put his phone in his pocket. "What's up?"

"It's about the house. Our house. Where we live?"

Seth gave her a funny smile. "Okay."

"I never told you, but . . . that house originally belonged to my grandparents. And then . . . then I lived there during my childhood. My mom, Kristen, and my grandmother. Until my grandmother died. That's when it was chopped up into apartments."

Seth's brows dipped. "You lived there?"

She nodded. "My mom sold it to pay for another round of Kristen's treatment. Anyway, I sort of stalked it until an apartment became available and moved in with a plan to buy it back. I thought that if I had that house, I'd be happy."

His expression was inscrutable.

She swallowed. "I was one of the buyers Mr. Contreras had."

"What?" He looked confused. And slightly annoyed. "But—"

"I know, I didn't tell you. Or anyone, for that matter. I can't explain, other than I was convinced it was something I had to do, Seth. I thought if I could buy back Grandma's house, I could put my life back together. And I didn't want any of you to know because, well . . . you all would have hated me."

"But—"

"But I'm not buying it," she interjected. "I'm not. I get it now—it's just a house, nothing more. It wouldn't have saved me."

He frowned. "Did you need saving?"

She sighed softly. "I needed saving from myself. Not from my past like I thought, but from my spiral of thoughts. Bean saved me. Then you and Liz and Martin came along and pulled me into the light. So did the people at Bodhi who helped me see what I was doing to myself. You all saved me."

Seth looked past her to Bean. "I wish you'd told us."

Lorna winced. "I wanted to."

He glanced off, his brow furrowed. Then he met her gaze. "You lived there as a kid?"

She nodded.

"What was it like?"

She told him the long sad tale of her life in Nana's house. When she was done, he didn't say much other than "Wow."

"Are you mad?"

"No, not mad," he said. "I'm not sure what I am. I have to think about it. I understand how complicated your emotions have been. I get that you'd boxed yourself into a corner. But I wish you'd told us."

"I understand. I'm so sorry." She hoped she hadn't ruined the best thing to happen to her in years. But if she had, she'd figure things out. She had walked into the light and she wasn't going back into the dark.

"If you're not going to buy it, then where are you going?" Seth asked.

"Well," Lorna said sheepishly, "I was thinking of checking out those condos you found. If . . . if that's okay with you."

Seth suddenly grinned. He took her hand in his and squeezed it affectionately. "Lorna Lott, that would be awesome."

It felt like her body cracked open and flooded with light when he grinned at her like that. *Yes, that would be awesome.*

Chapter 38

Lorna Is Forty-Three

IT IS BEAN'S NINTH BIRTHDAY, AND HE AND LORNA HAVE made a German chocolate cake. Bean has his baking badge now, the result of the chocolate cake he finally decided on.

There is to be a party at Seth's condo, which, how convenient, is just next door. When she bought her condo, she was a little nervous about the only unit left being next to his—familiarity breeds contempt and all. But Seth thought it was fantastic. "Are you kidding? We've been neighbors all this time. It's perfect." He's even put a gate in the fence between their small backyards so Aggie can come and go as she pleases.

Lorna is in a much better place. She's been to see Kristen twice since the first time. She has won the position of senior vice president at long last and received a substantial raise and signing bonus, which she donated to Kristen's care. When Deb told her the good news, Lorna shrugged a little. "It was a team effort," she said.

She has a much better working relationship with her staff, although she can still be a bit hard on them. But ever since she returned to work and adjusted the sales quotas and apologized to everyone, things have steadily improved. They are selling more than they ever did when she was mad at them all the time.

When she bought her condo, she had a housewarming party and invited them all, much to their collective surprise. But they all came—Suzanne, looking gorgeous. Lance and his wife. Sheldon and his boyfriend, who opened her drawers to look inside as if it were a perfectly natural thing to do. Lorna even invited Beverly Rich from HR, who, after seeing the boxes of Precious Moments figurines in the garage, offered to sell them on eBay for a cut. The arrangement worked out well for them both. The only one Lorna kept was of the lady, the boy, and the dog. The one Bean had handed her the first time she went in to see Kristen.

The most surprising thing of all is that, even though she now wears her hair naturally curly and wild, as Montreal called it, Lorna has not heard anyone call her King Kong behind her back. Suzanne has even complimented the dresses Lorna has been wearing to work.

Callie and her family have come for Bean's birthday party. Lorna and Callie are slowly making their way back to friendship. "Isn't it awesome," Callie said once, "that the friends you make as children can be the friends you want as adults?"

"Yes!" Lorna replied, beaming. "Does that mean you want me?"

"Sort of, but not if you make it weird," Callie warned her.

"I can't make any promises!" Lorna cried, still beaming.

Four of Bean's fellow Ranger Explorers have come for the party, and they can hardly wait to cram with Callie's kids into the bouncy castle that barely fits in Seth's backyard. "We should really take down the fence between us," Seth muses as he watches them set it up.

"We should," Lorna says. "It would make things easier."

Seth looks at her and winks. "Make what things easier?"

Lorna smiles back. "You know."

"I do. I just wondered if you did. You know, we could eventually knock out the wall between our dining rooms too."

Lorna smiles. There is something true between her and Seth, but it's a slow burn. There was a bit of a trust issue after they came back from Florida because she had not been forthcoming about the house. And she suspects he is still getting over the death of Jill. Those traumas don't clear out as quickly as one would like. She should know—she's still cleaning out her brain. But there have been a few dates, lots of hand-holding, and in the garage last week, he kissed her. Not just a peck, either, but a full-blown, *he's so hot* kiss. They are working their way up from friends to more than friends, and then they will be taking down fences and knocking down walls, and Lorna could not be happier.

Martin has come to the party. When he moved out, Lorna saw the enormous speakers that explained the noise she always heard coming from his apartment. Not a marching band after all, but the thump of heavy bass. He moved to San Antonio into another property Mr. Contreras owns and says it is in the same state of repair as the old place. "It's good to see everyone—even you, Lolo," he says with a grin, giving her a playful chuck on the shoulder. They started calling her Lolo after the Florida trip. It made them all laugh then, and still does, apparently.

Liz also bought a condo in this complex, a smaller unit on the other side of the property. But she comes to drink wine on Lorna's back deck from time to time, and Seth relies on her to babysit Bean when he and Lorna go out to dinner. She joins Lorna and Seth and Bean at least once a month when they volunteer at the soup kitchen. Peggy comes too. Lorna invited Candy to the party, but Candy told her she was crazy and she still hadn't forgiven her. Besides, she was busy that day, but maybe next time.

Liz's frequent visits have reminded Lorna of her mother and

Peggy, and then before she knew what was happening, Liz and Peggy became friends too. Peggy has come to the party with vanilla cupcakes decorated with little explorer hats she made from felt. "What are they?" Bean whispers, his brow furrowed as he examines them.

"Explorer hats, I think?" Lorna whispers back.

"*Awesome*," Bean says. "She could get a badge for that."

When it comes time to cut the cake, Lorna lights the candles and Bean almost takes too long thinking of the perfect wish before he blows them out. One of the boys asks what he wished for.

"I can't tell you," Bean says.

"Or he'd have to kill you," Lorna adds. There is a pause . . . Everyone looks at her. And then everyone laughs.

That's the other new thing about her life. Sometimes people laugh at her jokes.

As Seth hands around cake, Lorna asks Bean if he's finally decided what his favorite dessert is. "Yep," Bean says nonchalantly. "I decided a long time ago."

"What? You never told me!" Lorna says.

"It's birthday cake," he says. "It doesn't matter what kind, as long as it's birthday cake."

"Cake wins? Because I remember you really liked that gelato."

"I know, but my favorite is still birthday cake, because every time you eat it, your whole family is there."

Lorna wraps him in a hug. "You are really something, kid."

"I know," he says, and hands her his empty plate before dashing outside.

She is still holding the plate when Seth appears to take it from her. She smiles at him. "This is a great day."

"It's pretty great," he agrees, and their eyes lock in that way that makes her certain Seth will be around for a long time to come.

Her life may not have turned out like she thought, and it took her a while to get here, but she has no regrets after all. Regrets and fears have been banished. She's made her amends to herself and her loved ones, and now she only looks forward. There is no point in dwelling in the past. As Micah once said, it's in the past for a reason.

She is filled with immense gratitude at having found her family. Her *chosen* family. The people she wants to be near all the time. She is amazed at how happy she is, how free of guilt and anger she's become. She's amazed that all these people seem to actually like being with her, and no one has left the party yet.

She's found the best way to live, and she wakes up with hope every single morning. Hope for a good life. Hope for laughter and friendship and love.

She often thinks of her mother, who insisted Lorna look forward, not backward. She watches the kids running around in the yard, Aggie chasing after them. She sighs and looks heavenward. "You were right, Mom," she says softly. "But you knew that."

Acknowledgments

THIS BOOK WOULDN'T BE POSSIBLE WITHOUT THE SUPPORT of my agent, the inimitable Jenny Bent, or my wonderful editor Laura Wheeler, and the entire team at Harper Muse. They are small but mighty and are dedicated to getting good books in your hands. They have allowed me the absolute privilege of following my muse. You'd think every author gets that privilege, but that is not necessarily so. I am eternally grateful that women in this industry continue to take a chance on me and my ideas.

I must also give a hearty shout-out to Jane Estes and the staff at Lark and Owl Booksellers in Georgetown, Texas. Not only do they keep my books on their shelves and support me as an author in every way possible but they also support me as a reader. They've read everything, they know everything, and they never steer me wrong. As an author, I get lots of free books from the industry, but I cannot walk into Lark and Owl and leave without a couple of new books because the booksellers there are that good.

Discussion Questions

1. This book deals with the effect of one family member's addiction on the rest of the family. Millions of people live with this reality every day, which is why Alcoholics Anonymous teaches that addiction is a family disease. What did you think of the relationship between Lorna Lott and her sister, Kristen? Do you think there is a limit to supporting a loved one with an addiction? What could Lorna's parents have done to better support Lorna?
2. Lorna's mother is sandwiched between a mother who is an alcoholic and a daughter who is a drug addict. What could she have done differently with either of them? What are some things she did well? What are some things that made you cringe?
3. Bean is an innocent boy with an old soul. What do you think was the reason he and Lorna could connect so easily? If you were in Seth's shoes, would you have been wary of Lorna's friendship with your son?
4. Lorna attends a wellness spa with some different modalities of getting in touch with herself. Would you try some of the things she tried? Why or why not?
5. Lorna decides to revisit some past regrets with the hope of letting them go once and for all. Have you ever wanted to revisit any past regrets? What would you hope to achieve?

DISCUSSION QUESTIONS

6. Lorna finally makes some friends. How do you think her life might have unfolded differently if she'd had a best friend? How important are relationships outside of family to a healthy mindset?
7. Do you think Seth and Lorna will end up together, or do you think their relationship will remain in a comfortable close-friend zone?

From the Publisher

GREAT BOOKS
ARE EVEN BETTER WHEN THEY'RE SHARED!

Help other readers find this one:

- Post a review at your favorite online bookseller

- Post a picture on a social media account and share why you enjoyed it

- Send a note to a friend who would also love it—or better yet, give them a copy

Thanks for reading!

LOOKING FOR MORE GREAT READS? LOOK NO FURTHER!

Illuminating minds and captivating hearts through story.

Visit us online to learn more:
harpermuse.com

Or scan the below code and sign up to receive email updates on new releases, giveaways, book deals, and more:

@harpermusebooks

Now that Nora is not dead,
only one question remains:

What does she want to do with her life?

AVAILABLE IN PRINT, E-BOOK, AND AUDIO

About the Author

JULIA LONDON is the *New York Times* and *USA TODAY* bestselling author of numerous works of romantic fiction and women's fiction. She is the recipient of the RT Bookclub Award for Best Historical Romance and a six-time finalist for the RITA award for excellence in romantic fiction. She lives in Austin, Texas, with two teens, two dogs, and an astonishingly big pile of books.

• • •

Connect with Julia at julialondon.com
Instagram: @julia_f_london
Facebook: @JuliaLondon